Praise for Jackie Ivie's **Lady of the Knight**

"Compelling . . . dynamic . . . difficult to put down . . . with strong characters, sizzling sexual tension, plenty of passion, action, history, and great repartee, Ivie makes a strong debut and is destined to become a reader favorite."
—*Romantic ~~~~ ~~~~ ~~~~Kclub*

"Thrilling . . . excellent . . . ~~~~ ~~~~ ~~~~ ~~~~re pleasure."
—~~~~ ~~~~*ous*

"Beautifully writte~~~~ ~~~~ ~~~~ . . . a very exciting, excellent r~~~~ ~~~~ ~~~~o read again and again."
—*~~~~ce Reader at Heart*

"Prepare to be amused, entertained, and moved almost to tears . . . delivers all that a discriminating reader demands—lush passions, soaring tempers, revenge, royalty, and a lass with an uncommon talent for finding trouble."
—*Fallen Angels Reviews*

"Completely captivating! Ivie does a wonderful job of entwining sensuality, treachery, and romance.
—*Romance Junkies*

"Very hot! A page-turner [and] a wonderful debut novel."
—*Round Table Reviews*

"The sex scenes are some of the best this reviewer has ever read . . . highly recommended!"
—*Loves Romance*

Also by Jackie Ivie

LADY OF THE KNIGHT

Published by Kensington Publishing Corp.

TENDER
IS THE
KNIGHT

Jackie Ivie

ZEBRA BOOKS
Kensington Publishing Corp.
www.kensingtonbooks.com

To Glenn,
who never stopped believing in me

Chapter 1

AD 1876

There really was such a thing as one secret too many. Elise wouldn't have guessed it earlier. There was only one thing to do about it, too: give it up to its rightful owner. It wasn't her secret, anyway. It never had been.

Elise looked over the assemblage below, keeping the desperation well hidden beneath the cool, polished exterior that was all anybody ever saw on her face. She was so used to it, it was easy. For if coldness, conceit, and vanity were desirable traits, then Elise, the Dowager Duchess of Wynd, was a very desirable woman. She turned from contemplation of her own image in the mirrored disk at her wrist and looked at the staircase she was about to descend. Lady Elise always made an entrance. She always stopped what was happening, as others looked at her to see what outrageous, expensive, and scandalous ensemble she was wearing. It wasn't working tonight, but she didn't have to look far for the cause.

His dais was directly across from her, where he could host a vast number of society peerages, all lined up in a meandering band, like a misguided snake. Elise didn't falter. She pasted her society smile into place on her face, smoothed any stray hairs that might have escaped her coiffure back into place, and stepped onto the stairs.

If anything could be said to make her show emotion, this was it.

It didn't help to curse silently to herself, but she did it, anyway. She'd taken too long before making her entrance, and standing in that long queue was going to be her punishment. Elise checked the throng to see if there was anyone she could join up with to cut her waiting time proportionately. There wasn't. Her lips moved a bit at that and she stopped the motion. There wasn't anyone she ever sought out to join.

Elise's entrance wasn't going unnoticed, however. There was little for those waiting to concentrate on, except the new arrivals. She reached the dance floor to an almost audible sigh of relief and ignored the room-sized mirror placed at the bottom. This ensemble had cost her more than her entire hunting wardrobe of last season, but it was worth it.

As a young dowager duchess in a long line of plain-faced and large-boned women, Elise had taken it upon herself to be different. Gracing every social occasion with stunning, original gowns and remarkable jewels was the easy part. Elise walked, with her special sashay-style movement, to the end of the receiving line, aware of the froth of silver petticoats moving with each step. Diamond dust appeared to have been sprinkled throughout the material, and judging by the price, it probably was. She tilted her chin a bit and ignored the whispering about her.

She knew what they were probably saying, anyway. Scandalous. Spoiled. Emotionless. Daring. Heartless. Icy. She knew how she was described, because she'd worked long and hard at that very thing.

The line moved, and Elise moved with it. Then she saw Sir Roald Easton on the stairs and very nearly gave vent to the frustration as he crossed the floor to reach her.

"Lady Elise! How pleasant to see you again. I vow, you grow more lovely with each passing moment. You're a more breathtaking sight than a mere mortal can absorb." He'd started the effusive greeting before he'd reached her side, and he ended it with her hand raised to his lips. Elise listened to the increased whispering and longed to snatch her hand away. "I shall perish if you don't dance with me. Now. At once."

"I'm in the receiving line, Roald," Elise replied coldly.

"Why, so you are . . . which is highly unusual, if you don't mind me remarking on it."

"I do," she replied.

He tucked her hand beneath his elbow and turned them toward the dais. "Then allow me to escort you. Who is it we are meeting?"

"The new Duke of MacGowan, of course."

"The Scotsman? Good heavens, why? He's a heathen."

"Because it sounded amusing, and I could use a bit of that."

"Amusement? Well, if that's the case, I want you to know I've got the freshest cartload of peonies spread all over my home."

Elise's interest was perked. She tilted her head and looked up at him. "Peonies?" she asked.

He nodded. He really was devilishly handsome, she decided, not for the first time. "Peonies. Blossoms only, no stems."

"Why would you spread peonies all over your home?" she asked.

"To watch you wallow in. What else?"

Her gasp wasn't heard over those around them. Elise swallowed any reply, maneuvered her hand from his grasp, and practiced at a patience she was far from feeling. Tonight wasn't to be the night she told it, after all. It was almost a relief, until the weight of it started up again. Secrets had a way of gaining volume to them, and the one she had for MacGowan was a heavy one.

"That's a lovely dress, darling. I've not seen it before. New?"

"All my dresses are new, Roald. I wouldn't be caught in public in one I'd worn before. Imagine the lampooning I'd get," Elise replied.

"Imagine the ones you already get. Forgive me. Slight touch of envy. Cost much? Or just look like it?"

"Roald, your attendance on me is rapidly palling," Elise replied.

"Good. Otherwise, I'd think you bored. So, was it?"

"Was it what?" Elise asked, moving forward again with the line's movement.

"Frightfully expensive."

Elise watched as he looked her over. She could only hope the others about her weren't doing the same. Like the other ladies there, Elise's gown tightly followed her ribcage, but then it was split down the front to the floor. With the skirt's excess material, her designer had fashioned a small bustle at the small of her back. The man had then filled the gap in front with petticoats. This particular dress was made of a purple-hued taffeta, resembling the color of a storm-filled sky. She'd found the perfect amethysts to go with it, too.

"What do you think?" she asked, when he'd finished his perusal and returned to looking her in the eye.

"It's worth every quid. Double," he said finally.

It really was a shame. He was a very handsome man. Soulless, but handsome. They were a perfect pair. She ducked her head. It wasn't due to any shyness, it was to hide her expression. She may have been wearing the most beautiful, costly, and daring ensemble, but it didn't match her heart. There wasn't a material black enough.

"So . . . now that we've solved that riddle, answer me another. Why are we standing about, wasting this delightful evening, dancing attendance on a Scot's duke, rather than the waltz? Hmmn?"

"You don't have to accompany me, Roald," Elise answered. The line moved and she moved with it.

"Oh, that's the way of it. You're determined to mystify. Well, consider me properly intrigued. A Scot's duke? Fair enough. There must be a reason. Is he plump in the pockets?"

"He's the new Duke of MacGowan, Roald. You know very well he's rich. You read the papers."

"As a potentate. I know. Lucky bastard."

Sir Roald's voice was full of jealousy. Elise knew the cause. Everyone did. Sir Roald hadn't much money to his name, and what he did get, he foolishly gambled away.

She smiled slightly and looked away, as if disinterested.

"I've heard he's in the market for a bride," Roald leaned over to whisper.

"And?" Elise asked.

"You thinking of putting yourself in the running? This is news."

"I have nothing to say to such nonsense, Roald. Pray find a different subject to bore me with, or find someone else to address your presence to, someone who actually wants it there."

"Ouch," he replied.

"You still here?" Elise asked sweetly.

There were more twitters of amusement about them and more whispering. She ignored it. Roald's jaw tightened.

"It's a very good thing you're beautiful, Elise, because

you have the tongue of a serpent and the warmth of an iceberg."

"Careful, Roald, your flattery is slipping," Elise said, with a cool nod and smile to an acquaintance walking past. The line moved again. She noted they were halfway there.

"Oh, forgive me. I lost my mind for a moment. The beam of your presence shadowed everything else into insignificance. It's always the case when near a goddess wrapped in earthy tones."

"Too effusive," Elise commented.

He cleared his throat. "All right, then. Your radiance transcends Mount Olympus."

"Better," she replied, moving again.

He grinned, showing the dimples everyone ranted over. A lady could do worse than Sir Roald Easton for an escort, much worse. He was a wit, and he dressed in the epitome of fashion, from his dark coat to the exquisitely tied cravat at his chin. She'd hate to know how much he must owe his tailor this time.

"And all reason flees my mind when in the presence of one such as you. I vow, no mere man can keep his sanity and his words when faced with being near, let alone speaking with, you."

Elise pantomimed a yawn.

"It will never work between you two, Elise. I just told you he's looking for a maiden wife, and you . . . well . . . ahem."

Elise turned her head again. "And how would you know?" she asked.

He guffawed, catching more attention. "How do I know his wants? Or how do I know you're not maidenly?"

"Either," Elise answered stiffly.

"We belong to the same club. It's on the bet sheet. White's. I'm not entirely a pup, you know."

"White's?" Elise asked, then took a half step forward, although the line hadn't moved.

"Oh, yes. White's. They even allow me in. Fancy that."

"They must not expect payment up front, then." Elise had to keep her mouth from showing any gratification at such a reply. He deserved it after his maiden comment.

"I don't know why I stay at your side and put up with such abuse, Elise. Truly, I don't."

"Oh yes, you do, Roald. It's because I've got the widow's portion of the Wynd fortune at my beck and call."

"So?"

"And you don't," she finished.

"You're a very beautiful woman, Elise Wyndham. Very beautiful."

"Are we back to that again?" Elise asked. This time the line moved more than a few steps. She didn't bother to reason the cause. They were almost to the dais that the new duke and his retinue had been seated atop.

"I was just getting to the skin-deep part," he finished.

Elise's mouth twisted. "Your regard warms my heart, Roald."

"Impossible," he replied, "you haven't got one."

"I certainly hope, with a remark like that, you don't expect to ask for a loan toward your creditors from me again."

"Oh, bother!" he replied, beneath his breath. "What I said earlier about losing my wits? Well, it's true."

"How much this time?" she asked.

"Well, at least allow me to earn it first."

The gasps about them were more audible than before. Elise turned toward him. The dimples were out in force and the humor had extended to his eyes. Sir Roald Easton fancied himself a poet and a ready wit. He also had gray eyes, which, when he turned on the charm, warmed to the shade of gun-metal. Elise looked him over dispassionately.

"And how do you propose to do that, pray tell?" she asked.

His eyebrows went up and down several times. "With peonies?" he asked hopefully.

"Not a chance," she replied.

"Hmmn. A waltz, then. Maybe two?"

"I'm not interested in dancing tonight. I think my foot hurts. If I allow you to step on it, I'm sure it will." Elise kept her eyes on the dais in front of the couple before them.

"I'm a devilishly good dancer, and you know it."

"Careful. Your temper's showing," she reminded him.

"Oh, let me see . . . there's tea. That's it. Tea."

"Tea?" she asked.

"Will you be receiving at tea tomorrow?" he asked. "I'll be there. We'll drink a few cups. What do you say to inviting me?"

Elise had already decided this entire conversation was probably going to be a cartoon passed out on the streets tomorrow morn. She took a deep breath. She didn't let it bother her, much. She was used to being lampooned. It went hand in hand with being ostracized.

"I'm not entertaining for tea, Roald. I never do. There's so much better uses for my divan. You know that much."

He sighed, exaggeratedly. "Oh, very well. It will have to be with information. What do you want to know?"

"MacGowan. He wants a bride? Why?"

"The slick shard of your heart twists deeply into my own, Elise. I want you to know this beforehand."

"I never said I wanted the position, Roald."

He brightened. "Oh, well, then. Our erstwhile duke has been spending his time until now with his regiment in India. Of course, he had to resign his commission upon the news, lucky chap."

The couple before them stepped up onto the dais and started the introductions. Elise picked up her skirt with one hand and held to the railing with the other. She couldn't see the new duke from where they were standing, but the retinue about him had the bearing of army officers, to be sure.

"He's definitely not your type, Elise," Sir Roald hissed into her ear. "And, don't forget, he's in mourning."

"Mourning?"

"For his brothers. Drowning accident. Surely you read about it?"

"I must have missed it," she replied.

She wasn't fooling him, but she didn't care. Her heart was giving her more trouble than she'd own up to, and her throat was dry. She felt like a girl of fifteen again.

"The Lady Elise Wyndham, Dowager Duchess of Wynd. Allow me to introduce you to His Grace, Colin MacPherson Rory MacGowan, Sixth Duke of Gowan, Laird of MacGowan."

Elise heard her name and title and took the step up onto the dais. She held out her hand but had to let it drop when he didn't take it. She looked up; then everything in her head went right out of it. The new duke was enormous, he wasn't wearing anything that looked remotely Scottish, and he was looking at her with something akin to dislike. She hadn't counted on that.

He turned his head to one of his assistants. "This one does na' have much meat to her," he remarked.

Elise's mouth fell open and her eyes widened, and that was the only part she'd admit to. There wasn't a thing she could do about the flush taking over her entire body.

"I *beg* your pardon." Elise managed to find her voice.

He waved, and an unseen hand took hold of her

elbow and guided her. From somewhere she heard Sir Easton being announced. Then she was back on the ballroom floor, trying to find her legs beneath her. She did the only thing she could. She put her society smile back on her face and waited for her escort.

Chapter 2

Elise didn't sleep. She tried. Visions of her own mortification played with memories of the same, and every time she closed her eyes, she saw that great hulking barbarian announcing that she didn't have enough meat to her. And she was angry. Not with The MacGowan; he was a Scotsman and was supposed to be barbaric. She was angry with the fact that her wits and her tongue had completely deserted her when she needed them the most.

She was up, and almost wearing her riding habit, before dawn broke. Her maid, Daisy, would have to finish hooking up her stays, and promptly at the first sight of the sun, Elise rang for her. She didn't care if it was an ungodly hour to be out and riding. She had to escape any more time alone with her thoughts.

The Dowager Duchess of Wynd always rode in Hyde Park during the Season. It was one of the few pleasures none of her so-called friends shared. She needed the fresh air and the wind on her face. Elise found herself running the steps, and she had to stop to take a breath.

A groom awaited her at the front step, his hand

gentling a pure Arabian mare. Elise ignored his touch about her waist as he assisted her into the sidesaddle.

She'd grabbed the first thing in her wardrobe to wear and grimaced down at her newest habit, which was made of vivid blue satin with black piping. Seated atop her nephew's mare in such a color, she'd be impossible to miss. She was grateful it was early morn.

Elise actually owned nothing. Her late husband's nephew, Archibald Wyndham, owned the title and all the wealth being Duke of Wynd brought. Elise wasn't slighted, however. She had a stipend on her for life. It was something her father had been most insistent on when he'd, in effect, sold her.

Elise gathered the reins and set off, her mind still riding the morbid train of her thoughts, and that's why she didn't see what awaited her the moment she and her groom entered the park.

Good Lord! she thought the moment she saw the seven men astride seven horses. *He's even larger on horseback.*

The man bearing down on her from across the park could be none other than MacGowan. Elise tipped her head back, barely avoiding making any sort of a sound as he neared. She didn't question that he was racing to see her. There wasn't anyone else in the park.

She watched the hooves of the beast he was riding; they churned up sod with the way he halted it in, and she couldn't help but be impressed. Colin MacGowan had chestnut hair, nearly the same shade as his horse; his hair was thick and wavy and fell to his shoulders, *if* the muscled expanse inside his jacket was shoulders. Elise eyed the width of him while his horse breathed across on her and waited.

"Are you the woman known as The Ice Goddess?"

He held up a crumpled piece of paper in his gloved hand as he asked it. Actually, Elise had to rephrase it.

He wasn't asking anything, he was demanding to know. In his next sentence, she knew it.

"Answer me, woman! Are you the wench known as—"

"I heard you the first time," she answered, interrupting him.

"Well?"

He had a becoming flush to his face, and if she hadn't been overawed by the size of him the previous evening, she would have noticed the square jaw, Roman nose, and very brown eyes, bordered by very dark brown lashes. This MacGowan didn't look a thing like his older brother Evan MacGowan, she decided.

"Well, what?" she asked sweetly.

The six attendants he'd been out riding with formed a perfectly executed *V* behind him, with Colin at the tip. They all had their mounts' heads at an exact angle, their black ensembles perfectly matched, and not one moved by as much as a twitch of his horse's tail. Elise didn't let how awe-inspiring she found it show anywhere on her.

"Explain this."

He was shoving the paper toward her, and Elise sat immobile. Then she was motioning for her groom to go and fetch it. The young man's fright was apparent, and it helped to temper her own. It was obvious Colin MacGowan had every bit of the Scottish uncivilized arrogance, and then more as well. She patted her mare's neck and waited.

The crumpled piece of paper was a freshly printed cartoon. It was fairly amusing, too. She was depicted, shaped like a very slender icicle, while a mammoth-sized man was pointing down at her and shouting something about meat. Her lips twitched.

"Explain that," he demanded.

"Everyone at the Royal Palace must have been

busy," she answered, flattening out the paper on one of her blue-clothed thighs.

"What?"

"The Royal Palace. The family. You know. Prince Albert. Crown Prince Edward. Queen Victoria. Surely you've heard of them."

"I know who the Royal family is. What the devil does it have to do with me? And you?"

"I do believe someone found that what happened last evening between us was more amusing than the Royal house. They've decided to spare Queen Victoria. She's their usual target, you understand."

"Some wretch handed this to me on my own front steps! Right in front of my home!"

Elise shrugged. "It's a cartoon. We've been lampooned. Welcome to London, Your Grace."

"Well, I dinna' like it. Destroy it and stop any others from being distributed."

"You're speaking to the wrong person. Now, if you'd excuse me."

"You're to cease this immediately."

"I didn't have anything to do with it."

"Are you denying this is you?"

"Oh, it's definitely a depiction of me, Your Grace, and that's a very good likeness of you. Obviously the cartoonists have decided that I . . . make that we, are good fodder for their ink. It means nothing, really. They'll have another victim by noon. Now, if you'll excuse me."

"Don't turn your back on me, woman."

Elise hadn't turned yet. She looked over and across at him. "I have a name, Your Grace. And I don't take orders, I give them. Now, once again. Good day."

She had exactly six seconds to enjoy his discomfiture before she heard his horse again. The mare was trembling as that chestnut stallion bore down on their right and slammed them to a halt, which Colin then guaranteed by reaching across for her mare's bridle. Elise narrowed her eyes to look over at him.

The mass in his jacket probably was his shoulders, she decided, since it looked like the size of his thigh was equivalent to her hips. She eyed him uneasily. It was dawn, there were street vendors out, and this was London. He couldn't do anything to her. At least, she told herself he couldn't and hoped it worked.

"No woman turns away from me."

"I beg your pardon?" Elise answered in the same even tone.

"You heard me. I was na' finished, and you're na' dismissed until I am."

"If you don't wish to have your name connected to mine, Your Grace, this is not a very good way to manage that."

"What?"

"Chasing me down, preventing me from leaving, calling me names like wench, being seen with me. All told, I would hazard a guess you're going to see another cartoon about it."

"What are you talking of now?"

"Eyes."

"What?"

He really was fairly handsome, Elise decided, as his eyebrows rose and he puzzled that out.

"People have eyes, Your Grace. Especially the lower classes. It's what they do to even the field, I suspect. Everywhere you look these cartoonists get their scenes. Then they draw them, and then they print them, and then they pass them out. It's called socialism. The new order. If I'm not mistaken, that's a press chap right over there."

Elise pointed at a dark-clothed individual, who took off running the moment she did. She hadn't even seen him move, but one of Colin's guards was giving chase.

She watched him reach the street and turn back, empty-handed, before realizing she'd been holding her breath.

"Blast this nonsense! And you—"

He had a gloved finger pointing at her. Elise looked over at him.

"I had nothing to do with any of this, Your Grace, although I'm going to reap the results once again, no doubt. You shouldn't let it bother you so. I don't."

"You've been in these before?" he asked.

"Weekly, I'm afraid." She sighed. "It's the price of notoriety."

"Well, I have na'. I've na' wish to, either."

"There's not much way to correct that, I'm afraid."

"What?"

"Freedom, Your Grace. They can print what they like. You can let it bother you, or you can ignore it. I prefer to ignore it, which is a perfect lead-in for my *adieu*. It was ever so unpleasant meeting with you this morning. If you'd be so good as to release my mount, so I can proceed?"

"Is there *nae* way to stop this?"

"I'm afraid not. My mount?"

"If I'm seen in your company, enjoying your company, will that work?"

"Afraid not. I'm scandalous to be near. And you'll probably look like a barbarian again, but at least he'll have to invent the words to use."

"I'm *nae* barbarian."

Elise couldn't answer that, at first. She was afraid of the mirth bubbling just below the surface. She looked at him as levelly as possible until she got it under control. "I'll have to take your word on that, I'm afraid. Now, please release my mount and allow me to escape. I no longer feel any need for fresh air, or another moment of your company."

"I'll be escorting you to the Countess of Ipswich's dinner this eve. I'll call for you at eight. Be ready."

Elise's eyebrows rose. "I beg your pardon?" she finally managed to say again.

"The Countess of Ipswich's dinner. I'll call for you at eight."

"You're woefully out of your element, aren't you?" Elise asked. "And I'm afraid this isn't Scotland."

"I've na' been in Scotland for some years, my lady."

"Oh dear. I've advanced past wench. I hope that doesn't signify anything I don't want it to," she replied.

"You speak with riddles."

"And you don't speak, you shout. What I meant was, this is London, and here a lady is asked to be escorted, not told she will be."

He stuck his tongue in one cheek and looked down at her while his lips quirked. Elise's eyes widened slightly before she could help it as the strangest tingle ran up and down her spine. She told herself she was being ridiculous, and a moment later, she knew she was.

"Nonsense. I'll call at eight. We'll stop this at the source. If you're seen enjoying my company, they'll find someone else to draw."

"You seem to have forgotten something," Elise said.

"What?"

"I don't enjoy your company."

To her surprise, he tossed back his head and laughed, and he wasn't a quiet person when it came to laughter. As the sound died, she wondered if he did anything quietly.

"Eight. Be ready. I dinna' like waiting."

"You don't know where I live," she answered.

"Yonder. Pinkish house. Frilly decor all about." He pointed. She didn't look. He had the Wynd townhome pegged perfectly.

"If you're speaking of my Italian, iron-work balconies,

I'm fairly insulted, I think. Then again, they are
rather frilly."

"Be ready. Eight."

"I've not said I'll go with you."

"Dinna' make me chase you down."

"You'd do such a thing?" Elise asked.

"You doubt it?"

He released her horse with the question and
turned, walking away while the six men on horseback
filed behind him. Elise didn't move.

She'd never enjoyed getting ready for an evening
more in her life. Daisy helped. There was only one
gown that would do justice to an evening of thwart-
ing the Duke of MacGowan, and that was her white,
pin-tucked satin, with the light blue gauze overlay.
Elise watched the transformation taking place in the
mirror as Daisy coiled her ash-blond hair atop her
head and entwined silver filigree through the tresses.

There was some consternation about the heels.
Daisy didn't think heels would be necessary and
would end up doing more harm than good to Elise's
legs. Elise, on the other hand, knew that without
some height, she was going to be dwarfed.

She was ready promptly at seven, and in her own
coach at seven-thirty. She couldn't wait to see the Duke
of MacGowan's face at the Countess of Ipswich's soiree.
She wasn't accompanying a MacGowan anywhere. Elise
Wyndham didn't want, or need, any escort, for any
reason, especially not someone from the same family
that had helped ruin hers.

She hadn't counted on Sir Roald.

Sophie, the Countess of Ipswich, had a table set up
and arranged for her guests. Elise was in her assigned
seat, with Sir Roald slated to be at her side, when the
Duke of MacGowan was announced. She forced her-

self to sit stone-still and ignore all else about her as his presence filled the room. Despite everything she was trying, Elise felt him. She *felt* him! The hairs on the back of her neck were whispering where he was, and the shivers up her spine were confirming it.

She had her eyes open on the elegance of a swan formed from butter that sat in the center of the table, when she watched him pull out a chair opposite her. She blinked. He wasn't supposed to be near. She knew it. Everyone else knew it. The whispers started again as he seated himself, filling her vision with perfectly groomed and tailored maleness.

Colin MacGowan had found someone, somewhere, with fashion expertise, who could fit those broad shoulders and that torso with a starched white shirt and cravat, black jacket with tails, and a pleated, white silk, waist wrap. He had his wavy hair pulled back severely into a queue that met his jacket at his back.

She blinked. She swallowed. She adjusted the garland at her wrist. She turned to visit with the man at her other side.

Brown eyes watched every move.

Their hostess, Sophie Ipswich, took her seat at the head of the table, signaling the start of the dinner presentation. Her husband wasn't at the other end, nor was he anywhere near. Sophie's husband never left their country estate. She wasn't alone, however. She was gazing adoringly into the eyes of the man paying for all of this, the young Viscount of Beckon.

Elise had heard the gossip over his parent's reaction. She'd found it amusing. His mother was reportedly prostrate over this fascination with a strumpet, even if she was a lady of quality. Elise guessed it wasn't the fascination that bothered anyone as much as it was the funds the Viscount was expending on his pursuit of the *Incomparable* Countess Sophie Ipswich.

Elise didn't know where Roald had gone to, nor did

she care. Brown eyes were watching her, and they were cold brown eyes. Elise's thoughts hammered at her, not bothered by the size of the crowd about her. The size was intentional. Sophie preferred large gatherings. That way, she could show off her latest gown, jewels, or simply a large feast that would set her beau back a tidy sum. Elise suspected Sophie calculated her worth on the amount of gold her paramours were willing to spend on her. It was something Elise didn't bother with. Her self-worth didn't need to be measured by gowns or baubles. She knew exactly what she was worth. The amount the Duke of Wynd had paid for her.

Everything was crystal clear, and every sound was finite and too loud. Elise listened to silverware on porcelain, crystal tapping, and the conversation as it grew loud, then softened. There came sounds of liquid being poured and more than one exclamation of interest at the presentation of the main course; she thought it was roast boar, but didn't move her eyes to verify it, and swore she could even hear the butter of the swan when it was being carved on.

Through it all, brown eyes watched her.

Elise was trapped between Sir Roald's empty chair, a minor baron named Hampton and enduring a full frontal assault by The MacGowan. She told herself it couldn't get worse, and then it did.

"I'm prostrate at what you did to me, Elise."

Roald's voice preceded him as he pulled out the chair. She suspected he'd been gaming and drinking, or just drinking. Either one was bad. She didn't move her head as he seated himself, although her eyes widened before she could help it.

"And without one word of explanation. How could you?"

He dropped a folded square of rag paper next to one of her spoons. Elise closed her eyes, then opened them. Nothing had changed. She picked it up and unfolded it. The crude drawing was of the Duke of MacGowan, hoisting her atop his shoulders and riding off with her, dragging a chain of men who were each holding the preceding one's legs, starting with the man holding to the ends of her skirts. She recognized Roald, since he was the closest, and therefore the largest.

"Well?"

"It's not a very good depiction," Elise whispered. "And certainly not very accurate."

"You're denying this happened?"

"It's not worth the amount of time it would take to do so." Elise refolded the paper and put it back on the table next to Roald's unused silverware.

"May I?"

It was totally against protocol to reach across a table, but Colin's hand didn't disappear just because it shouldn't be there. Elise watched as Colin picked up the newest lampoon. She didn't look anywhere near his eyes; instead, she watched his lips tighten as he looked it over.

"Past paramours, I take it?" he asked finally, to no one in particular. Then he handed the page to the woman on his left.

Elise shut her eyes again as the cartoon went from hand to hand down the table, causing more than a few gasps and a chuckle or two. She looked down at the red spot her lip rouge had made on the napkin, before folding it quickly. A proper lady wouldn't resort to cosmetics, she reminded herself, then wondered why she cared.

"If you're trying to upset me, Elise, you're succeeding," Roald said.

"And if you're trying to ruin me, Roald, it's too late," she replied.

"I haven't tried that yet, although I'm definitely considering it."

"The cartoon means nothing. Nothing. I rode in the park. His Grace was there. We spoke, nothing more."

"I thought you said it didn't merit the time to explain," Roald said snidely.

"It doesn't."

"Last eve you didn't even know him."

"You're boring me," she answered, drawing out each word.

"And you're lying to me!"

He hissed the reply between his teeth. Elise had to consciously stop wringing her napkin between her hands.

"Don't play me for a fool, Elise. You won't like it."

"And if you say much more, you'll not like it. Or have you forgotten our little arrangement?" she asked. She turned to the drunkard at her left. He simply grinned and raised his goblet in a toast.

"Forgive me, Elise. I find all manner of emotion when I behold your face. The thought of you drives me mad. I must be mad to anger you. Pray, forgive me?"

"If you'll not wax poetic toward me, I'll gladly forgive anything."

Elise turned back to him and was startled by the look on his face. His eyes glittered strangely, and his brows met at the bridge of his nose as he frowned.

"Elise, you and I . . . we've much to remember."

"Yes, Roald," she replied automatically.

"I want more."

"You know I can't give more." Elise placed a hand on his arm and hoped it wouldn't be noticed. He reached his other arm across his chest and trapped her hand with his. She hadn't counted on that.

"You've put me off for two seasons, my fine lady." His hand gripped her wrist and squeezed until her hand was bloodless. Elise winced, yet he ignored it.

"I've endured countless times of talk, talk, talk. I've taken you to Picadilly, to Dover, why once we even went to the crossroads to see the hanged highwaymen, yet not once have you given me the slightest encouragement. Never once have you even given me a kiss! A small thing like a kiss! Never once have you given me one. Have you thought over what that does to a man? Any man? All I envision is you enwrapped in another's arms, and I go mad. I swear it!"

His whispered words weren't going unnoticed by anyone, especially the man across the table from them. Elise swallowed. Roald had held her gaze throughout the impassioned speech. She didn't dare look away. He might make an even bigger scene.

"You're hurting me," she whispered finally.

"Beware the singed pigeon," he replied. Then he rose from the table, releasing her as he did so. Elise hid her bruised arm beneath the table linen. She hadn't known he felt that way, and she had no idea what she was supposed to do about it.

And brown eyes were watching the entire thing.

Chapter 3

The best course to put rumors to rest was to escape London for a weekend and take as few with you as possible. The next best course was to be accompanied while you did so. Elise had an invitation to a hunting party at Barrigan's, which took care of the first part. She was planning to use the time to relax, recuperate, and figure out another tactic to get released from her secret, without further attaching her name to the Scottish barbarian's. The second part wasn't so easy.

The Countess Sophie had invited herself into Elise's carriage for the ride. Elise listened to the other's nonstop chatter with half an ear. She already knew Roald had an invitation. He was probably going to be there, and that worried her. Then Sophie told her about the Duke of MacGowan. He had been invited, too. That was even more worrisome.

The repository of Sophie's information, her young viscount, had allowed her to buy a beautiful, costly, emerald necklace. She held it closely in her reticule, bringing it out every so often to show Elise. Elise gave the proper response of envy, although her heart wasn't in it. Her mind was elsewhere, and she knew the price Sophie had paid.

Lord Barrigan was known for his excellent entertainment. His estate was bordered by forest at three sides. His wardens kept them filled with game. Ostensibly, this was a weekend party to hunt, fish, and escape the confines of society life. Actually, Elise knew it was simply an excuse for Barrigan to sport with his mistress amid his friends, while his wife was still stabled at London.

Elise had been to these affairs before. All the ladies and gentlemen on his guest list had. They'd been chosen carefully. The liaisons between them were whispered about but not common knowledge. Since divorce was unheard of, this was the next best thing, she supposed. Her lips twisted. Such behavior was yet another argument against the state of wedded bliss.

She knew she'd be given a bedroom adjoining Roald's. All the couples would have the same arrangement. Elise had always managed to handle Roald before. This time, however, she wasn't sure. She was sure only of one thing. It wasn't going to be very relaxing or recuperative.

"Well . . . good day, Lady Sophie, and I see you've brought that spark, the Dowager Duchess of Wynd, with you. I'm so pleased you both could visit my humble estate. Truly, I am. You brighten any gathering."

Barrigan's loud, booming voice met them at the landing. Elise looked it over critically. The architect had used a monstrous amount of marble and imported teakwood in the design of Barrigan's hunting lodge. It was as far from humble as could be described. Of course, Barrigan already knew it. That was the reason he'd spoken as he had.

Elise curtsied to hide the contempt. "My lord, your estate is most magnificent, as always. I'm thankful you thought to include me in your little entertainment this weekend."

Sophie echoed much the same at Elise's side.

"My thanks for your words, Lady Elise, but where have you eschewed Sir Roald? I thought him permanently attached at your side."

He winked at her. She smiled slightly and humorlessly.

"Sir Roald has other means of transportation at his disposal, my lord. I doubt he'd wish his name permanently attached to mine, anyhow, wherewithal the rumors."

"Have you had a falling off with Sir Roald?"

"Something of that nature," Sophie replied.

"Nothing of the sort!" Elise lightly touched Sophie on the arm with the edge of her lace pelisse. "I have only the highest regard for Sir Roald. And let's not forget his words. He does pen the most exquisite poetry, doesn't he?"

"I never read that sort of drivel," Barrigan replied.

"Spoken like a true man, my lord."

"He can be a devil at cards, though. I hope he comes with full pockets this time."

"Don't look to me," Elise replied. "I never bankroll my lovers. That sort of thing I leave to the moneylenders, although they'll not get as much for their coin, I'm certain."

Sophie gasped, while Barrigan choked on his amusement. "It's a good thing I've placed you beside Sir Roald, then. You had me worried. You won't find fault with my arranging?"

"Pray, don't let Lady Elise snow you, my lord. She'll have you thinking she admires the new Duke of Mac-Gowan next."

"I'll do nothing of the sort. For shame, Sophie. The next thing you know, His Grace's name will be even more firmly linked with mine. The poor man may never recover." Elise laughed lightly, and the others followed suit. "Although I will admit a penchant for attractive men who are lampooned with me. It helps share the fame. Where have you placed him, anyway? Has the duke a, shall we say, a companion with him?"

"Not to my knowledge. He arrived alone. I'll place him beside you for sup. That should provide enough entertainment for all of us. Come, ladies, my head housekeeper, Barton, will show you to your rooms. Until this evening, then."

Elise had sent Daisy on ahead, so she wasn't surprised to find her belongings already unpacked and her bed covered in her own linens. She dismissed the Barton woman after thanking her for the assistance.

The woman's stiff back answered Elise. She quickly stifled any emotion. All the staff at these gatherings seemed the same. They were snobbish and unfriendly, and they appeared to look down on the gentry they served. She ignored it.

Daisy helped Elise disrobe and don a fresh sleep gown, so she might lay down to rest before supper. It was probably useless. She now had the duke at one elbow and Sir Roald at the other. She was in luck that she'd wanted it restful and relaxing. She couldn't imagine what would have transpired had she wished for an exciting, eventful evening.

With her thoughts racing as they were and nothing decided, she was amazed that she actually slept.

When she awoke, late afternoon sunlight was warming the chamber. Daisy had been quietly efficient, as always. Elise's new maroon taffeta gown was pressed and hanging on the armoire door. A scented, warmed hip-bath welcomed her from beside the fireplace.

"Daisy, you are a wonder. Whatever would I do without you?"

The maid grinned and bobbed her head. "Get yourself in even more trouble. What else?"

"What trouble am I in now?"

Daisy clucked her tongue. "More than your usual, to be sure. And don't act all big-eyed and innocent with me. I was there. I got to bear the brunt of it when you left that fellow standing on the steps the other eve. Don't cow-tow to me. Here, hand me the nightie and sink beneath these bubbles. I've an ice goddess to create, you know."

"And which fellow might we be referring to?" Elise asked, as she shed the gown and let the afternoon sunlight touch her nakedness. The mirror reflected everything. Elise posed and turned, looking for any imperfections. She was slender, it was true, but she definitely had meat to her, and in all the right places, too. The man wasn't just a barbarian, he was a blind one.

"You're going to have to tell him. The longer you wait, the harder it'll get. Mark my words."

"I don't need a conscience at this late date," Elise replied.

"True enough. Go on. Get in. The bubbles? Wait! The hair."

Elise waited while her tresses were pinned atop her head before sinking into luxury; she leaned forward so the maid could wash her back with a large soft cloth, soaped by bath salts scented with lavender. Everything that touched the dowager duchess was the softest, most expensive item available. She sighed. Then Daisy had to go and ruin it.

"Now, don't go take that tone with me," Daisy said. "I've not finished with you, yet."

"What have I done now?"

"Deserved a spanking, but I'll forego it for another lecture."

"For what?" Elise asked.

"That man. Leading him on. Leaving him standing

on your doorstep the other eve, when he was dressed in a pure symphony of masculine taste. You should have seen him."

"I did," Elise remarked.

"Then you must have known how much trouble he went through to look like that. And how do you repay it? You leave him standing."

"He's a big, bullheaded, boorish brute bred in the barbaric boundaries of a backwater country."

"There's an awful lot of *B* words in there." The cloth slapped against her neck.

"Well, he is," Elise said.

"And all of that has nothing to do with what you owe him."

"I don't owe him the time it would take to embarrass him. On second thought, that much I do. I've yet to pay him back for the other evening. He was horrid to me. 'Past paramours?' he asks, before passing that cartoon all over the room. I'll not live that one down easily."

"You jilted him. It's you owing him, I would say."

"I don't do what a man orders me to do. Never again, anyway."

Daisy sighed. "Oh, very well. You still owe him the truth. He's got to know of the existence of the babe. It's his nephew, too."

"Good Lord." Elise sat upright. "We're related that closely?"

"Like you don't know each and every bit of it. Your sister, God rest her soul, wouldn't want that baby not knowing his own heritage."

"My sister had an illegitimate child, Daisy. I hardly think God had any part of *that*."

"It wasn't her fault. She was in love. He lied to her. It was his fault. All his. Every bit of it. His."

"So . . . you're saying it was a man's fault?" Elise asked innocently.

"That's what I've said and keep saying. It was completely and totally that Evan MacGowan's fault. That sweet Evangeline went to him pure and innocent, and he took it from her. He used her. Poor girl."

"Yes, poor girl. Poor Evangeline Sherbourne. Poor country girl. She gives herself to a big, barbarian, Scottish brute—one without a hint of a conscience, I should insert here—and how does he repay such a gift? He leaves her to face the ruin all by herself. And now *you're* lecturing me on how *I* treat one of them?"

"You're turning my words on me."

"And you're making it too easy."

"He's half Scots, you know," Daisy said.

"Who?"

"The babe. Your nephew. Rory. The light of your existence, or so you say every time you hold him."

Elise groaned. "Don't remind me."

"So when are you going to tell the duke and get this weight off your shoulders?"

"What weight?" Elise asked uneasily.

"The one you're always mumbling to yourself about when you think no one's listening."

"Oh," Elise replied, "that weight."

"It'll be easy. Just go up to him and say, 'Pardon me, Your Grace, but could I have a word with you? In private?' If you'd use your charms, I bet you'd have that fellow around your finger. You might even get him around your ring finger, unlike your older sister. God rest her soul."

Elise's eyes went wide. "Never. Ever. Never." She said each word and waited until the hint of sound evaporated before saying the next. It still felt awful. "Besides, you're forgetting, Evangeline wasn't good enough for one of them. What makes you think I would be?"

"Wishful thinking. And you should leave a bit of

room for doubt, you know. You're young. You're beautiful. You're healthy. You're rich."

"I'm heartless," Elise inserted.

"Only on the outside, love. Here, step out. You'll make wrinkles out of your skin if we don't get some creams rubbed into it before it dries. On the bed, facedown."

Elise lay on the large, fluffed out blanket of towels Daisy had warmed for the purpose. The maid started at her shoulders with yet another lavender-scented potion.

"There's something else you probably should know," Elise said, when Daisy finished massaging her lower legs and ankles. "I have tried to talk to him. He doesn't give me any time. If I open my mouth, he jumps right down my throat with some order or like insult, and I can't get in a breath, let alone a word."

"You? Tongue-tied? I'll never be able to show my face belowstairs again. Here, I've brought your striped stockings. Sit. Leg?"

Elise lifted a leg and helped pull the peppermint-candy-striped stockings into place on her upper thighs. She grimaced. "Why did I order such a loud design, anyway?" she asked.

"You wished a bit of attention drawn to your ankles should someone brush against your skirts. That's the same reason all your tastes are loud—attention. You thrive on it. Which does make it odd that you'd not pursue this Scottish duke fellow's company more."

"What are we talking of now?"

"Stand. Arms up." Daisy helped Elise pull a skintight, silken chemise over herself; then she strapped on a corset. "I saw the cartoons. Everybody did. They didn't do you justice; but then again, they never do. Deep breath."

Elise sucked in her stomach and winced as the

laces were pulled tight. "They were scandalous, Daisy," she managed to falter.

"Well! There's nothing like a bit of scandal to get you even more attention, and take a bit of it away from that Lady Sophie Ipswich. Now there's a woman who should be minding her manners and attending to her own home, not gallivanting about with boys a decade younger than she is. Like I've always said. Here, crinoline time. Stand straight. Taller. We'd best wear the heels again. That man probably dwarfs you."

"Probably?" Elise responded, watching the transformation taking place in the mirror. She didn't argue the points Daisy was making. It was a waste of breath. Besides, she couldn't breathe deeply enough to argue them.

"So do I have your promise?" Daisy asked, as she lifted the maroon dress down from the armoire door.

"What would I have promised now?"

"That you'll speak to His Grace. Tonight."

Elise groaned.

"You'll find a way to tell him. Tonight. Promise."

"He doesn't listen to anything I say, though. He treats me like a strumpet who lacks morals and a mind."

"You've got him where you want him, then. Good girl."

"What?" Elise asked.

"He'll not consider you marriage material, either. It works on just about every gent, except that poet-snake fellow. He'd take you with no questions asked. Of him, either, I might add."

"Poet-snake fellow?" Elise repeated.

"Sorry. Personal opinion. I have them. I do try to keep them to myself, though; otherwise, I'd find myself without any employ. Should you find my services lacking, of course."

"Never." Elise smiled. "There's not another lady of the peerage deserving of such service. But I think you denigrate Roald without reason. You forget, I enjoy his company."

"Not as much as he enjoys your gold."

"He's got a wicked sense of humor, Daisy. You do have to admit that. Come along, admit it."

"Wicked? Yes, that he is. Here, try this." The maid was holding out a maroon vinaigrette, a small bag for holding smelling salts and other ladylike necessities.

"Am I planning on swooning now?" Elise asked, raising her eyebrows. "What good will that do?"

"It's the coward's way. Try it. It might work."

"Daisy, I'm beginning to wonder at your sanity, and I've never been cowardly. I'm not about to start. The notorious Ice Goddess fainting? I'll never live it down."

Daisy clucked her tongue. "I put lavender-scented note cards in there. Put the words on one. Press it into his hand. They'll think it a love note. Take it. You might need a lifeline."

An hour later, Elise was pronounced ready and allowed to leave the chamber. Daisy had added more height by wrapping Elise's hair all about her head before placing a small ruby tiara in it. More of the same stones were set in a necklace that molded along the tops of her breasts, drawing the eye there. Looking there, no man could possibly think she needed meat to any part of her frame. The vinaigrette dangled from her left wrist with a note already written out.

Elise knew no part of her appearance could be faulted. It was a good thing. She needed it. She entered Barrigan's drawing room and Sir Roald was instantly at her side. Elise looked him over critically and could find nothing amiss, or snakelike. He was immaculately groomed, in stovepipe trousers, a high, starched cravat, and he had a small, linked chain draped to the monocle in his breast pocket.

"My lady, you eclipse the stars."

Elise tipped her head and glanced up at him. "I haven't forgiven you yet, Roald. Pray don't force it."

"I'm but a mere man, and such a lowly creature can never take note in the radiance cast from your own beauty."

Elise winced. "Pray don't bore me with such prose tonight."

"When should a man speak such things, then?"

"When they're requested, of course. Why look, there's Lady Beth. She does look spectacular, doesn't she?"

"You expect me to take note of other women when I've the most ethereal creature in the country at my elbow?" he asked.

"I'm warning you, Roald."

He sighed in an exaggerated fashion, then turned to look at their host's mistress. Lady Beth was graced with a complexion as pale as ivory, a font of light, auburn hair, and black eyelashes. That was a combination nature would never have gifted her with. Elise knew Lady Beth had liberally rubbed her lashes with watered-down soot to get such an effect. Elise knew because she wasn't above such artifice herself.

Lady Beth was wearing a peach gown and a resplendent, three-strand pearl necklace that must have set Barrigan back a few pounds. Elise wondered what Lady Beth's husband would think of his wife's new acquisition. Then she wondered, for the thousandth time, why she cared about such things.

"Bloody fortune on her, isn't it?"

Roald's venomous whisper startled her. "Don't begrudge it, Roald. Harry seems happy enough."

"Some women expect payment for services rendered. I'm in luck with you, am I not?"

Elise sucked in the gasp. "You dare much with such words."

He shrugged, and the tightness of his coat barely allowed the movement. Elise looked away. He was rapidly losing his attractiveness to her, if he'd ever had any.

"I've not much to lose, have I?" he asked.

"Sir Roald . . . Easton, is na' it?"

Colin MacGowan loomed right beside them and introduced himself. Elise guessed he'd been eavesdropping on their whispered conversation. She felt, rather than saw, Roald stiffen.

"MacGowan, I'm debating whether to shake your hand or call for my seconds." Roald tipped his head to look up at the other man.

"Seconds? A duel? Over her?" the duke asked, motioning with his head toward Elise.

Roald nodded.

"Why shake, of course. I've *nae* desire to kill a man when there's *nae* honor at stake."

Elise watched them clasp hands with a detached sense of fascination as to why Roald would put his fingers through the torment of such a wrenching handhold. She watched his fingers whiten, and then watched his jaw as he gritted his teeth. Then MacGowan released him.

Roald put the injured limb inside his jacket lapel, as though it belonged there. Elise was very close to rolling her eyes.

"I believe the lady shall be accompanying me to sup this eve. You may need to seek an assist with that hand, Easton. Lady Elise? Your servant." He was holding out an arm, awaiting her.

"Oh dear, you've learned my name. I'm not at all certain that's a good thing, Your Grace."

He grinned, completely opening a hole in the floor in front of her; then he winked, making it worse.

Chapter 4

There was something about this Scottish duke fellow, something Elise couldn't put her finger on. Just being next to him was the strangest experience. Everything sounded and looked more vivid, crisp, and bright, and felt more alive. Elise couldn't credit what it was, and she spent more than a bit of time trying to decipher it as they sat in a strangely companionable silence. It was as if someone had put magnifying glasses to her nose and she was looking through them at everything.

The first course was some molded confection made of salad greens in a jellied mixture that was neither sweet, salty, nor bitter. In fact, it was fairly tasteless and felt loose and insubstantial on her tongue. Elise tasted it, before putting down her spoon. Beside her, the duke devoured it. That course then was removed and everyone was served a hard, cold, blackened roll. Elise pulled off a bite, nibbled on it, and set it back down. They had baked large wheat kernels into the bread, making a crunchy texture that was tart tasting. Elise slid the bite about her mouth before swallowing. Beside her, she felt, rather than saw, the duke devouring that course as well. She didn't know why she cared to note what he ate, or how he did it. He hadn't grown to the size he was without eating.

The next course was a small Fillet of Whiting in a cream sauce. She toyed with the sauce, dribbling it over the fish, before bringing it to her mouth. It was perfectly seasoned with mushrooms and garlic pepper, and it was served at the correct temperature. The fish melted where it sat on her tongue. Elise couldn't remember having such sensations with food before, and then the man at her side opened his mouth and put a halt to the dreamlike sequence of it all.

"You eat less than a bairn," he said, startling her.

Elise slid her glance sideways, taking in the perfectly cut and tailored jacket, the crisply starched cravat, and now that she was so close, she could see his eyes sparkled with flecks of green highlights. She swallowed.

"Most gentlemen wouldn't remark on such a thing, Your Grace," she replied.

"Most men you've been around were na' gentlemen."

"I beg your pardon?"

"You always say that. I dinna' think you know what it means."

"I beg—" She stopped the exclamation herself.

"See?" His lips twitched. "I believe begging someone's pardon means you wish the words repeated because you canna' believe you heard them right the first time. True?"

She lifted a shoulder and felt the rubies slide across her breasts with the motion. She watched his glance flick there before returning to her face. Shivers accompanied it.

"So why beg it of me? You heard it right the first time."

"Your words are insulting. You're insulting."

His eyebrows lifted. "Am I now?"

"I'm beginning to think you take great pride in it, too."

"If I do, it's your fault."

"Mine?" She asked it with a bit of incredulity to her voice, and then she asked it again with more conviction. "Mine?"

"You specifically requested to have me placed right next to you this evening. Our host told me of it. For the life of me I canna' imagine why. Oh, yes, I do. It was to make your lover jealous."

Elise's eyes widened, but she caught the gasp as he leaned toward her to whisper the rest of it.

"You need na' bother. He looked jealous enough already."

Servants were removing the whiting and the duke had to lean away so they could do so. Elise turned forward and reached for her wineglass. They had served a Chablis. It was excellent with fish, she decided, letting the swallow linger in her mouth to rinse and refresh it.

"You like these society things?" he asked, when all she did was studiously look at the centerpiece of roses.

She put her goblet down in time for the servants to remove it. They were getting ready to serve the beef. That called for a wine change to a Bordeaux. She waited until it was poured to turn back to him. She didn't have any other recourse. Roald was still noticeably absent from his assigned seating, and Colin was ignoring the woman on his other side, giving Elise his undivided attention. To do anything other than converse civilly, when he was making this effort, would be *déclassé*.

"In what context?" she asked finally.

"These dinners. These clothes. The jewels. The flowers. The candlelight. The conversation. The funds expended on it all. *Ambiance*. That sort of thing."

Elise sighed. "I wouldn't be here if I didn't enjoy it, Your Grace."

"You've a strange way of showing it, then."

"I beg—" Elise cut it off again. She really did say it too much.

He grinned. The resultant blaze of fire through her chest frightened her, and there wasn't a thing she could blame it on. She had to look away.

"Don't think I'm fey. I'm na'."

"Fey?" she asked the roses.

"Sighted."

"Oh," Elise replied, although she hadn't the vaguest idea what he was talking about.

"I dinna' think you do much that you do enjoy, although you playact like you do. You're verra good, too. It's hard to spot."

Elise frowned at what he said, and then she frowned at the plate being set before her, which contained several folded-over, thin slices of roast beef. She knew exactly how it would taste by her enhanced sense of smell, and then she got to frown at that, too.

"I think you're overstepping yourself," she replied finally. The roast beef tasted just like she'd known it would, and Elise chewed thoughtfully on the four bites she allowed herself. Any more and she'd have trouble with the corset's confinement.

"I usually do," he said beside her, as he devoured his own platter. "Get used to it."

"Good heavens, why?"

He shrugged, and that movement in his tight jacket made the material go taut, defining sculpted shoulders for a moment, and then it was gone. Elise's eyes flew wide, and she was afraid to breathe.

"You asked for my company. You've got it."

"I never said—"

"You know most people who say they enjoy a meal actually eat it," he interrupted her, motioning to her unfinished serving.

"I am eating it," she replied, lifting her fork again.

"Like I said before, you eat like a bairn."

"And you eat enough to kill a horse," she replied, goaded into her own insult.

His eyebrows rose again. "How do you expect to create healthy ones if you dinna' eat enough to support them?"

"Healthy what?" Elise asked.

"Bairns."

She was reeling in place, astonished that she still sat upright, twirling her dinner fork, and extremely amazed that not one of the other diners appeared to have heard anything Colin MacGowan was saying.

"I believe I called you barbaric earlier, Your Grace. Allow me to embroider and refine that. When they invent the word, that is."

"I'm checking the market, dear lady. You're on it. You're making certain I take note of that. Very well, I am. I'm simply examining and testing the merchandise before the purchase. It's impressively arrayed, too, I might add. It's my prerogative, no?"

"No. Unequivocally, irrevocably, and inescapably no. N. O. No. Never. No." Her heart was pounding painfully against the little ribbon tie on the front of her silk chemise. She was afraid he'd spot it.

"Then why this game?"

"Game?" she asked.

"The courtship game. I was beginning to think you were playing it. Then you deny it. Is that part of the game?"

"The courtship game? I never thought of it—I mean, I never . . ." Elise stammered through her comment, and then put her fork down so the servants could remove her plate. She finished her words to the molded fruit sorbet that was being put in front of her. She didn't dare look anywhere toward him. If she held her breath, counted to ten, and kept her voice low, she was ready to blurt out her secret, and then she was going to run, as fast and as far as she could. She started counting.

"What are you doing?"

"Counting to ten," she replied without thinking.

"Why? It's na' going to change things. You're very good at the play of it. Very."

"The play of what?" she asked.

"The courtship game. Intrigue. Witty remarks. Entrancing displays. Catching interest. Holding it. You catching mine. Literally."

Elise lost her inheld breath, every bit of her nerve, and any ability to answer. Little needles of reaction felt like they were racing her body to reach her toes in the heeled shoes Daisy had made certain she wore. She'd never felt anything like it. She didn't think she liked it, either.

"Everywhere I've been and everywhere I go, there you are. Are you following me?"

Elise swallowed and turned to him. "Not because I want to," she replied.

It was his turn to gape, and she watched those brown eyes widen. She'd slighted him before. He was actually extremely handsome, once one got past the first impression of the man. It was a shame he was the one man who, not only would she never play any sort of game with, but whose clan had decreed her unfit for even the participation, just as they'd already branded her sister. Pariah. Jezebel. Unwed mother. Harlot. Sinner. Her pious sister, Evangeline, forever labeled a sinner?

Elise's lips tightened; she turned back to her sorbet and watched with a strange, detached sense of dread as Roald's chair was pulled out for him and he dropped into it. She rather fancied he'd been drinking. When he opened his mouth and started speaking, she knew it.

"Elise?" Roald pushed away the serving placed

before him. She caught the motion out of the corner of her eye. She sighed and tipped her head toward him, because there wasn't anything else she could do.

"Yes, Roald?" she replied, excruciatingly aware of the male on the left side of her. She noticed Roald wasn't using his right hand yet. In fact, he had it tucked beneath the table linens.

"You can cease avoiding me. I'm contrite."

"Roald, I've been dining. You've been absent. That hardly constitutes avoidance on my part."

"You know what I mean." His left hand snaked out for the wine goblet. Elise watched it.

Beside her, she heard Colin chuckle, although the sound was barely discernible. "Something amuses you, Your Grace?" Elise turned her head back to him.

"These society affairs can be amusing. Na' what I'm used to. I believe I can understand your sentiment about them."

"I never said—" Elise stopped the words herself, and there was an awkward silence, for it seemed conversation stopped as those diners across the table from them listened, too.

The servants were removing the sorbet, preparatory to serving the next course, which her nose alerted her was going to be a meat-filled pastry. Murmurs of appreciation accompanied the presentation of each plate, where an individual pie had been formed from paper-thin shells of pastry, and then baked into a small custard cup.

"My only regret is that I canna' linger much longer. I'm anxious to return to my home, Castle Gowan," the duke said, from her left.

"But you've not gained what you sought," Roald said loudly, on her right. Then he looked sidelong at Elise. "Or have you?"

Now Colin was looking steadily at her. Elise didn't bother to check. Her heightened senses were telling her exactly what he was doing. Her stomach lurched queerly. She gulped. Then he was talking loudly enough for everyone to overhear, easily deflecting the attention from her. She listened to him do it and knew what he was doing without asking—he was rescuing her. Elise didn't betray herself by so much as an eyelash flutter as she examined the rose centerpiece with minute detail.

"That may seem a puzzle, Easton, but I find myself longing for the burn I used to fish in, a good round of golf, and the stables. My father improved the Mac-Gowan stock some years back. I'm told we compare favorably with any in the South, something unheard of, if you ask the right Englishman. I'm na' slackard in the saddle, either, and I miss a good ride. That'll most likely be the first thing I do when I return, although I've probably grown too soft for the clime, now."

The duke . . . soft? Elise contemplated his tight-fitting jacket, the cuffs at his hands, and from there to where the black trousers molded and defined his thighs. He didn't look a bit soft. The instant she thought it, Elise had to move her glance back to her entwined fingers.

Roald answered, "You're in luck, Your Grace. I understand there's to be a foxhunt on the morrow. First light. There will be plenty of time to show off your prowess at riding . . . a *horse,* that is. As an Englishman, I look forward to seeing it."

Elise went white and then dark pink with her blushes. She knew it, too, because her skin was cold, and then flushed with heat. She hadn't been slighting Roald earlier to Daisy. He had a wicked sense of humor and a rapier-sharp tongue. She just hadn't had it turned on her before.

Elise heard the gasps and then the twitters of amusement about them. She took a deep breath.

She had to do something. "You say nothing of your home, Your Grace. Do you miss it as well?"

She batted her eyelashes up at him, pleading silently for him to ignore Roald's taunt. Elise's eyes widened as he winked again; then he smiled, and those green flecks sparkled at her. Elise had to force herself to continue looking at him without showing that it was affecting her, and very much so.

"My home? Why, I miss Castle Gowan the most, of course."

"Why is that, pray tell?" Elise hoped the lighthearted note was in her voice as she placed a hand on Colin's sleeve. She didn't have to look to know how Roald was reacting. The entire grouping of diners across from them told her. She was more afraid of the way her fingers curved ever so slightly about the duke's forearm, molding to and learning the muscled curvature it felt like he had, even there.

"Castle Gowan, situated as it is on the shore of Loch Elnore, was originally built to protect against Norse raids. Only one tower and the old gatehouse still survive from that time, although outer walls still encircle the grounds. The keep itself was rebuilt after Culloden. The duke at the time had wed with a Douglas heiress. She brought a dowry that paid for most of the upkeep and repairs. Prince Charlie's war nearly bankrupted the MacGowans, as it did most the lairds. Her dowry was their salvation, I'm sure."

Elise nodded as if she knew what he was talking about. He rolled his hand into a fist, cupped by the other hand, and the motion made the arm beneath her fingers move and tense. She felt each ridge of muscle in his forearm as he did so.

"Oh, do tell me more," she said, with a breathlessness she wasn't far from feeling.

Colin leaned toward her, nearly touching his head to hers as he bent down to whisper. "I can talk of

Castle Gowan all eve, but it will na' prevent your paramour from glaring at me."

He didn't give her time to respond to his latest insult. Besides a deep intake of breath and gripping his arm, she didn't know how to react to it, anyway. Colin lifted his head away.

"My grandfather also wed well. My grandmother's dowry refurbished most of the rooms. Why, Castle Gowan rivals anything you'll find here. Easily."

"I find that difficult to believe. Surely you exaggerate, and I must dispute the point. Any Englishman worthy of the name would do the same," Roald said from the other side of her.

"Perhaps I'll proffer you an invite, Sir Easton, once I'm settled, and then I'll have *nae* further reason to argue it with you, will I?"

"Here now. How's that? Did I hear you extending an invitation to Sir Roald, Colin? What's the bugger done to deserve that, I wonder?"

Barrigan's booming voice toward the end of the table inserted itself. Elise closed her eyes tightly as it felt like everything and everyone paused in order to watch and listen. She'd known they'd be the entertainment for the evening. She'd as much as set it up that way.

"Why, I extend Castle Gowan's hospitality to you also, Lord Barrigan," Colin replied. "Of course, it's a hellish journey to reach it, and one that takes nigh on two weeks if the weather holds."

"Two weeks?"

Someone asked it, and Elise removed her fingers from his arm as delicately as she could while he answered. She knew what she was going to do. She was going to take the coward's way out. She reached down for her little bag and palmed the lavender-scented notecard by feel alone.

* * *

Night mist chilled her arms and Elise rubbed at them to still the shivers racing through them, before resuming her pacing. Barrigan had installed several Eastern-inspired pagodas throughout his garden. It was a romantic, enchanting sight, if anything could be. She reached the side of the structure, pivoted, and started back across.

Lilac bushes obliterated the sides of the pagoda, just as Elise had remembered, creating the privacy she needed. Unfortunately, it was also unsettling and unnerving to ladies who should be abed, rather than waiting to unburden secrets they shouldn't be a party to in the first place. Elise listened to the rustle of leaves and the strange sounds of the woods about her. Barrigan really should fence his property, she decided, and then she wondered how much longer she was going to have to wait. It would be just like that man to make her wait, too. Her note had been most specific: MIDNIGHT. PAGODA CLOSEST TO THE WOODS. ALONE.

Her lips twisted. It was now ten past, and knowing her luck, he probably still hadn't opened it!

She stilled as a man silhouetted himself in the framework.

"Your Grace?" Elise whispered when he appeared. It was difficult to see him. His presence was only visible due to the lighter shade of darkness about him.

"Even you could not be so cruel, Elise."

Roald's voice cracked intentionally as he approached. Elise stumbled until her back touched a pole.

"I . . . I am meeting the duke on a private matter. You are not to interfere. I have something I have to make him aware of."

"What could be of such import that you seek his company here, at night . . . alone and unescorted?"

"It's none of your concern," she replied.

"It's of every concern to me."

"You're not to follow me, Roald. I won't have it! Now go!"

"You expect me to ignore this pursuit of him?" he asked.

Elise stuck out her jaw, pushing her lower teeth past the upper ones. He couldn't see it. "You're mistaken, but I won't explain. I don't have to explain my actions to anyone. That's the way I like it."

"How many times have I asked you, Elise? Do you feel nothing for me? Nothing for my . . . suffering?"

His voice, as much as his words, would have been wrenching had she not already eavesdropped on just such a speech before. Roald had once hidden her in a cupboard at his apartment when one of his many women came to see him and listen to the same wrenching words.

"Roald, I'll have no man. I've told you often enough. None."

He dropped to one knee before her. Elise could just make out his face and the glint of his eyes in what light slithered through the gazebo's widely spaced poles. She stiffened.

"Marry me, Elise."

"No."

"I'm . . . begging you," he beseeched, making his voice faltering and shy sounding.

Elise's features froze. "Don't. It doesn't become you."

"I'll die without you."

The man should have been on the stage. She'd often thought it. Now, she knew for certain. "Put the thought to paper, and perhaps I'll read it, Roald," she said coldly.

"Do you care nothing for me?"

"Oh, please. Stop this. I've heard this same speech from you too many times and to too many other

women. You needn't start boring me with such stupidity at this date. I'll not listen. Now, get up."

"You think you know me, don't you, Elise?"

"Not as well as I thought, obviously."

"You think I'll just leave him the clear field?"

"You're mistaken, Roald. I'll not repeat it again. Is
this the way you wish to end our friendship . . . and
your loans?"

"You think I'll just let you go?"

"You've little choice in the matter. Get off your
knees and allow me to retire to my chamber."

"I love you, Elise."

"As I've already heard you say such a thing many
times over, and in the same convincing tone, to lots
of other women, I'll not repeat that, either. See me
back to the house, Roald, and let's end this."

"But this time I mean it. I swear!"

"Oh, please. How much do you need this time?
Own up. I'll pay it, but never again, understand?"

"That isn't what I want, and you know it."

"I'll find my own way back to the house. Good night."

Wreathed in moonlight-strewn mist, Barrigan's
property was romantic and enchanting. It was also
rough and unkempt. Elise made it back to the house
without one misstep. He didn't try to stop her. She
didn't think about that until later.

Chapter 5

Saturday dawned bright and sunny, darn her luck. Elise looked out morosely at the beauty of dawn-highlighted fields. They'd let out the fox any time now and her horse was fidgeting. Not as much as those that Sir Roald, His Grace, and Barrigan were fighting to control, but enough to keep Elise occupied.

She checked the glove's buttons on the backs of her wrists again and silently cursed that move, too. She knew they were still fastened. Everything was still in place. From the chignon at the back of her neck to the thirty-nine buttons on each boot, she was still perfectly dressed and groomed, and as it appeared, so was every other guest.

Only Lady Beth had resisted the invitation to the hunt. Lady Beth's auburn hair was loose on her shoulders, her pearls still entwined her throat, and she looked fresh and relaxed in her peach gown and like-colored pelisse, sitting in an open coach. Elise envied her.

Elise had learned how to ride two years earlier, when one of her men had tired of pretending to be a lover and amused himself teaching her. She knew well enough how to stay atop a horse, but only for a nice, elegant ride through Hyde Park. This was something else.

Elise patted her mount. Thankfully, Barrigan had allowed her to pick it out herself. She'd opted for an older gelding of a gentle nature. Their barely hidden smiles hadn't changed her mind, either. She didn't have anyone to impress. Not with her riding, anyway.

The fox shot from its cage, and Elise realized her luck as she didn't have to spur her mount; he'd done this before.

It wasn't as different to race through the meadow as she'd suspected. Elise was flattered and a bit pleased to find herself in the midst of the riders. She could see Colin MacGowan was leading the field, although Roald hung directly behind him. Elise would have been disappointed if it were any different, and she was disgusted to admit that much to herself.

The Duke of MacGowan was ignoring her. He had to be. The dark crimson of her habit wasn't difficult to spot. Elise had made certain when selecting the shadow-striped, silk material that any ensemble sewn from it would be as eye-catching as it was.

She knew her appearance was spectacular. The first reaction told her as much, but it did nothing to soothe her vanity. The duke had studiously ignored every opportunity to speak to her, or even to look at her. Roald wasn't much better. He wasn't importuning himself with her, but she caught his glance on her more than once.

He wasn't through with her, that much she knew. She wondered how much it was going to cost her to pay him off and be rid of him. The situation was ridiculous. No lady of the realm paid off her sham lovers!

How had she allowed such a thing to happen, anyway? She sighed, then answered her own question. She'd spent too many evenings holding her admirers at arm's length, that's how. She hadn't noted when they became fewer and fewer. Sir Roald had been the only hanger-on. Elise wondered how she'd manage the many society functions still ahead of her without a ready escort to help alleviate the boredom.

The hounds bayed from beyond a hill, out of her sight. Now, she got to wonder how that had happened, too. One moment she was amidst the chase, the next she was by herself.

"Oh, well."

She said it aloud, then sighed dispiritedly. Her heart wasn't in the chase, and she didn't want to see the duke win. She had no doubt that a MacGowan would excel. They always did.

Elise let the horse have its head and wasn't surprised when all it did was bend to munch on the unkempt grass beside the fence. Barrigan really should send his groundskeepers to mow some of the overgrowth away. It was obvious they were a lazy bunch, she told herself.

She was doing too much thinking anymore. It wasn't like her. She was supposed to be enjoying the Season. She was supposed to be putting the gossips on their ears. She was supposed to be setting an example of self-absorbed, self-serving, and lustful ways that couldn't be topped. And she was supposed to be making certain the MacGowans knew that their precious Evan had left an heir, albeit an illegitimate one. That's what she was supposed to be doing, and what had she managed? To sicken herself with thinking of their laird.

Perhaps she'd go to the Wyndham Villa in Monte Carlo. She could be early this year. No one would expect that. Everyone would be expecting her to supplant Roald in her affections with another male conquest. She was tired of the stupid, unspoken rules the *ton* followed. Monte Carlo was fresher, less restricted, more open. There, none would expect her to posture at will. Perhaps there she could be herself.

If she remembered who that was anymore.

A red animal streaked past, startling her horse. Elise grabbed for the mane to hold her seat as dog after dog raced by.

"Blast it! Watch your—!"

Elise hadn't had time to do more than put her hands up as the duke's mount flew over the fence and landed beside her. The ground thudded, chunks of dirt flew, and her horse reared. Elise didn't know the earth was that hard, or that the sky above her was so blue. She couldn't remember why she'd want to know, either.

"God's blood, Madame, but you are the most reckless, stubborn, and stupid woman of my acquaintance!"

Her collar was nearly wrenched from its exquisite sewing as a massive hand grabbed it and yanked her to the fence. She would have screamed when he pulled her beneath the bottom rung, too, except the field of horses leaping the fence and landing where she'd just been silenced her more effectively than a gag.

"Have you *nae* sense?"

Elise grabbed onto him, holding his jacket so tightly her fingers felt enmeshed with the leather lapels on his tweed jacket. She had her eyes squeezed shut, too, to stop the frightened tears. She was barely stopping the screams. Didn't he have enough sense to know that much?

"I asked you a question."

His voice was harsh with the exertion he'd just been through. From where she was held, directly atop him, she could feel every bit of brawn, every deep breath, every nuance. Elise shook her head and pulled closer to him. "Don't . . . say anything more. Please."

Another clod of earth hit her in the back and she whimpered. The tall grass was shielding them better than anything else would have, but she trembled anew at every ground tremor. She didn't dare open her eyes. The MacGowan would know how near tears she was, and no one ever saw such an emotion from the notorious Dowager Duchess of Wynd.

"Spoiled . . . beautiful, irresponsible, little twit."

Fingers touched the area beneath her chin, lifting it, and then his nose matched against hers. Elise didn't have time to do anything other than suck in a gasp as his lips found hers. Then she lost the ability to control anything—her thoughts, her reactions, or her body. Liquid heat washed over her in waves of tremors, blocking out the terror of a moment before.

The ground wasn't thudding with hooves anymore, but her body wouldn't cease shaking. Shivers flew down each limb and were followed by more of them, over and over, time and time again. Warm, hard lips pulled her own awry, as he turned his head in order to more fully possess her mouth. Elise moaned, and with the movement her lips parted. Colin used the opening to flick his tongue against her own. Elise's entire being pulsed at the sensation, and from some instinctive flight of fantasy, she recognized it. She joined him breath to breath, as they grew in cadence, strength, and volume. Without conscious volition, her fingers left the lapels of his jacket, smoothed up over those massive shoulders, and started raking through the tail of hair at his neck.

Now, it was Colin's turn to moan, and the arms about her tightened, stealing her breath and crunching her corset against her ribs. Elise didn't even feel it. Hard. He was hard. Covered with tweed and muslin and cotton duck, he was still hard. And lumpy. Her body molded to the parts of him she was touching, sliding sinuously atop him as his hands started moving, claiming, teasing . . . damning.

Her moan wasn't audible, but she knew what it was as he roamed his hands all over her back, uncrossing his arms when he reached her buttocks in order to cup them and assist her with her writhing motions. Then he was moving them back up, pressing her so tightly to that mass of chest, she was in danger of having the boning from her corset permanently embossed onto her torso.

A loud shout came, stopping everything for an encapsulated, frozen, infinitesimal amount of time. Elise halted every motion at the same moment he pulled his head away, releasing her mouth. Those wide-open, green-flecked brown eyes were glazed with something akin to shock. She'd never seen such an expression.

She had to look away; her mind was devoid of anything she had to make it do. She looked down, past the freshly shaved, strong chin of his, noted that the brown tie was pulled loose, and stopped at the opening of his button placket on his muslin shirt. How had that happened? She focused on an open buttonhole. What had she been doing? What was she thinking? *Oh, dearest God!* she begged. Then, it clicked. She was the Ice Goddess. She was emotionless. Heartless. Ruthless. Arrogant. Merciless.

"Well. . . This is a surprise. You're good. You're verra good." The duke's voice growled at her ear, as well as echoing from the mass of man she was perched upon.

Her mouth opened to say something disdainful. Nothing came out. She had to close it again.

"No answer? Interesting."

Her lips twisted. She opened them again. Nothing came out . . . *again.*

"A woman of few words is a thing of beauty. Or so my father always used to tell me. Damn me, if it isn't true."

He chuckled, making her body, where she was still clasped against him, experience it at the same time. That was so foreign, anything she could have thought of answering flew completely out of her grasp. It was worse than the dinner had been.

Her eyes narrowed to make it harder to see. It didn't work. The experience, sight, smell, and sound of him were too large and perfectly focused to ignore. She could swear she could evaluate the looming quality of the tweed material of his jacket simply by the feel of still being clasped to it, and the texture of every strand of his hair beneath every perfectly manicured fingernail, from the queue she was still holding on to.

"Have you naught to say?" he asked.

"I . . . no." Her voice didn't sound right. That was worrisome. Everything was, especially where she still lay, enwrapped in the Duke of MacGowan's arms and with her bent legs ensconced between where his own had opened, and then closed, trapping hers.

"Well, I have plenty."

Elise turned her head slightly and watched the grass in front of her face that was still shielding them. It was akin to being in a small, intimate, hidey-hole—with the one man she daren't be. She frowned. His chest rose and fell. So did she. The shivers from that contact flew her arms to her fingers, and down her legs to her toes, before she could figure out enough about why to stop them. She was going to cry; but that would be so much worse, it was incomprehensible. She gulped the emotion back, closed her eyes, and gulped again. She was afraid he'd spot her trembling, and then he spoke, confirming that very thing.

"You can cease this. There's *nae* one about to posture to that gives a damn. I certainly dinna'."

She began pulling her fingers away from each strand of that wavy, reddish hair, trying her level best to keep him from noticing it. He moved an arm from her back, cursing her with the instant chill from its absence, and placed it beneath his head, trapping her fingers exactly where they were. Then he lay back, sealing her hands in his, as if there was nothing further about it than that.

"They've . . . gone." She whispered it, yet still had to swallow between the words.

"True," he answered.

"You can let me up now." Her voice was still breathless sounding, but it was stronger.

"Is anything broken?" he asked.

My facade is. Does that count? she wondered. She shook her head.

"That's one good thing, I suppose. You've ruined my hunt."

Elise opened her eyes.

"Was that your plan?" he continued.

"I was knocked off my horse. I was nearly trampled. I couldn't plan that."

"Everything you do is carefully planned, woman. Everything."

Elise's eyes widened on the grass.

"They'll probably send a search party for us when the race is won and I'm na' the man winning it. Then they'll notice you're missing, too. This might prove difficult to explain. Of course, that Easton fellow might not care, now that he's nipped me to the post. Oh, what am I saying? The man is dying of love for you."

She put a carefully constructed look on her face by arching her brows and shuttering her eyes before she turned back to him. It didn't help that he hadn't moved, and she was close enough to feel his breath on her cheek. "You're reading the wrong cartoons, Your Grace."

"I heard him with my own ears, last night. I just dinna' understand why you gave me a note making certain I'd be there to hear it. I've been puzzling it and still canna' figure it. Well?"

Elise took a deep breath. "I . . . have a secret for Your Grace."

"Oh, I'm fairly certain you have several. I'm just cursed to be on the receiving end of this one."

She couldn't stop the movement as her eyes widened, pulling them from the disinterested look she'd attempted.

"Surprised? Dinna' be. You're fairly transparent. You wanted to make Easton jealous so he'd propose. I understand this courtship game. I dinna' like playing it, as anyone in my old regiment could tell you, but I do know how. You will na' like it if I start, either. Trust me."

"I play no game."

"Right."

The one word made it sound like she never told the truth. Elise stiffened, and then she knew what was worse, as every bit of her came into contact with every bit of him. Even through her riding habit, gloves, and buttoned boots she felt him. Her heightened senses made certain of it, as hard humps of chest smashed further against her bosom, an entwined conglomeration of ropelike stomach pressed against hers, hard hips supported hers, while legs resembling iron bars were locked so effortlessly about hers it might as well have been a permanent condition.

"I suppose you're going to say this is na' a game, either?" he asked, his breath catching strangely midway through the words.

Elise forced herself to relax every part of her body that was touching him. "Let me up, please."

"I'm na' holding you,"

Beyond the thinning of her lips, she let that one pass. "Please?" She tried again.

"Explain yourself, first."

"What?"

"The courtship game. Why are you still playing it with me?"

Elise looked heavenward before returning to his

face. "Just because Sir Roald came upon me doesn't mean I'm playing anything."

"Then why did you set it up . . . and then turn him down?"

"That isn't what happened."

"I already told you, I heard it. I trust my own ears more than a woman's lies. I just dinna' understand why you did it. Enlighten me."

"I don't have to say another word to you."

"Do you wish to be free?"

The fingers locked further on both of her hands, imprisoning her against his queue. Her eyes went wide before she could help it. Then she had to shutter them and blink before he saw it. She'd been stupid earlier, she realized. Instead of trying to work her fingers loose without disturbing strands of his hair, she should have been pulling them out.

"Were you trying to make him pant for you more than he already does?"

"I beg your pardon!"

He grinned, and the gesture destroyed every bit of her constructed personae. She knew he saw it, too. He wasn't leaving her in any doubt as he winked. "Trust me, lady. You heard it exactly as I said it."

"If you say another word, I'm going to hit you."

"With what? I've got your hands." He tensed the one hand behind his head again, proving it.

"My knee."

She went to move it, but the legs she'd already compared with iron bands flexed, sealing off any move. That put everything that was male about him against everything that was female about her. Elise's gasp wasn't heard above the absolute roar of sound in her very own ears.

"Care to try again?" he asked. His eyebrows were raised, and when he was amused, his eyes were definitely more green than brown.

Elise swallowed, but it was more a gulp.

"So . . . are you ready to enlighten me?"

Tell him about their siblings and Rory? *Now?* Elise nodded. She gulped the excess moisture from her mouth, then had to suck more moisture in when it dried too much to speak.

There was another loud shout, followed by several more. The duke moved his head, craning his neck to listen, moving Elise with it. Her eyes fell to where his button placket had come undone. He was a tan color, even where the skin disappeared beneath his shirt. Something happened. Something twinged deep inside her, and Elise surprised herself by actually catching the gasp that was accompanying it. She'd never felt the like, but if it was what she suspected it was, there was absolutely nothing worse in the world that could happen!

He had bands of sinew going from his jawline, down his neck, and right into where his shoulders were still hidden beneath his shirt and jacket. Elise went limp before she embarrassed herself forever by putting her lips to the flesh he was displaying for her.

"You keep looking at me like that and we're going to be in an even more compromising position when we're found."

Like what? she instantly wondered, but already knew.

His voice had echoed from the chest she was perched atop. Everything in her wanted to put her head down, snuggle against that neck, bury her nose against the heartbeat she could see pulsing through the skin, and experience everything he'd made her feel the first time he'd kissed her. None of which she was ever going to show.

Elise closed her eyes, found the core of strength she'd always had deep inside of her, and counted to ten before opening her eyes. She was labeled The Ice Goddess for a reason. She looked into those greenish brown eyes with the coldest expression she could manage and hoped it worked.

"I don't think I like you very much, Your Grace," she said.

"The feeling's mutual. Does this mean you will na' be expecting a proposal of marriage after this ravishment?" he asked.

Marriage proposal? Ravishment? Her mind replayed the words. Her heart decided it would continue beating, and she'd have given anything to be able to stop the blush that was heating all the way to her forehead and back.

"Oh, I forgot. It's unequivocally, inescapably, and a few other fancy, big words . . . no."

"I'll . . . never marry." She had a voice. It was breathless, young, innocent sounding, and everything she'd destroyed when she married the first time. She frowned. "I mean . . . remarry."

"Right. Why, please?"

"Why?" she repeated automatically.

"Yes, why? Women marry. Men get trapped. Good God, this is na' a trap, is it?"

He lifted his head, instantly releasing her hands. The look of shock was back. Elise giggled, then felt him go taut beneath her, making her body rise a bit with the movement. That was interesting, she decided. Almost as much so as the flush infusing his cheeks and making the flecks in his eyes even more green-looking as he stared at her.

"I'll never consider remarriage, Your Grace. It's the one thing I won't do."

"Truly?" He relaxed, moving her body again with that motion, and then he blew the sigh over his forehead. All of which she was extremely aware of. "That does leave other options I'll have to think over. You'd na' think it amiss if I escort you to dinner again?"

"I'm not in need of an escort. I believe I already have one."

He snorted. "Let's run along and see if Sir Roald will mind, then."

Elise frowned. "In that event, I think I've quite lost all appetite, Your Grace. I believe I'll dine in my rooms tonight."

"Alone?"

"Hardly. I have my maid with me."

"*Nae* one will think it amiss if I attend you, instead. Order it."

"In my rooms?" Elise asked, showing every bit of her own shock. "I'm certain my maid will," she answered finally, with a choking voice.

"We're about to be discovered." His voice dropped to a conspiratorial whisper. "You should try to look a bit disheveled from your fall and na' my lovemaking."

Elise had to look away. She was afraid he'd spot the sudden moisture in her eyes that she couldn't staunch quickly enough. "I'll do my best, if you'll let me up."

"There's naught holding you," he answered.

"Your arm?" she asked. "Your legs?"

"How the devil did that happen?" His voice was quite merry as he lifted his arm from her and opened his legs.

Elise pulled away from warmth and didn't enjoy the tremors being away from it caused. She went onto her heels to look down at herself. Strands of ash-blond hair were trailing about her face, showing the condition of her coiffure; there were more rips in her habit than could be resewn, mud about her elbows, and lip rouge on Colin's lips. Elise found her handkerchief and handed it to him.

"I need this?" he asked.

"Not unless your lips are always that red."

"You use that kind of artifice? Too?"

"Of course. Doesn't every woman?"

"Na' the ones I grew up with. Is it gone?"

Elise couldn't prevent the snort. He'd smeared it worse than before. She held her hand out for the cloth. Colin gave it to her. "Hold out your tongue," she commanded.

"Why?"

"Must everything be explained to you first? I can't get the rouge off without moisture."

"You lick it off, then."

Elise pulled back as though stung. "I . . . can't," she whispered, finally.

"Why na'? You put it there."

Elise set her jaw, wrapped the handkerchief about her finger, and put it to her mouth. He stopped her with a quick hand and pulled the handkerchief away from her lips.

"Against the rules, Elise," he said, clicking his tongue, and his eyes were as cold brown as they'd been the first time she'd seen him. "I said lick it off."

"What rules?"

"The courtship game. I told you I knew how to play it."

"You can't possibly mean . . ." Her voice stopped exactly when her thoughts did.

"Oh . . . and canna' I?"

Shouts and calls carried to her, and they both heard them. They were closer. Colin hadn't changed position, but she could swear he'd gotten larger. Elise shut her eyes, but when she opened them he still hadn't moved. She couldn't believe what she was hearing.

"I thought . . . you didn't like me," she said.

"I dinna'. Much."

"Then why must you make me do this?"

"Let's just call it payment for a bit of lampooning I've had to endure. And it's rather amusing, I think. Dinna' you?"

She closed her eyes again and took several calming

breaths. There hadn't been one gentle line to his body when he'd said it, either.

"You can open your eyes, too. I'm na' going anywhere."

She did. If anything, he'd gotten closer when he lifted his head atop his bent arm.

"That's better. Really, woman, you dinna' have much time. We're about to be discovered, and I'm covered with your lip paint. I'm fairly certain they'll know how it got there."

"So? I've been whispered about before."

"Well, I have na'. My reputation is impeccable. Until my name got linked with yours, anyway."

"That's the price of a title, Your Grace." She shrugged and tried to look at anything except him.

"Do you know what you're about, Elise? You claim you dinna' want a marriage proposal? Very well. Get on with it. You know you canna' just compromise an eligible bachelor and expect to get off with a by-your-leave. We're both too well-known. I'll be forced to offer you my hand in wedlock. Or is that what you want?"

This isn't happening to me! She was not being threatened with marriage by the Duke of MacGowan, she just wasn't.

"Oh, Christ! It is, isna' it? I had the clue in my hands and dinna' even see it. I'm more dense than a sweep! That was the reason for your note, and your acting last night, and this! You expect a proposal from me. Not him. Me. Damn you."

She swallowed hard. "Just shut up, Your Grace."

"Give me the rag." He didn't wait. He reached over and plucked it from her, licked it, and slashed it across his lips. His eyes never left hers, and there wasn't a bit of green to them.

Chapter 6

"Up you go now. Don't mind this steed, my lady. His Grace has him in hand. Your Grace?"

Elise couldn't share her inner anguish with anyone, so she simply let herself go limp as Barrigan's groom lifted her up to the duke's arms. It was more of her rotten luck that her gelding had returned riderless to the stables after her fall, and that MacGowan's had stopped the moment his rider jumped from his back.

"Relax. Pretend you enjoy this. I know I am. Pretending, that is."

"Why?"

"Why am I pretending, or why should you, also?"

Elise put her teeth together. She didn't answer. It didn't matter.

"I'm pretending I enjoy it because it was my rescue. You were in distress. That's an oddity none can believe. Or so they keep saying. I like that. Colin MacGowan, chivalrous rescuer of maidens in distress. Oh, pardon. You're *nae* maiden. I keep forgetting."

She stiffened further, but that just made her back ache more.

"And you should pretend to enjoy it, because it appears to fluster your man-friend."

"You've a lot of gall, Your Grace."

He chuckled above her head, and the chest she was staunchly keeping away from moved with the motion. "That I have, to be sure."

Elise sat with her legs overlapping one of his. He had the reins in his left hand and his right about her waist to steady her seat. She wished it didn't feel as warm and right and safe as it did.

Four of Barrigan's grooms were accompanying them, along with Barrigan, Sophie's viscount, and Sir Roald Easton. The last, Elise was studiously ignoring. Nothing about him appeared to be flustered.

The sun was directly above Barrigan's lodge, making every shade of color almost painful to look at. Colin felt hard and sturdy beside her, and the horse's rocking motion made her back ache unduly from the taut posture she was forcing on it. How she longed for the luxury of a good cry! She sniffed and hoped he wouldn't notice.

"You can lean back. *Nae* one's looking, and I will na' take it as a personal insult."

"Everything you do is an insult, Your Grace."

"That's the nicest thing you've said to me thus far."

"You've gained full measure for any slur to your name that my presence has caused you. Does that satisfy you?" she asked.

He shrugged. "You're the one setting the scenes. You tell me. I've yet to compliment you on today's effort."

"I had nothing to do with nearly being trampled!"

"You put your horse directly in my path. You knew exactly what you were doing."

"Is that what you think of me?" she asked, in a little voice she hated the moment she heard it.

"I dinna' think of you at all."

She sat stiffer at his words. The horse slowed. Elise wiped quickly at a tear. She was stupid to allow self-pity now, besides, it would make her blackened eyelashes a mess of wet soot. It was because she was suffering from reaction, that's what it was. That's all it was.

"That's all what is?" Colin asked, as if she'd spoken aloud.

"I—I don't believe I'm ever speaking to you again, Your Grace. You may unhand me."

"If I were to do so, you'd likely fall again. Why dinna' you tell us you could na' sit a horse?"

"I sit a horse just fine. I wasn't expecting stallions to come leaping from the sky."

"Nor a gallant gent to rescue you, either, I presume?"

"Is that what you call a rescue?"

"Actually, it was more along the line of a lesson."

"I don't need, or want, any lesson from you, Your Grace."

"Just settle back like a good lass, will you? I'm having a bit of trouble with Thunderbolt here."

Elise tightened her lips but knew he wouldn't spot it. The horse wasn't giving anyone any trouble. She shut her eyes and allowed herself to lean a bit against him. Colin's chuckle greeted her action.

She sniffed again and turned her face away.

"You still have your handkerchief?" he asked.

She nodded.

"Good. I dinna' like to be wet with woman-tears."

"You need to worry more about being blackened, I should inform you," she answered.

"You use artifice there, too?"

"There's not much of me that isn't artifice, Your Grace."

"Hmmn, interesting thought. Is that a challenge?"

"To what, pray tell?"

"Find out."

The pillow that was his chest moved as he reached about her, pulling her more securely against him. This sort of intimacy she could do without. She'd sworn it after watching Evangeline cry her heart out for a man who could not care less about her. Elise would never let that happen to her. She'd vowed to die a virgin. She'd sworn never to feel anything for a man. And never, ever, to be near enough to one to feel anything.

Especially a MacGowan.

She lay abed after dining in her chamber, much later than usual. She'd had only Daisy for company, because His Grace, the Duke of MacGowan, had seen her to this chamber, and then ordered it that way while he told all who would listen that she had to recuperate from her ordeal. She didn't want him seeing to her well-being. She didn't want anything more to do with him . . . and she still hadn't told him of Rory!

"Damn him, anyway!" she swore, then smacked the covers.

"What was that, Elise?" Daisy looked up from her sewing to ask it. Elise looked away.

"I'm talking to myself. Pray, don't pay me any mind."

She didn't need the extra coddling Colin seemed to have ordered for her, either. She didn't need or want his horrid lesson. She especially didn't need the recollection of how warm and secure he'd felt. She only wished she could banish that memory.

"Will there be anything else, then?"

"How about a sleeping powder?" Elise asked.

"Does your back hurt you that much?"

"Actually, it's another part of my anatomy with the larger bruises, Daisy. And, no, I was teasing. I don't need my head to ache all day tomorrow, should I take one now. You know how they affect me."

"Are you certain you don't wish me to sleep here tonight? I can have the trundle set up again in no time."

She gestured to the connecting door and Elise

glanced that way. Roald wasn't interested in her anymore. The duke's behavior seemed to have settled that.

"As long as you've locked my door, there's no
need," she replied.

"Sleep well, then, Elise."

"I shall sleep soundly and well, I assure you."

"No adventures, mind. And no mad dashes about
the countryside in breeches. Nothing of that nature?"

"I'm far too tired and bruised for such tomfoolery.
Trust me."

"You're certain you wouldn't like me to stay? His
Grace said you might need—"

"Off with you, Daisy," Elise interrupted her. "Get
your own rest. We've a long day tomorrow. We'll
leave early. I have things to see to. Wake me early."

The door closed, taking the light with it. Elise snuggled down into Barrigan's feather mattress and fell
asleep again to images she'd never tell a soul about.

"Elise?"

The drunken whisper filled her bedchamber, arous-
ing her instantly. "Are you awake, my love?"

"Get to your own rooms, Roald. Let me be."

"Not this time, my fine lady. Oh no, not this time."

The bed gave slightly as he fell onto it. Elise struggled out the other side simultaneously. Her limbs
weren't awake yet, and the clumsiness was hampering
her search in the dark for her dressing gown before
she gave it up. It was delaying her too long.

"Elise? Wait! Damn!"

He swore and lunged at her, trapping her with fist-
fuls of her cotton nightgown in his hands. Elise pum-
meled him and swung her face away from the kiss he
was trying to give her.

"No, Roald!" she screamed. She felt the nightgown
ripping from her shoulder as he tossed her to the bed.

She was pummeling and struggling, and he acted like it was nothing.

"I've dreamt of this moment, Elise! You've . . . no idea."

His open, wet mouth landed on her collarbone and a shudder of revulsion filled her, draining her strength for a moment. It was getting dim. She saw him as a darker blackness than the room as he lifted himself above her. Then she was swinging at him again.

"Stop that! I won't hurt you. I only want to love you. You'll enjoy it. I promise. Now stop! I'm going to make love to you, Elise. Then I'm going to marry you! And then we're going to spend the Wynd fortune!"

She heard his clothing rustling through her frantic breathing as she inched her way from him to the headboard, and then to the lamp. She'd noticed how heavy and awkward it was earlier. It was all she had. They'd been stupid. They'd locked Roald's door, but she hadn't been safe. They hadn't locked the other door.

"All I ever wanted was for you to love me, Elise. I swear it! I've waited, postured, and pleaded. I can't wait any longer. Tonight, I'll force you, by God!"

He was shouting it as he fell onto her legs. Elise slammed the lamp onto him. He didn't know what hit him. She pitched the lamp from her with both hands, and then had to contend with his weight. There was warm, sticky liquid everywhere. She seemed to be covered with it. It got worse as she pushed and struggled to get free. The thump as she fell from the bed was loud. Then she was on her feet and she was shaking. There wasn't a sound from Roald.

"Oh my God! I've killed him!" What started as a whisper, ended on a shriek as Elise wrapped her arms about herself. "What can I do? Where can I go? Think, Elise, think!"

She could leave. She could get a groom to saddle

a horse and race for London. No, that wouldn't do. She had to find Daisy. She had to have help to escape. It's all she could think of. She'd have to run. There was too much blood in her chamber. She didn't need to see it. She could still feel it on her nearly everywhere.

"Oh, God, help me. Help me!"

She was whispering the prayer over and over as she went through the connecting door into Roald's chamber. She didn't think beyond her objective, and she didn't question why. She had to get to Daisy.

She knew where the servant's quarters were, although she'd never been there. The hall was empty and frighteningly dim, with soft, yellowish light glowing slightly from each oil globe. Elise stumbled once, and then forced her body to hold the shock inside where it wouldn't show. She wasn't going to be able to save herself if she gave into hysterics. She took a deep breath and ran to the door leading to the stairs that the servants used. She opened it.

Then a large body was there, blocking her, and arms wrapped about her torso as she was lifted. Elise was struggling and pummeling again, and for the same reason.

"Stop that, Madame! Stop!"

A door was kicked open, and Elise was shoved into the light of an unfamiliar bedchamber and lowered onto her feet, although he kept her locked in his arms. Elise's heart was beating so loudly and in such a disjointed rhythm, it was hampering her own breathing.

"What the devil is this?"

Elise's heart ceased pounding and felt like it moved to lodge in her throat as she recognized MacGowan's voice.

"I caught her running the halls. In this."

"Just this?"

Elise forced herself to turn her head. The duke hadn't been sleeping. He'd been sitting, contemplating a deck of spread cards, and he was wearing a red, green, and black plaid robe that actually reached the floor when he stood, knocking over his chair.

Then he was looming, all towering strength and anger. Elise actually hugged into the man still holding her.

"What have you got to say for yourself?" he asked in an ugly tone.

Elise turned around.

"What the hell?" he burst out.

"I—" Elise opened her mouth, but little more than that came out.

"What happened?" He was asking the man holding her.

"I told you, Your Grace. I caught her at the servants' stair, like this."

"You're both covered in blood. Explain. Now!"

"I did as you said. I watched. She was out, like you said she might be. I caught her."

"Then, whose blood—?"

"Roald," Elise answered, interrupting them as they just got louder and louder, with angry words that seemed to swirl above her head.

"Easton?" He lowered his head and asked it, and nothing about him was soft or caring, or anything other than intense and brutal and frightening.

She nodded. She didn't think her voice would work.

"What happened? Quickly! I canna' do something about it if you dinna' tell me."

"I—" Elise stopped; a sob stilled her voice as trembling overtook her for a moment. She watched his face harden further. "I . . . I have killed him. Dearest God . . . I've killed him."

"What? Why?"

She watched him shove the robe off, imprinting a large, extremely defined masculine span of chest and belly onto her eyes, and then he was shoving his arms into a black coat. Then he was covering the

whole with a black cape and lifting the hood to
shadow his features. Elise wondered stupidly, if he was
trying to disguise himself. It wasn't going to work if
he was. There wasn't another on the estate his size.

"Where is he?"

Fresh tears obliterated everything for a moment,
then they cleared as she blinked them into existence
down her cheeks. *His features may as well be carved
from stone,* she thought.

"Well?"

She was surprised at herself, and for good reason.
She hadn't been so naive since she'd been sold into
wedlock. Surely an attack like Sir Roald had perpet-
uated was reason enough to defend herself. What had
she been thinking to run as she had?

She willed strength into her legs, but they just
shook more as she tried to stand upright. Everything
wavered for a moment, then cleared. It was as crystal clear as everything had been since she'd met him.

"He's . . . in my chamber. In—in my bed."

That reply got her MacGowan's enlarged nostrils,
heavier breathing, and a snarl, too. Elise opened her
mouth and kept talking.

"He . . . came to me! He wouldn't leave. I—I didn't
mean it to happen, I swear it!"

"There's naught that happens about you that you
dinna' plan, down to every excruciating detail." He
lifted his gaze from where he'd pinned her in place
to speak again to the man at her back. "Was there
anyone else about, Mick?"

"I dinna' see another. She was alone."

"No one about? No witnesses?"

"None."

"You were at your post all eve?"

"Aye."

"Then how did he get in?"

"I—"

"Stop this! You don't understand!" Elise burst out, stopping the arguing male voices that just kept getting louder and louder. "He tried to—! He—!"

"Yes?"

She had his attention again, and for the life of her she didn't know why she'd wanted it. There wasn't a soft bone anywhere on his body. He reached out and lifted the front of her nightgown where it was torn, then put it back on her shoulder, where it stayed plastered to her with the adhesive of drying blood.

"He wanted to—! He ripped my gown!" She was shaking and sobbing and stammering. It surprised her that he understood.

A nerve in his jaw tensed out one side, defining the strength and shape of it, as well as every bit of his disgust. Elise recoiled from it.

"Dinna' you dare leave these chambers."

"But I—" she began.

"That's an order. Mick?" He was looking over her head again.

"Your Grace?"

"Get cleaned off. Burn those. Get that off her, too. Call the guard."

He was leaving. Elise watched as the door opened in seemingly slow motion, before slamming shut with a precise cannonlike boom of sound that should have reverberated everywhere, but rather felt like it throbbed in waves to penetrate to where she was still, miraculously, standing.

"You heard him. Gown."

Elise stumbled out of the strange enclosure of Mick's embrace. Her legs were just as insubstantial and weak as she'd suspected. She went to her knees, and the jolt scraped skin that had never felt the like. Mick didn't move.

"You heard him. Gown," he said again, with the exact same inflection in his tone.

"I don't obey him," she replied to the Aubusson carpet at her nose. That was odd. She had fallen inches away from padded luxury.

"You will. You heard him."

"Stop saying that!"

"Then give me your gown."

She shook her head, denying every blush that heated everywhere on her.

"I'm to take it from you. You heard him."

"You wouldn't dare." She whispered the words to the floor.

"Don't make me prove it, lass. Gown."

"Is . . . there a privy closet?" she asked.

"Yonder. Lift your head. Get me the gown. You heard him."

If he said that one more time, she was going to scream all her vexation and anger, rage and shock at him. Elise bit her tongue to still it. Then she stumbled to her feet again. She shouldn't need the hint. Colin's bedchamber had the same arrangement as her own.

She forced her legs to get her around the wooden slatted divider that screened the water closet.

"I've na' got all eve. We may be caught before I can get them burned. Hurry, lass. Hurry."

Elise's hands belonged to someone else, as did the entire episode. She couldn't believe the last half hour of her life. She'd killed Roald, and then what had she done? She'd managed to involve the Duke of MacGowan. And then what was happening? He was hiding the crime.

Elise's hands shook before her eyes as she squelched the screams that came from being a party to what Colin MacGowan was doing. But what else could she do? Wait for the discovery of the body? And then her blood-stained body in the duke's chamber? What could everyone say had happened, but a lover's spat? Or even worse, a fight over her?

"Dinna' make me come in there," Mick said.

Elise gripped her hands into fists, cracking the dried blood, and tried to control her own body. It wasn't possible. Everything on her looked to be a dried reddish color. Horror overwhelmed her. *I've taken a life!* she thought, before gagging on it.

"I dinna' hear any cloth moving."

"I've got to get clean." Elise stopped her own throat's motions, swallowed, and then managed to whisper the words.

"I dinna' hear any water, either."

Elise grabbed the pitcher. She spilled water onto the walnut-grained cabinet as she poured. The empty ewer tipped over when she set it down. She ignored it.

She spilled more water onto the wood as she shoved her hands into the bowl. She didn't care. Elise splashed water again and again onto her face, chilling her and making it difficult to breathe. She felt for Colin's soap and started scrubbing. She couldn't seem to get clean no matter how much soap she used or how many times she rinsed. The soap slipped from her hands, and Elise's tears started up again as it fell into the water.

Oh, dear God, I've murdered a man! she thought.

She wiped the moisture from her face roughly with a towel. The tears wouldn't stop, no matter how she sponged at them. Elise buried her face in the towel. She'd killed Sir Roald. She'd broken the number one commandment. There was no penance for that. There was no going back. No salvation for her. Ever.

She recognized the horror in her eyes when she moved the towel away and looked at herself in the mirror. Her mouth fell open to scream, but no sound came. Her nightgown gaped to the waist, and more of Roald's blood was staining her bared breasts.

She started ripping the gown from her, and the

more of it she got off, the more she ripped and pulled and cried.

"I did warn you, lass."

The hulk of a man was in the space with her, his mouth a slash of a line, his teeth clenched, and his face averted. Then he helped, lifting her out of the mass of cloth at her feet, before setting her back onto them.

Then he was gone, his head bowed, and his back hunched as he backed from her. Elise heard his steps, then the door, and then complete and absolute silence.

Chapter 7

There was a stag head mounted above Colin's unlit fireplace. Elise studied it when she wasn't tossing playing cards onto the table in front of her. The stag's eyes were on her. They had been all night.

She knew the duke had been gone for hours. The clock, out in the hall, chimed every quarter hour. According to that clock, it was nearing four in the morning. It would be dawn soon, and still Colin hadn't come with further information for her. That didn't bode well.

Her hands wouldn't warm. No matter how much she rubbed them together, she couldn't keep them warm. She'd had the same trouble with her feet, until she'd rifled through the duke's armoire and found two pairs of socks. He wasn't going to like that, she supposed. He probably wouldn't like the fact that she was wearing his cast-off dressing robe, either. It was made of a fleece-type material softer than any fur. It was also patterned in red, green, and black plaid, as was most of his wardrobe. There was an embroidered crest of the MacGowans on the right front yoke. Elise felt the weight against her skin like a rock. There was probably real gold in the thread. That would explain the weight and rigidity of it, and why it chafed her breast every time she moved her arm.

She wondered what he was doing and how he expected to get away with it. Was he hiding the body, adding his sin to hers? How were they supposed to explain that? Sir Roald Easton couldn't just disappear. He'd be missed by someone who cared. Surely there was someone, somewhere, who cared for him. Elise was ashamed to admit that she didn't even know if he had family who would care.

Was this another lesson she needed to learn? Was the duke, even now, awaiting the arrival of Barrigan's constable to have her arrested? *And why won't my hands warm?* she wondered.

Elise had been watching the wrong door. She had no warning as the ornate chamber door opened and the hulk of man that was Colin MacGowan entered, attired in yet another plaid dressing robe that reached to the floor.

"Forgive me, darlin'. I could na' prevent this."

Elise's eyes went wide at the endearment, her hand went to her throat, and she pushed away from the card table to stand. It gave her a little courage as four men followed on the duke's heels. Elise met the Viscount of Beckon's gaze for but an instant; she ignored Lord Barrigan and his watchman. She put her full attention on the rotund figure of a man she recognized as a constable.

At this hour of the morning, the man already looked overworked in his rumpled greatcoat and unshaven cheeks. Then she realized he probably hadn't slept. He'd spent his night gathering evidence to arrest her. Elise didn't have to ask it. The man seemed emblazoned with it.

From the back of her mind, she registered that the clock was chiming the hour of four. If she'd known the duke was bringing a roomful of observers, she'd have prepared herself better. She'd have been wearing something more suitable than Colin MacGowan's plaid robe and two overlapping argyle socks on her feet. This was not how the Dowager Duchess of Wynd's social prominence was supposed to end.

The entire sequence of her thoughts took but a fraction of time. Elise kept her head at an arrogant tilt and put as much disdain in her eye contact with all of them as she could. At the final chime of Barrigan's clock, she moved from behind the table. She watched dispassionately as Colin seemed to follow her direction to walk across the Aubusson rug to her.

Then he reached out, and with one arm pulled her so completely against his side, she felt melded to it. Both her arms came out instantly and defensively. She put one hand at the small of his back, wrapping her fingers about his belt, and the other hand went to his chest to steady herself. She had no choice but to look up at him. His eyes shoved green sparkles at her.

And from what sounded like very far away, she heard him say, "I told you, gentlemen, that it would na' be necessary to disturb my wife."

The shock stilled her in place, and the weight and intent of his arm guaranteed it as he tightened his grip, lifting her slightly from the floor, where she hovered on tiptoes. The hand at the small of his back went into a fist about his knotted belt to stabilize herself.

"We know, Your Grace, but there's still some questions."

Someone was talking. Elise could sense it, but she couldn't fathom what was said or who said it. All she could see was Colin's jaw as he faced them, and all she could hear was the breathing of the man it looked like she was clinging to. He said something else, and all she heard was the rumble of sound through his body. She frowned, and for some reason he looked back down at her.

"You . . . you told them—" Elise stammered, but he was interrupting her before she finished.

"Aye."

One word, and then he was grinning down at her, dissolving the floor, the walls, and every person in proximity, and making everything very, very cushiony and warm and protected feeling. Elise's eyes widened and her mouth dropped open.

"I'm afraid they will na' accept the obvious, however. They want to hear it from your lips."

"What?"

The word didn't make it to sound, but he heard it. He had little laugh lines all around his eyes, too, she noticed, as his smile reached there for the first time she'd ever seen.

"Tell them, my love."

"Tell them . . . what?" she echoed. *My love?* she wondered in absolute amazement. She was ashamed to realize the twinge deep within her was back, in force, and was shortening every bit of ability she had to breathe. She was taking short gasps of air to compensate. It wasn't working. *My love?* she repeated in her thoughts.

"Why, that you've been in here tonight, all night."

He was lowering his head a bit and raising her at the same time. Elise lost touch with the floor, but she hadn't felt it for some time, and her eyes went wide with the surprise as he put a nose against her cheek.

"With me," he finished, whispering it against her skin.

Someone cleared their throat, dropping her back into the reality that was Colin MacGowan's arms, his bedchamber, and the murder of Sir Roald Easton. She knew then exactly what the duke was about, and his ability to playact was incredible, and very, very painful. He was saving her, just as he had at dinner, what now seemed a century ago. She meant nothing to him. She never had, and she never would. He was simply saving her. Again. It was extremely stupid of him, and she wondered if he knew what he was doing.

With every bit of skill and strength at her command, Elise made herself withdraw from what her body was experiencing, taking every bit of the twinge, the overly focused senses, and the burning at the base of where her heart should be, and she hid them. Deep. Deeper. She had to close her eyes partway to make it happen, for the look on Colin MacGowan's face was making the blood gush through her ears with a force that made them ring.

"Elise?" he whispered.

She tilted her head and looked him over critically, and with every bit of loftiness she could. Then she smiled, coldly, calculatedly, and mechanically. "What *have* you been saying, again?" she asked, as clearly and perfectly as The Ice Goddess always did.

"You've been in here with me."

"With you?" she asked.

"All night."

"All night?" she repeated, automatically.

"I'm afraid they need some convincing." He tipped his head, motioning to the others in the room.

"I hardly think—"

"That it would be necessary? I know, I was hoping it would wait until the announcement reached London, too."

"Announcement?" she asked.

"I'm afraid that is na' possible now. There's been a dreadful accident in your chamber."

Elise felt her face drain and her knees wobble, but she didn't give a sign of any of it.

"It was a prowler, we think. Dinna' we, Lord Barrigan?" Colin turned his head back to their audience. Elise followed suit.

"It appears Sir Easton must have heard him and went to investigate," Lord Barrigan explained.

"Is he—?"

"He's unconscious. We don't know the extent of it yet."

Elise was so grateful for Colin's continued embrace, she would have kissed him if he had been any other person on the face of the planet. As it was, she didn't have any feeling left in the hand wrapped about the belt at his back, or in the other that was curved about his lapel in order to remain standing.

"I'm afraid my man, May, here, has a few questions for you."

"He does?"

"It's rather unfortunate that the incident happened in your bedchamber. Or, rather, what we all assumed was your bedchamber."

Barrigan's voice hadn't lost a bit of volume. He was loud enough to wake anyone sleeping. Elise touched her glance on him and he grinned, before nudging the viscount at his side.

"I guess congratulations are in order, MacGowan. The devil knows I should send my condolences to the entire male population of England along with it, too."

"My Lady? I mean . . . Your Grace?"

The constable cleared his throat. Barrigan's chuckles died as Elise looked back at him. Beside her, she felt Colin stiffen.

"Yes?" she asked steadily.

"You say you were in this chamber all night? With His Grace, the Duke of MacGowan?"

"I already told you that she was," Colin said in a low, menacing growl of sound.

Elise moved her hand up the lapel of that fleecy robe and touched his chin, moving his face toward her. The contact burned, or her hands were ice cold. She was afraid it was the latter. She had no choice. It was self-preservation now, and she was going to let the dominoes fall where they would. She sincerely hoped he knew what he was doing.

She smiled lovingly, but none of it reached her eyes. "Of course, you did, dearest," she said softly and poignantly.

The words would have been choking her if she hadn't closed off every emotion, and the slight pursing of his lips didn't help. She was afraid he was enjoying this. She just didn't know why. He was damning himself, too. Elise turned her head back to their audience and smiled across at them. "And it's true, gentlemen. Every bit of it."

"It's true that the Duke of MacGowan and you are wed? You agree?"

Elise looked back to Colin. He hadn't moved from the position she'd put him in. Her fingers still on his chin were probably the reason. She rubbed a thumb subconsciously across the slight scratchiness of his chin and watched the flicker of green that went through his eyes. Then it was gone, leaving nothing but an opaque brown glaze.

He nodded, but it was such a small gesture, if she hadn't been holding on to him, she wouldn't have known it. Elise turned back to the others.

"Whyever would you doubt his word, sir? I don't believe I'm hearing this correctly," Elise replied in her coldest, most arrogant voice.

The man flushed before replying. "Well, it is a bit of a tangle, I'm afraid. You see, it appears your bed was slept in. Since you weren't using it, that makes it a problem for me. There is also the matter of a woman's robe still there. Unless you'd given your chamber over to another lady without letting your host know?"

The man was obstinate, and Elise narrowed her eyes before looking back up to Colin. She sighed loudly. "I'm afraid it's not going to stay secret much longer, my love," she said to him. Then she released his chin

to move her hand to a span of shoulder no man
should own.

Nothing about Colin was moving. She watched him
watch her. She unwound her hand from his belt. She
was already thinking through the ramifications. Annulment? No, too severe, much too spicy to stay the gossip.
It was a mistake? No. Too much imbibing the night
before? No. A bet gone wrong? That was going to be
it. A bet.

With whom?

She was already calculating the amount and extent
of it, and who she'd have to pay to advertise and
start the propaganda, and Colin looked like he knew
all of it. Elise sucked in on her lower lip and slowly
lowered the hand that was still ice cold, despite being
in such close proximity with him. Then she was turning her body, still keeping his arm about her but
making it more of a conjoined defensive stance than
an embrace of love. Colin's arm dropped to encircle
her waist, and he brought his other one to join it as
she moved in front of him.

That was disturbing, but she let it go. Everything
about the episode was. His Grace was a barbarian from
a barbaric country. He didn't know what he was doing,
or what it was going to cost. She did. She released her
lip to smile wryly at the floor. That was strange. The
wood flooring looked the consistency of sand.

This was going to cause more of a stir than her
trysting with the Marquis of Quorn had, once the
story broke; consequently, she'd now have more whispers attached to her name. That might not be all
bad, she decided, remembering Roald's words. Any
notice was better than none.

She lifted her head, facing everyone from a position in front of Colin. She felt every bit of him as his
breath touched her neck.

"You must see, don't you? We didn't wish the explanations . . . yet. It—it all happened in such a hurry, you understand. I set the stage to look like I was there all night. That's why I left my robe, so my maid wouldn't question anything about my absence. I'm sorry it caused anyone such worry, and I'm exceptionally sorry about Sir Easton. Although, now that I think of it, I feel rather lucky that it wasn't me there instead."

Colin's arm tightened about her waist, and Elise fought the urge to struggle as his interlocked hands made certain she couldn't move.

"You agree you are wed?"

"How many times must I say it?" Elise replied.

"Well, that would seem to sum up everything, for certain, my lady . . . I mean, Your Grace. There is one last thought, though, almost not worth the mention. Would it be impertinent of me to ask when it was that you and His Grace wed, and perchance what church? For the record, you understand."

Her heart sank. She lost her color. She gulped on the excess spittle choking her. She looked down, although the floor didn't have any answers. Elise shut her eyes.

"Surely that is inconsequential, May," Colin replied. His voice was louder and had more of a brogue than usual. "For is it na' Scottish law that to claim to be man and wife before a magistrate of the law makes it legal and binding? And you did all hear us, didn't you?"

There was a gruff, snortlike sound from Barrigan that drowned out Elise's gasp. Colin spoke again, interrupting her from what she was certain was going to be a bout of hysteria, followed by screaming.

"And you are a magistrate of the law, are you na'?"

She didn't hear the reply. She should have simply fainted, she told herself, and wondered how women went about it.

"That should be proof enough for any man."

The duke was still talking, for the rumble of sound

accompanied it, and she was still conscious as she heard the announcement that damned her.

"By Scot's law, the Lady Elise Wyndham is now my wife, the Duchess of MacGowan. Congratulations are in order. As is some privacy due my wife and I. Gentlemen?"

Chapter 8

Elise woke to bright, midmorning sunlight as Daisy pulled the drapes wide.

"Well . . . for an adventure-free night, you are a wonder."

Elise was struggling with leaden eyes. The bed-chamber looked vaguely familiar, as did the embroidered crest on her pillow. She felt, rather than saw, her maid's amusement.

"Daisy—?"

"No, let me ramble while I puzzle this out. My lady settles into her own bed to sleep. Sir Roald Easton, the poet-snake fellow"—she stopped and wagged a finger at Elise—"why, that gent ends up with a nice scratch to his noggin' and is found in my lady's messed bed."

"Daisy—"

Elise tried again but didn't sound authoritative even to herself. The motion to rub the sleep from her eyes wasn't helping her, either. She neither resembled a powerful lady of the realm nor an employer. She probably looked like a child.

"But does my lady lie ravished in her chambers? Oh nay, not her. She is declared wed to the richest Scot on record and found in said duke's bed, instead!"

She stopped for a bit, as if for dramatic effect. Elise couldn't meet her eyes.

"However did you manage such a restful night?"

"Could you offer me a little water? My head aches."

"Well, that I wouldn't doubt for a moment. Why, I swear when I was first told the story, I denied it could have happened. I know how you feel about men. I thought they frightened the daylights out of you. I thought . . . well, I thought I knew you. I will admit, though, that His Grace does seem to be a fine specimen of a gent, now doesn't he?"

Elise caught Daisy's glance in the chamber mirror.

"Why, it's fairly easy to see why my lady would melt in that man's arms."

"Wrong story," Elise informed her, in a nondescript tone. She busied herself with patting the pillows into a mound for support behind her back while she waited.

"Then where is your clothing? Answer me that. Why would your cotton skivvies be missing while you're wearing nothing more than His Grace's robe? Did he pull them from you with much passion? That might explain your actions."

"Burnt."

Elise watched as Daisy assimilated that.

"Burnt?" she asked.

"Probably tossed to the winds by now."

"What man burns his wife's clothing?"

"One who's hiding blood stains."

"So . . . that's what happened," the maid said.

Elise turned her face away.

"I should have stayed and beaned the rascal for you! Why, he'd be out cold for a week, instead of suffering a mild concussion as Lord Barrigan's physician man says he has. How dare he?"

"Sir Roald . . . has a mild concussion?" Elise was choking on the words.

"He soaked up the housemaid's attentions with it, he did. Foul-tempered he was, too, so I was informed."

"A . . . mild concussion?" she repeated.

"As I've already said. Are you all right, my lady?"

"I must speak with MacGowan. I've got to stop this nonsense. This instant. No, I'll need something to wear first."

"Already been seen to, my lady. I suppose it's to be Your Grace again, isn't it?"

"Oh no, not if I can help it. My clothes?"

"I'd certainly choose the blue daygown if I were you. It's the best choice of what we brought. I didn't pack enough, but that can't be changed at this late date."

"You packed sufficiently as always. I already complimented you on it," Elise replied, lifting the covers to step out.

"You're going to need more than we brought in these four trunks."

"What? Why?"

"Your new husband has sent word to close your townhouse. All of your immediate belongings are to be packed and transported without delay."

"He—what? When? On whose orders?"

"This man is efficient and expects orders obeyed. He doesn't wait for you to catch your breath. He has so many servants, I quite lost count. They've been preparing all day . . . since just after four this morn, anyway."

"Preparing for what?" Elise asked, almost against her will. She didn't want to know. She really didn't.

"He's ordered his traveling carriages prepared. He's readying for the journey to his home. Seems he's got to be in Scotland as soon as possible. And if you think I'd drop everything and go to the Highlands in a moment's notice for anyone else, you're sadly mistaken."

"Oh no, he didn't. He couldn't."

"Not only could he, but he did."

"But he knows nothing of the particulars! Nothing."

"I don't think he quibbles particulars."

Elise smacked the pillows. "I haven't even told him, though!"

"You got him to wed with you, and you never even told him of Evan and Evangeline? Or Rory? You are a wonder. I'm impressed."

"I didn't have time!"

"You spent the night in his arms and didn't have time? Lord bless us!"

The maid lifted her apron over her face. Elise set her jaw to stop the sound of vexation. It was a wasted effort. Her voice sounded it. "I wasn't in his arms! Well, maybe I was, but it wasn't what you think. None of this is."

Daisy dropped her apron. She didn't answer. She didn't have to. Her look said enough.

"Oh, Daisy, this is ridiculous," Elise said, with a nervous giggle.

"Just as I told that Barton woman when I was informed of His Grace's plans. According to Barton, who got her information straight from your husband's man, Mick, His Grace isn't staying another moment longer than necessary. He's delayed long enough already. Seems he was only staying in London long enough to choose himself a bride. Now, thanks to the poet-snake fellow, he's gone and got himself one."

"I must speak with him. I must stop this! At once! Hurry!"

"The blue?"

"Anything, and quickly!"

Elise was more in Daisy's way than helpful. The entire episode had gotten out of hand. That's what she got for her bout of feminine squeamishness last night. Sir Roald was suffering a mild concussion. She'd joined her name with Colin MacGowan's for absolutely nothing. She should have lit the lamp after she'd hit Sir Roald with it. That would have been the smart thing to do.

Elise had purchased the blue satin daygown because the color made her eyes stand out. It was trimmed with small pearl buttons that gave the dress an elegant air. She cursed those same buttons under her breath as she fumbled with those at her wrists, while Daisy fastened those up her back. She should have used hooks; they would have been faster.

Daisy refused to let her from the chamber until her hair was pinned up, too. Elise couldn't keep still long enough, and the result wasn't as artistic as she usually prided herself. Still, it was off her shoulders and atop her head in some semblance of order, which was proper enough.

She met Sophie and Lady Beth in a sitting room. They were sitting beside each other and sipping tea.

"Have you seen the duke?" Elise rushed to Sophie, ignoring all the social pleasantries as she did so. She didn't have time to exchange polite chitchat. She had to stop this madness.

"Your gown is stunning, Elise. How much did it cost you?"

"You can have it, Sophie. Only tell me where the Duke of MacGowan is!"

Lady Beth looked shocked for a moment, and then giggled behind one gloved hand. Sophie allowed her eyebrows to raise slightly at Elise's outburst. "Your new husband has been directing orders from the library like he was still in the military."

"My new hus—?" Elise bit off the word. Colin MacGowan was not her husband, but she wasn't about to unburden it to anyone. Just a hint of what had happened would be more than either woman would keep secret. Elise was determined to prevent any further scandal until she could start her own propaganda.

"Thank you," she said calmly, and then she smiled her society smile at both ladies.

"Oh, your dress will be payment enough, I'm sure."

Sophie burst into laughter at the end of her words. It was ringing in Elise's ears as she hailed a footman to show her to the library. She'd never been in Barrigan's library. She was rarely in anyone's library. The Dowager Duchess of Wynd had little use for books.

"Her Grace, the Duchess of MacGowan."

The footman announced it loudly as he opened the door. Elise made a fist. She listened for the door closing.

"Elise, my dear, take a seat."

The duke had glanced up from a desk before looking back down again. Elise watched him as she waited what seemed an interminable amount of time for his attention. The drapes had been opened behind him, and sunlight highlighted Barrigan's grounds, where she could swear she saw the top of an Oriental gazebo. She swallowed in reaction to the sight.

Colin was dressed in a rich, brown tweed jacket, white shirt, and brown leather pants, which were tucked into his boots. He wasn't sitting at the desk, either. He was perched on his haunches while he wrote. That maneuver was spreading his arms wide and easily showing the size of him. He had leather epaulets sewn onto his jacket shoulders. They perfectly matched his trousers. His hair really was the color of roasted chestnuts, and it was curling upon his collar. She knew exactly how it felt between her fingers, and for some reason her fingertips tingled at the thought.

She cleared her throat. "Was that a request, or an order, Your Grace?"

"That's too formal, Elise. You have to start calling me Colin. And it was a request."

He still wasn't looking up at her. She dropped her eyes

to the list he was looking over. His penmanship wasn't the best, and she couldn't decipher it upside down.

"Your—Colin, I need to speak with you."

"I'm listening."

She took a deep breath. "I can't go to Scotland," she said.

"It's na' open for discussion."

Elise's eyes widened at the same angle as her mouth did. He scribbled some more, as if she'd disappeared. She took several calming breaths before trying again. She guessed he was treating her like he would a member of his regiment. She didn't like the feeling.

"You don't understand," she said.

"No, you dinna' understand, Elise." He looked up then and frowned, putting two furrows into existence in his brow. "You should take more time with your attire, my dear. You're barely proper."

"I beg your pardon?" she responded.

"Unless you wished to look like you'd just come from a good tumble. That should certainly put some truth to what they're saying about us. I believe I stand corrected. You did well. I applaud you."

Elise felt the blush clear to the roots of her hair. She glared at him and couldn't think of one witty, demeaning, or biting thing to say. He went back to his paper. She watched as he dipped his quill into the ink pot and began writing again. She knew what he was doing. He was listing necessities for his journey. Elise choked on the angry words she longed to screech at him, swallowed, took another breath, and tried again.

"You're wasting your time and mine, Colin. I don't like you. You don't like me. Remember? Stop this farce before it goes any further. I'm not going to Scotland. I refuse." Her voice wasn't as calm and cool as she was trying for, but it wasn't full of anger, either. She was proud of that.

"You have *nae* choice, Elise. You're mine now. Mine."

"I am not!"

"Oh, but you are. You said so yourself. A magistrate heard you. Your feelings dinna' matter with it, although it would be nice if you felt something besides dislike for me, I think. Perhaps na'. It might actually be better this way."

She was choking and couldn't blame it on anything but the shock of what he said and the way he said it.

He ignored her reaction. "Either way, it does na' matter. You are my wife. I'm leaving for my home. So are you."

"You can't just abscond with me. You can't."

He sighed, those shoulders moved with it, and Elise's mouth was failing her as it dropped open. Then he carefully put down his quill and stood, making the library look very small and cramped. She watched as he smoothed out the wrinkles in his leather pants, where they were molded to his thighs, before looking back toward her.

"Very well. I'll try this your way. Dinna' push it."

"My way?"

"The English way," he replied snidely.

"And what way would that be?"

"With words."

She frowned, but at least her mouth closed.

"You expect an explanation. Very well. I'll do a bit of them. I'm needed at my home as the Laird of the MacGowans. That's quite a responsibility and goes back centuries in tradition, in case you missed your history lessons. Everything with a Scot's clan hinges on the laird. Everything. I've been shirking returning to it for a reason . . . a very good one. I dinna' wish to wed the MacKennah lass. Now that I've been freed of the obligation, I'm ready to return."

"Your . . . obligation? The MacKennah lass?"

Her voice was starting to crack. Colin smiled. She

was afraid it was because he'd spotted the emotion she was hiding.

"The eldest MacGowan was betrothed to Mistress Mary MacKennah at a ceremony nearly a score ago. You, Elise, are my salvation. You have my eternal gratitude, too."

"You—you said we were wed . . . in order to escape a betrothal?"

Elise stumbled before collapsing onto the edge of a wingback chair. Her legs were giving her trouble again. She, who had never experienced a moment of the vapors, thought she might actually need smelling salts. Colin didn't say anything for so long, she had to look to see why. He was silhouetted in the sunlit window, with both hands on his hips, lifting the jacket ends effortlessly as he studied her.

"Dinna' I protect you?" he asked softly.

"But he was hardly injured!"

"You're correct. In fact, Easton has already been sent back to his abode in London. I dinna' want him near you, just in case."

"You tricked me!" She was losing the battle with her own body. Elise couldn't stop the panic from coloring her voice.

He moved to one side of the desk and placed one leg atop the corner as he studied her. Then he shrugged. He was too much man, arrayed too handsomely, and caused wondrous things to happen to her pulse and a whole slew of other horrid things.

"Perhaps, but I prefer to think of our marriage as a mutual agreement. It has a nicer ring to it."

"Mutual agreement?" She bit back all the rest of it, but it was difficult. Her fingernails were biting into her palms.

Colin acted like he knew it, too. His hazel eyes didn't move from her. Elise had to look away first. He was right about her attire, too. She wasn't properly dressed. The pearls weren't fastened from the elbow to her wrist on the right arm.

"I don't want to be your wife." She spoke the words to her arm.

"Is it that you dinna' want to be a wife? Or just mine?"

How am I supposed to answer that? she wondered. Elise had never had to think it through before. The silence grew. She actually began wishing he'd go back to his writing again. She undid the fists her hands were in and started fastening the pearls one at a time, as though that's all she had to do all day.

"Very well, dinna' answer. Sometimes, that's answer enough. Besides, it's too late."

"You're not aware of my reasons."

He sighed again loudly. "Well, let me list some of them, then. You're a very beautiful woman, Elise. So beautiful it takes a man's breath away; but you know that. You've always known it. That's why you dress as you do, act as you do, and set up everything like you do. You want to order and control everything and everyone. You're missing something, though. You dinna' seem to have a heart anywhere in that perfect body of yours. Am I getting warm?"

The pearls shimmered. Elise shrugged very, very carefully.

"And you're a tease. You play the courtship game without a hint of the consequences. Last night showed me. You treat men like playthings, without any care to what you do and who you hurt. You're called The Ice Goddess in those cartoons. You probably know that, too. You seem to be punishing all men for something. It makes me wonder which of your legions of lovers hurt you that badly."

Elise wasn't in control of her fingers anymore. She was focusing all her attention on each pearl. It was the only way she could stop the tremor of her fingers.

He snorted, and she heard the desk creak as he relieved it of the burden of his weight. "Or you are a consummate actress. I'm beginning to think it will prove highly interesting to find out which it is. Lord knows my home can get boring, if you let it."

"I have another reason that makes me unsuitable, Colin."

"Too late."

Elise glanced from beneath her lashes at him. He had his back turned to her and was looking out at the lawns, ignoring her. After saying what he had, he ignored her? She'd caught her breath when he'd first started talking. He'd called her beautiful. Perfect. The twinge had come so swiftly and brutally, it was almost painful. Then he'd kept talking, stealing her breath, making her nose run, and hurting her chest.

She'd never felt the like. It was taking all her will to keep him from guessing how his words had affected her. She'd give anything to keep it her secret.

"Colin?" she whispered to her hands.

"Too late," he answered.

"You won't listen?"

"Too late."

"But you don't understand! I have to tell you—"

"We leave tomorrow morning," he interrupted her. "And I shall na' enjoy having to force you. You may leave."

Chapter 9

He didn't have to force her.

As cowed as she felt, he didn't even have to send his man Mick to escort her. She'd have gone without him. Elise glanced sidelong at Colin's man and looked away before he caught her at it.

She was paler than usual, and that made the blue of her eyes look darker. Her reflection had already shown her how spectacular she looked in the fox-trimmed traveling ensemble. Hadn't she chosen the russet-dyed silk, interwoven with golden threads, for just such an effect?

It wasn't wasted. Elise had borrowed Lady Beth's maid, and she had to admit the woman possessed an artist's touch when it came to hair arrangement. There were no less than four wraps of her pale-blond hair encircling her head, while ringlets fell down her back. The maid had entwined miniature red roses throughout Elise's tresses. She thought it was a nice touch.

Apparently, it was going to be a beautifully calm morning, so she wouldn't have to shroud her head with her hood, either. Her toilette had taken up a major portion of the morning. Elise hoped that His

Grace was annoyed at the wait, but there wasn't any sign of him.

Elise made her farewells to the staff and Lord Barrigan's guests. She was reminded of her promise to Sophie of the daygown amid the other woman's giggling, and then she was ready. Another of Colin's footmen assisted her into the carriage. Elise ignored him and occupied herself with arranging her skirts.

"Your reticule, Your Grace."

She thanked the servant with a stiff smile. Normally, Daisy would have possession of her purse, jewelry, and such. Elise would just have to make do without her maid's services.

"My thanks for the stay, Lord Barrigan. I shall not forget your hospitality," she said.

"We'll not soon forget it, either, Elise, my dear! I vow we've not been so entertained in many a season. Remind your new husband of his promise of a berth to me should I ever venture that far North, will you? And tell him of my chagrin. I knew there was a man out there to melt your heart, I just wish it hadn't been a bloody Scotsman."

The man's voice hadn't lost any stridency. Elise winced before she caught the action. They were all laughing at her. There was more said, but Elise didn't want to listen, so she didn't. She pulled back into the coach and dropped the curtain, shutting out the entire thing.

There had been at least a dozen outriders milling about the ducal carriage when she'd been escorted in. Elise hadn't seen Colin, but that was no guarantee of his absence. She hoped he'd choose to ride outside with his entourage. She wasn't certain she could maintain her ice goddess facade with as little sleep as she'd received.

That was her fault, too. She sighed, lost in the remembrance.

She could have stayed alone in her new chamber, dressed in what wardrobe was available to her, gone to bed, and slept. That's what she was supposed to do, but she was finished with doing what she was supposed to do as the Duke of MacGowan's newest property.

Property. How Elise hated the word! Why, if she hadn't sent Daisy on a desperate mission to fetch Rory the moment she'd arrived back in the bedchamber yesterday morn, the maid probably wouldn't be allowed to follow Elise's orders, either.

Colin hadn't had one more word to say to her yesterday in the library. Elise had clamped her lips tightly together to keep the shrieks in as she'd left him. He hadn't even turned around.

He'd force her! She'd repeated it in her thoughts until her head ached worse than any headache powder could cause. He'd force her? Everything that was being done to her was forced! Why should this be any different?

He hadn't known how she'd raced back up Barrigan's stairs. He wouldn't have guessed that she'd dodge around the room where Sophie and Lady Beth were still sipping tea. Why, Colin shouldn't have known anything his new wife was doing. So how had he known she'd try to flee him last night?

Elise had forced herself to wait until the hall clocks were chiming one-thirty in the morning before sneaking from the room they'd given her, which was directly connected to The MacGowan's. It hadn't been an easy wait. She'd paced her room. She'd found her young gentleman's costume, dressed in it, checked and then rechecked it. She'd pouted and complained about everything and to everyone with whom she came into contact. She had been wrapped in an already hated, large, red, green, and black plaid robe about the whole of it, and when left alone, tossed it all off to recheck her costume.

She'd guessed there would be more staff, due to the prowler story, so she'd avoided the main stairs. This time she'd been much more careful, too. She'd checked the halls first. There wasn't any large, lurking guards about. Then she'd used the servants' stairs, clung to the walls, and tiptoed through the entire house. All she'd had to do was get to her own carriage. She hadn't known until later that Colin had sent it back to Wynd, along with her servants, while he replaced them with his own; but that wasn't what had made her escape fail.

Barrigan's house party had continued, unabated, and with more ribaldry than earlier. She hadn't been allowed to attend, even if she'd wanted to. She wasn't being allowed to do anything other than what he said. She was as much a prisoner as she'd been the first time she'd wed.

The ignominy of it made her grit her teeth, but Elise wasn't sitting still for it. She knew how to sneak about. She'd been doing it for years. She was surprised that Colin hadn't checked her trunks before having them moved. If he had, he would have known there was a young gent's pants, shirt, hat, and overcoat in one of them. He'd also have known exactly what they were for.

Now, in retrospect, she guessed that he had checked them.

Elise hadn't even made it to the kitchen, when Colin's big, hulking mass of a personal servant blocked her path. He hadn't said anything, he'd simply put up his finger and wagged it back and forth. Elise's snarl of anger hadn't done anything except bring a smile to his face.

That she could do without. She hadn't needed his escort back up the staircase, either. Elise had heard the distinct sound of a lock when she got back there, too.

Then she'd tried the window, although it was a full two stories above the ground. Two dark-clothed men had looked up as soon as she pulled the casement open. The duke was having her guarded there, too! That was truly too much.

Elise longed to forget the entire episode, but it was lonely in the carriage. She couldn't stop remembering. Her mind kept replaying it for her, and each time it was more mortifying.

After seeing her guards beneath the window, she'd slammed the window shut and used a string of the basest words she knew in her anger.

"Elise . . . my dearest, I'm shocked."

Elise had pivoted to face him. Colin was leaning on the wall, next to the open door, wearing what could be the same robe he'd been in when declared wed last night, and from the looks of it, not much more.

"I'd *nae* idea you had a penchant for strolling about in the dead of night. Although, now that I think on it, last night should have educated me, should na' it?" He'd reached over with an arm and flicked the door closed, belying the weight and unwieldiness of it with the nonchalance of his motion.

"What do you want?" she'd asked.

"No social pleasantries? No warm-sounding, but false, words on my appearance?"

Elise had smiled tightly, although swallowing had been a chore. "Forgive me, Your Grace. I'm quite overwhelmed at your appearance, and in *dishabille,* too. I'm speechless, I am." Elise had placed a hand to her throat. Her stomach had actually roiled when she came into contact with the gentleman's stock she'd tied at her neck.

"I believe you're the one in costume, and I always dress this way when I'm preparing for my bed. Your answer now, please."

"You can't sleep in here." Her voice had given her away, almost as much as her trembling.

"Why na'? It's part of my chamber, you're my wife, and you're avoiding my unspoken question."

"I'm not . . . I can't . . . I won't—" Her voice had just stopped, annoying her, as well as embarrassing her.

"Let me put it into words. What on earth are you doing dressed so . . . interestingly and revealingly?"

He'd then unfolded his arms and raised his right hand to place his index finger against his cheek, while his chin rested on his curved middle finger in order to study her. "I've na' seen legs that curved and slender on a gent afore. I'm surprised you actually think this sort of outfit disguises you."

"People see . . . what they want to see," she'd replied.

"That's probably the most intuitive thing you've ever said."

Elise had looked away quickly so he wouldn't spot the instant surprise in her eyes. "Can't you let me rest in peace, Colin?"

"This is what you call restful?"

"I've been apprised of my guards now. I believe you can call them off. I'll not leave."

"Really, Elise, you expect me to believe that? Besides, I canna' return to Barrigan's festivities. Na' like this, anyway."

"Well, you'll certainly have to dress more appropriately," she'd replied with as much sarcasm as she could find.

"Oh, I am dressed appropriately, for what I have in mind."

Elise had felt her heart stutter, and she had to consciously force herself not to show it. Colin wouldn't know of the gooseflesh flowing her back, or of the sweat beading on the nape of her neck.

"What . . . would that be, if I may be so bold?" she'd managed to ask, pushing the words past cold lips.

"Oh, this?" He'd moved his hand down the closure of his robe and watched how her eyes were following the motion. "I'm supposed to be clinging with passion to my new bride. That's the real reason we dinna' wait for a proper ceremony. We lusted so for each other, that we could na' control ourselves a moment longer. A preacher would have been a nuisance to us."

She knew she was losing what color she'd managed to keep. She also knew she was swaying in place on shaky legs. She hadn't anything to hold on to except the window casement at her back, and he'd know of it if she did.

"I don't . . . lust for you," she'd managed to say around the obstruction in her throat.

"Would you like to put it to the test?" He'd raised himself from the leaning position against the wall.

Elise hadn't waited to see him move. She'd swung back to the window and couldn't stop her cry, although she bit on the knuckles of one hand to staunch it.

"I take it that's a *nae*?"

He had kept talking, in a calm, modulated tone, and she hadn't heard most of it. She had watched his reflection with wide eyes as he'd bowed. He was leaving?

"If you have need of further strolling, you'll not take it amiss if I accompany you, will you? I'll just be in my chamber. You recall where it is, surely?"

He wasn't going to force her? Elise had sagged in place, and was in luck that he hadn't seen it. Her legs had still been shaking with relief when she'd reached the bed.

Chapter 10

The carriage stopped for a late luncheon. Elise had just begun wondering if Colin meant to see her fed at all.

The carriage was comfortable, the best sprung she'd ever been in, Archibald Wyndham's included. Elise had settled herself against the cushion support at her back and side, careful not to disturb the roses in her coiffure. She had almost managed to sleep.

She could feel more of the carriage seat than she should have, but that was no great burden. The Mac-Gowan coach seats were stuffed to an exactitude, she was certain. She could feel the seat because her ensemble was supposed to be worn with no less than ten petticoats, to gain the proper volume and width. It should have taken up much more of the seat than it was. She'd opted for only four petticoats, instead. She would never have managed all of it without Daisy to assist her. Then again, she'd not known that the cushion under her posterior settled after a spell, and she'd have to rearrange herself constantly on it or risk an ache in her back.

It would also help if designers would give women a little breathing room. The bone-stiffened corset

kept her from being able to take deep breaths, as well
as making it difficult to slouch against one side,
where it would have been the most comfortable.
She'd debated not wearing the corset this morning,
but Lady Beth's maid had been shocked enough.

Elise wouldn't let unspoken censure stop her next
time. The corset was an uncomfortable device of tor-
ture. It was digging into her ribcage; it was itchy, too.
It was also getting warm.

She'd already removed her pelisse and placed it on
the opposite seat, where a traveling companion should
have been. She should be grateful that she was traveling in such comfort. She could be atop a horse in
the open, like the duke most likely was.

She wondered if he was riding his chestnut horse.

"Damn it!" Elise cursed aloud, annoyed with herself.
Just because she was being sentenced to solitude didn't
mean her every thought had to be on His Grace,
Colin MacGowan.

The coach stopped in the yard of an inn. Elise
barely had enough time to sit back, as though uninterested, when the door opened.

"The duke has reserved a private room, Your Grace.
If you'd follow me?"

She gathered her skirts and followed Colin's man.
She was turned over at the front step to a servant girl
who wouldn't meet her eyes.

"Your Grace."

The girl mumbled the title and swept into a low
curtsy. Elise grimaced, then she found herself in a bedroom and watched while the girl poured water for her.
Elise soaked her handkerchief and sponged her neck
and face. The girl watched silently as Elise studied herself in the chamber mirror.

Other than the slight drooping of her roses and the
wrinkles along the back of her silk skirt, she looked exactly as she had when they'd started out. She probably

had the corset to thank. Perhaps she'd best quit cursing the designers of her clothing, she told herself.

"My thanks. I'm ready." She tipped the girl and tried to match her smile. *Such an innocent, young thing,* she thought. Elise wondered if she'd ever looked like that.

Colin was already in the inn's private room, awaiting her. Elise halted the instantaneous start of sensation as she hesitated in the door, before forcing her feet to continue moving. She'd only seen him in lofty rooms or out in the open. In this little dining room, he was even more immense—larger, stronger, more inescapable. There was nothing she could do about it.

She also had to admit that he looked fairly impressive in traveling attire of butter-colored trousers tucked into knee-high boots and an open vest worn with a thick, muslin-type shirt. He'd shed his jacket, and he wasn't wearing cuffs. He'd taken the resultant material at each arm and rolled it almost to his elbows, showing every tanned bit of sinew and muscle he possessed, even in his forearms. She knew exactly how it felt, too. She'd already had that sensation. No wonder he'd felt so hard! Everything that was female in her stopped and sighed; then every bit of her that was The Ice Goddess rose up in protest.

Elise consciously halted her own thoughts. She wasn't sighing over him. She was never even considering him, ever again. He wasn't her type, much as Roald had said, what now seemed years ago. Colin wasn't a dandy. He wasn't born to wear white gloves, black trousers, and a high, starched cravat. He wasn't a self-assured sophisticate, whose tongue dripped with sweet nothings for no reason. He wasn't like that at all. He seemed much too rugged for such niceties.

He wasn't as dark as Elise preferred, either. Her men were usually dark haired and swarthy. That made them a perfect foil to her.

Colin was tanned, it was true, but his eyes were golden brown with greenish flecks that sparkled sometimes, and his hair was reddish in the window's light. Now, why should she notice that? She winced and hoped he wouldn't spot it.

"You've journeyed well, thus far?" he asked.

"Passably, Your Grace." She moved gracefully to her seat.

"Always in control, are na' you?"

His whisper made her start as he watched her arrange her skirts. Then the door opened and the inn-keeper entered, bowing so low that Elise couldn't see his face. He was followed by the tantalizing aroma of roasted beef. Her mouth watered.

"Your sup, Your Grace."

"I may even find it edible, my good man." Colin's bored tone was as insulting as his words. The innkeeper's head shot up.

"My Sarah's every bit as good a cook as them you'd find in London."

"That remains to be seen. You may withdraw."

Colin waited for the man and his helper to leave. Elise couldn't believe what she'd just heard. As the door shut with more force than seemed necessary, Colin turned his warm brown eyes to her. She caught her breath and looked away.

"Am I passing your inspection yet?"

"My . . . inspection?" she asked the wall.

"I can act as convincing a fob as those you seem to prefer. I've na' taste for it, though."

"I have no such preference."

"Surely, you jest. I spent some time scanning the papers yesterday while you slept. You're featured in quite a few of them. You're quite famous. I dinna' real-ize that before."

Elise ignored him and helped herself to a slice of freshly baked bread. The innkeeper was right in his esteem of the unseen Sarah's skill. The inside of the loaf was soft and heavy with aroma, whereas the crust crunched in her fingers. She tore off a bite and spent the next several moments evaluating it.

"I'm trying to have a conversation here, Elise."

"His cook is extraordinary."

"Perhaps you'll do it justice and take more than two bites, then?"

"I always take more than two," she replied.

"All right, three."

Elise looked across at him. "I'm making polite conversation. That is what you wanted, wasn't it?"

"I said naught about being polite. I prefer you when you're brutally honest. I will admit, though, that I'm a bit stung at the parts where you dislike me."

"You want me to like you, now?"

"I dinna' particularly care how you feel about me. It's of no consequence one way or the other. It simply irritates me when you hide behind teasing phrases and flirtatious glances."

"Flirtatious glances?" She laughed her society laugh and put the crust back on her plate. "Such enticements would surely be wasted on you, Colin. That much I already know."

"From our near-collision? Why? I mean, I did kiss you, and on such short acquaintance, too. What more would you have had me do?"

"I'm afraid you're losing my attention, and this Sarah is a very talented cook. You really should try some."

"Are you such a coward?"

"Let us end this farce, Your Grace. I have my own estate, one that isn't linked to Wyndham's. Although it's not large or assuming, I could disappear. I swear it. You'll never hear of it again."

"You actually think we're na' the topic of conversation at each and every gathering? And in every house? I just told you how famous you are. Really, Elise, I expected better of you."

"I'm begging you."

"Dinna'. It does na' become you."

Elise sucked in air as she recognized her words to Sir Roald. She held her breath for several heartbeats as she calmed her reaction. Then she lowered her head and glared at him from beneath her lashes.

"That's better." He leaned back, folded his arms, and smiled across at her.

"This playacting can't continue, Colin." She had such a tight rein on her emotions, her voice cracked.

"Oh, I quite agree."

"You . . . agree? But you just said—"

"To the playacting. I'm in agreement that it canna' continue. I'm still waiting to meet the woman that's my new duchess."

"That's just it! I don't want to be your duchess. I don't want to have any part in this!" Elise had promised herself that she'd not give in to any emotion, anger or otherwise. Yet here she was with her voice rising, her hands clenched, and angry words just beneath the surface.

"What is it you do want?" he asked softly.

"I want to be left alone!" She was very close to shouting and was hard put not to shove from the table.

He didn't answer. Aside from heightened color along his jawline, he didn't exhibit any sign of even hearing her. She watched him load a platter with beef and vegetables. Then he applied himself to buttering his bread with more aplomb than was necessary. There was a self-satisfied grin on his face the entire time. Elise knew why. She'd played right into his game and come out the loser.

He had every right to gloat over her lack of self-control. He was the one who had reminded her of

The Ice Goddess title. She shouldn't begrudge him the victory. It wasn't like her.

She bent her attention to unfolding her fingers, one at a time, and flexing them. If she kept her mind on simple things, she'd get back her calm facade. She knew that much.

"You must admit, we could deal famously together."

He was watching her, so Elise looked away. She didn't want to know what expression he'd have on his face. Her calmness was barely working, and he would probably know of it.

"That sounds just like every other proposal I've ever received, Your Grace. I'm surprised at your lack of originality." Her voice dripped with sarcasm and boredom. She lifted her hand to her mouth to cover a pretend yawn. She was very pleased. Then he had to reply and send ripples through her facade again.

"My reasons should be different from your usual. You see, I dinna' truly want a wife. I certainly dinna' want you. Oh, I know, I postured and put out the story that I was looking for one, but it was a sham. I've but recently acquired my title. It came with a lot of sorrow and pain attached. It also comes with a bloody fortune, something you probably already know. I've yet to acclimate myself to that. I'm wealthy beyond my wildest dreams and I'm but twenty-eight. That's young yet, even to a woman of your age and experience. I had *nae* wish to be fettered to anyone, especially someone like you."

"Then, why—?"

"Hear me out, Elise. You canna' learn much if you're constantly interrupting."

She bit her tongue and forced herself to smile vacuously at him.

"Where was I? Oh yes, my assumption that you're exactly what's needed at this point in my life. Let's start with the obvious. You've mirrors. You're a lovely woman. It's a pleasure looking at you. From any angle, you're almost inhumanly lovely." His voice warmed. Elise was afraid she did, too. "Looking at you, I can understand this ice goddess thing, only it's na' just due to your coloring and the fragile quality about you, is it? Dinna' answer that. Let me."

He probably said the last because her mouth had dropped open, and not to say a word, either.

"It's na' only your beauty, it's the entire thing. Everything about you. You're perfect, almost beyond imagination. Exactly what I need. It was fated, if you will. It fell into my lap, and I dinna' take opportunity for granted. I never have. Do you want me to go on?"

Elise didn't move. He smiled, and his green-flecked eyes smiled, too.

"Verra well. As I already told you, sometimes a nonanswer is an answer. You're perfect, and na' just because you're beautiful and have a perfectly formed body. You happen to carry an impeccable title, you exhibit all the social graces, you have your own fortune, and let's na' forget the most pertinent—you, my dear, were a lady in trouble. I rescued you at enormous cost to myself and my very own future. It was an act of chivalry that has cost me dearly. Why, I canna' possibly wed the MacKennah lass now. And the best part is, there's *nae* man in my clan who can fault me for what happened, and consequently having you foist upon me when I least expected it."

"No, I—" She stopped her own instant response because the pain-filled voice didn't sound like her. If it hadn't come from her own throat, she would have disowned it.

"Careful, you're in severe danger of cracking. That's what decided me, actually. You're The Ice Goddess. You're cold. You're heartless. You're bloodless. Perfect. Ask any man looking for a society wife. There's too much theatrics with normal women. There's tears and trauma and jealousy and emotional scenes. Let's not forget those. Most women send a man to his grave early with such scenes. Na' you. Oh *nae*. You never make a scene, do you? And then there's Karma to consider."

"K-k-karma?" she asked through lips that trembled, making it a four syllable word.

He smiled coldly. "Karma is fate. The solution fell into my lap. It's a double-edged thing. I want you to know that. I'm still assimilating it. The opportunity to seal all the leaks in my life was carted into my room that night, and I spent some time mulling it through and setting it up. You were there when least expected. You put yourself into my life. On purpose. Constantly. You must need me. Have you thought through that one yet? Dinna' bother. It's too deep for you at present."

"Colin, I—"

"And then there's the most important thing," he interrupted, as if she hadn't said a word. "As a man, I hold absolutely no interest to you. You've made certain I know that, at every opportunity and with every gesture. All of which leaves me free, and, in an odd sort of way, so are you. I canna' think of a better-suited couple, can you?"

Elise could feel the wave of tears filling her. She was afraid every exposed portion of her body was showing it. Colin was describing everything she already thought and hated about society marriages; at the same time, he was making her heart grow heavy with an ache she didn't think she could support. He was wrong, too. And not just about her interest in him. It wasn't true that she didn't want marriage, although she'd never admitted that to anyone except herself.

She did want to be married; but she wanted love more.

Elise began to think she didn't have the ability to

remain aloof, after all. The tablecloth was wavering before her eyes. Breathing deeply wasn't doing the trick, nor was counting, nor was paying close attention to every facet of her fingers. Nothing was working.

"Beside which," he continued, as if everything he was saying was normal and insipid and bland. "It is a definite feather in my cap that I have managed to wed the most notorious woman in London. I quite feel I've risen in the world. You should read the congratulatory notes I've received already from Barrigan and his friends."

She made a choking noise. She couldn't help it.

The innkeeper knocked and Colin looked to the door. Elise dabbed at the corner first of one eye, and then the other. She tipped her head to allow the moisture to soak into her handkerchief. She was glad she hadn't put a bit of soot near her lashes.

A stout woman followed on the innkeeper's heel. Elise knew it was the cook without asking. She turned her face away from them and surreptitiously slid her handkerchief back into her reticule.

"You found your meal satisfactory, Your Grace?" The man seemed to have lost some of his awe at having such illustrious customers. His words and tone were confrontational and clipped.

Colin pushed back from the table. "My thanks. The meal was that and more. Your Sarah is quite a cook, just as you said. I'm afraid Her Grace has lost her appetite, though. The swaying of the coach, you understand. Would you be so kind as to prepare a hamper? My man will see to the arrangements."

The couple at the door groveled at Colin's changed personality. Elise sat, frozen in place, and watched.

"Have you *nae* cloak, my dear?" His voice was as warm as a love-struck husband's should be. She knew it for the act that it was.

Elise tried to face him. She could only hope that he

wouldn't notice that she wasn't meeting his eyes. "I left it in the carriage," she answered, in a whisper.

"I see that I'll have to look after you better."

He had his head lowered toward hers and was whispering as he helped her to rise. She wondered why he bothered posturing for her. The couple at the door couldn't overhear what he was saying.

She put her hand through the crook of his arm, settling her fingers on rock-hard flesh, and let him escort her to the carriage. It shouldn't have been difficult. She simply had to put one foot in front of the other and hold up her skirts with her free hand.

Elise was shaking when they got to the coach door. Colin stopped, turned to look down at her, and waited. At this point, she was supposed to let go of her escort, take hold of the carriage handle, and step up. It wasn't supposed to be difficult.

What was wrong with her?

Colin had said a lot, most of it untrue. He'd been right about one thing, though. The imperious Dowager Duchess of Wynd never, ever caused a scene. It was Elise's unspoken code of honor. Yet here she was, holding up the entire retinue, because the man she'd proclaimed to the world as her husband that night didn't want her at all. She was beginning to fear that she had a heart, after all.

"I've decided to ride inside now, Mick."

"Very good, Your Grace."

She heard the exchange between Colin and his man, but it didn't sink in what Colin was about until he put his hand atop hers. She guessed he was physically removing the contact.

"Elise?"

She touched her glance on his and quickly looked away. He was too astute when it came to guessing what she was feeling. He'd probably recognize her expression for what it was. Her dreams were dying, and there was no one she could tell.

She'd never get the chance now to correct anything.

"You dinna' have to fear me . . ."

He said more words in a strange language in her ear. Then he lifted her and entered the carriage, with her in his arms. Elise could have done without the intimacy. She kept her eyes shut tightly the entire time and struggled with her instincts. How she longed to simply turn her head into his shoulder and hold on to the experience! She hadn't had this much physical contact with anyone since her childhood. She was afraid he'd guess that, too.

"Do you want me to hold you?"

The gentleness of his voice existed only in her dreams. She shook her head and moved off his lap, and to the other bench, before she could change her mind. It was still just as hard and lumpy as she remembered.

Chapter 11

Colin had made arrangements to stay with Lady
Sophie's husband their first night, and it was bound
to be uncomfortable. Elise could have warned him
how straitened the circumstances were at Ipswich
Manor, if he'd asked.

In the vague light cast from the ducal carriage
lanterns, the cobbles looked overgrown and dangerous for the horses. If, as Colin had already alluded,
his new duchess was the type to be ill at carriage
swaying, she'd have been prostrate by the time they
arrived.

It made as good an excuse as any other, she decided,
eyeing the untouched hamper of food. She wasn't
hungry; besides, she'd been pretending to sleep.

The family of Ipswich had resided in Barton's
Abbey ever since their own manor had burnt shortly
after Sophie's marriage. It was apparent that the
funds to rebuild weren't available.

The lights were on, however, and the entryway was
inviting. Elise followed Colin down from the carriage. She didn't need him to stand so close to her as
she did so, but it was her fault. Everything was her
fault, but that didn't make it better.

"Your Grace, and Elise, my very dear Elise! So wonderful to have you stay. Welcome! Welcome!"

Sophie's husband was round and jovial. He held his arms wide in welcome. She smiled in return and held out her hand.

"Howard, you are doing well? How are the boys?"

"Doing fine, the lads are. Fine." He held her hand for a moment.

One of Colin's servants took his coat, while Elise looked about for a housekeeper.

"Have you seen Lady Sophie lately? She's still well? Come in, come in. Dinner is almost ready. We've been sending out invitations all day, and quite a gathering it's turning out to be. My thanks for sending such an amount of food, Your Grace. I feel certain you wouldn't begrudge a bit for the festivities. You couldn't possibly eat all of it, even if we had the time to prepare it all. There will be a vast amount to send on, I'm afraid."

Colin turned and helped Elise with her pelisse. He handed it to one of his footmen, winked at Elise, and then turned to Howard.

"I would na' hear of it, my lord. What arrived will only spoil if I tried to keep it further. I'll hear no more about it. Is there a chamber for Her Grace to freshen up in? Then you and I can talk about horses."

If Colin had wanted Howard's complete attention, he couldn't have said anything more perfect, Elise thought wryly as she followed Colin's servant up the stairs. She knew how boring Sophie found her own husband's continual talk of horses. When Elise had first met her, Sophie had made it more than plain.

Hers was an arranged marriage, just as Elise's had been. After Sophie had gallantly given her husband not one but two heirs, she had then left, to enjoy herself in London. Elise wasn't in any position to sit in judgment of anything Sophie took into her head to do. Elise had met Howard twice before this. Both times she had found him jovial and consumed by talk of horses. Of that, Sophie hadn't exaggerated.

The chamber Elise was shown into was adequately sized but intimately bare. Great beams crossed the ceiling. Her presence, together with the fire, made the room effectively warm. She looked about and frowned. There was a dressing table with a stool, a bureau, a cheval mirror, and a very large bed; but that was all.

She crossed to the mirror and began unwinding her hair, pulling flowers from it as she went. She was doing her best to ignore Colin's trunk on the floor beside her two. A knock on the door brought her a maid who was almost too old to walk unassisted. Elise helped the woman lay out her evening wear. She was going to be overdressed, but that couldn't be helped. She had only the contents of her trunks from Barrigan's house at her disposal.

Perhaps His Grace, the Duke of MacGowan, shouldn't travel with such haste, she thought snidely.

She was careful to choose the plainest gown, but it looked ornate lying atop the bedstead. Elise had this one fashioned of gold-tone brocade, with black satin oversleeves and tonal golden embroidery about the waist. It also required six layers of petticoats. Elise helped the maid pull the garments from the trunk and stifled her cry of dismay at how crushed they all were.

"I'll just see these ironed, Your Grace, while you bathe."

The woman held open the door for a tub. Elise recognized the MacGowan livery on the men bringing her heated water. That was interesting. It appeared the Duke of MacGowan was thoughtful and organized. She supposed she had his lists to thank for that.

Elise had never been one for lists. She wanted spontaneity and instant gratification in her world. Lists required too much thinking, which she avoided; besides, she told herself, looking about, everything she could possibly need or want always seemed to materialize without her request. She'd had Daisy for that.

She missed Daisy's efficiency when she was left to contend with shedding the traveling ensemble by herself. It would help if the hooks weren't up the back, she told herself more than once as she wrestled with them.

She didn't hear the door opening, for she had the tight-fitting jacket wrapped about her neck and ears. She had no trouble hearing the laughter, however. She pulled the material back down and whirled to face him.

"Is there something I can do for you, Your Grace?" Elise tried to sound supercilious, but it came out breathless and agitated to her own ears. She lifted her chin to glare at him. It worked only because he was taking up the space across the room from her.

"Would you be needing the services of a lady's maid?" He folded his arms across his chest, raised his eyebrows, and waited.

"Don't be obtuse. It's rather obvious, isn't it? You didn't happen to employ me one, did you?"

"Turn around."

"No."

He took the nine steps across the room, put his hands on her shoulders, and turned her around. Elise clenched her teeth shut as he deftly undid the last hooks. Her eyes widened as he tossed her jacket to the bed and began pulling on the laces of her corset.

"You can stop there, Colin! I never said that I—"

"Who would you like to undo your underthings, my dear? If my touch is so horrid, perhaps you know of someone else? I suppose I could send up Ipswich. He would na' take it as a personal affront if I asked it of him. He'd probably be delighted, and I might na' even challenge him."

Elise was gasping, and it wasn't his words that were causing it. He'd stopped pulling laces but kept his hands where they were. The near touch of him was stealing her thoughts and stilling her tongue.

"Well?"

"Finish . . . quickly, then."

"I'll try, but I seem to be all thumbs tonight."

He was wrong about that, for she felt certain more than a thumb had brushed against her spine. The remembered warmth was spreading, too. Elise stiffened her legs and held her knees together.

"Where is it that your own maid went to? She did na' desire a trip to the Highlands, either?"

"She'll be meeting . . . up with us . . . at Crewe." Elise would have given anything to take back the stammering of her voice. She couldn't seem to catch her breath, though, and Colin's finger traced her backbone while she was trying to.

"Crewe?"

The word was breathed against the nape of her neck. Elise jumped.

"I . . . I—"

She stopped the stupid stuttering that was her voice. It was next to impossible to think through what she was supposed to be replying to. He touched her ear, and she could have sworn it was with his lips. Her thighs were turning to water. Elise willed the sensation to cease, but her body wasn't listening.

She took a deep breath and started speaking. "I thought surely you would travel by train. I mean, the roads North aren't passable much of the year, and the MacGowans do own a train. You do, don't you? I . . . well, I felt Crewe would be the most convenient stop for such. That is where the rail line goes into Scotland, isn't it?"

He didn't say anything for so long she nearly tipped her head to see why. His fingers had stalled on the corset, too. She should have kept silent, she told herself.

"You surprise me, Elise."

When Colin finally answered, his voice was so soft she could have reached out and touched it. Surely he'd spot her shivers now. *This is monstrous,* she told herself.

He cleared his throat, and then he was speaking in his normal tone again. "Of course, the MacGowan train stands ready for us at Crewe. I dinna' think you interested enough to advise you of it. I thought you dinna' think of me at all."

"It isn't what you—" she began, but he interrupted her.

"What is this contraption made of? I'm having a bit of trouble with the bottom. You're knotted. What idiot would do such a thing?"

He didn't finish what he was saying, but he did pull back from her. Elise put a hand out to steady herself on one of the bed's posts. This was worse than embarrassing. She was probably flushed a rosy pink, too. She supposed if she was facing the mirror she'd know for certain. Her eyes widened.

Perish the thought! Having to watch him as he unclothed her would be more than she had experience to deal with.

"I'll have to cut it."

He was fishing for a knife, no doubt. The longer he stayed away from her, the easier it was to breathe. Elise held the front of her corset to her with her free hand and tried to ignore what that might mean.

"It probably will na' be wearable now. My regrets. You'll have to make do without one for a spell."

He cut the last stay away as he spoke. If she hadn't been holding the whalebone-stiffened piece to her, it would have sprung off. Colin's voice had lost its carefree tone, too. He sounded as short-tempered and curt as he had to the innkeeper. All of which was her fault, she supposed. She was the one who had tied it in knots this morning.

"I . . . have more with me."

"Whatever for? You're slender as a thistle already."

"Propriety?" she answered, making it a question.

His snort was her answer, and she did turn her head at that. Colin wasn't even near her, nor was he looking her way. He was looking at his own reflection in the mirror, although he had to bend at the knees to do so. He was also unwinding the stock from about his neck.

Elise's heart sank. It was a very good thing she hadn't eaten luncheon. It made it easier to quell her stomach's rebellion. "Colin, surely you aren't . . . you wouldn't?"

"Would the thought of it upset you so much?"

He was speaking so softly that, if she hadn't seen his lips moving, she'd have thought she imagined it. She met his eyes in the reflection. He pulled the neck cloth harshly from his neck and flung it over the top of the mirror.

"Your face speaks for you. Dinna' fear. I'll na' spoil your bath with my presence. I should have paid better attention to your press."

Colin had full lips, but he'd thinned them as he spoke. The lines about his eyes weren't the ones from laughter, either. She made some sort of noise he could take for whatever he wished and put her hands to her face. The corset fell to the floor.

Ida was the elderly maid's name. Elise knew that, and more, before she was dressed. She hadn't washed her hair. It would have taken too long to dry. She was glad she'd had such foresight as Ida continued her meaningless prattle, like the amount of underclothing Elise was bent on wearing. Ida was appalled by the neckline, too. Elise wasn't comfortable with it, either, but the maid's nonstop criticism had her actually lowering the edge. Even Ida couldn't help an intake of breath when Elise clasped her topaz-studded necklace in place, though.

"I have to admit, Your Grace, that you do these old eyes proud to look at you. The abbey could use a bit of gaiety now and again. Makes my heart sad to see his lordship pining out his heart for that wife of his."

Howard . . . pining? Elise wondered with raised eyebrows.

"Not that she cares a fig for him, or for the estate. Why, with the funds she spends in town, his lordship could have had his home rebuilt by now. And those boys . . ."

Elise helped pin her own hair up in order to escape further revelations. Ida obviously hadn't placed the new Duchess of MacGowan as Lady Sophie's companion, the notorious Elise Wyndham, yet. She wasn't about to enlighten her, either.

As it was, Elise received an earful about the staff's sufferings, the boy's sufferings, his lordship's sufferings, and why everyone else on the estate was suffering according to Ida. Through it all, Elise stayed silent. What answer could she make? It was Sophie's right to enjoy the Season away from her husband, if that's what she wanted. It was every woman's right who'd been forced! Besides, Elise reminded herself, she knew where the money Sophie was spending actually came from, and it wasn't from Ipswich.

The abbey boasted a large dining room. The table was graciously arranged, and fresh flowers adorned each place setting. Elise found herself making small talk with a squire and his wife while she awaited Colin's presence.

She wondered where he had dressed. Then she told herself that it didn't matter, as long as it was far from her.

All the squire wished to do was talk of horses. Elise gave him what she could of her attention, because the wife's eyes were on her neckline the entire time. It took every bit of her will not to reach to touch the topaz strand and cover herself more.

"I see punctuality is another of your virtues."

Colin stepped from behind her, interrupting the other woman's inspection. Elise turned to look up at him and found her eyes admiring the man beside her with every bit as much fervor as the squire's wife was. In tight-fitting, black-checked trousers, superbly tailored jacket, and starched white bow tie, he was every bit a gentleman.

She tried not to show her surprise, for he couldn't have picked a better match to herself. She no longer looked out of place or too richly dressed. She looked like she was the Duke of MacGowan's Duchess. She was proud to stand beside him and introduce him as her husband.

She hoped it didn't sound in her voice.

He had their complete attention as he lifted her hand to his lips in seeming adoration, before turning to the squire and his wife. Then his conversation went immediately to the MacGowan stables.

Elise pursed her lips. She should have known.

She noted that the wife's eyes were on her now for a completely different reason. Elise recognized envy, and she looked sidelong to the man at her side, who was causing all of it. He seemed unaware of what was transpiring beneath his nose, although he should have been. There wasn't a bit of that elegant ensemble that was hiding a bit of the man beneath it all.

"That is a lovely piece of jewelry."

Elise didn't realize he'd finished his conversation. She started, tipped her head, and then skittered away from his glance. The twinge came again, in full force, startling her into a gasp as she dropped her gaze to the floor and owned the entire flame of her blush.

Oh no. No. Never. It was horror fighting with giddiness,

while anger, fear, and dismay sidled right alongside anticipation and such a feeling of euphoria that her eyes burned with unshed tears at the beauty of it. Elise had to close them on the stone flooring of Ipswich Manor's dining room. *This is the absolutely last thing that can happen!* she thought, while her heart hammered in fear. She wasn't going to allow it. She refused to feel anything for a MacGowan! Ever. Never. She wasn't finding him stirring her senses, and he wasn't anything other than the stranger she'd been tricked into wedding. Nothing more. Ever.

"A souvenir from some love-struck swain, I gather?"

Elise reached to touch the stones, grateful for his words, for her thoughts had stalled the moment he'd spoken again.

She'd selected the necklace when it was presented for her inspection. Very few knew that the Dowager Duchess of Wynd bought her own jewels, usually on a whim, but sometimes with her eye to a good investment. That came from another of her past friendships. She'd been helping one of her previous amours catch another lady's favors with baubles very much like these. Elise twined her fingers in the topaz-studded gold chain and smiled glassily at the little scar on his chin.

"I'm pleased you like it," she answered.

"The MacGowan gems will look splendid on you. Perhaps that will compensate."

"For what?"

"For being unable to wear the ones you have on now, or the rubies, and let's na' forget those little purple ones from the first night."

"You recall . . . what jewels I wore?" Elise's head was spinning with what he'd just said. He remembered a small thing like that? Her heart stumbled, pumping more blood into her face than she could staunch, and she didn't even have a fan to hide behind.

"Of course na'. You were described in one of the papers."

She deserved the look he was giving her. Elise took several barely noticeable breaths to calm herself. Such a reaction belonged to the girl she'd been, not the woman she was. How stupid of her to have forgotten it. She narrowed her eyes and pursed her lips sweetly at the man parading as her husband. "You live in the past, Your Grace. I have every intention of wearing my own jewels in the future, just as I do now."

His lips thinned, and the nerve twitched in his jaw as he seated himself beside her. "Must you fight me at every turn?"

"Until you release me from this farce, yes. I'm finding it immensely entertaining, too."

"How do you know that you will na' like Scotland? You have na' seen the green of the moors, felt the wind on your face, fished a burn—"

"All delightful pursuits, I'm sure," she interrupted him.

"You know, unlike most of the clans, the Mac-Gowans fought against land clearances. That means there's a lot of old-fashioned Scots for you to meet."

Elise knew what he was really saying. If she insisted on such stubbornness as wearing her own jewelry, she'd not find Scotland a very welcome place.

"Land clearances, Your Grace?"

The squire's wife claimed Colin's attention. Elise listened as he explained how once landowners had found out how profitable raising sheep was, they'd cleared their own people out of their crofts and forced them off the land. Some of the clansmen had been sent, ill-prepared, out into the night without so much as a warning. Some had even had their possessions burnt to the ground as they watched, to make them leave.

"It sounds barbaric and horrid, Your Grace," the squire's wife said.

"Perhaps I should also explain that most of the affected properties belonged to English landowners."

Elise used every repertoire in her book to keep the grin from settling on her mouth at the woman's expression. She knew her lips would betray her eventually, though. She cupped a hand over her mouth to hide it. Then she caught Colin's eye. He was suffering the same thing, she was certain of it.

Elise didn't have any experience of the thrill sharing her amusement with him was causing her. It was like being doused with cold water, yet set afire at the same instant. As if he knew it, Colin's grin slowly faded. She had to restrain herself from bolting from the table.

"How is it that your clan survived and prospered, then?"

Elise thought it was Howard asking it, but the question simply joined the humming sound in her ears.

"The MacGowans have always wed well, my lord."

Colin didn't turn his head to answer. He didn't let go of her gaze. His eyelashes were fairly lush and shaded those golden eyes to deepest brown. How had she missed that? His glance moved from hers, down her nose to her mouth, and back again, in less time than it took to catch another breath. Then he did it again, only this time he licked his lips.

Someone cleared their throat and her eyes widened before she choked on the reaction. Colin saw every bit of it, too. She looked hastily to her lap. Those were the same fingers, the same nails, the same rings: everything was the same, yet different.

She was acutely aware of Colin seated beside her. Unless she kept her eyes closed, she had no choice but to be. What could only be very large thigh muscles were clearly defined beneath his trousers. He had small diamonds on his cuffs, and his hands were tanned against the starched white of his shirt. She caught her lower lip in her teeth.

She twisted her napkin without thinking. She wished she dared to dip it into her water goblet and dab at her temples.

". . . on your honeymoon, Your Grace? Your Grace?"

"Elise?"

Colin was whispering it, and Elise concentrated on untwisting the linen square in her hands. She lifted her head and looked toward the head of the table. Lord Ipswich seemed the safest, and she thought it had been he speaking.

"Forgive me, I must have wandered," Elise spoke up. "It has been . . . a long day. You were saying?"

The squire's wife now was looking at her with what could only be dislike and real jealousy. Elise studiously ignored looking that way again. She couldn't meet the woman's eyes. She'd thought herself born to the art of the double entendre. She'd been four years in society, and was a master of the quick, brutal set down. She was known for her wit. She was never without partners at any social gathering because she had a rapier tongue and a quick mind.

It was laughable. She felt as shy and insecure as a schoolgirl.

". . . the continent? *Nae.* We've na' any plans except returning to my home. We were wed so quickly, we dinna' have time to think on it. Did we, my dear?"

Elise mumbled something after Colin answered for her. It was all she was capable of.

Chapter 12

It was a relief to get out of her finery, but Ida's chatter was giving Elise a headache. Perhaps it was only intensifying the one she already had. She listened to how lucky she was, how charming her new husband was, what a lovely couple she and Colin were, and felt like screaming.

How could I have been so brazen? she asked herself for the hundredth time. It didn't help that her reflection wasn't answering. Ida noticed nothing amiss. If she did, it didn't stop her prattle. Elise waited placidly while the maid brushed her hair into a waterfall that reached the seat of her cushioned chair. Then she dismissed the woman. She couldn't stand for one more idle remark or complaint about the sufferings of the Ipswich family.

Elise had her own demons to face.

She stared at her reflection. She hadn't changed, although it felt like she should have. She should look even older than usual. She should have dark circles beneath her eyes and lines of dissolution about her nose and mouth; but she had neither. With her hair down and her face bare of cosmetics, she looked more like a girl of nineteen. She looked like the fresh-faced country girl she'd been. It was a shame Colin Mac-Gowan would never see it.

As if she'd called him, the door opened. His Grace walked in, pulling the tie from his neck as he shut the door behind him. Elise met his eyes squarely in the looking glass, although the girl in the mirror flushed. The heat spread up her neck to her cheeks. There wasn't anything Elise could do to stop it.

No one ever saw her this way. She wouldn't have been able to act the part of the imperious, heartless duchess if they had.

She watched as he took in the length of her hair, the plain cotton of her high-necked nightgown, and the hand she clasped to her throat. What she wouldn't give for a bit of rice powder to temper the blush staining her cheeks!

He smiled and cocked his eyebrows. "This is a becoming change."

"I wasn't expecting you."

"That much I can see for myself."

"What do you want?"

"You'll have to forgive me, but it will look strange if I waste any more time away from my bride. Forget I asked that. I dinna' think I want your forgiveness, after all."

She didn't answer.

"You'll na' run in terror or shriek in fright, will you?"

"I'm not afraid of you, Colin."

"You're afraid of every man, myself included. I'm bright enough to guess that and experienced enough to know it. Next lie, please?"

He slung the tie onto the dresser without leaving her gaze. Her eyes widened a hair. Not enough for him to notice, but enough that she knew of it. She picked up the brush for something to do.

"Do I have your assurance?"

He was undoing the buttons of his jacket as he spoke. Elise started brushing. She needed both hands to do it properly. She had to consciously force her hand to let go of the ribbon tie at her throat. Colin put his hand to his sleeve as if to pull his arm free.

"You can't sleep here." Her words stopped him.

"Why na'? Are we na' hopelessly in love with each other? So much so that we could na' even wait for a proper ceremony to wed?"

She shut her eyes to still the emotion he'd see. She had no right whatsoever to be hopelessly in love with him, or even pretend to it. He was a MacGowan, and she'd sworn to hate them forever. Yet the longer she knew him, the harder it was. Colin MacGowan wasn't supposed to be charming. He wasn't supposed to have greenish brown eyes that had sun-enhanced laugh lines at the edges. He wasn't supposed to make her laugh. He wasn't supposed to make her feel like her feet weren't touching the ground. He certainly wasn't supposed to be undressing in her bedchamber while she couldn't seem to move her eyes.

Elise had some thinking to do about it. She didn't want to. That much was obvious. Colin had already given her the time, and she'd wasted it. He was right about one thing, though. He'd said it was too late, and it was.

Elise was beginning to understand how her sister had felt. She knew now why Evangeline had tossed everything away in order to be with a MacGowan. Elise was stupid to flirt with the same feeling. She didn't wish to know how the betrayal and rejection felt, too. Yet here she was, ignoring every vow she'd made. It was amazing how small and wretched it made her feel.

Not only was Colin a MacGowan, but he was *the* MacGowan. He was the laird of their clan. As such, he was the imperious judge of who was acceptable and who was not. He was the epitome of everything Elise hated and feared.

Her sister, Evangeline, was probably turning over in her grave.

Elise opened her eyes and met his. He shrugged out of his jacket next and hung it on a peg beside the door. Inside, Elise was screaming at him to stop; outwardly, she smoothed the brush through a lock of hair that ended in her lap. She had to lift it with one hand as she did so.

"You're showing remarkable restraint. My compliments."

She didn't answer. He didn't seem to be expecting one. His evening attire included a stiffened, pleated-front shirt, too. Elise watched as he unclasped the diamonds at his cuffs and set them atop the dresser. Then he began slipping the buttons on the front of his shirt from their holes. He wasn't watching what he was doing, either. He was watching her.

He wasn't wearing proper attire, after all. He didn't have anything on beneath his shirt. He also had more muscle than she'd ever seen, or had known existed. Parts of his chest flexed strangely as he pulled off the shirt. His flesh wasn't wasted and white. He was lightly tanned and had chestnut hair spreading from a line up his belly to the two mounds of his chest. He looked every inch a man, and an extremely virile one at that.

Elise couldn't hide the width of her eyes. She knew he'd spot it but was beyond that. She put the brush back with a hand that trembled so badly it clattered on its tray.

"Your lack of courage is showing."

"Colin, please?"

He sighed, and it lifted the hair from his forehead. It also moved everything on his chest. *That,* she could have done without noticing.

"Believe it or na', I'm na' fond of rejection. Hard

to believe, I know. I have a suggestion for you. Have you ever heard of a bolster?"

She shook her head.

"I'll explain."

She had to turn from the mirror to watch him, which was worse.

"We roll up the top covering, like this, until it makes a long divider."

Elise tried to follow along, but the humming sound in her ears was making it difficult. She was afraid it had something to do with the sight of the Duke of MacGowan, clad only in tight, black-checked trousers and standing about six feet from her.

"Then we place it between the sheets, making a nice wall between us. Will that suit, do you think?"

He was putting action to word, and Elise watched his thigh muscles moving with that motion, too. The Duke of MacGowan wasn't a man of leisure; that was a certainty.

"Will this meet with your approval?"

She knew he was asking something, but she hadn't actually heard any of it. Maybe if he'd put his shirt back on, she'd find her mind functioning again. Elise had to force herself to look from the ropelike structure of his stomach, up his chest, to his face.

He was grinning. She looked to the floor, where it was safer.

"Well?"

"I've never heard . . . of such . . . a thing," she stammered.

"That's because you hobnob with the elite classes. You have to come down a peg or two in the company you keep if you want to find common sense. It's sadly lacking in the upper crust."

"But—"

"I know, I'm a member now. I've been dutifully

informed of it, too. It will take some time to polish myself enough. I'm a bit rough about the edges."

A bit? she wondered.

"I told the solicitor fellow as much. Everyone will just have to bear with me in the meantime. You included."

She was glad she was looking at the floor. He wouldn't be able to spot her smile. She didn't want him to know she shared his humor. She already knew where that had gotten her. She bit her lip and tried to find her voice.

"Your bed awaits, Madame. I hope it meets with your satisfaction."

The plain wood flooring below her was hard to focus on. He sounded so friendly and so safe. How she wished she were naive enough to believe it!

"I suppose it will have to do," she said, with her haughtiest voice.

His quick intake of breath was her answer. Elise avoided what that meant as she walked to the opposite side of the bed from him and slipped beneath the covers. She turned toward the wall and tried to ignore him.

She knew by the shadow on the wall that he hadn't moved. For some reason she was ashamed at her own actions. Angry tears filled her eyes. She blinked rapidly. She didn't need a conscience at this late date. Maybe Colin should have paid better attention to some of the cartoons about her. The Dowager Duchess of Wynd didn't have a conscience, and she didn't have a heart.

"If I had another option, I'd take it. I want you to know that."

"Very well, I know of it," she told the wall.

His answer was in the same strange language she'd heard him use before. His shadow was moving, too. Elise shut her eyes tightly, squelching every emotion. When she opened them again, she couldn't see any shadow. She didn't know where he was, and it was making the flesh on her back tingle. She turned her head as quietly as possible, found him, and caught the cry before it sounded.

Colin was standing before the chevel mirror, brushing out his hair. He had to bend down in order to do so, and he wasn't paying the slightest bit of attention to her. He put the brush back and bent to check something on his face. Elise fought the smile. She hadn't known that men primped.

He'd shed his evening trousers and was wearing only skin-tight drawers. Either his wardrobe was too small, or men's underdrawers were supposed to end at the calf, she decided. Then he stood and stretched, lifting his arms above his head and making his shoulders and back undulate. He had entirely too much muscle, and in too many places.

She wondered if it felt as hard and strong as it looked, and could swear her fingers tingled again with the same sensation of want. Elise couldn't believe what she was doing, nor could she imagine the reaction in her entire body. The same inferno was igniting every nerve, including those in her feet. She was in serious danger of having to consider revamping her viewpoint of what handsome was.

Colin dipped at the waist and began doing some strange contortions as he rolled himself back and forth like a pendulum. She imagined he was exercising, but it didn't look like anything she'd ever seen or heard of.

With his legs bent perpendicular to the floor and his arms clasped in front of him, he began bending and circling. He wasn't in any hurry to finish his movements, either. Each time he lifted a leg or held out an arm, he did it with precision and grace. It looked like some strange dance, without benefit of music.

Or was there music? she asked herself, trying to still her heartbeat so she could hear.

It wasn't the humming sound. Elise sharpened her ears, for it was a very light melody. Then she knew; it was Colin. He was making strange singsong noises as he moved. She was so spellbound, she forgot to blink, until her eyes watered. Such a mundane thing as blinking didn't occur to her.

He'd finished and stood, his chest heaving as he looked to the floor. Then he lifted his head and looked straight at her. Elise strangled a cry, threw her head back down, and slammed her eyes shut. It was too late, though. The image was burned onto her eyelids to resurface without any effort of will.

She knew the heated goosebumps covering her were from the embarrassment, but it was something else, too. He was so stirring! He hadn't been His Grace, Colin MacGowan, whom she'd sworn to hate. He'd been some strange creature she didn't know enough about to name. She'd been lost in some erotic realm of fantasy and desire, and he'd gone and caught her at it. There wasn't a hole big enough to hide in.

She didn't open her eyes when he dimmed the oil lamp. She refused to acknowledge that he was there. She was doing her best to stop the dry sobs that shook her.

Something wasn't right. It was good, though.

Elise snuggled closer to the warmth behind her back and ignored the lighting of the room. She felt rested and secure, although she was lying in a strange position and on her left side. Always before she had slept on her right, curled into a small ball. She couldn't remember the last time she'd slept this way. She also couldn't remember ever feeling so protected and warm. Then she knew why. Her eyes flew open in alarm.

Colin's right arm encased her, scooping her into the

enclosure he'd made with his body. She tried not to feel the contours of his legs against hers, or his stomach against her backside, or his chest against her shoulders, but her skin was awakening to every inch of him. She even had her head pillowed on his outstretched left arm.

Elise blinked once, and then again. The view wasn't changing. Her eyes widened at the sight of the bolster roll in front of her nose. She was the one on the wrong side of the bed.

Oh, dear God! How had that happened? she asked herself.

Colin's rhythmic breathing along her earlobe tickled. Elise scrunched her shoulder up and stirred away from it. The arm about her tightened. Elise held her breath until his breathing pattern resumed.

It would never do to have Colin awaken to this. He'd think things of her that she couldn't allow. She had to reach her side of the bed, and before much more time passed. With an effort that felt foreign, she turned onto her back, moving as carefully as she could. Colin's arm rolled with her. She kept her eyes on him, expecting at any moment to see him open that greenish brown gaze at her.

She'd never been so close to anyone in her entire life. From the distance of his forearm, she could pick out each and every eyelash curving on his cheek. He did have a scar on his chin, making a groove that resembled a small cleft just above the square end of it. He also had a vague sprinkling of freckles across his nose. She hadn't noticed that before. Of course, that was because she hadn't looked closely enough at him. How could she? He was forbidden. She knew that much from Evangeline.

Elise wished she hadn't awakened yet. Awareness brought thought with it, and she didn't want to think. She avoided it at any cost. That was what lightning-fast conversation, expensive parties, wild midnight excursions, and free-flowing wine was for.

She slipped from beneath his arm, pushing into the mattress beneath her in order to do so. Colin groaned and rolled onto his other side. The loss of his warmth chilled her. Elise had to fight the urge to move back against him, and that was what scared her into rising.

The only chair was as hard as it looked. Elise settled into it, pulled her knees to her chin, and stretched her nightgown over her toes. It still wasn't as warm and comfortable as sleeping with Colin's arm around her had been. She hadn't known how it would feel. No one had told her, and she hadn't asked.

Evangeline was Elise's only sister. They hadn't been close. Elise realized it now for the loss it was, with a feeling akin to the force of a stomach blow. It was too late, though. It had been too late the moment Evangeline had come to the Dowager Duchess of Wynd for help. Elise hadn't been much help. In the predawn light of Ipswich's guest room, she realized she hadn't been any help.

Evangeline was supposed to have gone to London for her Season. She was supposed to get only one but had stretched it to three. That was dangerous, as well as stupid. Any woman could have told her that. Evangeline was supposed to do exactly what her younger sister had done. Find and catch a rich husband to support her. That's what a Season was for.

She certainly wasn't supposed to fall in love with one of the MacGowan clan. Nor was she supposed to turn to her little sister for solace with a broken heart when Evan MacGowan stomped on it. Evangeline had been so stupid! Women didn't gain in this world, only men did, and the last thing a woman needed with such lopsided odds was a broken heart and a swelled belly.

By the time Evangeline had come to her, Elise had convinced herself that she didn't have a heart. How could she have commiserated with anyone? Why, she hadn't even been there for Evangeline when she'd passed away, at the Wyndham Villa in Monte Carlo, while birthing Rory.

Only a heartless sister would have done that.

Colin snorted something, and Elise glanced at him before shying away. She'd superciliously thought Evangeline had deserved everything that had happened to her. You don't fall in love with a Scotsman, especially with their arrogance, lineage, and sense of tradition. It was the height of stupidity. It was inviting heartache.

How she longed to undo the past! To just once hold on to Evangeline's hand, look into her eyes, and tell her she understood.

Colin rolled onto his back, turning his profile to her. Elise told herself not to look, but it didn't work. Dawn light played across the planes of his face, defining it. Either he was getting more handsome, or she was losing sight of reality, despite every trick she'd used.

She didn't want to be in love with him. She refused! She didn't want to love anyone. She wanted to be The Ice Goddess, the woman who the press claimed had discarded more lovers than most men claimed. It was simpler that way. She didn't want the heartache, for Colin MacGowan would find out the same thing his brother had, eventually. He'd find out, and then he'd look at her with something akin to disdain and disgust and rejection, because she wasn't any more suitable to wed than Evangeline had been.

It was a shame to discover that she really did have a heart.

Elise watched Colin MacGowan sleeping, and her heart lurched fully and painfully, filling her eyes with stupid tears. She couldn't blink them away fast enough and bowed her head to her knees. No wonder she detested thinking.

She should have already told him of Rory, too. She should have told him everything. Now it was too late.

"Prayers, Elise? I would have thought them beneath you."

She shuddered through a breath, and then another. The material covering her knees was wet, but it would hide her loss of control well enough. She'd just have to be stronger in the future. She'd just have to withstand the onslaught of a masculinity she hadn't known existed.

She wasn't going to stay with him, and when he found out, he'd think she wanted it that way. She was stupid to lose sight of her future. She was heartless, ruthless, and ice cold, wasn't she? She took a deep breath, held it several seconds, and looked up.

"There's a lot you wouldn't have thought of me," she replied finally.

"Of that, I'm certain. You slept well enough? I dinna' disturb you too much with my snoring?"

"You . . . don't snore."

It was harder to answer him when he sat up, tucking the sheets about his waist and acting as if he were wearing full Scot's regalia, instead of a pair of shortened knickers. Colin MacGowan was a very handsome man, after all. He was also powerful, educated, sophisticated, honorable . . . and he was not for her. Elise let the hurt soak in and narrowed her eyes at the sight of such masculine bounty.

"Do you always rise this early? We'll make verra good time if we manage to get this kind of start."

"I'll try not to slow you." She tossed her hair over her shoulder and faced him as squarely as possible.

"You dinna' mind the bolster? It worked fairly well, dinna' it? We may have to resort to this type of thing again."

"It . . . was an acceptable alternative."

"Oh, it was more than acceptable."

He was chuckling as he said it. Elise reddened. He hadn't known, had he?

"I dinna' suppose you'd turn aside while I rise, would you?" he asked, his voice losing some of its amusement.

"Why? I very much doubt that you have anything I haven't seen before," she replied.

"True enough. You have na' seen me, though, and I could have sworn you quailed at that very thing. I'm only warning you. I dinna' wear proper attire last eve when I finally gained the bed. I wear verra little when I sleep. You can watch again, if you like. I will na' mind."

She lifted her chin and met his look without flinching. It would be petty of her to argue. It was the truth. She'd simply have to endure being with him, and then move on. She unfolded her legs and swiveled on the bare wooden seat of her chair, and that's when she saw his discarded knickers slung across the dresser top.

She clapped a hand to her mouth.

Chapter 13

"Tell me about your first husband."

Elise gulped. "Good heavens, no," she answered, with more strength than she thought she had at her disposal.

"Why na'?"

She decided to be airy and false with her tone. "It's ancient history, Colin. I've quite forgotten him."

"Interesting bluff and almost believable, if you were na' clenching your sewing as if it were going to run off, that is."

"Oh." It was all she could manage.

"Wynd. Tell me about him."

"Why?"

"Well . . . I might decide that I'd like to turn this farce into a real marriage. I'd need to know in that case, would na' I?"

"Perhaps you should have held out for a real wife, then," she answered.

"Oh, you are my wife, Elise. It's as legal as they come. The law was put into effect centuries ago, but never re-scinded. Perhaps you should brush up on your history."

"That isn't what I meant."

"You meant, perhaps, that you dinna' wish to be anyone's wife, and therefore are na' going to be mine?"

"Something along that line," she admitted.

"You've a strange way about you, then."

"Pardon?"

"I'm just remembering last night."

She flushed, but since she was looking down at her sewing, she knew he wouldn't see it.

"So tell me about him."

"Surely it isn't far to Storth Hall. I've heard the Marquis of Quorn is in residence. I find that strange. I thought he enjoyed the Season."

"I just finished reading about that scandal. Seems you kept this Marquis Quorn fellow company the entire time he was in London last year. As that's the case, you should know better than I what he enjoys . . . *and* you're changing the subject."

Elise frowned at the mess she'd just sewn before answering. "His home, Storth Hall, boasts a snuff box collection second to none, too. I believe Queen Elizabeth's historians made note of it."

"Somehow I dinna' think Quorn's snuffbox collection was the main topic of your conversations with him, but I could be wrong."

Elise was silent. It was better to ignore his little insult; but for some reason it wasn't as easy as it should have been.

"So tell me of Wynd. I'm a captured audience for the afternoon. The least you can do is entertain me."

"How . . . do you expect me . . . to do that?" Elise's voice stumbled. Her mind had already filled with scenes she'd never admit. His exhibition last night was featuring prominently in each of them, too.

"A bit of pleasant conversation, perhaps? A bit of knowledge about the woman sharing my name? I dinna' know, enlighten me."

"If this is your idea of pleasantly conversing, I can

see some decidedly lonely evenings in your future. Insults and innuendoes are hardly considered proper, you know."

"Present company only, I assure you."

"Why single me out?"

"I already told you yesterday."

"You're speaking riddles, and you know it. I hope you don't intend to fill the hours with such drivel. I may scream my vexation."

"That would be an improvement."

"My being vexed would be an improvement?"

"*Nae,* your screaming would be."

Elise set her lips and frowned. He wanted her to scream? He should have better comprehended what he read about her. She'd never allow such a reaction; it was for the innocent masses that possessed emotions. She'd settled all that with herself this morning.

"An improvement to what, pray tell?" she asked airily.

"To the fluff-filled, meaningless words you fill everything with."

"You should have tried poetry, Colin. You're quite good, you know."

"I'd be a dismal failure, I'm afraid. My penmanship would scare all but the stoutest heart away."

Elise fought glancing over at him. She should have known she'd fail at it. He'd crossed one leg over the other, folded his hands over the upraised knee, and raised both eyebrows as if he had nothing better to do than pursue this type of torment.

"Surely you can find something of interest out the window, instead?" she offered.

"Well, since you've decided to ignore me, I've had little choice. I'm beginning to think the entire countryside is boring, though. I hope my home is still as free of the plow as it was when I left. I'd hate to see the entire landscape riddled with cornrows, too. Na' that I mind a field or two, but here there's naught left untouched. Why, everywhere you look anymore some-one has been carving up the land or building another estate. It's quite depressing."

"Civilization annoys you?"

"Civilization? *Nae.* Why, I've never seen as many people as there are in India. You would na' believe it. It's impossible to count how many. And they seem to speak so many languages, all at once, that the marketplace is quite a cacophony of sight and sound.

"Once you leave the cities, though, it's different. It's barren and lush, colorful and yet dull at the same time. I've seen jungle so thick, you could na' spot a man-eating tiger from an arm's length, and I've seen desert so vast, it's like being at the ends of the earth. It's such a contrast. You can travel for days without sight of an-other person. I rather liked that. I miss it, too."

His voice softened as he spoke. Elise swallowed, lifted her sewing hoop, and spoke her next words to it. "I still can't tell you, Colin."

"About what?"

"Wynd."

"That would be a shame, to be sure." He sighed loudly. "So now that you know of my boredom, what would you like to talk about?"

"For some reason I didn't think it was the height of my ambition to keep your interest, Colin."

"Then you should na' try for such an air of mystery. I've already made mention of how intriguing I find you. If you dinna' wish my interest, you'd na' hide your past so well. It was quite difficult to trace it, you know."

This time when she swallowed it was more a gulp-ing motion. "There's nothing remotely intriguing about my past, Colin. It's quite dull, unless you pos-sess an active imagination. I'd not heard that of you, but I didn't listen to all your gossip, so I might have missed it."

"You're na' as old as you would like some to think, are you?"

"You're rather fond of asking questions a lady shouldn't have to answer, aren't you? That is distressing. I hope you'll curb that facet before our next visit with anyone."

"Dinna' fear, Elise. I would only ask such personal questions to the woman sharing my name. I'd rather na' know how old most of the Grand Dames in England are. You probably know, though, dinna' you?"

"Today seems such a lovely day to ride. I'm surprised you'd rather stay in this airless carriage with me."

"Let me just part the curtains here and allow you some air, then. You should have said something earlier."

He was putting motion to word. Elise gave her attention to shoving the needle into her fabric. She didn't even care if it was in the right place. She watched him tie open the curtain on the door. He was right about the view. The instant glance she had of the landscape was of little more than harrowed fields.

"Better? Well, now that I've solved the airless problem, tell me just how old you are."

"Colin . . ."

"All right, let me answer for you. Let's say that you are twenty-five."

Elise snorted.

"Twenty-six?"

She sighed heavily, since snorting hadn't worked.

"I'm na' even close? Well, for the sake of my little story, let's go with twenty-five. Fair?"

She shrugged. "It's your story. Make it whatever you wish."

"I've heard tell that you've been widowed four years. Was I listening to the right gossip on that one?"

"I really wish you wouldn't do this."

"No doubt, that's what makes it so damned amusing. This stretch of road could stand some of that, I think."

"This isn't amusing."

"You're wrong there. I'm finding it verra much so. It's entertaining, too, watching you massacre your sewing. You're na' much of a seamstress, are you?"

"One of my lesser talents, I'm afraid."

"So . . . what are your higher talents?" he asked.

"Not the ones you're assuming."

"Really? And just what is it that I'm assuming?"

Elise looked sidelong at him again. One thing was certain, he did look amused. "You tell me," she answered.

"Perhaps I'll ask Quorn. Is he the forthright type?"

"I'll never tell."

"You're discreet. That's admirable, it really is. That must be one of your talents. Glad to have found one. Where was I, anyway?"

Elise lifted her head to meet his gaze. The laughter showing in those brown eyes was almost more than she could withstand. Nothing she'd said was swaying him from his little inquisition. That much was obvious. She was beginning to think she'd more than met her match. It was an unsettling feeling in the pit of her stomach, too. She tried to swallow it away. She wasn't going to be ill, and she wasn't going to scream. She was going to get through this with her emotions intact. Colin MacGowan didn't have the right to open closed wounds. No one did. He grinned, and she had to look back down.

"Oh, I remember now. The baiting, hooking, and netting of the illustrious, and very wealthy, Duke of Wynd. Quite an accomplishment, that one was. You must have been about twenty or twenty-one then. It's rather odd that *nae* one had heard of you afore your wedding. Why is that, do you think?"

"You tell me," she said, without any inflection.

"Do you come from the wrong side of the blanket?"

"Am I illegitimate? Not that my parents ever let on."

This time her voice cracked a bit, despite the effort she was expending.

"Perhaps you were dreadfully poor? That would account for it."

Elise had to put down the hoop. The knotting was probably permanent. She was becoming too agitated to work at it.

"And na' one had ever laid eyes on you until that wonderful day when Wynd laid eyes on you and made all your dreams come true."

She was losing. He may have said more, but she wasn't listening.

It had been twilight, nearly five years ago. Elise had stayed too long at the vicarage. She and Evangeline had been going there for lessons since they were small. It was a two-mile walk from their home and back, but it was worth it. Sometimes Elise had thought it was the only escape she had.

Evangeline was seventeen then, and so beautiful. She hadn't accompanied her little sister that day. Their aunt, on their mother's side, had promised them each a Season when they were old enough. Evangeline had stayed home to put together some sort of wardrobe to travel in.

Elise hadn't been afraid of the walk home, but she'd hurried. Father would have his whip out if she wasn't back before dark. In her rush, she'd missed seeing the entourage bearing down on her in the village lane and hadn't avoided being knocked down by an outrider's horse. She'd sat in the roadside and stared. She'd never seen a real duke or a ducal carriage. It looked like something the king would travel in.

Then she'd seen him. The Duke of Wynd was ancient; his face was carved into so many lines he looked like he was frowning. He also had the strangest odor emanating from him.

"Come here, child." He'd commanded it in a frail,

shaky voice, and Elise had obeyed. She hadn't known enough not to.

"I've discovered your secret, have na' I?"

Colin's voice broke through her nightmarish reverie. Elise stared stupidly at him. "You . . . what?" she asked.

"You dinna' pay attention verra well, do you? That is definitely na' one of your talents."

"I don't want . . . to talk about . . . it." The strain on her voice was obvious now. The last word resembled a sob to her own ears.

"Verra well. Since it's hours yet before we'll be at Storth, what do you want to talk about?"

"The weather has certainly been nice this time of year, hasn't it?" She spoke just above a whisper. She couldn't change it. She didn't have any moisture in her mouth to swallow with.

"It's been that, and more. I only hope we dinna' run through a spring snow, or two, but I'm na' counting on it. We've some miles to travel yet. My homeland is na' known for its mild weather. I'm na' used to it anymore. I'll probably need extra woolens. So will you. You were bought, were na' you?"

"What?" Her eyes were as wide as her mouth.

"Bought. Purchased. You know, as with a bride price. It was a common practice in the Middle Ages. A comely daughter would bring a large settlement to her parents. That is still how most marriages in India are accomplished. I'm quite familiar with it."

She was choking and he didn't even seem to notice.

"You dinna' still communicate with them, do you? I would na'. I'd wish them off the face of the earth. You can tell me. I will na' be surprised if the answer is *nae*."

"My mother's dead." So was Elise's voice. What little sound it made was croaked through the dryness of her throat. It didn't stop Colin.

"Your father sold you? Your own father?"

Colin's face glittered through the blur of unshed tears. Elise gagged on a reply. Nothing was going to stop him.

"You were terrified of marrying Wynd, were na' you?"

"What would you know of it?" She was trying for a cold, unaffected voice, but she sounded like she was chewing on pebbles. Colin understood it, though.

"You were afraid of him, and yet you still wed him? Were you punished? I find that hard to believe. More like you went for the money and ended up paying more than you bargained for."

"Stop! Please, please stop!" Elise put her hands to her ears and held them there. She'd found her voice, too, for she was screeching. Shuddering filled her. Colin's eyes had changed, softened somehow, and she couldn't face him anymore. She stared out the window and let the tears fall. "You didn't know my father. You can't have known how much I hated him. He beat me. Do you hear me? He beat me!" The words were slurred with her anguish. Elise wasn't in control of it. The young girl she'd been was the one talking.

"I would never have married Wynd. He was old. Do you hear? I hated him. That I was wed with him and had to share his bed . . . dear God! It makes me ill to recall it!" She was gagging as she said it. "He smelled. The entire room smelled. Don't you understand? He was an old man!"

"But you wore the strawberry leaves. You were rich; you were a duchess, with an army of servants at your beck and call."

"You think I cared? If I could have walked after my father beat me, I would have run. I would have done anything. I would have killed myself before I let the duke touch me!"

"Elise . . . Elise."

Colin slid forward from his bench and reached for

her. She was incapable of resisting him. She collapsed onto his chest and sobbed into his shirtfront. She couldn't control the shaking that had overtaken her.

"I dinna' know. I'm sorry," Colin whispered.

"They had to carry me to the altar. They had to carry me to the duke's chambers, too. I didn't have any fight left in me. I was only fifteen! What did I know of it, anyway?"

"Fifteen? Good God!"

"He died that night, after . . . I can't finish, I can't!" Elise tried to push from the safety of his lap, but he held her too tightly.

"You dinna' have to finish, Elise."

"Don't say another word, Colin MacGowan. You wanted this, didn't you? You wanted me screaming? Well, take notes, then."

"I already said I was sorry."

"I would have done anything to keep this secret . . . anything!" She was gripping his shirtfront and trying to shake him. It wasn't working. "Is this what you wanted, Colin? Well, is it?"

"Na' especially."

"Well, you're going to know every morbid detail now. You're going to listen through the whole horrible thing, and then you're never asking about it again. Do you understand?"

"Stop it, Elise." He may have thought he commanded it, but his voice was too soft and gentle sounding. It didn't make any difference to her tears or her trembling, however.

"He died. And I watched him do it. I spent my entire wedding night next to a . . ." She was gagging and had to hold a hand to her mouth. "I couldn't move. My bandages had come off. I hurt so badly, I couldn't even move."

"That's enough, Elise."

"I'll say when it's enough! You asked for this, remember?"

"I dinna' know."

"Of course, you didn't know! No one does. The entire staff at Wyndham is ignorant of it. Do you know why? Because they'd been ordered to stay away no matter how much I screamed."

"The bloody bastard!"

Since Colin's arms about her had tightened, she felt the movement of his chest as he swore. Elise took a gulp of air, and then another. *I am not perched atop Colin MacGowan's lap, while he tears my carefully constructed persona apart!* She just wasn't! It was too strange to consider. Stranger still was the fact that she wasn't in fear of it.

"I see you dinna' wear bootblack on your lashes today. That's a verra good thing for me. I'd hate to arrive at Storth with black stains all down my shirt-front."

Colin may have been trying to sound his usual, carefree self, but he had to clear his throat midsentence to lower the octave. He let go of her with one arm and began searching the greatcoat beside him. The shifting of his thighs beneath her was startling. Elise shut her eyes and her mind to it.

It wasn't working. She knew just how muscular his legs were. She'd had a very good look at them last night. She couldn't believe what she was doing! She should be prostrate with guilt, not thinking of the man beneath her.

"You can put me down now, Colin," she whispered.

"And you can shush, too. I've found it, thank God. I was beginning to think my man absent in his duties. Here."

Elise had to open her eyes. Colin was proffering his handkerchief. She shoved it to her eyes.

"Thank you for telling me. I understand now. You

dinna' wish to be any man's wife, again. It would na' have mattered if it was me or that Easton fellow."

"I let him die, Colin. I must have wanted him to."

"The man got *nae* more than he deserved, if you ask me. *Nae,* that's too mild. He should have suffered an agonizing death, na' one from bedding a beautiful girl."

His matter-of-fact tone and words were calming her. Elise wasn't shaking anymore, and the handkerchief was mopping away not only the tears, but the desire to cry. She took another shuddering breath.

"You can set me down now."

"As we've already gone over that particular conversation, I'll remind you of how dull it sounds when repeated. Perhaps I dinna' think you're sufficiently recovered to sit by yourself."

"I am." She sniffed after saying it, and then moved the handkerchief away to prove it.

"All right, I'll come up with another reason. There's the matter of your youth. You had me fooled on that score. I just found out that I've nearly a decade of age on you. That will require some adjustment on my part. If you think I dinna' have much experience with society women, you should see my lack of it around lasses as young as you are. You're barely old enough to be wed."

"I don't want a husband, Colin, elder or otherwise."

"That's most likely true. Unfortunately, as I've told you, you're already most legally wed . . . to me."

"I can't consummate it, though, Colin. I just *can't!*" Her voice rose and there wasn't anything she could do about it. She refused to meet his look, too.

"Well, that would certainly open the door to an annulment later."

"You won't force it?"

"I am neither old, ugly, nor unsuitable bedding

material. Of course, I will na' force it. What do you think me?"

"A man," she answered.

"True enough. Are you quite recovered now, then? Good. I've quite lost feeling in my lower extremities."

Elise slid from him, swiveled, and sat on her own bench. She had weeded all but one petticoat from her traveling attire. It made the movement easier. It had also made it easier to feel every bit of him when he'd been beneath her. He hadn't felt like he'd lost all feeling. He'd felt hard, strong, and warm. She didn't know what to make of that.

The sewing hoop was still there, and she stared at it uncomprehendingly.

"You've been honest with me. I must be the same with you. I've already sent news of our marriage to my clan. I've *nae* wish to look a fool, and a cuckolded one at that. May I make a bargain with you?"

"What kind of bargain?"

"Let's give this charade six weeks, *nae* longer. At the end, I'll let you leave Castle Gowan and petition for an annulment if that's your wish. I can always blame it on the English lack of good sense."

"Do I have a choice on the matter?"

"Of course. Unlike your prior experiences, I'd na' force a girl to do anything. It's inbred. I'm asking you, as a favor to me, to pretend to be my wife. Six weeks. You can na' have anything more pressing at hand, do you? I've gotten a bit of insight into the life you've led. It has to be boring at times. Besides, the older you look, the thinner you'll find the ranks of available men to wreak your vengeance on."

"I beg . . . your pardon?"

"Forgive me, I'm thinking aloud. Stop me when I'm wrong."

"Colin—"

"All right, stop me now. I'm due for a bit of a nap, anyway."

"A nap? After forcing me to tell you about Wynd, you mourn a lost nap? You are unbelievable. Now, you want me to agree to parade as a wife, to God alone knows how many Scotsmen?"

"And Scotswomen. Dinna' forget them. They'll spot a fraud the moment they see one."

"I don't love you."

"Well, I've still got ten days to make you do so, dinna' I?"

"I—I refuse your bargain, then."

"Why? I'll do my best to be charming. You do your best to resist. It sounds verra entertaining and should make the rest of our journey fly by."

"I won't do it."

"Why? Afraid you'll lose?"

Yes, she answered silently. That was exactly what she feared. "I refuse to answer that, because it's beneath me to do so."

Elise picked up her discarded hoop and tried to locate her needle. Normally, it would have been easy; she could simply follow the loose thread. Unfortunately, there were no less than four large loops of loose thread, and none of them had a needle attached. Colin had been right about that one, too. Sewing wasn't one of her talents.

"Coward."

He didn't seem to expect an answer, and Elise wasn't going to give him one. She tried to ignore him as he put on his hat, and pulled the brim forward to shade his eyes. Then he propped himself into the padded corner, which her corset wouldn't allow her to do, and slept.

Chapter 14

"For some reason I dinna' think Quorn is very fond of you, my dear. I can na' imagine what you did. You dinna' throw him over for another, did you? The papers seemed to think quite the opposite."

Elise smiled behind her gloved hand. "I think it was more because we used to gossip critically of those at court. I believe his story was that he hid his wife away from society so that none others would steal her from him. He never expected me to see the truth. I think that's more the reason for his behavior toward me today."

"Well, he has naught to fear from me, I assure you."

Elise giggled her reply.

"The Quorns do have a spectacular snuffbox collection, though. Now that, he'd best keep guarded."

"I wouldn't know," Elise answered, as she let Colin lead her to the indoor conservatory.

The Quorns hadn't accompanied them, nor had their other guests, so Elise had Colin MacGowan all to herself.

Almost before his wife opened her mouth, it had been obvious why Quorn preferred the thrill of London. Elise knew Colin had spotted it just as she had, for he'd met her eyes and winked. The Marquise had a spotted complexion, a rotund shape, and rotted teeth. She'd looked incongruous beside the tall, dark, dapper figure of her husband.

When they'd arrived, Elise had been afraid that she'd unseated her hat, destroyed her gown, or at least had dark circles beneath her eyes. She wouldn't have been able to hide it, if she'd looked worn, wearied, or just plain emotionally drained, for the entire front of Storth Hall was lit. It hadn't been necessary of yet, because the sun was just sinking. It was probably for the effect.

Colin had assured her she looked fine, and she'd had to trust him. It wasn't necessary, though. Neither Quorn had glanced her way at all, and the greeting had been curt. Colin had escorted her up the front steps of Storth Hall and into a massive hall. It was very impressive. Elise had to look away when she'd first seen the Marquis with his wife.

Correct social decorum dictated that their hosts bow first. Colin wasn't having any of it. He hadn't waited for the majordomo to introduce them, he'd done it.

"Quorn! So nice of you to have us visit. I recall Storth Hall from the last time I was here, but that was some time ago. Allow me to introduce my wife, the new Duchess of MacGowan, Elise MacGowan."

"We've met," the Marquis said coldly.

Elise inclined her head, hid the smile as best she could, and said something inane.

She and Colin had been given adjoining state bedrooms on the second floor. It was quite an honor. Elise prepared herself as quickly as possible, for the Quorns had assembled a small soiree for the evening on behalf of their guests.

Elise had been grateful Colin had kept to his own room. She needed the privacy. Although the Marquise had donated the services of a maid to her, it had still been after eleven when Elise descended the steps, clad in the next-to-last evening gown she'd had with her.

Colin's attire couldn't be faulted. It was difficult to believe he had this type of wardrobe available to him from the one trunk she'd seen. He'd exchanged his brown traveling suit for black pants and a matching jacket. The cummerbund about his waist was of a distinctive red and green plaid on a background of black. Elise remembered it from Colin's dressing gown. She wondered if that was the only color of plaid he had with him.

He should have looked outlandish amongst the local gentry, but he didn't. He looked just like a Scottish laird in English attire would.

Now, accompanying Colin into the conservatory, she wondered about that. What would those clanspeople of his think of such a wardrobe on their laird, if they'd fault her the jewels she wore?

Storth Hall actually had more than a conservatory. Quorn had been remarking on it at dinner. He was trying more for a topiary garden, where one shaped the trees and shrubs as they grew. She could see what he meant the moment they entered. Glass walls about the room let in the moonlight, so the little globes of light dotted about the walls weren't really necessary.

Elise held her breath. She'd gone straight from the luxury of an English manor to what was, in essence, a rain forest. Beside her, she felt Colin's surprise, too.

"The Marquis has every right to be proud of this."

"It quite takes the breath away, doesn't it?" she replied.

"That and more. It looks like the perfect spot for a kiss. I dinna' suppose you'd oblige, would you?"

"You'd best be joshing with me, Colin."

He sighed beside her. If she could have seen well

enough, she'd have sworn he looked heavenward for a moment before returning to look at her.

"Give me your hand."

"Why?"

"So I dinna' lose you, why else?"

"It's not that dark."

"You are na' still afraid of me, are you? I thought we'd settled that this afternoon."

The soft Scottish burr he spoke with tightened her throat. Elise shook her head and changed the subject.

"I've noticed that you wear the same plaid every time, Colin. Isn't there another color scheme you'd wear?"

"Of course na'. It's my family colors. All my clansmen wear the same. I happen to like it. The pattern goes back so many centuries, I've lost count. My Aunt Lileth can enlighten you, though. As the Matriarch of Clan MacGowan, she weaves the ceremonial sett after checking the placement on the castle's muckle wheel."

"Are you talking in a foreign tongue, Colin? I didn't follow any of that."

"Another of your nontalents? They seem to be multiplying."

"Fine, don't tell me."

"Every clansman is recognized by the plaid he wears. This is the MacGowan sett. Every MacGowan clansman wears these same colors. I'm required to do so. It's tradition. I'm the laird. As such, my clan owes me their fealty; in return, I owe them my protection."

"I know what a clansman is," she said, trying not to sound defensive.

"My apologies. What dinna' you understand, then?"

"The muckle-thing. What is that?"

"A muckle wheel is used for holding the spun wool before it's woven into the plaid. Always the same. Same width of bands. Same positioning of colors. The pattern of any plaid is called a sett. The privilege of weaving ceremonial setts goes to the matriarch of the family. Aunt Lileth is the matriarch, since she's my father's only surviving sister."

Elise was beginning to understand Evangeline's situation even more. With such old-fashioned customs, no wonder she'd been beneath consideration to wed into their clan.

"Is everything so . . . rigid, then?" she asked.

"Aye, you'll probably have to don the colors, too, Elise. On ceremonial occasions, anyway."

"Black has never been a good color for me. It's quite theatrical with my coloring."

"Does na' matter. It will be expected."

She sighed. "How many of them are there, then?"

"Ceremonies? Three, four a week. Sometimes more."

"What?" Her voice rose with the word.

"I'm teasing with you, Elise. You may wear whatever you like, whenever you like. I'd prefer it that way, actually. I would na' change anything about you."

She had to turn aside so he wouldn't see any part of her face. They'd been strolling about a huge statue of some mythological god in the middle of Lord Quorn's indoor garden. There were some Grecian-inspired benches along the wall, too. She wasn't surprised to be led to one. She was actually grateful. Her knees felt quite weak and shaky at what he'd said.

Colin sat beside her and leaned forward to rest his forearms on his thighs. He wasn't touching her, but it felt as though he was. He clasped his fingers together, and then he sighed.

"Now what?" she asked.

"Quorn has designed a masterpiece. I'm quite envious. Na' that I can na' build my own at Castle Gowan, you understand. It will take time, though, and I have na' much. I have na' even gotten you to agree to the six weeks, yet."

It felt like her heart was the lump that lodged in the base of her throat. She had to clear her throat in order to speak. "Yes, it is lovely, isn't it?"

"It's beautiful, peaceful, and romantic, Elise. If I look at it just right, those trees there resemble a garden in Darjeeling. I used to go there when I was na' on duty. If the moon was full, anyway."

"Darjeeling?"

"Capital city of India. Sorry, I was rambling."

"No, please, tell me more."

"Why?"

"Something to do. I don't know."

"I've got better things in mind if that's your worry."

"No, wait."

Her words stopped. He was turning toward her. She knew he was putting an arm along the bench behind her at the same time. She was trying to concentrate on how to divert him. Then his knee touched hers. Elise knew then that her gown wasn't made of thick enough material. It couldn't be, or she'd not feel the warmth spreading up her leg.

"Colin." She was supposed to be strongly protesting, not whispering the name with a voice she didn't recognize.

"Did you wear lip rouge tonight?"

"I can't—"

His arm pulled her to his chest, and the rest of her sentence failed her. She didn't know how the ruffled front of his shirt would feel against the skin above her bodice; nor did she guess how heated the hand he raised her chin with would be. He didn't give her any time to assimilate any of it, either.

Colin murmured some strange words against her mouth. Elise started shivering. She couldn't understand a bit of it, but she didn't need to. The gentle tone of them touched her heart and started a stab of tears to her eyes.

Her hands had stabilized her against him; her fingers gripped to the plaid wool of his belt. She could feel the ridges of muscle in his stomach flinching against her knuckles. Then his lips took hers.

Her mind stopped. Elise moaned, but it was covered up by the sound of his. Fast-moving waves crashed into her stomach, and then flooded right from there to her breasts. She couldn't stop them as he moved his lips against hers. She could hardly believe they existed.

More of his soft-sounding words were mumbled against her cheek as he moved his kiss to her throat. She tipped her head up to let him. She'd never felt such trickles of emotion as the ones that took the place of the wave, sensitizing her breasts and belly. It was incredible.

And it was wrong.

"Stop, Colin. We must . . . we can't—Colin, stop, please."

Elise moved her hands from his cummerbund and pushed at both humps of his chest. It was against every instinct she had. She longed more to hold to him and never let go.

He lifted his head and looked somewhere above her. Elise's eyes widened at the heaving of the chest in front of her. It took an act of will to remove her hands from it. She watched him through a gloss of tears. She was afraid to blink.

He was still looking above her head, but his arm loosened. Elise had to will herself to move from him. She stood on legs that resembled sticks of wood and met his eyes. What emotion she was holding in check stalled as drops of moonlight touched the moisture on the surface of his eyes. Elise licked her lips with a dry tongue. His jaw was set, his lids were narrowed, and he didn't look at all gentle.

"Do you treat all of your lovers to this torment?"

She made some sound he could take for whatever

he wished and turned her back to him. "You don't understand," she whispered to the statue.

"Try me."

He was right behind her. She could see his shadow
on the tiled floor beneath her; it began climbing
the base of the statue. The hairs at the nape of her
neck were telling her, too.

"I don't want to love you, Colin."

"Is it that you dinna' want to love anyone? Or just
me?"

Elise pushed her fingers into her mouth to still the
cry. Colin came from around her, and she didn't
move. He didn't say anything. He just stood there,
watching her. Elise willed herself to tell him the secret.
It was the perfect time, but the words wouldn't come.
She knew why. She may not want to love him, but it
was too late.

"You're na' going to answer that, are you?" he
asked.

She shook her head.

"Are you still so scarred by Wynd?"

She shook her head again.

"Then what is it? You confuse the hell out of me.
I'm fairly certain I dinna' like it, either."

"I'm . . . sorry."

"Your body begs for my touch, your eyes plead
with me for it, and your lips definitely answer mine.
Yet, when you have all that, you push me away. Why?"

It was no use. The tears slid from her eyes and she
bit on her fingers to still the sob. She couldn't tell him,
yet. She didn't wish to see him turn from her, like
Evan had her very own sister, and his unborn son.
She didn't think she could bear it. Then she knew the
truth: She knew she couldn't bear it.

Stupid girl! she called herself. She was no more suitable to be the wife of a MacGowan than her sister,

Evangeline, had been. The worst part was, she'd known it beforehand.

"Here, dinna' cry, Elise. I think I've made you do that enough for one day."

"I'm sorry."

"As you already said that, and in a convincing enough tone, I have *nae* choice but to believe it. Here."

He was handing her his handkerchief again. Elise pulled one hand from her mouth and took it.

"I'll have to stock more at the rate you're starting to go through them."

"I'm sorry for that, too." She mopped at her face as she spoke, and then sniffed. She hadn't resorted to any cosmetics. With the amount of emotion Colin was raising in her lately, it was a very good thing, too.

"Dinna' be. I've an army of seamstresses to sew more, if need be."

"It's a good thing, too. I've not much talent with a needle."

"So I noticed," he said wryly. "You're very talented at some things, though, I must admit."

"What things?"

"Human conditions. Hardly worth mentioning."

"Human . . . conditions?"

"Lust. Desire. Want. Need. Heat. Those kinds of things."

Each word made her eyes widen further, and the sob caught in her throat. He sighed heavily.

"Come along, Elise. The night is na' getting any longer, and we've a full day ahead of us. Quorn has promised me a grouse hunt on the morrow. If we've any luck, we'll feast on them for supper. He's also scheduled a ball in our honor. Surprisingly generous of him, considering how much he dislikes us."

"A ball? I can't attend one."

"Why na'? I'll bet if you were in town, you'd be attending several."

"I don't have enough wardrobe for a ball."

"Spoken like a true woman. Na' to worry. I've seen to it already."

"I've more luggage arriving? Perhaps my maid . . . uh, Daisy, has arrived?" Elise tried not to stumble over the name but failed.

"Na' to my knowledge. I've simply arranged for a gown for you. It should be ready afore you are."

"You—?"

"Got you a gown? Yes."

"Of all the nerve! You don't know my tastes, you don't know my accessories, and you don't know my measurements."

"Oh, please, Elise. I've seen almost all of you and envisioned the rest. I know the width of your waist is less than my hands can encircle, and you've got softness and womanliness right where you're supposed to. Blast! Stop me before I turn into a maudlin pup, like that poet fellow."

"I thought I didn't have enough meat for your taste."

"First impression. Taken out of context."

"I was there. I heard you."

He groaned. "I got into this conversation because you asked of your new gown, and here it is turned on me. Do you wish to know or na'?"

"Very well, finish."

"What I meant was, it was na' difficult to get it sized. It was harder to find the talent to get it sewn as I designed it."

"Why would you do such a thing?"

"I'll tell you tomorrow."

"Why not tell me now?"

"It will give you something to dream about."

She didn't need any ideas on what to dream about.

That much was certain. Ever since she'd met him, she'd thought of little else.

"Come, I think it's time I escorted you to your chamber."

He held out his arm, and she tucked her hand into the crook he'd made. He matched his steps to hers, although she was taking two to his every one.

"Will you do me a favor before you retire, Elise?"

A frond was shading his face when she glanced up at him. She should have known that what light there was would fall on her. He licked his lips as she nodded. She didn't trust her voice.

"Lock the connecting door between us. And take the key."

Chapter 15

"You look very nice, Your Grace." Jane, the maid who Elise had borrowed for the evening, smiled and bobbed her head while she gave her opinion.

Very nice? Elise wondered. Jane needed a larger vocabulary if that was the best she could do. Elise thought she looked ethereal, innocent, and very fragile. She wondered where Colin could have found such material. She was also questioning why he had gone to such lengths to make her look akin to a vision come to life. No other phrase fit. She didn't have anything else to compare herself with.

The state bedroom mirrors were large, but they weren't showing her enough. She stood between two mirrors and held a smaller one in her hand; she couldn't believe what she was seeing. She knew now that, despite the expenditure in the past, she hadn't come close to showing herself to full advantage.

It was surprising that Colin had known how.

Elise wasn't a tall woman; she barely grazed Colin's shoulder when standing beside him. Yet, with what the hairdresser had done, her neck had never looked longer, and she had never looked so regal.

It had come at a cost, though, and she rubbed her

neck with the instant memory. She'd spent the better part of the day sitting patiently while the hairdresser woman sent up from the village worked magic.

Daisy never would have been able to accomplish it. Elise's hair had been pulled back to the crown of her head and crimped into such a mass of curls, it looked like a veil down her back. It was totally against the fashion mode. She wondered if Colin had ordered such an effect. She didn't look sophisticated or grand, or anything like the Dowager Duchess of Wynd; instead, she looked excruciatingly young.

Colin also had sent several strands of tiny diamonds, six in all, and it had taken over an hour just to entwine and pin them into place throughout the curls. The effect had taken her breath away, but that was before she saw her gown.

She couldn't imagine where Colin had found such material. Elise was familiar with real silk from the Orient, and had worn it before; but this silk was different. It was softer and less wrinkled. The only stiff sections of it were where the artist had woven star-shaped motifs into it. Elise had never thought of the people who wove cloth as artisans. She'd never thought of them at all.

She looked so different, and so amazing, that she was afraid to leave the chamber. Her dress was stark in design, barely claiming a bustle at the small of her back. Colin hadn't been perfect with the size, but he'd been close. It had only taken a bit of sewing to fit it exactly to her. She felt nearly naked, though. The only difference was that it looked like liquid silver skimmed her without the slightest offsetting color to distract it.

"They'll be expecting you by now, Your Grace."

Elise put the hand mirror down and smiled uncertainly. It was going to be impossible to miss her. She looked like she was encased in a streak of moonlight, and whichever way she turned, she sparkled. If there was such a creature as an ice goddess, she certainly looked the part.

"The duke has asked me to see that you attend him in one of the salons when you've finished."

"Can we get there . . . unseen?"

"We can take the back stairs, but it's not proper."

"Forget propriety, just get me to the duke. I can't face anyone looking like this. It's too strange."

"Begging your pardon, Your Grace, but you don't look a bit strange. You look very nice, very nice, indeed."

Jane really did need more descriptive words. She was one of Quorn's maids, a little slow, but efficient enough. She also helped Elise reach the salon down the servants' stairs, something an older, more experienced maid never would have allowed. Once there, Elise had to take several calming breaths before letting the girl open the door for her.

Colin was in profile to her, examining the miniatures dotted all over a section of wall. He was bending forward slightly, with his hands clasped behind his back. Elise coughed discreetly.

He slanted his glance to her, and then turned fully and stared. The look on his face said everything. His mouth dropped open, his eyes widened, and then he hit himself in the chest with a sideways fist. Elise couldn't meet his eyes. She looked down and tried to curb the smile hovering at her lips.

She couldn't seem to face him, either. She flitted her eyes to him as he moved. He walked toward her, and then he stopped. He started talking softly in that strange language of his before circling slowly about her. She knew now why she'd spent so long at the mirrors. It was to achieve that look in his eyes and on his face.

Elise couldn't stop her own eyes from widening, and then narrowing repeatedly, as Colin moved. She pursed her lips to stop the smile from breaking into a grin, but nothing was stopping her blush.

Colin stopped in front of her and said one final word before quieting. Tension grew in her as he just stood there, unmoving. Elise moved her glance up his pleated shirtfront and met his gaze before shying away. She had to do it several times before she dared keep her eyes on his.

He was definitely getting more handsome, she decided. The lamp above them was causing the shadow from his eyelashes to dust his cheeks and was sending the cleft of his chin into prominence.

"I'm afraid to touch you, Elise."

"Afraid?"

He licked his lips and looked away. She watched him suck in air; it was an erotic motion. "We've still a banquet to attend."

She gasped, looked down, and grinned at the carpet beneath her. "You're pleased, then?" she asked.

"Pleased?" One word, and then he lapsed again into that strange language.

"You always do that. Why? What are you saying? Is that the language they use in Darjeeling?"

"*Nae*, it's Scots . . . the Gaelic of my ancestors."

"What are you saying, then?"

He cleared his throat. "There is na' a proper English translation for it, I'm afraid."

"Try for one." Elise watched in amazement as Colin flushed clear to his eyebrows. He wouldn't meet her eyes, either.

"You'll think me a fool, like that Easton fellow."

"Are you speaking lovely words, then?"

"More or less."

"Colin—"

"Do you have to do that? You say my name like a threat, and then dinna' finish what you're threatening. You do it all the time."

"Are you changing the subject? My ears must be failing me."

"*Nae.*"

"Then tell me what you said."

"You dinna' want to hear it. I'd bore you."

She stomped her foot. "Is there something you don't like, then?"

"I already told you I canna' touch you. What more do you want to hear?"

"I want to hear what you said. I want to hear all of it."

"I just *can na'*."

He was looking somewhere over her head. Elise cocked her head and pursed her lips. "Did you tell me I look beautiful, then?"

He cleared his throat, and when that must not have been sufficient, he put a finger behind his bow tie and pulled it from his throat. "You're making me regret speaking."

He wasn't getting out of it that easily. Elise narrowed her eyes. "Let me repeat myself. Did you say I looked beautiful?"

"That . . . and more."

"What more?"

"It's getting stuffy in here. I'm ready to gain the banquet hall if you are."

"Why did you want to see me in here, then?"

"Oh, I nearly forgot. I've a present for you."

"Beyond this dress and the diamond strands woven into my hair? You've a generous nature, Your Grace. You do like what has been done with my hair, don't you?" Elise pirouetted before him and grinned at the choking sound he was making.

She stopped right before him and watched his gaze fly from her bosom, to the top of her head, then to the area around her nose. Elise knew he was avoiding meeting her eyes.

"Colin?" She reached a hand toward him, and he

flinched back a hairsbreadth. She was close enough to see the nerve in his cheek twitch. She could also feel his breath on her cheek. It was making strange things happen to her knees and the backs of her thighs. "Fine, don't give me my present, then."

"I already told you I dare na' touch you! Jesu', woman! What more can you wish of me?"

"You can tell me what you said. Start with that."

"Oh, hell."

"I'm fairly certain you weren't swearing through it. I would have recognized that word."

"Here."

The word was terse as he fumbled beneath his jacket to hand her a slender jewelry case. Elise let her fingers touch his as she took it from him. She could actually see the shudder that shook him. She couldn't believe her eyes. The familiar humming was joining the sound of her own heartbeat in her ears, too.

She opened the box and gasped. There, on a bed of velvet, was a necklace of little linked diamonds shaped like stars. "Oh, Colin," she whispered.

In answer, he seized her upper arms and pulled her against him, lifting her to tiptoes. The jewelry case snapped shut at the contact, but she barely heard it. She recognized his curse when she heard it, even if it was in Gaelic, and then he slammed his lips against hers.

Elise actually saw stars behind her closed eyelids, but she gave as good as she got. It was her tongue flicking against his and her tormented moan blending with his. Colin let go of her arms and wrapped his about her, molding her to him. One hand held to the back of her neck as he sucked on her mouth. Elise tried to help by blending into his shirtfront.

"Sweet Jesu', but you're an angel come to earth. Oh, Elise . . . my sweet. There are *nae* words lovely enough to describe you. I've *nae* talent for finding them if there are."

There was more, and he murmured them into her
ear, shoving the hair from his way as he kissed her
there, too. Heated shivers ran up her spine and settled into her breasts. Elise couldn't believe that. She
couldn't believe any of it. She had caused him to do
this. She didn't know how to stop it, either. She had
teased him to this, but she hadn't known this type of
excitement existed.

Who was she supposed to have asked? She hadn't
known she had such a wanton side, either.

Elise pushed on his chest, and at the first touch he
groaned so deeply that it made the hair on her arms
stand up. Then he yanked his head from her to look
at the lamp hanging from the ceiling above them. She
watched him fill his chest with great gulps of breath,
and then hold them before he exhaled. After the third
one, he lowered his head and pushed her his entire
arm's length away from him.

Her legs were shaky, and he seemed to know it, for
he waited before releasing her. She couldn't meet his
eyes to verify it. She was amazed that she still held on
to the jewelry case.

Elise looked at the clock on the wall and couldn't
believe so little time had passed. Her entire world had
been upended in so little time? *Where is the justice in
that?* she wondered.

"I'd apologize, Elise, but I did warn you."

"I wouldn't accept one."

"Truly?" he asked.

"That was as much my fault as yours."

"True enough. It's big of you to admit it. Another
of your talents, no doubt?"

"Thank you for the necklace. Thank you for the
dress, too, and the diamond strands."

"And for mussing it all up, too?"

"I am not mussed!"

"You're right, you're na'." He ran his gaze to her toes and back up to her hair. "Na' much, anyhow."

"Colin—"

"See? There you go again."

Elise smiled. It was a relief from the tension of a moment before. It took a bit before Colin returned the gesture.

"Will you be able to clasp my necklace?" she asked.

"I would na' even attempt it. I'll stand patiently while you have a go at it, though. Looking as you do, I'll na' let you get far from my sight, anyway."

"Since there doesn't appear to be any mirrors, will you tell me if it's straight, then?"

"How the devil are you supposed to get a necklace crooked? And use the windows. They work well enough."

Perhaps she'd rather he spoke in Gaelic, since he was making her feel like a schoolgirl. Elise lifted the necklace and clasped it adroitly. She ignored him and walked to one of the windows. Colin was right; it was easy to see herself. He had probably been preening there before she arrived, she told herself and smiled.

Then she brushed one side of her hair over her shoulders and met the reflection of his gaze. He hadn't moved, but he didn't need to. He was glaring at her, and his chest rose and fell with each breath. Elise couldn't move. Her mind was barely functioning.

"Are you na' done admiring yourself? The sup will be cold afore we get there."

"You don't have to be rude."

"And you dinna' have to be so damned desirable."

"Pardon?"

"You needn't ask. You heard me, exactly as I said it."

Elise turned and kept her eyes on the area of the carpet where he stood. She didn't dare let him see. He'd know then that she was fighting what had to be the same frustration and longing. It wasn't fair, either. At least she knew why.

"Thank you . . . for . . . everything, Colin."

"You're welcome. Can we go now?"

He was being curt, but Elise forgave him. "I've never seen silk such as this. It's so soft and—"

"I've *nae* wish to hear it described at present. I already know exactly how it feels. That's why I selected it."

Colin's voice lowered, and Elise had to tip her head up to hear him.

"Did you pick it from the marketplace in Darjeeling, then?"

"Something of that nature," he replied.

"You have excellent taste."

"So I've been told. Are you ready yet?"

Elise glided across the room to stand at the door. "I'm sorry I kept you waiting. If you'll give me your arm, we can proceed."

"My . . . arm?"

His voice was low but choked sounding. Elise smiled. "For an escort. You do wish to escort me, don't you?"

"Perhaps we'd best wait until we reach the others."

"You're being silly."

"And you're being naive. Would you like another taste? I've had a bellyful of staying a correct distance, as it is."

"Why are you acting this way?" she asked.

"Because I can na' act the way I'd like. Not yet, anyway."

"You're speaking . . . riddles, now." She'd lost her breath midsentence. He couldn't possibly be implying what it sounded like he was.

Colin walked past her and shoved open the door, before going out with it. "Oh, Elise, my dearest, with the way you kiss? It's a riddle that you're still looking as untouched and innocent as the moment you stepped into this salon. And that I have na' made certain of how that dress feels . . . or rather how you feel in it."

"You're being very familiar, Colin. I'm not certain that I like it."

Elise didn't think she sounded like she was chastising him, although that was what she was trying for. When a sly half-smile curved one side of his mouth and he raised his eyebrows, she was certain of it.

"All right, I'll wait, then. It will be midnight soon enough."

"Colin—"

"That again? It's na' going to work. I've already said too much. It's a surprise."

"What's a surprise?"

"Are you coming?" He was tipping his head as he spoke and gesturing with a hand at the same time.

Elise knew her eyes were worried. She couldn't disguise it. She kept her gaze on the hall flooring as she stepped past him, and she kept walking. She didn't know what she was supposed to do now. She hadn't kissed him that way on purpose, but she'd not been in control of anything. She couldn't think, either.

She followed the low murmur of conversation and slight strains of music and tried not to be aware of the man behind her. It was impossible.

"It will look strange if you enter the room as if I'm chasing you, Elise."

"What?" she asked, wrinkling her brow.

"I'm your escort. You're running."

"Oh."

Colin held out his arm, and the hand she placed on his sleeve shook. He sighed in an exaggerated fashion. Elise glanced up. The look in his eyes sent her stomach reeling, it was so tender.

"You, Madame, are a minx. It's hard to believe you're a lass of less than a score in years. It truly is."

"If I want insults, I'll sit beside the Marquise, thank you very much. At least with her, I know why."

He placed his other hand atop hers and turned to

her. "You wish to know of the dress, Elise? Verra well, I've had the material some time. I dinna' know what had possessed me to buy it, at first. I dinna' know until . . . well . . . ahem." He stopped and cleared his throat.

"Until?" she prompted.

"Make me answer that later, fair?"

Elise nearly responded with his name in a threatening fashion, but she caught herself. He probably read it on her face.

"Anyway, I've had a bolt of it with me. I had a devil of a time getting it designed, sewn, and sent here in time, too. Took me another bit of time picking and choosing your jewelry, too. Dinna' think that was na' difficult."

"In time for what?" she whispered.

"Our marriage." He was watching so closely that he saw her immediate reaction. She couldn't keep it from him. "Does it frighten you so much, little one?"

Elise swallowed. He thought her frightened? She was horrified, yet filled with joy at the same time. She actually felt quite giddy. "What about my . . . six weeks?"

"A valid question, to be sure. Any others?"

She couldn't do this, and he wouldn't let go of her hand. She'd have to tell him, after all. The words felt stuck in her throat. "I—I may not be a . . . fit wife for the MacGowan Laird. What of that?"

"Is that your lone objection?" he asked, raising his brows.

"I'm serious."

"My clan has my protection. They dinna' have rights to my bedchamber, too."

"Colin!"

"Admit that you feel naught for me. Tell me that you dinna' feel it. I dinna' choose to want you, but I can na' deny I do. I can na' deny the passion, the heat, or the desire. I'd like to hear you try. Go ahead."

She didn't have any voice with which to answer. He was naming every emotion she felt.

"I can na' keep my hands from you even standing here, and we've got an audience right in front of us to parade for. Tell me you've *nae* regard for me whatsoever, and I'll try to honor it. Tell me you feel naught. Tell me. Go ahead, Elise. Tell me."

They'd been spotted, for she could hear the announcement of their names and titles. She heard clapping, and then there was silence. She and Colin were causing a stir and Elise didn't even give it a thought.

"Tell me." Colin mouthed the words, for no sound came with them.

The majordomo was opening the door wider, probably to see what was keeping them.

"If I did so . . . it would be a lie," she answered softly.

Chapter 16

"It'll probably be cold."

"Well, I think it's dreadfully romantic."

"It has potential. It's obvious you're a newlywed."

"We're all quite envious of you, my dear."

"Well, I—" Elise started to mumble something, only to be interrupted.

"Come now, don't be shy. We saw the way you two act. So in love, you look. I wonder if Herbert and I were ever that way."

"Not that we ever saw."

The Duchess of Argyle dissolved into giggles and the others about her did the same. Elise frowned instead. She wasn't listening to their chatter. She was watching the clock. Midnight was but a half hour away, and her palms were getting clammier the closer it got.

"I've not seen Colin since he joined the regiment. I tell you, I've never seen him so happy, either. You're to be congratulated, Your Grace."

"What?" Elise asked, turning from the mantel clock.

The ladies had left the men to their port, as usual. Elise hadn't been able to meet Colin's eyes as she'd followed the others. She'd been grateful that he'd been placed beside the Marquis in a place of honor.

It seemed like every one of her heartbeats was repeating over and over what he'd said.

For our marriage . . . for our marriage . . .

"I quite like how you've done your hair tonight, Your Grace. Are you attempting another fashion coup?"

"I've left those days behind me, Lady Beckon."

Anyone within hearing distance could tell a snide tone colored everything Lady Beckon said to Elise. Elise let each and every one of her comments pass without one sly, biting, or querulous answer. It was unlike her, but everything felt like it was anymore. She hadn't known that Sophie's viscount's parents would attend. Anyone who read the papers would have known that it would cause a problem. Perhaps that was what the Marquise had in mind when she'd created her guest list. Had she hoped to discomfit Elise for her reported dalliances with her husband, the Marquis, last year?

If she had, it wasn't working. Elise glanced at the clock again. She'd lost another minute!

"Your husband told me at dinner about his plans. It is so very romantic," Lady Norwich said.

He did? Elise bit her tongue to still the question. She'd barely found out what Colin intended, and he'd told others as well?

"Why, my husband hasn't taken me on a moonlit drive in . . . well, never."

Again, the women giggled, and Elise closed her eyes.

So she was going on a moonlit drive. A drive that would include a preacher, a pulpit, and a real wedding ceremony! Her palms were wet with worry, and she didn't have anything to wipe them on. She wondered what Colin would say if she feigned an illness and returned to her chamber.

The choice was taken from her as the men arrived. Colin wasn't the first through the door, so she scanned for him. The Quorns had filled their banquet hall with guests. There must have been forty, but there could have been four times that number and Elise wouldn't have noticed.

Colin's eyes went directly to hers the moment he entered. He didn't move at first; he simply stood there with his eyebrows raised and one hand on the back of a settee. Elise felt her heart jumping and was powerless to stop it. She couldn't tear her gaze away.

He smiled slightly and started walking toward her. Elise froze.

"It's truly romantic, my dear. You're to be congratulated, you really are. Oh . . . for the good old days when my Herbert . . ."

Lady Norwich was whispering right beside her, but Elise couldn't hear it over the humming sound.

"Elise?"

Colin had reached her; he bent a bit to assist her up. The entire room seemed to be watching. Elise put every effort into controlling her trembling as she put her hand in his.

Colin closed his fingers about hers and lifted her hand to his lips. She shut her eyes, but that made it worse. The sensation of warmth was radiating the exact same way from him. Elise's trembling increased.

"Would you be caring to drive with me? I understand the moon will be full over Crewe tonight. The view is considered by many to be extraordinary."

He was giving the entire decision over to her. Elise understood it the moment she opened her eyes. He hadn't moved at all. He was still holding her hand beside his lips and looking at her down the length of her arm.

Elise wasn't one for smelling salts. She didn't even know what they smelled like. But the longer she looked at him, the closer she came to knowing, she was sure. She hadn't known that a ring of green encircled the brown of his eyes, or that he could look so intense and yet so unsure at the same time.

All she had to do was say that she was tired, or that the night air would chill her, or any number of things. He wouldn't force it, of that she was certain. It was all her decision.

"Aye," she answered, then stood.

The night was cold, just as had been predicted. Elise pulled the fur-trimmed blankets closer to her neck and wondered at her sanity. In one moment of impulse, she'd agreed to be his wife and to everything that stood for.

She glanced up at him. Colin was wearing a great-coat and hat; his breath fogged about his head each time he exhaled. He had great hands when it came to handling horses, but she would have guessed that already. She wondered if that was the only thing he had great hands for, gasped, and looked away.

Beside her, Colin chuckled, as if he'd known what she'd been thinking.

With her nose outside the fur, the cold instantly frosted each indrawn breath. She wondered how Colin could sit and embrace it as if it was nothing. He didn't look a bit cold.

"Having second thoughts?" he asked.

Elise glanced up at him again. "If I am?"

"We're na' there yet. You've still time. The reverend is expecting us, but he said he'd wait all night, if need be. The Abbey at Crewe is very well-known about these parts. It has a thirteenth century vestry. It even survived the Cromwellian uprising. It's very old and has a verra sanctified air about it."

"You're a font of information. How do you know all this?"

"I was na' grouse hunting all day."

"Oh." On the last word she pushed her nose back under the edge of the fur blanket.

"We do this, and there's *nae* chance I'll retire to my own chamber tonight. You do ken that, dinna' you?"

She groaned and twisted her hands together. He was putting into words what she didn't dare imagine.

"You'll be my duchess in every sense of the word, and unlike that Easton fellow, I'm na' one to be trifled with. You do understand what I'm saying?"

She was choking too much to answer.

"I'll most likely survive the night, too, unlike your first husband. I'm a trifle younger, and you already ken I'm in better shape. I also dinna' care how much you scream. I intend to make certain of it. You do ken what I'm talking about? Or were all your lovers inept?"

"Colin!" The first syllable of his name was an octave higher than the last. Elise was a lot warmer all of a sudden, too.

"You want me to stop? Will na' happen. I'm making certain you ken exactly what you're doing. I dinna' want the recriminations later over too much wine, lack of sleep, you felt beholden to me, or some other nonsense excuse. I want you as I've never wanted anyone. Ever. I've had too many sleepless nights for wanting you. I'll na' be put off by screams, or tears, or pleas, or any other feminine wile."

"Are you trying to make me rethink this, Colin?"

"*Nae.*"

"Then shut up."

His grin answered her. The star-filled sky was beautiful above them, and Elise watched it. She was no longer the slightest bit cold.

"We've arrived. Do I hitch the horses, or drive around some more to convince you?"

"You'll need a lighter manner, if that's the case."

"I dinna' frighten you?"

"I didn't say that. You frighten me just fine. I may find that I like it. I may even tell you of it."

"You *are* a minx." He tossed the reins to one of his

men and jumped from the curricle. He didn't allow her time to get down. He didn't wait while she stood, so he could escort her down, either. Instead, he folded her into the blankets and carried her into the church.

He'd been right about everything. Elise looked about her in awe once Colin set her on her feet. The wrapping about her fell to her ankles, but she ignored it. In some long-ago, almost-forgotten time, she'd imagined just such a setting for her wedding.

Candles glowed from the first-floor joists, the end of each pew, and all about the altar. The worn wood of the aisle looked thirteenth century, easily. Colin tossed his greatcoat to another of his men before turning to her. He held out his hand, and Elise gave him hers.

"As God is my witness, you'll na' regret this."

He pulled her toward him and leaned down to touch his lips to her temple. Elise's eyes filled with tears. She had to wait for them to subside. She didn't dare blink.

She hadn't known love felt like this.

Colin's man Mick stood beside the altar stone. The reverend behind it looked official and very kind. Beyond that instant glance, Elise couldn't tell. She didn't even think she was walking, yet they were there. Two pillows were at the base of the altar, and she knelt beside Colin on one.

Elise ran her free hand across her lashes but stopped short of wiping it on her dress. Such silk was the stuff memories were made of. Every time she looked at it, she wanted to recall every moment.

When it came time to answer, she spoke in a voice that trembled. Colin didn't seem to have that problem. His vows were even, deep, and in a humbling tone. Despite her every effort, as he spoke, the tears filled her eyes again.

Colin didn't let go of her hand until he had to. She

watched him take the signet ring from his little finger and place it on hers. He didn't let go when he'd finished, although now his thumb and middle finger twirled the ring where it sagged on hers.

I've just married the Duke of MacGowan! Elise had to close her eyes at the thought. There would be no chance for an annulment after tonight, either. Of that, she was certain.

When it came time for the kiss, Elise felt so light-headed that she leaned into him for that reason. Colin caught her against him easily, although he had to let go of her hand to do so. Elise tipped her face up to his. He narrowed his eyes. She watched the shadows lengthen on his cheeks as he did so. Then she shut her eyes as well.

Colin's kiss barely grazed her lips, and then it was done. He was standing and taking her with him.

"Congratulations to you both."

The reverend was all smiles, and so were Colin's men. Elise didn't have the choice as her new husband picked her up and walked back down the aisle with her. He set her on a high stool beside the registry book and handed her the quill.

"I'll na' be long."

He whispered it in her ear, then he left her. She felt the loss immediately. The church wasn't as warm as she'd thought.

Elise looked across at the entry and saw that Colin had already signed his name. *When did he do that?* she wondered. His penmanship was still atrocious. Elise's lips twisted as she lifted the pen. The signet ring was heavy and kept sliding about. She moved it to her middle finger, where it fit better. The clerk smiled.

She signed beneath Colin's name with a flourish and more elaborate loops at the end than were necessary. That made the clerk's smile broaden. Elise returned it.

She watched him sand the ink and moved her feet to the upper rung. That way, she could wrap her arms about her knees. Now, she really was the bride of The MacGowan, and by her own words, too. Nothing was ever going to change that.

"Oh, Elise, darling, you look such a child. Here."

Colin had crept up behind her and started wrapping the blankets about her again. Elise couldn't meet his eyes.

"What is it?" he asked.

"Nothing."

"You expect me to believe that? Come on, you can tell me." Colin was hoisting her as he spoke, and Elise fought the urge to burrow into him. Then she simply did it. "Well?"

"You left me." Elise kept her nose against his neck while she spoke; it made her feel braver.

"I was gone only a moment or two."

"You didn't kiss me, either."

His laugh was so low, she barely heard it. "I dinna' dare. We are in a church and on consecrated ground, Elise. I'm just hoping I can get you back to Storth Hall without ravishing you. It's a mite cold out yet."

He climbed aboard the carriage and kept her in his lap. Elise pulled her nose from the comfort of his neck to see why. Colin's man Mick was holding the reins; he tipped his hat to her. Elise hid back against Colin.

"Mick's driving. Better that way. Oh, Lord, dinna' sit there. Na' there, either." His words were getting more blunt and spoken at a higher pitch as she settled against him. It wasn't her fault that it was a precarious seat atop his lap; but she did wriggle a bit more than she had to. The way he was sucking in breath was gratifying, too. "Elise?"

"Yes?"

"How do you expect to rejoin the others if we—stop that!"

Elise's fingers stilled against his chest. "Do we have to rejoin them? Now?"

"We've been on a drive, remember? There's still dancing and such to do tonight. Bother that. We're na' dancing. We've got to stop in and let them know that we returned unharmed, though."

"Must we?"

"For the sake of gossip? Yes. For my sake? *Nae.* For our host's sake? Yes. For God's sake, stop that!"

Beside them, Elise heard Mick snorting through his laughter.

"I didn't do anything," she complained.

"Get us to the hall, Mick, and stop laughing."

"Yes, Your Grace. Oh, immediately, Your Grace. Anything you say, Your Grace," the servant answered.

"I'm going to remember this, Mick."

Colin was probably trying to sound threatening. Elise looked over at Mick. He looked like he was turning red with withheld laughter.

"*Nae* doubt," the man replied, and that's when she started giggling.

The lights were bright, the music seemed especially loud, and there were too many people waiting about the entryway to greet them. Colin swore so rapidly and vehemently that Elise didn't have to.

She didn't dare look at her husband when she entered the ballroom in front of him. She didn't dare dance with him, either. That would require too much contact. He was too intense for his own good, she decided . . . and he was all hers.

The thought was absolutely thrilling. She was afraid he'd guess at it, too, and that would make the wait more unbearable.

Since he'd called on all the saints' wrath to fall on everyone's head, it was surprising that the wine was still flowing and the conversation was just as mindless as always. Elise dropped into a high-backed chair on the dowager's dais and studied her new ring. Colin's initials were engraved along the side, and what had to be his family crest adorned the top. It was quite heavy.

From across the room, she felt him. She raised her eyes and caught his stare. Although he leaned nonchalantly against a pillar and held a glass of wine in his fingers, she felt the emotion. When he narrowed his eyes and nodded at her, she was sure of it.

"Your Grace?"

A manservant stood beside her. Elise had to tear her eyes from Colin to attend to him. "Yes?" she replied.

"Your maid has returned. You left a message to be informed immediately should that happen."

Reality intruded like a slammed door. Elise didn't think she'd be able to stand, at first. "Of course, thank you. Can you tell me where she is?"

"I'll take you. If you'll follow me?"

Elise wasn't surprised when she was led to the third floor, or when she was shown into the nursery, but she stood at the door, waiting for her mind to function before she could act.

"Oh, Daisy. Thank the Lord you've arrived in time! How was the trip?" Elise rushed to Daisy's side.

"Passable, Elise. Only I don't think his wee lordship had as good a time as we did, eh, Nanny? He's been fussing most of the time. It looks like he'll keep us up again tonight."

"Oh, Nanny, I'm so pleased you could come, too. I don't know what I would have done." Elise turned to the older woman.

"Now, don't go and upset yourself, Your Grace. I've been on worse trips than a little jaunt North. It will do me good, it will."

The baby in Nanny's arms had stirred at Elise's voice and raised his chubby arms to her.

"Oh, Rory, darling!" Elise cried.

"Now, don't take it amiss if he doesn't take to you right off. Babies are a bit like that, they are," Nanny warned her.

Daisy stopped Elise from lifting the baby until there was a linen secured on her shoulder. Despite Nanny's warning, Rory settled easily into Elise's arms. She felt the same heated pull on her heart that she'd felt when she first saw him. "Such a little love you are," she told him.

He lifted his head to give a toothless grin.

"He's grown stronger, hasn't he?" she asked.

Reddish brown curls covered the baby's head. At eight months old, he was a very strong and healthy babe. Elise was very proud of that. Watching over Rory was the only thing she'd done right for Evangeline. She listened to Nanny as she commented on Rory's advances.

"You little darling." Elise was still crooning to the babe. It felt like all her prayers were being answered, and the weight lifting from her made her feel buoyant. She hadn't dared to hope that Nanny would be willing to accompany Rory, but she'd forgotten the woman's love for Evangeline. It hadn't been easy to locate her when Evangeline had died, leaving Elise with an infant nephew, but it had been done.

The Quorns' nursery boasted cream walls that reflected the fire's light warmly about them. It turned Rory's hair more red than before. She could see that he wasn't the least bit sleepy, either. Elise gave her condolences of that to Nanny.

"I'm sure I can find me a young housemaid or two that will spell me. It was all we could do to make it to these rooms without half the staff holding him. Makes him more spoiled than you already do."

Elise grinned and ignored the barb. "Was it difficult, Daisy?" She swiveled with the baby to ask the question.

"Shutting the place down? Well, you'd think that I had orders to sack everyone by stealing the baby away. Isn't that right, Nanny?"

"I have to admit that Rory has brought new life to the old manor. That's a fact."

"Did you provide for everyone, then? The signed vouchers were enough?"

"Now, Elise, you should know me by now. I followed all your instructions to the letter. Everything will be fine. The place will be kept homey for you. Caretaking isn't their normal line of work, but you gave them plenty of funds."

Rory cooed in Elise's arms, and she hugged him. He had grown and she tested his weight.

"Forgive me, Daisy. It was stupid of me to doubt you. I was so afraid that something would happen to prevent this. Life sure turns out strange, doesn't it? You've both done a wonderful job. He looks even healthier."

"When that boy's walking, I'll need help to catch him."

Elise chuckled at the image of Nanny chasing anything; then the amusement died in her throat.

"Oh my, Your Grace." Daisy's voice sounded strangled as she curtsied toward the door.

Oh no! Dear God, no! In less time than it took to turn around, Elise said the words in her heart and in her mind. God wasn't listening, though.

Colin stood in the doorway; his eyes were as hard as agates, and his entire body stiffened in disgust. Elise interpreted the sudden graying of his features and knew she was correct.

"Oh, dear God, no. Colin! Wait!" She shifted Rory to hand him back to Nanny. It took too long to hand him over. Elise silenced the cry when she reached the stairs; Colin was nowhere in sight.

"Oh no . . . no! God, no!"

Elise was pleading the words aloud as she ran down

the stairs. There was no sign of Colin. He wasn't in their rooms, the ballroom, or the banqueting hall. She hadn't hidden it on purpose. She was going to tell Colin. She was always going to tell him. He had to know. It was his secret as much as it was hers. She should have told him before. Now, she was too late.

The majordomo was the one who informed her that the duke and his men had left the hall. He must have taken pity on Elise's face, for he offered to get her assistance. She waved it off. There wasn't anything he, or anyone else, could do for her. All she could do was wait.

She couldn't even cry.

Chapter 17

The summons came before the sun was up. Elise listened as Daisy answered the door.

"Her Grace is to proceed to the stable yard immediately."

"But she isn't dressed proper!" Daisy replied, in a scandalous tone.

That much was a lie. Elise was still wearing the silver-starred dress. It was wonderful fabric, too, just as she'd suspected, for there were few wrinkles. Then again, she'd not sat still long enough to test it.

"His Grace is na' in a waiting mood, Miss. I've orders. Perhaps you'd best see to the bairn upstairs."

"He won't be awake yet. This is highly irregular."

"I've orders," he repeated.

Elise turned from watching the predawn light through her windows and walked to the door. "Don't argue it, Daisy. See to Rory, please."

Daisy's mouth set in a thin line, and her eyes narrowed, but Elise ignored it. She turned to the man at the door.

He was standing in the shadow of the hall. Elise was hard put to hide the instant cry. He stood more than a head above her and probably tripled her weight, too.

He wasn't pasty faced and fat, either. He was huge with muscle, unshaven, and dressed strangely.

Although she'd not seen it, she was certain she was looking at a clansman in full MacGowan regalia. She knew, without asking, that her presence wasn't a request. It was an order, and it would be carried out by force, if necessary.

"See to Rory, Daisy. Thank you for staying with me all night. I shall let you know what the plans are as soon as I know them."

Daisy's expression mirrored every one of Elise's emotions. She'd never felt so alone, lost, exhausted, and unsure. She only hoped she didn't look it.

Elise started trembling before they reached the main landing. The man at her side wasn't following any social strictures. He was escorting her by holding to her arm just above the elbow and propelling her down the steps at an unseemly pace, and then out the door with him.

Elise tripped on a clod of dirt turned up by the amount of horses in the yard. Her escort kept her from falling but didn't slow his steps. Elise was left to stumble along until she was upright again. She had lost one of her glamorous evening shoes, and she was going to be bruised on her arm. The man didn't even bother to notice.

She hadn't been treated this roughly since she'd lived with her father. She was afraid it might show on her face, too. That, she wasn't going to allow.

He didn't stop at the stable yard. It would have been too confusing there for any kind of a meeting. He marched her into one of the outbuildings and dropped her arm. She heard the doors being shut and the long bolt being pulled behind her, but she didn't dare look to verify it. She was determined that none would find her anything save gracious, calm, and as emotionless as ice, no matter what happened.

The last was closer to reality, for the mud she'd stepped in was cool on her bare toes. The straw beneath her felt cold, too. She could blame all of that for her continued shivering. As much as she tried to stop it, her trembling was obvious. That couldn't be helped. Elise rubbed at her bruised arm as several lamps all about the rafters were brightened.

She was glad the motion had put her in a position to clasp her arms. It gave her something to hold on to. Elise held the gasp inside as more men than she could count pulled themselves upright from the walls to encircle her.

She thought her heart was going to pound its way right out of her breast. She'd promised herself not to show her fear, but it wasn't working. She was being surrounded by men as strangely dressed as the first one had been, most sporting full beards, and all nearly matching Colin in height and weight. She felt like she'd been sent back several centuries in time for her sin. She didn't know what the punishment was supposed to be, either.

"I want you to meet my Honor Guard, Elise. They've been shadowing me since I was reached in Darjeeling."

"Colin?"

Two of the men swiveled, and Colin stepped through them. He wasn't dressed like the others. It made him stand out more. Deep lines appeared to score his cheeks, and his lip was curled a bit in derision. It could have been the lamplight, but Elise knew different.

"If I gave you leave to use my name, I'm rescinding it. Women of your ilk are na' fit for such." He'd reverted to such a thick brogue, it wasn't easy to understand all of it.

"It isn't as you think, Colin! It—"

"If she speaks again, silence her."

Dead quiet greeted his softly spoken words, and

Elise's eyes widened. He wouldn't dare! "You don't understand! You've got to give me time to explain. I'm not—"

He'd gestured slightly with his head as soon as she'd begun. It felt like iron bars seized her from behind, stopping her plea. She was dragged backward and slammed against what had to be a chest; then a wad of material was forced into her mouth.

Elise's eyes filled as they gagged her. She didn't move a bit while the cloth was wrenched tight behind her head. She kept her eyes on the duke and let the tears slip from her eyes.

"That's better. I dinna' listen to lying whores. Not anymore. You, Madame, have set back my opinion of the fairer sex more than any woman alive. I thought I knew of your type from Ira. I thought I'd be able to recognize one when I met up with her. I was a fool. And now I get to pay. My entire clan does."

He stepped closer to her. The light didn't allow one bit of illumination to touch his eyes. They didn't look warm or cold. Elise tried to maintain eye contact with him, hoping he'd read what she couldn't tell him. The effort made her eyes burn, but she refused to blink.

"Go ahead, hate me. I've little care. It's na' more than I feel for you."

She blinked as rapidly as possible but couldn't stay the flood of fresh tears at the ugly words. She knew he saw it, for he sneered.

"My oldest brother always kept a wench or two. Often, he'd share his women with any man willing to risk the pox. I was na' that desperate. I thought them lying, unscrupulous, black-hearted, and filthy. I actually hold them in higher regard than I do you."

"No!" Elise screamed the denial through her gag, although little could be heard.

"You dinna' do what you did to me, Elise."

She shook her head vehemently until his image

bobbed with the motion. *You're wrong, Colin! So wrong! Please don't do this to me! I can explain Rory! Please?* Her mind was shouting the words at him, and he must have known of it. He frowned, and the look on his face was like he'd smelled something repugnant.

"If she can na' be quiet this way, silence her further."

His soft words frightened her more than anything else. Elise stopped trying to communicate and actually pushed back into the man holding her.

"You can foist a bastard on a thousand men, but na' the Laird of the MacGowans. Our thirst for vengeance goes back centuries. It's the one thing I'm counting on. Right here. Right now. I want you to know this."

Elise couldn't look at him any longer. She was afraid he'd see the absolute terror she couldn't hide. She bent her head, although it pulled the hair trapped behind her, and looked down at the beautiful silver dress. She watched as a tear splashed onto the fabric, staining it, just as she'd guessed it would. She didn't care. The beauty of the abbey and the sanctity of her wedding felt like they'd happened to someone else.

He spoke again, as if reading her thoughts.

"Perhaps you should ha' thought of all this before weddin' with me last night. Now, you're my property by law—any man's law, even English law. I can do whatever I wish with you, and none will stay me."

She squeezed her lids shut and shook with the reaction. She didn't care that they all saw.

"Get her from my sight. Put her in the rail car with the bastard. Send Quorn our apologies for na' staying. And, Martin? Try na' to bruise her overmuch."

Elise had to remind herself that she'd never fainted in her life. It was a luxury she couldn't afford, she used to tell herself. She knew it must feel like the strange needles of sensation pricking her nose and the queasiness of her stomach as the man named Martin marched her to the MacGowan coach. He didn't like touching her, she could tell. It was apparent from the scowl on his face and how he held her a good forearm's length from him.

The sun had come up, but it was still early. Elise knew it was useless to cry out. All those about the stable yard wore the MacGowan red, green, and black plaid. None of Storth Hall's guests would be awake this early, and it was doubtful the servants would interfere.

If she had wanted to flee, it would have been impossible. There were at least two dozen of Colin's Honor Guard about her, too. Martin stopped. The coach door was opened; she was picked up by the waist and set onto the floor of it. Then the door was shut, a bolt thrown, and the horses started up.

Elise tore at the material about her head, until she realized it was a slipknot and came undone easily. Why had he had it done that way, and why had they used one of Colin's embroidered handkerchiefs?

She sat on the floor of the carriage, buried her face into the material, and wept.

Elise was in command of herself when the carriage halted an hour later. She wasn't going to let anyone guess at what had happened to her. It was going to be her newest secret, and she was very good at keeping those. She was stupid to have told Colin any of her past secrets. She was stupid to have trusted him with anything. He was proving himself to be everything she'd already been told that he was. How had she forgotten about Evangeline? Her sister had told her often enough of the MacGowans' callousness, their judgmental nature, and their heartless ways. Elise should have been a quicker study.

Colin's train consisted of four cars and an engine. Elise sat in the carriage for what was left of the morning and watched the loading. She was a prisoner, and they'd bolted her in to make certain she knew of it.

The first car appeared to contain baggage, whereas the second was given over to Colin's servants. Some of them were members of his Honor Guard. Elise was certain of it, although they weren't dressed in tartan anymore.

The third car was where they put Nanny, Rory, and Daisy. Elise pulled back from the carriage window as Daisy glanced her way. She had rarely been able to keep anything from the maid before, but she was determined to keep this to herself.

The end car was the one reserved for The Mac-Gowan and his family. She knew it without watching all the flowers, food, and activity about it. Colin's car was more ornate than the others and gleamed with fresh black paint. Elise had to shut her eyes when she saw his trunks being loaded.

She could tell when they were readying the engine, too, for more steam than before came from the engine. The whistle blew loudly, causing her to jump. Then she saw the contingency of men coming toward her. Colin didn't need to send so many guards for her. What did he think her?

Elise put her hands to her mouth to still the cry. She already knew exactly what he thought of her. She pushed her hair off her face with hands that trembled. She didn't like wearing it down. She'd have to ask Daisy to help her pin it up.

The bolt pulled, and Elise put her aloof facade in place. She kept her eyes above their heads as they opened the door, and then she slid out without assistance.

"I can walk," she informed them.

She was ignored as one of them gripped her upper arm and made her stumble along at his pace. It wasn't the one called Martin. The rail yard didn't have the same soft mud as Quorn's stables. Elise set her jaw further as she bore the brunt of the pace on her shoeless foot. If he noticed her limping, it didn't show, for he didn't pause.

She already knew which car she'd be assigned to. There wasn't any other choice. Elise scraped her instep on a rough piece of the ladder step into the third car but hid the sharp gasp of pain. Her escort didn't appear to note it, for he released her arm the moment she gained the floor, and then pushed her skirts inside to slide the door closed. She heard the lock being turned behind her.

Elise took stock of her prison. The car had been divided into two separate parts by a beautifully carved, wooden screen. Elise noted that it had been attached to the wall on both sides, but she could see through some of the scrollwork to the other side.

I'm not even allowed the companionship of others? she wondered. Oh, Colin was going to regret it when he found out the truth. She just hoped that she was as far from him as possible when he did, too!

"Elise? I've died a hundred deaths, I swear it! He hasn't mistreated you, has he?"

Daisy's whisper brought a wince to Elise's face. She limped to the wall. "I'm fine, Daisy, just fine. He's a bit angry with me, is all."

"Did you tell him?"

"He didn't give me the chance."

"I'll tell his man."

"Oh no, you won't. I forbid it, do you understand? Let him think exactly what he does. I rather like it this way. It keeps him away from me." Elise colored her voice with the proper amount of anxiety. Daisy knew only of Elise's fear of men; she knew nothing of last night and the wedding.

"I'll not say a word. I promise," the maid said.

"I'd like to rest now, I think."

Their words had gotten louder as the train had begun

moving. Elise didn't know that train travel came with such an abrasive sound. She hoped Rory wouldn't be disturbed by it, especially as Colin had made certain she'd not be able to comfort or hold him.

She stopped the tears that welled up. It was just self-pity now, and she'd not bow to that. Colin may say she was his property, but he was wrong. With the right magistrate and enough gold, Elise could get an annulment easily enough. They hadn't consummated anything.

Her prison had a long bench against the wall, but nothing else. It had cushions on it, though. She wondered if that was for her comfort, or if he'd forgotten to order their removal.

Elise lay on her bench, watched the ceiling of the car above her swaying, and tried not to think.

Chapter 18

The train halted at a town called Preston. Elise had two windows, both facing the side opposite from the town. She watched as the coal was loaded and heard the activity beyond the wall. They were allowing Daisy and Nanny out for a comfort stop, but not the new duchess? She narrowed her eyes and sat back down on her bench.

Her bolt lifted, the door slid open, and a hamper was shoved in.

"With His Grace's compliments."

It was Mick, Colin's personal servant. Elise turned her head to the wall until she heard the bolt fall. Then she moved. Stubbornness wasn't going to help her now. She limped over to the basket. She didn't dare eat, but a few sips of water wouldn't matter. There were freshly baked buns, a slice of warm ham, a napkin, and a flagon of liquid. She wrinkled her nose when she tasted the lemonade, but that made it easier to take just two swallows. She replaced the container, put the cloth back over the feast, and returned to the bench.

When the others had feasted and returned to the

other half of the car, Mick came back for the basket. Elise kept her eyes on the wood wall.

"His Grace has made arrangements to stay at Castle Kinlochlan, just across the border."

"Why tell me?" she asked.

"Orders. Prepare yourself for when we arrive."

With what? Into what? Using what privy closet to relieve myself? Elise almost said the bitter questions aloud, but instead bit her tongue. She'd rather starve. She heard Colin's man sigh, and then heard the sound of her prison door closing and locking again.

Nothing happens by chance. Elise had been told that by Sir Roald in one of his sonnets. It wasn't true. It couldn't be. She'd wanted Rory to be with the MacGowans. That was where he belonged. But had she truly created this ignoble situation in order to make that happen? It was too ludicrous to consider.

The train started back up, and she ran a tongue over her teeth, tasting the bitter residue of lemonade. Colin should have simply sent water. He was an inconsiderate jailer, too.

Lord Kinley's carriages were waiting at the station. Elise had Daisy to thank for that information, and more. They'd arrived at Carlisle Station in good time. Rory was enjoying the swaying of the train and was turning into an excellent traveler. Nanny was complaining a bit about her gout; otherwise, all was fine.

Daisy kept Elise informed through the scrollwork. Elise hadn't asked. She'd tried to sleep in the three hours since Preston. It hadn't worked. Her foot had started throbbing, along with her headache, her stomach was rebelling at lack of sustenance, and the only thing keeping that sensation at bay was the need to relieve herself. She couldn't recall ever being so miserable.

She didn't bother to ready herself, as she'd been ordered. It hadn't seemed necessary. She thought she'd have plenty of time, once they stopped. In the span of a few hours, she was getting used to being treated as an afterthought. The lock turning surprised her, and she had to struggle into a sitting position to face the door. She shoved the ungroomed mass of hair off her shoulders at the same time.

"I'm to see you to the laird's carriage."

Mick spoke from outside the car. He was waiting at the steps, so only the upper third of his body was in her doorway.

"Perhaps you'd best put me in some other conveyance," she replied.

"Orders."

Elise set her jaw. She was learning to dislike that word. "Oh, very well. Let's not tarry, then."

She stood, and the blood rushing to her scraped foot made it almost too tender to bear her weight. She limped over to the door and held to the frame of it while the strange dots in front of her vision cleared. Her innards pained so much, she couldn't stand upright. She wondered how she was going to be able to withstand a carriage ride.

"What have you done to yourself?"

Elise lifted her chin to look at him down her nose. She lifted one side of her upper lip at the same time. "It's none of your concern, that I can tell."

"Can you walk to the carriage, then, or will you be needing my assist?"

"I'd sooner touch a snake than a MacGowan clansman. Now, step aside, so that I can proceed. I'd not like His Grace thinking this delay is my fault."

Mick backed up a step, folded his arms, and cocked his head. Elise bit her lower lip between her teeth and stepped down the steps. Perhaps she should have requested water instead of lemonade. She could have used it to bathe the muck from her injured foot.

She was hunched forward, and each step was accomplished in a gingerly fashion, but she reached Lord Kinley's ceremonial carriage on her own power. Getting into it was a separate problem, though.

Elise stood beside the small ladder and debated whether her injured foot would bear her weight long enough to reach the lower rung, or if she'd be better served trying to pull herself up onto it. She might have to ask Mick for assistance, after all.

Colin forestalled her. "Put her in the carriage and stay this stupidity. I've better things to do than watch."

Elise cried out as Mick lifted her. His grip about her waist was painful, as was the motion of setting her onto the carriage floor at Colin's feet.

"Perhaps you would na' be so weak if you ate what was given to you."

His unconcerned voice stiffened her back.

"Only an idiot sends food and liquid to a prison with no comfort room, Your Grace. I'd have been stupid to eat or drink." Elise forgot her own vow as she answered, and then felt like a fool. If it killed her, she was going to gain her own bench, and without any assistance, either.

Colin answered with some of his Gaelic words. He was probably deciding her punishment for calling him an idiot, she guessed.

Elise ignored him and slid her back to the opposite bench. If she pushed with her good foot against his bench, it wasn't going to be too difficult.

"Come along, then. I've na' got all day to await your needs."

Colin stepped over her and leapt from the carriage. Elise closed her eyes in disgust at herself. The entire Honor Guard would be informed of her weakness, no doubt.

"Do you need assistance, again?"

It was Colin. He hadn't any inflection to his voice. Elise masked her own. "I'd not accept it, even if you were the last—"

"What have you done to your foot?"

Elise hid it quickly beneath her hem, turned her head, and spoke to the bench at her nose. "When a man is ordered to escort a lady, and she trips on the way, he may want to stop and check why next time. It could be because she's lost a shoe, and consequently doesn't have any protection on her foot for the forced march on rough surfaces."

Colin frowned, and Elise hated herself for turning and looking at him long enough to know of it.

"It was na' my intent to harm you, Elise. You should ha' said something earlier."

Elise wasn't fond of his way of responding, especially the part about silencing her. She didn't answer that. She didn't have to. She met his eyes levelly and half-lidded hers, to take him out of focus. Then she looked away with as insulting a gesture as she could manage.

"I'll go for your woman."

Elise knew the tears in her eyes were from anger at herself. She blinked them rapidly away before Daisy arrived. She was embarrassed. In the first test of her inner strength, she'd found out she hadn't any.

Castle Kinlochlan wasn't large. There were only two floors throughout, and she guessed at four in the great tower. Lord Kinley and his family occupied the first two floors. Colin's party was being given the tower. Elise knew that much from the whispers she could hear. She also knew she was being stared at and openly gossiped over.

Anyone with her recent marital history would be.

That and Colin's obvious treatment of her guaranteed it.

Elise didn't move her cloak and check, though. As horrid as she looked, it would simply cause more comment than any could fight. At least she wasn't limping as openly and could keep up with the men all about her, encircling her like a shield.

Daisy had helped Elise with her foot at Carlisle Station. It hadn't taken long before she gained the carriage again. Colin had been waiting. She'd thought about thanking him but didn't. He'd looked her over before turning his head. He hadn't said a word. Elise returned the favor.

It was chilly in the bedchamber Elise was assigned to. The water in her hipbath was cold, too.

"I didn't know you were his prisoner, Elise. You didn't tell me."

"I don't know what you're talking about. Stoke the fire; it might warm this place a mite."

"There are four of his men outside this chamber as we speak. They all snap to attention whenever I open the door. They're quite well-trained, like puppets. Would you like to see it?"

"They're members of his Honor Guard. We met this morning. His Grace is just keeping me safe."

"I don't believe that, and you know it. Furthermore, there's little that will dent the chill in this tower. It's a Scot's castle, and they all feel this way."

"How would you know?"

"I've heard tales."

Elise was breaking one of her own rules. She never washed her hair right before a dinner engagement. Not only was it nearly impossible to dry, but it was unmanageable, too.

Of course, she had no idea if she was attending.

She had to take several breaths before she was brave enough to sink into the water. She was beginning to think she'd never warm. She wasn't disguising how cold it was when she came back up.

"And then there's the matter of your wardrobe. I've not been given access to any of it. All I've got is this silver gown. It's seen better days. What do you wish me to do with it?"

"Leave it."

"Leave it where?"

"Anywhere!"

"If I tidy a room, I need to know how and where. This room is bare of just about anything. It resembles a cell. Oh, I forgot. You're not being held prisoner. It can't possibly be a cell."

Elise sighed loudly.

"Well, help me out. It's no cell, you're no prisoner, you've no creams for your skin, no potions or hair picks for your coiffure, and nothing to clothe you with, save these soiled undergarments and a very soiled gown. Tell me what this looks like to you."

"Will you just leave it?"

"The words or the gown?"

"Both," Elise replied.

"You can't just leave a dress like this lying about."

"Must you go on and on about it?" Elise asked bitterly.

"I think it's salvageable. It just requires a bit of an airing, and maybe a paste of salt on the worst stains. Give me a couple of days; you won't even be able to spot them."

"Leave it. I'll take care of it."

The maid cocked her head. "You? Did I hear right? You?"

"I've got special plans for that dress, Daisy."

"This should be good. What are they?"

"I'll tell you later. Now, assist me. I've got to ready myself for the festivities. In case I'm attending."

"In case—!" The maid bit off the exclamation.

"Very well, I'll assist you; but I'll have you know it's under protest."

"Now what are you protesting?"

"I've nothing to coordinate you with. No attire. Exactly what are you planning on wearing? In the event you're attending, that is."

"They'll send something up."

"Oh, that's right. I've been told whatever you require will be sent up. How would they know what you require? What you feel like wearing? What color scheme we want to accomplish? Of all the nerve!"

"Hand me some soap, Daisy. I neglected to bring some."

"I've not got any, unless you consider the boiled lard they gave me soap. It turned my hands red. I don't think your skin will be able to survive it."

"Only one way to find out. Quit complaining and help me," Elise said.

"Not until you tell me what to do with this dress."

"Tie it in a knot. Toss it out the window. Save me the trouble."

"You wouldn't! You couldn't!"

"Not only would I, but I definitely will."

"But it's beautiful. Special. I've never seen—"

"It's a reminder, and there are some things I don't want to remember. Thank you very much for helping me make up my mind. Bother this. I'll wash my own hair. Hand me the soap."

"I'll not be responsible for the damage."

"To what now?"

"You. Why, they even took your entire trunk of creams and gels, out of my own caretaking. I haven't seen it since. What am I supposed to rub into your skin? Use on your hair? Why can't you have access to those, I ask?"

"That's a good question. I'm not sure. I might be able to rig up an escape tool, I suppose."

"I thought you weren't a prisoner."

"I'm not," Elise said, without inflection.

"You only need escape if you're being held against your will."

"You don't have to accompany me to Castle Gowan."

"Don't turn your sarcasm on me. I'll not give you over to them. Not without a fight, anyway. They've never seen an English lady's maid when she's angry. They'd best watch their Scottish backs! That's what they'd best do!"

Elise giggled as Daisy began scrubbing her hair. She was right about the lye soap. It was harsh. Her hair would be like a cloud of white ash about her.

"Will you be able to pin it up?"

"The hair? You need worry over getting it dry enough first. And don't you fret. I'll have you back to the notorious ice goddess in no time. That's my mission, and I'd never shirk from my duties."

"Oh, thank you, Daisy."

"Ice goddesses don't cry, you know."

The maid's voice had softened, and Elise pulled in a shuddering breath. "Yes, I know," she whispered.

When the knock came, Elise was ready. Her hair was still damp, and that made the tendrils about her face curl as they dried. There wasn't a sign of the silver dress anywhere. She couldn't even see where it had landed among the bushes bordering the tower. She'd had to wait until the tub was taken away, and Daisy was busy with her attire, to toss it. She was half-afraid the maid would try and stop her.

She was wearing one of her older gowns, a simple affair in peach organza over cotton sheeting. It was something she'd wear to visit with women-friends, or for a morning of strolling about a country garden. It certainly wasn't something she'd choose to wear to meet and dine with the influential families of Carlisle.

She met Daisy's glance in the mirror, and they both smiled.

"His Grace must not want to see you at your best. That is a puzzle, to be sure."

"I look fine," Elise replied. "A bit understated, but fine."

"Understated? You? Isn't this the self-same castle that our great Queen Elizabeth had that Scot's Queen Mary imprisoned in? And aren't you married to one of their very own grand Scottish lairds? Yet they wish you gowned this plainly?"

"The gown is fine. I wish I had my pearls with me, though."

Elise had purchased a single strand of apricot-hued pearls in France last year, when she should have been attending Evangeline at the birth of Rory. She put the thought aside the moment it surfaced and gazed wistfully in the mirror.

"You'd think a great Scottish duke would know when he'd met his match. I have all your jewels, love. They've been in your reticule. Just let me go and get them for you."

Elise watched as Daisy opened the large tapestry-covered carpetbag. She had to blink the emotion away as the maid came back with not only her necklace, but the bracelet and earbobs as well.

"There. An improvement, to be sure. I'm quite proud of you, I am."

"Do you want me to cry?"

"Of course not. I want you to give them all the hell they can stand. Let me see if that Honor Guard is still napping at your threshold. Oh, bother. They've been joined by His Grace. Pardon me, Your Grace, we weren't expecting you."

Daisy had opened the door, then slammed it shut

again. Elise had to stifle her laughter at the maid's actions. She had her face composed when the door opened again from the outside. Daisy was busily picking up the discarded towels and straightening an already straight bed. Elise was grateful she was there.

"Thank you for being prompt, Elise."

Colin took one step into the room, and four of his men filed from behind to flank him. It was effective. It was obvious they considered her the enemy. What were they protecting him from, a bar of lye soap?

Daisy snorted from her position beside the bed.

He looked Elise up and down, then he frowned. "I dinna' send jewels up."

"Inform His Grace that I'm wearing my own pearls." Elise motioned to Daisy, who stood obediently and spoke for her.

"Her Grace is wearing—"

"I heard it, and I'll na' allow it. She already knows that. Take them off, or I'll have them cut off."

Daisy's indrawn breath spoke for her.

"If she refuses?" Elise asked quietly.

"I've a certain position in Scotland, as one of their lairds. It's one of the oldest and most sacred of duties. All my countrymen are aware of my marriage by now, without receipt of clan permission. They also know I wed an Englishwoman, which is worse. I have *nae* choice now but to produce my wife at every occasion. Dinna' test that choice, for I will na' hesitate to send you, under guard, to Castle Gowan, with the bastard, and let the gossips be damned."

Elise started unclasping her bracelet.

"They're just pearls, Your Grace," Daisy said.

"This is Scotland, Elise. Kindly tell your maid that in this country a man's wife is his chattel, and her servants are his. They can be dismissed at my whim, and they will be."

Elise had pried the earbobs from her ears and it

smarted. She ignored it. She was afraid Daisy would be sent packing if she said another word. The maid didn't know what Colin MacGowan was capable of. She turned to the maid. "Thank you, Daisy. You may attend to Nanny and Rory, now."

Daisy met Elise's eyes before she curtsied. She'd been asked to do the impossible, and Elise knew it. Daisy couldn't pass by Colin and his men, but she didn't say another word, either.

"I am ready now, Your Grace."

"I see that you are."

Colin turned on his heel and walked out into the hallway. His men formed a line behind him. Elise walked past them with her head high. They were all wearing their kilts, and all the strange accoutrements that seemed to accompany an outfit of that nature. They were a barbaric-looking lot.

That was the point, she was sure.

They didn't frighten her. She was The Ice Goddess, wasn't she? Their laird was simply putting more ballast into her hatred of him. It was going to be highly enjoyable when he found out the truth. She might want to be around, after all.

Chapter 19

"What do you want?"

Elise looked up from the chair beside the fire as the duke entered. Her words hid the instant fright the sight of him had caused her. He was wearing a long plaid robe with the MacGowan crest.

"You sent for your maid," he answered.

"What of it?"

"She's na' available to you tonight."

Elise's heart sank, and she had to fight to maintain her color. He wouldn't have dismissed Daisy, would he? And if he had . . . why? Elise had postured at being an obedient, quiet, and subservient wife at the sup. Lord Kinley had even complimented Colin on his choice of a bride.

"Why not?" Elise looked down at her hands as she asked it. She was preparing herself for the answer. She knew she wouldn't be able to hide her reaction if he was looking.

"She's tending to the bastard."

"He has a name, you know." Relief was what made her words so harsh and quick.

Colin didn't say anything for so long, Elise looked up to see why. He had such a look of disgust on his features, she immediately looked back to her hands. She was grateful he hadn't been looking at her and had missed her motion.

"Your nursemaid woman was na' up to a jaunt North. I let her go. Along with a nice stipend, I might add."

"You dismissed Nanny? You've overstepped yourself. He needs her. You have to hire her back."

"I'm afraid I dinna' quite hear that. Perhaps you'd be carin' to do a bit of a repeat?"

Elise sucked in a breath, held it, and then spoke. "My mistake, Your Grace."

"I suspected as much."

How she longed to scream at him! Instead, she contented herself with examining her nails.

"Now . . . as to what I'm doing here," he said, drawing out the words.

"I would prefer to be alone."

"With *nae* one to assist you with your undressing? I've already seen how far that gets you."

Elise caught the sob in her throat at the brogue-filled words. She didn't want any of those memories! She was more certain of it now than when she'd tossed the silver-starred dress from the window. She didn't want any reminders of Colin MacGowan.

"I'll not allow you to touch me."

Silence greeted her whisper. Despite her every effort, Elise glanced sidelong at him from beneath her lashes. He hadn't moved. He had a strange look on his face, too. She looked away quickly before she thought about what it could be, but knew she was too late.

It was self-hatred. She knew it too well.

"I've *nae* desire to be anywhere near you, Elise."

"You're wasting your time," she replied coldly.

"*Nae*, I'm not. I dinna' say I'd be assisting you. I just said you had *nae* one else who would."

"What do you want, then?"

He took a great, lung-expanding, chest-enlarging

breath. Her eyes burned with watching it, and then her ears joined.

"To assure myself that I'm not a simple-minded whelp. To ken that my foolishness was na' without cause. To remind myself that there were verra good reasons for wedding with you." He stopped and pushed the rest of his breath out. "And to help me sleep. You're a verra beautiful woman. Verra womanly. Verra."

She gagged on the cry and fought the rush of gooseflesh along her limbs.

"It's na' difficult for any man, myself included, to see why I married you and why it's affecting my sleep. I'm here now because it's my own special hell that I have to ken for certain."

"I care not how you sleep, or if you do," she replied.

She sat in the chair closest to the fire, but at the present moment was so cold, she couldn't feel it. She wished he'd leave, so she could crouch beside the flames. Or, now that she knew she'd be sleeping in her evening attire, she'd crawl beneath the heavy quilts and let them warm her. She knew it wouldn't work, though. It wasn't the chamber's chill that she was suffering from.

"Why dinna' you tell me of him, Elise?"

His whisper raised every bit of nerves she was fighting to still. Elise molded half-moons into her palms with her nails as she clenched her hands.

"I can understand hesitancy at first . . . when you kissed with me. I can even give you embarrassment at Barrigan's. I suppose I can even give you Ipswich, but you could have said something at Crewe."

His voice cracked. The hands beneath her blurred with the onslaught of tears. Elise hated the emotion and hated herself for being weak enough to have to suffer through it. She took several deep, even breaths and blinked the moisture away before she answered.

"Perhaps I was afraid of how you'd react, Your Grace. And look here, I wasn't far wrong, either."

"You think my treatment harsh?"

"Right now? No, but you do seem to have forgotten to bring along some of your Honor Guard. Perhaps you should open the door and invite some of them in."

"Oh, I dinna' think so. I dinna' want observers at present."

Elise knew it was her heart sinking this time. Her eyes widened to their fullest extent, and the hands on her lap shook. She had to clasp them together to stop the motion. She didn't dare take her next breath for so long she started to feel faint. "Now, you're wasting my time," she said coldly.

"Since your time belongs to me, as everything else about you does, I fail to see waste. If I want to see you, I will. If I want to hold you, I will. If I want to use you to slake my lust, there's none to stop me from doing so. You're mine to do with as I see fit, remember?"

Oh, God! Elise screamed it silently and lost any pretense to the contrary. She held her hands over her eyes and shook.

"That's what a whore is good for. You ken that much."

"Don't do this, Colin . . . please?" To her own ears, the plea sounded broken and defeated.

"You've na' received permission to use my name. Dinna' do it again, or reap the penalty."

Elise pulled her hands from her face and stood. She knew she was ashen. She knew, because it took an effort of will to stay upright. "You don't want me, Your Grace. You don't. I know you don't."

"How do you ken anything about me?"

"I . . . I have foisted a bastard on you, remember?"

His jaw tightened. "How can I forget?"

Then he was walking across the room toward her, looming larger the closer he got. Elise backed away until her feet were on the hearthstone. She couldn't go any farther without getting burned, but she actually considered it. She opened her mouth and started talking.

"His name is Rory. He's eight months old. He was born at the Wyndham Villa in Monte Carlo last summer. There is no record of his birth. I thought it best . . . for all concerned."

Her words stopped his advance. Elise watched the conflicting emotions cross his face. The closed, unreadable one was replaced by such loathing, she arched from it, the back-cracking motion stopping only when she reached the mantel.

Colin swore and spewed his Gaelic words before spinning about. Elise watched him pace her chamber; turning once he reached the door to glare at her.

"Damn you, Elise MacGowan. Damn you, and your ilk, to hell."

The door slammed, reverberating through the room. She found she preferred his Honor Guard, after all.

Colin had ordered a privy chamber constructed in the corner of her prison. Elise looked at it without any emotion; she'd spent every last bit of that last night, after Colin had left.

They'd awakened her at dawn, and a strange maid had assisted her into a plain skirt and blouse. It hadn't been comfortable sleeping in her corset and all the clothing beneath it, but things could have been worse. Colin might have stayed, and then where would she be?

Elise knew where she'd be. She'd been fighting thoughts of it all night. She'd be at Colin's side, in his arms, and in his bed.

Whereas two nights ago, when it had been her

wedding night, she'd longed to surprise Colin with her virginity, now she was doing her utmost to keep it from him. He'd not know the truth from her lips or her body. His treatment of her had sealed that vow. He didn't deserve to know *that* secret.

"Elise? You slept well?" Daisy poked her finger through the scrollwork as she asked it.

Elise walked over to her. "Passably. What happened with Nanny? I thought Rory was everything to her."

"She complained once too often. I couldn't keep her silent. I tried. Please don't think I didn't try."

"That's a silly request, Daisy. I know my husband's ways. He's a harsh man. A barbarian. A brute. A boor. And all those other *B* words I used so long ago. He's reverting further the longer we travel North, too. He's a harsh man from a harsh world. I was a fool to forget it. You're not overburdened by yourself?"

"I've four housemaids assisting. The duke hired them away from Castle Kinlochlan for the rest of the journey. It's actually quite crowded over here."

And too public, Elise finished in her thoughts, before sucking on her tongue.

Colin MacGowan was a worthy adversary. He either didn't wish Elise to have any company, or he was aware that she'd try to escape him if given a chance. Either way, she'd lost her confidante for the time being but had gained some insight.

Colin MacGowan wasn't a man easily thwarted.

They separated the train at Glasgow. Daisy described it for her. The only view from her side of the car was of rain-blurred trees, caressed by a low-lying mist that seemed to be held in the air by drizzle. It made the forest look more sinister than it could possibly be. Daisy told her there were eight more cars lined up behind another engine. The extravagance was stunning. Nothing the Wyndham family had could compete.

"They're sending Rory on ahead, Elise! What am I to do? He's lost Nanny, and he doesn't know anyone here. He's crying. Here, baby, that's a love."

Elise heard Rory's cries, but she couldn't do anything through a wooden wall. She was losing Daisy. She'd shown how much that would matter to her, and now he was using it. She shouldn't begrudge it. She was the one who'd given His Grace the weapon to use.

"You'll accompany him, of course. I can make do without a maid for the time being. It will be rough, but I've managed before."

"I can't leave you alone with him, Elise! Hush, Rory."

"The baby's already lost too many, Daisy. He knows you. He'll be safe with you. I won't listen to another word. Besides, I'll be right behind you, I will. I promise."

Elise wasn't so sure of her words, when Mick came for her. The MacGowan train had been reduced to two cars, and the others were nowhere in sight. The closer she got to Colin's carriage, the more worried she grew.

All about her there were big-boned, unkempt-looking horses and men wearing the MacGowan plaid. Elise didn't bother to count, but the ranks of Colin's men appeared to have doubled.

"Where is Rory?" Elise broke her vow of silence to ask it. She didn't think he was going to answer for a moment. Then he looked down at her with something akin to pity on his face.

"The bairn is on his way to the castle with the bags and such. They'll be there nigh on a week afore we arrive."

A week? she thought. Elise set her lips and narrowed her eyes. "Was a guard sent with him?"

"The Honor Guard stays at the duke's side. There's outriders. He'll be safe enough."

"He sent my baby away without a guard, yet kept so many for his own use? You've got to stop him."

"The bairn will be safe enough. None will attack the MacGowan train. The name's too well known."

"There's nothing I would put past your country. There's probably a robber behind every tree, and—and a kidnapper at every stop!"

Elise knew she was acting hysterically. She also knew it was horrid to consider, but she couldn't stop the instant vision from catching her breath and twisting her belly with worry. What was to stop Rory from disappearing, and saving their laird at the same time? She didn't know what Colin was capable of anymore.

She watched as Mick shrugged. "It will be safe. Come, you waste time. His Grace has to put in an appearance at the Castle Dunvargas yet today. It's a long ride."

"Why can't we stay with the train?"

"The tracks to Inverness go through Grampian Mountains. It's rough country. The duke will stay to the valleys."

"Why? Is it safer?"

Elise watched the man narrow his eyes and sigh heavily. He was probably attributing her fears to womanly weakness.

"I promise you it's safe. The train runs year-round. Nothing happened to it getting here. Nothing will happen to it going back."

"They weren't carrying a baby, you backwater-bred idiot."

He didn't like that title. Elise could tell by the way he clenched his jaw as he opened the carriage door for her. She didn't care.

"Go tell Colin—I mean, His Grace, that Rory isn't just any baby! He's Evan MacGowan's illegitimate son. He's too precious to be sent off like unwanted baggage. Go! Tell him. He can't send that baby without a guard. I won't allow it."

"That bairn . . . is a MacGowan? He's Evan Mac-
Gowan's son? The duke's brother, Evan?"

Mick was choking on the words and looking at
Elise with such horror that she smirked. "I just told
you he was."

"And you said naught of it to the duke?"

"Oh, I had so much time for that in the stable
building, now didn't I? Don't stand there like a dolt.
Go and get an Honor Guard for Evan's son. Worry
about what His Grace says later! That's an order."

Elise couldn't believe her eyes when Mick turned
on his heels and ran from her. She glanced about
quickly. Dressed as plainly as she was, no one seemed
to be paying her any attention. Since she was also clad
in calf-high boots that she'd been given that morning, the mud wasn't a problem. She didn't have any
trouble getting around to the back of the carriage.
She'd have called it luck, if she still believed in such
a thing. What was it Roald had once penned? Nothing happens that isn't meant to. They were going to
be the words she lived by from now on.

She'd done what she had to, no matter the personal
cost. She'd given Rory to them, and she'd made certain they knew who he was. There was nothing left to
keep her. She didn't even have to see Colin's face
when he found out.

She acted like there was nothing odd about taking
a stroll to the edge of the woods. She knew the town
of Glasgow awaited her on the other side of the trees,
although she couldn't see it, and Glasgow was well advanced, considering it was in Scotland. Elise should
be able to access some of the Duchess of Wynd's
wealth. Even here, where it felt like the very ends of
the civilized world, there was probably a bank willing
to advance her Wynd funds, wasn't there?

The foliage beneath her feet wasn't as muddy or as
damp as it was around the rail station. Elise hadn't

thought she'd be able to get away, and yet it was easy. She had to wait for her heart to calm, so she leaned against a tree.

The waste of time seemed stupid, but it was necessary. Colin would be searching for her, and he'd most likely look for her beyond the railyard. He'd suspect she'd run. Any woman treated as she had been would be running. Elise forced herself to wait. A quarter hour passed, then another.

The woods about her were wet and quiet, instilling a sense of security. Although she was less than a hundred yards from the station, and all the MacGowan clan were there, it was still. Elise had to hug herself to keep the joy inside. She was in charge of her own destiny again.

And she was almost free of Colin! Once she had seen a magistrate to make certain of it, anyway. She refused to decipher what the thick, hurtful pressure near her heart might mean. She felt nothing for Colin MacGowan anymore. He was as harsh and barbaric as his clime.

She'd forgotten about Daisy, though. Elise pushed from the tree and started walking, going down the gentle slope. She was going to have to wait to fetch Daisy. Rory needed her more right now. Elise would send for her, once she was able to.

The forest floor was thick and wet. She appreciated the boots more the farther she walked. Her skirt was getting wet clear to the knees, but that couldn't be helped. She couldn't lift them. She had to use her hands to clear a path for herself.

The trees thinned, and she recognized rooftops through them. With any luck, she'd be in a warm bath, writing notes to her staff, before the sun set. Elise took another step, brushed aside foliage, and stopped, swaying back into place. She hoped her face didn't show the severity of her disappointment.

The three MacGowan coaches sat on the roadway directly in front of her. Horses, their coats thick with unshed hair, milled about, and His Grace wasn't hard to spot. He stood in his leisurely pose against the back wheel of his carriage.

Elise was starting to shake. She hadn't realized how wet her outfit was becoming. From all about her, she could feel their censure. She did the only thing she could. She took a deep breath, lifted her head high, and stepped through the last of the greenery.

"It's lovely country, Your Grace, but a trifle damp," she said loudly and unconcernedly, as she walked to his side.

"Get in. Now."

He was livid. Elise didn't need to look at him to know.

"Perhaps . . . I'd best wait for assistance," she stammered the words.

In reply, he gripped her about the waist, lifted her, and shoved her in. As much as she hid it from herself, the sensation from his touch had begun immediately. Why couldn't it have been Sir Roald, or another of her men-friends? Getting that reaction from any of them would have been preferable to the Laird of the MacGowans!

Elise busied herself with arranging her skirts about herself. It wasn't for effect, or to keep the wrinkling to a minimum, it was to put the driest sections against her legs. She wouldn't let him know of it, though.

"We've more than two hours' journey ahead of us. You'd best spend some of that time explaining, starting now. Right now."

Elise ignored him and started rubbing her hands together for warmth. She'd been so stupid! She hadn't waited long enough, and then she'd taken the direct path to Glasgow, when any woman in her boots would have done the same. She must not have wanted to escape.

Elise's thoughts stalled.

I didn't want to escape him? It couldn't be true. It was too ludicrous to consider. She put her hands to her face and blew warm air on them.

"Well?" The one word was harsh and biting.

"I'm not speaking to you, Your Grace."

"Oh yes, you are. You're na' going to finish until you've explained everything."

"Explanations are—" Elise started, but he interrupted her and filled the small enclosure with a slew of bitter words that wouldn't stop.

"First, you're going to explain what you're doing with Evan's son. You're going to explain why you dinna' tell me about him the very first moment you saw me. You're going to convince me as to why you trapped me into a marriage. Even if we wed, the boy remains a bastard. You're smart enough to know that.

"Then, you're going to entertain me as to what it was that Evan saw in you. Ira? Yes. He always did know a good whore when he saw one. But Evan? *Nae.* Evan was intelligent. He was fastidious. He would na' have given a woman like you his child, and then allowed you to carry it! We've got more than two hours in this bloody carriage, and you're going to do a damn sight more than speak with me, woman!"

Elise had caught her breath in shock more than once throughout his speech, but she hadn't interrupted. Her mind was in denial, but her ears heard every word. If she'd thought the space in her chest hurt before, she'd been a fool. It now felt like her heart was in someone's fist, and every time it beat, they squeezed.

He hadn't moved, but it felt like he'd grown in stature. Either that, or she was in serious danger of possessing an overactive imagination. His eyes weren't

green flecked or brown, either; they were an indecipher-
able shade of black. It was dim in the coach's interior.
Those strange dots hampered her vision again, too.

"I'm waiting, and I'll na' wait long. You dinna' do
what you've done to me, or to Rory. You're unfit to
mother anyone."

Elise wasn't doing a good job of keeping her tears
at bay. It could be due to her wet clothing, or her failure at escape. She could attribute it to her lack of sleep
last night, or the experience of hearing what he
thought of her. It could be a myriad of things. She
didn't have to feel cowed and weak and beaten, but
she did. She couldn't stop the stream of tears. She
licked them from her upper lip.

"You should simply get your guard . . . to manhan-
dle me again and save yourself the trouble."

What was supposed to be a sarcastic, self-assured
answer had her anguish flavoring every word. Elise
couldn't stop shivering.

"You lying, scheming, little—"

Elise didn't hear the rest. For the first time in her
life, she knew how it felt to faint.

Chapter 20

"Come along then, Elise. Elise?"

The fuzzy feeling about her face was fading. It took a few seconds before she realized it was the Duke of MacGowan speaking to her. It took another few to notice that he was undoing the buttons down the front of her blouse.

I'll not allow this! she thought. "What do you think you're doing?" she asked feebly.

"Getting you air, of course. What else?"

He had her blouse undone completely and didn't need to pull it from the waistband of her skirt, because it wasn't on her anymore.

"I have quite enough air already," she replied.

Elise's voice was getting stronger. She was getting control of her limbs again, too. She gripped the blouse placket at her breast together and held it that way. Colin pulled the ends from her, as if she wasn't holding it, and pulled the garment roughly off of her. Elise congratulated herself that she hadn't given sound to her cry of protest.

"You're soppin' wet. In this country, that can mean death. I had to strip you to your knickers. They're verra pretty ones, too. Frilly. Not much for warmth. Here, I've finished. You can protect your modesty."

He deftly pulled the ends of a blanket about her and propped her into the corner of her bench. Elise noticed that he wasn't looking anywhere near her as he seated himself. He looked a bit white about the mouth, too.

The blanket was warm, but it didn't compensate for losing the heat that seemed to come from his nearness. Elise guessed the look on her face was from the worry and confusion. Her own body wasn't listening. She'd vowed not to feel anything for him, and everything mocked her. The pulsing sensation was back, deep in her belly, making a throb that wouldn't ebb; the slightest scrape of her nipples against the satin made an accompanying tempo of shivers to join the pulsation, and the entire mass of it felt like a series of far-off drumbeats.

"You've got color back. It's an improvement. You've such pale hair and skin that when you faint, you look a ghost. Did you ken that?"

"I don't faint," she replied.

"Excellent time to start, then. My compliments."

"Save them for one of your clansmen."

He sighed hugely, which made his chest rise; Elise averted her eyes, although it was difficult. It was because he had such strength evident in every line, she decided. He was a massive man. He stood apart from others. She'd never seen one as well-defined and muscular. His Honor Guard were all large men, but none would be mistaken for the laird.

"Are you recovered sufficiently, then?" he asked.

"Sufficient to what? And, to whom?"

"Answering questions, of course. You do remember that was the reason for your performance of a few moments past?"

"Performance? I fainted," she replied.

"You did it well. Timely."

"You're an insufferable prig, Your Grace," she said sweetly.

"As I recall, your opinion was na' one of my questions. I dinna' think I want that one asked or answered. I think I'll excuse you from another of them as well. I've already decided the answer myself."

Elise's mouth tightened, but that was the only sign she gave.

"I see verra well why Evan was enamored of you. You've a quick wit, and you're a verra beautiful woman. Verra. Especially the parts hidden beneath your clothing. Evan always did have exquisite taste."

Elise sucked in a breath and glared at him. He wasn't looking. She watched as he sat upright on his bench, unbuttoned and pulled off his own jacket, then started on his shirt. There was an erotic motion to it she'd not suspected existed before. She lifted the blanket's edge to cover her mouth and demanded her eyes to cease looking.

Colin creased the clothing precisely before laying it atop the bench beside him. Elise didn't move her eyes. Then he started removing each boot, taking more time than was necessary to slip the laces. She was holding her breath when he finished with one and prayed he wouldn't notice. She wouldn't allow him to do this! *Whatever it is he's doing,* she told herself.

After Colin had the pair lined up exactly to the edge of the carriage door, he stood. The carriage wasn't tall enough for him, and Elise barely kept her gasp silent as he undid the trouser buttons at his hip. She pulled the edge of her blanket clear to the bottoms of her eyes. He didn't notice. He bent forward, faced the carriage door, and then pulled down his pants, for all the world like she wasn't there.

Elise couldn't seem to control her own eyes as he sat on the opposite bench and finished removing his slacks. He was wearing another pair of calf-length underdrawers. Her sigh of relief made it to sound, and she shoved the fingers of one hand into her mouth.

This was inexcusable . . . incorrigible! Just because His Grace, Colin MacGowan, had a physique of a Grecian god wasn't any reason to stare like a love-starved ninny! Elise reprimanded herself, and lost out.

He was pretending she wasn't there, but it was a lie. She could tell. The strange half-smile on his lips was giving it away.

"You can look now. I'm na' going to ravish you."

"What?" The word was garbled. She should have removed her fingers first, and the quick look he flashed at her told her of his knowledge of it.

"I've better things to do with my time."

Elise told herself she wasn't insulted, but it wasn't true.

Colin bent his legs onto each other in a strange sitting pose on his bench. Elise watched with eyes that had seemed to have forgotten again how to blink, as he straightened his back and took several deep breaths. Then he placed his hands together, palm to palm, bent his head forward, and leaned his forehead onto his entwined fingers.

Elise knew that she no longer existed for him. She could have been stark naked and reclining on the bench, like she'd seen once in an illicit drawing, and he wouldn't have noticed. She sensed the calmness and peace that started radiating from him, and she was jealous. She grew warmer, too. It had to be the fleece-lined, woolen blanket he'd wrapped her in. Her mind and experience were telling her that much, but her intuition knew better.

There was something about this man. Something that existed only for her. It was the same thing that had aborted her escape attempt. It was as if an invisible cord threaded the space between them, and she didn't know enough about it to cut it.

She recognized the humming sound, although it was fainter; it seemed to be coming from Colin's side of the carriage. Elise was annoyed with herself. She had better things to do than watch the Duke of Mac-Gowan and think fanciful thoughts. She really should have been better at her sewing hoop, she decided.

When they arrived at the courtyard to Castle Dunvargas, Colin was again fully attired. He'd come out of his strange trance a quarter hour before they'd arrived. He hadn't seemed tired or sore, although she could've sworn the indentation of the cushions at her back and legs were permanently imprinted onto her.

The reason for his care when undressing was apparent, too. While her cast-off apparel was in a heap on the carriage floor, he looked as fresh as when he'd first entered the carriage. His clothing fit without a wrinkle, belying the need for creasing, and he hadn't a hair out of place. He'd made certain of it in a small mirror he carried. Elise could have kicked herself for knowing all of that, too.

"No doubt, they'll have the usual reception prepared for us. You're na' attending."

She didn't answer. She was afraid it would give her away. The fist wrapped about her heart was squeezed tight, making it painful and bringing self-pitying tears too near the surface.

"It's na' due to any disagreement between us, you understand. I'll na' start a scandal of that nature. I'm still staving off any the bastard's presence started. The introduction to my household of my nephew could have been something I'd planned easily enough. I'm simply leaving out any maternal relationship at present."

"Do as you wish. It's what you're best at." Elise wanted to snatch the words back the moment she spoke them.

"You appear to be learning. Excellent. By the time we arrive at my home, you may even surprise yourself at your ability to obey me."

"Forgive my earlier description. You're not a prig. You're an egotistical, insufferable boor. I'll not stay beyond my six weeks."

"My offer is withdrawn," he informed her.

"Excuse me?"

"The reverend at Crewe effectively canceled it. You were na' payin' attention to the vows? There's a *'til death* part, you know . . . or were you na' listening?"

"Nothing has been consummated, Your Grace. I can still attain my annulment. You know it."

He sighed heavily. Then he smiled. There was nothing humorous about it. "I keep forgetting how young you are. It's na' entirely my fault. Your abilities are ancient. You are na' attending the reception because you seem to have lost your attire during the ride, inside this carriage—with me. I assume they'll make the proper connection."

The strangled cry she stifled was the best she could do.

"Oh, good, we've arrived. Try to hold a temper until I've finished carrying you to the rooms."

"You're not carrying me."

"Oh yes, I am. And it's na' due to any want on my part. It's a mark of ownership and a certainty of obedience. You're to hide yourself. Tomorrow, I have to produce my duchess, and you're going to look every inch the woman who ensnared two MacGowans. Are you clear on that?"

Elise hadn't access to a mirror. She had her hair pinned up, but it was bound to be in disarray, and she didn't have anything except her chemise on. He knew that was how she'd interpret what he'd said.

"Prepare yourself. The curtain's rising."

The carriage had halted, and Colin tapped his hat on. The door opened. Elise pulled the blanket over her head as she sat up.

"Now, come into my arms like you want to be there."

She gritted her teeth and slid forward. There was going to come a day when Colin MacGowan would regret every little insult and every uncivilized ploy. She was going to make certain of it.

He held her to his chest; it felt like he made it closer than was necessary. She didn't do anything about it. She tipped her nose into his neck and listened to the commotion about them.

"Your Grace! Such a pleasure to have you stay. I can na' tell you how thrilled my wife is to be one of the first to meet your new spouse! She reads every paper. I can na' stop the woman. She probably knows more about your bride than you do. Congratulations to you both. Is this her, then? Open the wool. Let me greet her properlike."

"She's a bit indisposed, I'm afraid. The English dinna' travel well." He sighed. Elise moved with it. "My luck. Mick? Show me to my chamber, and have Her Grace's clothing fetched."

"We've so longed to meet her. You have *nae* idea. Is her hair really the color of moonlight? My wife says it's nigh impossible, but I'd rather defer to experience . . . and that you have. Well?"

"I believe I'll let your own eyes be the judge. Mick? My room? Her Grace grows heavy as we tarry about."

Elise scrunched her eyes shut to the entire brightly lit entryway. She wished she could shove cotton into her ears, too.

"She'll be well enough to attend tomorrow's banquet?

It's held in both your honors. There'll be quite a turnout. *Nae* one could believe the notorious Ice Goddess would move this far North, although that's where ice belongs, eh?" The man was laughing at his own wit. No one else was.

"If I dinna' get her some rest, my lord, she may na' be able to leave her bed. She's English, you ken. Allow me to see her settled, then I'll be down directly to discuss it."

"Forgive me, Your Grace. I would na' delay your wife's rest another moment. Wilson! Show them their chambers. See them settled. Will I be seeing you again this eve, Your Grace? I've sent out notices. We've got guests."

"You've whiskey?" Colin asked.

"Of course, Your Grace, only the finest."

"In that case, I'll be back. I'll not delay. Mick?"

Elise had spent four years of her life making certain she'd never be treated to the experience she'd just gone through. She never wanted to be at any man's beck and call. She'd never wanted to know how it felt to have a man speak for her, decide for her, and direct her every movement for her. She'd wasted all that time making certain no man could do what The MacGowan presently was doing.

She should have married the first spineless sop she met.

The experience of being held in Colin's arms while he climbed stairs was especially unnerving. She could feel each breath on her cheek, and it was getting longer between each of them. He wasn't breathing any heavier from the exertion of carrying her. That much, she guessed.

She watched the slight growth of whiskers on his chin before she dared glance higher. Even with the hatred and disgust he spouted at her, he still had beautifully formed lips. She wondered what would happen if she broke her vow and told him before he could stop her.

She licked her lips and caught the lower one between her teeth. The indecision was an effective gag.

"Stop that, Elise."

The harsh note in his voice decided her, and she lowered her eyes back to the blanket.

"Where did he put me? In the bloody turret?" Colin grumbled.

"The stairs grow longer the more you stand about, wasting time, Your Grace. Either that, or you should have rested on the road."

Colin bit back the retort. She heard it in his throat and hid her nose against his neck again.

"You've been given rooms on the second floor, just as Lord Dunvargas ordered. Your Graces? Your apartments."

The strange voice probably belonged to Wilson. Elise heard some conversing between Mick and the man, and then footsteps as Wilson left. The sound of a door yawning open was next.

Colin set her down the moment he went through it. It took a moment for her legs to function. He obviously didn't enjoy carrying her, which was fine with her. She told herself that she liked it even less.

"See that she stays here. See that she eats all that's sent up."

"Aye, Your Grace. It will be as you order, Your Grace. Oh, anything you say, Your Grace."

"I should have sent you ahead and kept Martin. Either that, or had that Wilson see to my needs."

Mick winked at Elise and her eyes widened. Then she opened her mouth and started talking.

"Colin—uh, I mean, Your Grace? I have some requirements of you before you go."

She'd surprised him, as well as the four men at his heels. Elise had to turn her head and hide her smile at the five identical expressions. Only Mick was grinning. Elise knew why. His Grace, the Duke of Mac-Gowan, had overplayed his hand. He was the one who had wished it to look like they'd been occupied with each other the entire ride, not her. Now, it was going to be her pleasure to use it.

"Requirements?"

He was choking on the word, and Elise had to get control of her expression before she turned to him. It wasn't easy with Mick stifling laughter on the inside of the door where Colin couldn't see him. She tossed her hair and turned to look at him over her shoulder. She used her most seductive voice.

"I'm going to need a hipbath of warmed water. I'll need my trunk of . . . well, the smaller one, with the ebony inlay. It contains my creams. I'll also need a gown and all the flimsy things that go under it. My knickers aren't the only frilly little things I wear, and you know it."

Absolute silence was her answer, except for Mick; his face was red, and strange, chortling sounds were coming from him. The door he was holding was swaying, too. Elise was surprised Colin didn't notice.

"Go now, and have the creams sent up first. I have to get them rubbed into my skin, for the proper silk-like feel. You might want to fetch a lady's maid to assist this time. I'd hate to overtire you again. Run along, and take your men with you. I've no need of an audience."

"You're na' to leave these rooms." His face was stiff, and his mouth was a slash of ugliness.

"Oh, I wouldn't dream of it, Your Grace. I'll be far too busy. I am the notorious Ice Goddess, you know. I have to get ready for the part. It's going to take a while now that you've gone and mussed it up, too."

His face hadn't changed, although now it looked

carved of stone. "You're to stay, and you're to eat everything I send up."

"I'm certain your man, Mick, will see that I do."

"I'm na' leaving Mick here with you."

"But you already told him he had to stay at my door and make certain that I ate. You're confusing me, Your Grace."

Elise was attempting her most innocent look. She let the blanket slip a fraction off her shoulder, and then pulled it back up, modestly. His Honor Guard was no longer looking at her. They were studiously watching anything but her, except for Mick: he was stone-faced, too.

Elise knew her color was heightened, but she met Colin's gaze evenly and didn't shirk at the anger written on every feature. He'd started it, and two could play this game.

"I'll na' stay with Dunvargas all eve."

He was speaking in a low, threatening tone. Elise lifted her head.

"I'm gratified. I'd hate to think his lordship's company, and his spirits, hold your interest more than my charms do. You'd have me thinking I'm losing my touch."

"You mistake me."

The four members of his Honor Guard weren't at his heels anymore. They were fading quite nicely into the shadow of the stairs behind him. She watched them do it but couldn't hear a sound. For large men, they were amazingly silent.

"Do I? As I recall, it wasn't me setting any stage this time. It was you. Now, you're just going to have to live with it. Just like I do."

"By all that's holy—"

"Oh, please, Your Grace, don't start that up again. I'll be obedient, I promise. I'll have a nice long soak, get creams massaged into my skin, eat my sup, and find my bed. I won't even wait up, if that's your wish."

"That's na' my wish."

"You want me awaiting you, then? I wish you'd make up your mind, Your Grace."

"That isna' what I said."

"But you did. You said—"

"I'm going to go get uproariously drunk, Elise. If you're awake when I return, we'll find out then, will na' we?"

He snarled after he said it, as if the entire thing were her fault. Elise didn't have to answer. Mick's choked exclamation did it for her. Colin spun on his heel.

Elise stood at her chamber door and debated her options. She knew she was looking her best. That wasn't the problem. She was wearing her blue day-gown, her hair was pinned atop her head in a mass of curls, her gloves were buttoned, and her shoes were shined. She had lightly dusted rice powder across her nose, touched such a small amount of rouge to her lips as to be nonexistent, and enhanced her lashes with watered-down soot.

The maid who been assisting her had watched all of it and said nothing. She didn't have to. The distaste on her face was obvious. Elise was glad when the old, sanctimonious woman left, although she'd had to knock to be let out.

The reason for Elise's indecision was obvious. It was the retinue of MacGowan clansmen who were bound to be outside her chamber door. Colin had instructed her on how she was supposed to look, but he hadn't said when. The last thing she wished was to be sent back to her chamber like a misbehaving child.

Elise took a deep breath, then turned the knob.

Mick looked up from studying the stone at his feet

and smiled. Elise almost returned it. She scanned the hall. Only Mick stood there.

"Where is the Honor Guard?"

"The laird dismissed the rest."

"Why, please?"

"Most like, he dinna' wish any observers."

"Observers to what?"

He shrugged.

"Where is Colin—I mean, His Grace?"

Mick's lips fought another smile at her lapse. He gestured with his head to another door.

"Is he awake, then?" she asked.

"Doubtful. He was na' in a wakeful mood."

"He wasn't? Then he can't stop me, can he?"

"Depends on what you've in mind to do. We've orders."

"There's that word again. I was planning on finding myself a bit of repast. That's as shifty as I wish to be this morning. Maybe after I've breakfasted, I'll feel differently. I'll let you know my plans, then."

"I've orders," he replied.

"Is he thinking to starve me?"

"*Nae.*"

"Then why can't I see to my breakfast?"

"I've *nae* objection," he answered.

"Good." Elise made as if to pass him, but he reached out and put an arm across her path, stopping her. "I thought you just said—"

He interrupted her by putting a finger to his lips. "If what I'm about to tell you becomes common knowledge, I'll na' longer be accepted by my clan. Do you ken what that means?"

"Perhaps you'd best not say it, then."

"Someone has to."

Elise frowned. "I really shouldn't waste time like this. Imagine what His Grace would say if he saw it. Besides, there's certain to be eggs and some gruel on the sideboard. Such things are best served warm."

"I've been watching you," he replied.

"That isn't surprising, considering your orders."

"It isna' true what they say of you. It canna' be."

Tears glittered in her eyes and she looked away before he saw them. "Perhaps I'd be better served having a tray delivered to my room. You'll see to it, won't you?" Elise turned around and went back to her chamber door. Mick was a more effective guard than all the others combined, she decided.

"There's something more you're hiding from him. I dinna' know what it is yet, but there's something. I only hope it isna' going to hurt him more than I can repair, this time."

"Hurt him? Hurt? His Grace? We are obviously not discussing the same man. I'm sorry I stepped out. And trust me, you've no reason whatsoever to fear for your position in Clan MacGowan from me. Good day to you."

"Tell me you're na' being wronged, then."

She was on the inside of the door, with the doorknob in her hand, and had to avert her face. "You're verra . . . perceptive," she whispered.

"Colin is very important to me. I've had the care of him since he was a lad. You've the wrong idea of him."

"Oh, really? I think I've got him, and his reasons, directly in my sights. He makes certain of it, too."

"You gave him na' other choice!"

"Oh, this is priceless. I suppose next you'll tell me that I gagged myself in the stable building and locked myself into a railroad car."

"He has to treat you as he does. Being the MacGowan Laird gives him *nae* other choice. His entire Honor Guard, and most of the clan, know what you did by now."

"Having Rory wasn't something I did to His Grace."

"I'm na' speaking of the bairn."

"No? This should be even better. What is it, then, that I've done to His Grace, the Great Laird of the MacGowans?"

"Taken the heart right out of him and defiled it."

"I beg your pardon?" Elise said.

"I saw you at the abbey. I was there, remember? If what I saw was false, you had me fooled, too."

"I've decided I'm not hungry, after all," Elise said, in a tight little voice.

"Do you know where he spent his wedding night, after seeing you and the bairn?"

"I don't want to hear this," she answered, then shut the door. She wasn't quick enough, though. She heard the answer, then leaned her head against the wood. She would have given anything not to have heard it.

"Grievin' in my arms, that's where."

Chapter 21

The indecision was the worst part. Elise knew it, as scene after scene played through her mind. If she gave into the picture of Colin that his man Mick had just painted, she couldn't hate him. If she didn't hate him, she had to name the other emotion she felt for him. If she named that, she'd go to him; and if that happened, she'd have to face what she already knew. She still wasn't good enough for a MacGowan, and when he found that out, the penalty would probably be worse.

Probably? she wondered. Her heart already knew it was; only the mind was in doubt.

She'd spent the better part of the day pacing her chamber, and it wasn't getting her anywhere. She glared at the fireplace as if it were at fault and twirled about.

The gown, which had been pressed and sent up for her to wear, was loose fitting. It hadn't been that way when she'd purchased it, but Colin's treatment of her had effectively stifled her appetite. It was an odd feeling to have the sway of her skirts a fraction of time behind her. If she hadn't already dismissed the cranky old maid they'd lent her, she'd get a stitch or two put into the waist. That would solve her problem.

Stupid girl! she thought. Nothing short of the truth would solve her problem! She grimaced at her reflection and turned back around.

Elise had bought this black satin dress, with a heart-shaped neckline, for the visual effect. Petticoats shimmered down the front, all in descending shades of gray. It would look perfect with Colin's star-shaped diamonds, but she'd sworn never to touch them again.

She cursed Mick again in her mind, before crossing to her reticule. It didn't take long to clasp the necklace. She didn't have the skill to weave the star strands through the one long braid that went down her back. It was a moot point. Colin probably wouldn't even notice.

"His Grace requests your presence in one of the antechambers. I'm to see you there."

Elise had bade the MacGowan man to enter when he knocked. They didn't exchange further words as she followed him. It wasn't his fault he'd been given the duty of escorting her. Elise counseled herself not to take out her temper on him. He was just relaying the message. He couldn't be faulted for Colin's behavior. She glared at his back, anyway.

After the third hall, she was glad she had the Mac-Gowan man to follow. She hadn't any estimate of the size of Castle Dunvargas, but it wasn't small. Colin's words while carrying her last evening made sense now. She'd given them a different meaning entirely, and actually blushed at the fantasy. She'd suspected his trouble had something to do with having her in his arms. She really was turning into a fool.

Her guard opened one door of many and waved her in. Elise listened for the sound of a key turning behind her, before she shook off the fancy. Colin wouldn't wish that scandal.

The duke wasn't awaiting her in the room, a stranger was. Elise was familiar enough with the MacGowan full dress to know a different clan immediately upon seeing one. Her eyes widened at the clash of colors he was presenting.

"Please forgive me, sir, I must be in the wrong room."

"You're the Sassenach."

His words were clipped with anger and said in such a thick brogue that Elise frowned as her mind replayed it for her.

"I beg your pardon?"

He spouted some of the Gaelic dialect and glared at her. Elise could sense waves of emotion emanating from him, and she took a step back toward the door.

"You've *na'* learning, have you?"

Elise narrowed her eyes before answering, and she put a touch of sarcasm to her words. "That depends on which subject you're referring to. For instance, you're demonstrating your lack of learning in manners, as we speak."

"I've na' need of lessons in that."

"Not unless you normally make gentle-bred ladies faint." Elise fanned herself briskly with her glove. The man was tall, but no more so than Colin. He was leaner, too. He was wearing what had once been a bright yellow tartan with an interwoven sett of blue and brown. His hair and eyebrows were an unattractive orange-red color. He was probably in luck when his beard grew in black, she decided.

"You feel faint, then?"

"I guess I'm not gentle-bred enough. What is this nonsense of a . . . what did you say? A Sassenach. What is that?"

"English. You're the damned Sassenach."

"Well, I may be English, but I'm not certain I'm damned, to boot. Even if I were, I'm not the only one, by any means. You don't get out much, do you?"

When he flushed, it was a purplish shade of red. His

eyes narrowed, and he strode across the room in less than ten steps. Despite her best intentions, Elise backed away another step toward the door.

"I dinna' need a lesson, Madame."

"Oh, I'd say you're in need of several. Starting with how to properly introduce oneself. My name is Elise MacGowan, the new Duchess of MacGowan. And you are?"

"You dinna' know what you've done."

"Aside from a bit of banter, you're right, I don't. I was looking for my husband. Since you are obviously not he, darn my luck anyway, I must be in the wrong chamber. I really hate to leave such charming company, but—"

"It'll be thanks to you the killing will go on."

He punctuated his words by aiming a forefinger at Elise's forehead. Her eyes crossed as she followed it.

"I'm afraid I don't know what you're talking about." Elise shook her head to uncross her eyes before pulling her head back to meet his glare again.

"A fancy piece. That's all you are." He spat the words.

"You know, I would've thought even Scottish dukes kept their guest lists free of lunatics, but there you go. What do I know? You, sir, are in dire need of more lessons than I care to teach. Good morn."

"Colin should have just bedded with you and left. It'd be what his brothers would have done. There never was a way of talking sense to that stone-head."

Elise narrowed her eyes again. She already knew what Evan was capable of. It sounded worse to hear it put to words, and to know that it was no secret. When she spoke again, it was with a brusque, cool, uninterested tone.

"You appear to know my husband. All well and good, then. He was supposed to be waiting for me. I really think I'd best find him. He'll be looking for me by now."

"Aye, I know him. Grew up with him. He was a thickheaded brat, then. Still is. Always was one for games of brawn and contest and *nae* sense. He's gone and proved it now."

"Oh, let me guess. This has something to do with me, no doubt?" she asked, in a sweet tone that dripped with sarcasm. It was lost on him.

"He should have had sense enough to uphold clan honor. That's what a real Scotsman would have done."

"Upholding clan honor? My Colin? You are mistaken, sir. He's an expert at that. This is the second time I've discussed my husband with others who are apparently clueless to his real nature. It seems to be a curse today. Now, if you'll excuse me? I really must go."

"You twist words like a woman."

"That's very observant of you. Would you like to try for two? I've been known to dress like one, too."

He leaned toward her, and his nostrils flared with each breath. Elise looked at him as though he held as much interest as a dust mote. She held her eyelids halfway closed and hoped he'd know contempt when he saw it.

"You've spirit, have na' you?"

He surprised her with his instant smile. Elise raised her eyebrows a fraction before she replied.

"Among other things, yes."

"When I first laid eyes on you, I thought a slight gust might knock you over. You're as colorless as a ghost, you know."

"Your compliments turn my head. That, they do. What do you do for an encore, pray tell?"

"It's a shame. That's what it is."

"What is such a shame? My coloring? My country? My marriage? Your existence? Be specific, if you please."

He tossed back his head to laugh. Elise watched the fringe hanging from him sway with the motion. She noticed the tassels on his socks were of a coordinating color scheme but in a smaller sett. With such an array of color, it was no wonder he thought her pale.

"Name's Torquil."

He bent at the waist and bowed in as courtly a fashion as any she'd seen in London. Elise didn't say a thing as he picked up her hand and brought it to his lips. She snatched it back.

"Torquil Brennen MacHugh Douglas MacKennah."

"All of that is your name?"

"Only son. My parents made up for lost opportunity."

"I see. Relation to Mary, I presume?"

"Little brother."

"My, my. That does explain your comments. Some of them, anyway. I really must be going now, Lord MacKennah. I'd stay and make small talk, but that pleasure has already palled on me."

"Call me Torquil. I give you free leave of it. I'm going to call you Elise. You can blame it on my lack of manners."

"I'd like to think there's no reason to call you anything. I'll not be entertaining much. If you're a close neighbor, I don't think I'll be entertaining at all."

"The MacKennah property marches next to the MacGowan."

"In that case, if I do entertain, I'll just have to scratch your name off of my guest list."

"I'll have to use my other middle names, then."

"Good heavens, you've more?"

"Only son, remember?"

Elise giggled. She couldn't help it.

"It really is a shame. I can't get over it." He was shaking his head as he said it.

"I take it we're talking about my marriage now?" she asked.

"That, and you're a Sassenach. I can na' blame Colin, though. If I'd seen you first, I might have been tempted to taste you myself, and clan honor be damned."

Elise sucked in a gasp. *Scotsmen!* she thought. "Allow me to dissuade you from continuing this conversation. I have a tidbit of information for you. I'm not very tasty, and I don't like Scotsmen."

"Nary a one?"

"No."

He raised his eyebrows. "Na' even your husband?"

"Oh, him." Elise frowned.

"I'm a mite tempted to put that to the test. Right now. Right here. You and me. A stolen kiss? What do say you?"

Elise gulped. "I thought I wasn't colorful enough for you."

"I've been amending my opinion."

He took a step closer. He was definitely as tall as Colin but about a third less in bulk. The instant thought calmed her. She narrowed her eyes up at him.

"Oh, please don't bother on my account."

"Why na'?"

"I'm pale, a woman, and horror of horrors, English to boot."

"That is a problem, to be sure."

"I'm already wed, too. The MacGowan. His property."

He sighed and backed up a step. "I'd as lief na' know of it, especially now that I've met you. I dinna' wish to take a liking to you. All I wished to do was warn you."

"Now, I'm certain that I don't want to stay a moment longer."

"It's not to be taken lightly, lass. The clans are up in arms."

"Over what?"

"You being a Sassenach and marrying a Highland laird. More specifically, *that* particular Highland laird."

Elise's heart might be the painful ball twinging at the pit of her belly. It also could have been the lump that moved to stick at the base of her throat, making swallowing difficult. She almost put her hand there.

"Explain, please." She choked over the words.

"I just did. You're a Sassenach."

"Yes, I already know that part."

"He was the chosen husband to my sister."

"I know that part, too."

"You knew he had a betrothed? Yet you still wed up with him?"

I wasn't given the choice! Elise almost said it aloud.

"You're Sassenach all right. All pompous arrogance and crazed with power, with heads full of their own importance and such, and sporting a lust for bloodletting. As long as it is na' theirs, that is."

"This is ridiculous. I'm in a castle, surrounded by gentlemen and ladies. I am not listening to this. I'm not."

"You like killing?"

"I've never harmed a thing in my life," Elise replied.

"Then why did you do it?"

"Do what?"

"Wed up with him! Stir the clans! Have you *nae* concept of it?"

"I believe I've had enough of your company. You may leave. Bother that, I will."

Elise moved as quickly as she could. She felt the dress sway a hairsbreadth of time behind her. His hand slammed against the wooden door at her temple, stopping her. She swiveled.

"You can't continue this, you know. I'll be missed. He'll miss me."

"You think I dinna' know that?"

"Then let me go. You don't have to face his wrath."

"Not until you understand."

Elise took a deep breath to calm herself. It almost worked. "The last I heard, Scotland and England weren't at war. Of course, I'm not one for politics, but there you have it. Colin and I met, fell in love, and then we wed. I don't think my being English bothers him. I try to pretend the same about him being a Scotsman."

"We may na' be at war, but a man would na' be a true Scot if he forgot Culloden."

"Culloden? I've heard that name. Who was that?"

His breath whooshed out with his disgust. "Not who. What. And where. It all started with the Stuarts. The throne belonged to Bonny Prince Charlie, it did. With all the clans rallied behind him, he was sure to gain it. Dinna' happen, though. Near everyone was wiped out. The Sassenach saw to it. Killed and maimed even the women and children. They nearly wiped out the clans, at Culloden. The MacKennahs have never recovered. The MacGowans did it the easy way."

"When was this?" Elise asked, her eyes wide.

"1746."

"What? More than a century ago? Oh, please. That's it, I'm leaving." She turned and pulled on the door handle. His hand was still holding it in place. Elise had no choice but to spin back around.

"Are you enjoying this?" she asked.

"We Scots never forget."

"Or forgive, obviously. All right, have your say. That's what you want. Very well, talk. But you'd better start making sense. What has any of this to do with me? I can understand anger over a broken betrothal, but now you're tossing in a battle that's decades old. I wasn't born. You weren't born. We can't change it. Why bring it up?"

"So you'll see the festering of it."

"Of what?"

"Hate."

Elise looked up at him. "Can the MacKennahs really hate me so much because I'm English?"

"It's na' just the MacKennahs you need worry about. The moment news of Colin's betrayal reached the clan, the feuding started up again. I can *nae* more stop my clan, than The MacGowan will be able to stop his."

"Feud? Am I hearing this right?"

He stepped back and looked a bit sheepish. "Well, it's mainly been an ewe, or two, gone a-missing, so far. Just enough to keep the borders busy. It's not as bad as before."

"Before what?"

"The jilting of Mary, of course. My clan's na' about to forget it. There's been bad blood since it first happened."

"First happened? Oh, of course, Ira. I keep forgetting that he was the original bridegroom."

"Ira? *Nae*, he was a wastrel. He wasn't fit for any woman's husband, least of all my Mary. She wanted Evan. Even when he petitioned the Clan MacGowan to wed that Sass—I mean, that English lass. Even then, Mary still wanted him."

"Evan MacGowan petitioned his clan . . . to marry an English girl? Excuse me, Torquil. I think I need to sit down now."

Elise ducked under his arm and forced her legs to continue supporting her until she reached a chair. Now that she knew what fainting felt like, she had to put her head down on her lap and breathe rapidly to stave it off. Evan had petitioned his clan to wed Evangeline? Every part of her seemed to hurt at the thought; then it decided to center in her head.

"You're looking a mite peaked there. Worse than before. Here, drink this up."

Torquil opened the round bag at his belt and twisted off the top of his flask. Elise tipped her head back and gulped. Then Torquil came to her rescue as the liquor burned her throat, but it had worked. She no longer had the fuzzy feeling about her nose and cheeks.

"Why dinna' you tell me you had na' the constitution for good Scot's whiskey?"

He asked it between blows to her back. Elise couldn't decide which was smarting more. Her head was pinging with needles of ache, her throat and chest were burned, and her back was suffering the bruising force of his blows.

"Stop! My thanks, I think. You can stop now. I'm fine, truly. I'm rather grateful I didn't have any brothers. Are all their ministrations so brutish?"

"You've got your color back, have na' you? It was just some good Scot's whiskey. I always carry a nip, or two, in my sporran."

"I'm grateful, truly. Finish your story, so I can get this little meeting over with. Ira MacGowan wasn't a fit husband, and then Evan MacGowan jilted Mary. Was that what started it?"

He walked over to look into the unlit fireplace.

"It actually goes back to Culloden."

"Surely there's been peace made since then?"

"There was a chance for the MacKennahs to recoup the losses from Culloden. The battle bankrupted my clan, as well as many others. Only the MacGowans came out ahead."

"Why did the MacGowans fare so well?"

"The MacGowan Laird was betrothed to a MacKennah. He violated it by wedding with a Douglas heiress, for her dowry. The feud hadn't even a good start when the duchess died of chilblains. Then, not a year later, he up and wed with a bloody Sassenach. Again, for her dowry. The MacKennah lass killed herself."

"She loved him that much?"

"Love? Are you daft? She could na' bear the humiliation."

"Well, that certainly educates me on where affairs of the heart stand with you Scots. Be still, my quivering heart."

"What?"

"I'm talking to myself, obviously. Go on. Finish your story. Let's get this over with."

"The MacKennah Clan swore revenge. Many's the clansman who has been rewarded by bringing a Mac-Gowan to justice!"

"I'm not certain I want to know how. Do you have to tell me?"

"We ransom each other all the time. Only trouble is, the MacKennahs can na' pay much. That's why we offered Mary's hand in the first place. It was a ransom payment from twenty years ago."

"You . . . ransom each other?"

Elise stumbled over the word. She was afraid her expression mirrored the shock she was feeling. She knew now why Colin had treated her as he had. They were all barbaric and uncouth and uncivilized. They'd only follow a leader who was the same.

"Aye, only sometimes it gets a bit out of hand, and well . . ." He stopped for a moment and took a draught from his flask. He wouldn't meet her eyes. "Whenever a clansman disappears, and there's *nae* ransom demand, we suspect the worst. The land's dotted with lochs, and they rarely tell a tale on a man."

"I'm not certain I wish to hear any more. You honestly expect me to believe the lochs hide—? I'm not listening to another moment of this conversation, Lord MacKennah. I'm going to wish you from my existence, forget I ever met you, and find my husband; then I'm going to dine elegantly on the Duke of Dunvargas's gold-bordered plate. I will not allow you to stop me. Do you understand what I'm saying?"

"Spoken like a true Sassenach."

"You'll allow me to leave?"

"Nae."

The pounding of her head was taking over her

existence. It should be obliterating everything, but it wasn't. "Why not?" she asked, tartly.

"Well, aside from wanting to warn you, I was thinking a bit of an abduction might go a long way toward gaining my clan's respect."

"Abduction? Now?" She was reeling in place, yet nothing about the room looked it.

"I've since changed my mind. You're more trouble than you'd be worth. You probably can na' even sit a horse, and you choke on good Scot's whiskey."

He winked at her. Elise closed her hands into fists and longed to beat the table with them. It was almost laughable. She'd been trying to escape, and the MacKennahs would have helped her do it. They were all set to kidnap her! If only she'd stayed in her room this morning and not listened to Mick, she'd be assisting them at it. Right at this very moment. Now. She put her hands to her temples to soothe the ache.

"Oh, where were you yesterday, Torquil?" she asked.

"Perth. Why?"

"My own purgatory," she whispered. Elise didn't feel the slightest bit like answering loudly enough for him to hear. The knot in her throat started to uncoil. She took small gasps of breath as she felt it. She knew why. Her decision was being made for her.

"How would you have done it?" she asked.

"It would na' have been hard. This is my country, too."

"You've a way around the MacGowan Honor Guard?"

"You're in here visiting with me, are na' you?"

"The man who brought me here wasn't one of them?"

"MacGowan plaid comes in handy at times."

"Dunvargas doesn't even know you're here, does he?"

"He's got a good cellar, full of stock. It has a nice, well-built tunnel directly to it, too."

She looked across at him. "You're incorrigible."

"Aye." He grinned.

"You'll need to plan it better than this."

"Verra well, I will."

"If I disappear before we arrive at Castle Gowan, it would go well with you and your clan. Perhaps even with the MacGowans. That's what you're telling me, isn't it?"

"I'd claim innocence, of course."

"Oh, of course," Elise repeated. "And, if Colin were granted an annulment, that would go well with the clans, too?"

"Annulment? On what grounds?"

"That's for a judge to decide, isn't it?"

"English courts dinna' cotton to Scottish troubles."

"Let's just say an annulment is granted. Would she have him? This isn't 1746 anymore, you know."

"Mary's had her eye on Colin MacGowan, too. She'd wed him."

"I can't believe I'm thinking like this. It's silly."

"You'll save a lot of grief, and mayhap some lives, too. That's why you're thinking this way."

"Do all Scottish men treat their women like stuffed dolls? They tell us this is what you're wearing, this is what you're thinking, this is what you'll say, and this is how you'll act."

"There's another way?"

He looked like he was serious. "Believe it or not, Torquil, if I agree to help you kidnap me, it will be because I have my own reasons."

"I respect that."

"I'd have to write two letters: one to my bank and one to Colin. Can you get them posted?"

"Your maid's name is Lydia. She's a MacKennah. Give them to her. She'll see to it."

"That certainly explains her attitude," Elise replied, without a tone.

"She's a good woman. She can get a message to you, too. Can you be ready by Inverness?"

"I didn't say I would do this, Torquil."

"You dinna' say you would na', either."

She lowered her hands to look across and up at him.

"And you dinna' scream, cry, or sound the alarm on me. All of which I would have expected."

The door opened, and the man who had brought her there stuck his head in. "They've noticed her missing, my lord."

"Verra good, I'll be out directly."

"One minute, maybe less." Torquil's man shut the door.

"I have to go now. I'm flirting with capture as we speak. You'll think on it?"

"More than I want to. And, Torquil?" He stopped at the door and waited. "I can sit a horse."

Chapter 22

"Here she is! We've found her, Your Grace."

Elise looked up and caught the looks Colin's men were giving her. They should have passed Torquil MacKennah in the hall. She composed her face to look innocent as several members of the Honor Guard assembled about the doorway.

"Elise? Thank the Lord."

Colin shoved through his men, and it was hard to believe the thankful words had come from his mouth, with the angry expression that was on it when he spoke again. "How the devil did you get here?"

He had to say it twice before she heard it. She was blaming it on her headache but knew the real cause the moment she saw him. Colin was in Highland evening wear, and the tight-fitting, black-velvet doublet, cascading lace jabot and cuffs, atop a kilt of red, green, and black plaid was making everything hum out of rhythm to the pulse in her head.

"What?" she asked.

"How the devil did you get here?"

"Oh." Elise stood but held on to the table for support. "I walked, of course."

"What are you doing here?"

"I'm waiting for you. I don't understand the dramatics, Your Grace. I did nothing other than what I was instructed to do."

"How did you get past my Honor Guard?"

"I didn't. I followed one of them here. He told me to wait for you."

Elise watched them mumbling amongst themselves. That much of her story was true. She heard snippets of their discourse. It was hard to keep the amusement at bay. She concentrated on her headache. It wasn't as severe as before. That was odd.

"The MacKennahs? Here? In the open?"

"They're a craven bunch of game-playing fools."

"That Torquil is the worst of them."

"Double the guards. I will na' have her abducted. I dinna' care how many went on with the bastard. Call on more." Colin turned back to her, and Elise pretended complete ignorance. She was having a difficult time meeting his eyes. She didn't wish to decide the reason.

"You're na' to be out alone. It's na' safe."

"I didn't harm anyone," she replied.

"I will na' have anything happen to you."

"But I tell you it was a MacGowan who came for me!" This scene wasn't calming her head, but she would never admit it.

"It was a shyster in MacGowan clothing."

"How am I supposed to know who to follow, then?" she asked.

He pulled himself to his full height and put his hands on his hips as he considered her. The cut of his coat was responsible for the deep funnel shape of his torso, she decided, eyeing it. Then he spoke again.

"You dinna' recognize the Honor Guard yet?"

"I've tried not to take note of any MacGowan about me, Your Grace. Any. It's enough that I recognize the sett, isn't it? Or do you wish me on more familiar terms with them?"

"*Nae* and *nae*. Dinna' this experience teach you anything?"

"What experience? I followed your man to this room, and then I got to patiently await your presence. I fail to see the harm."

"That was *nae* MacGowan, and I dinna' have time for this. We're late for the banquet as it is. I've enemies in Scotland, Elise. Why do you think the Honor Guard is necessary?"

"Protection from me, perhaps? How am I supposed to know? I'm just a Sassenach." She bit her bottom lip on the last word, but it wasn't soon enough. She could tell by the quick intake of breath.

"I'm na' arguing this a moment further. Come."

"I'm not arguing. You asked questions and I answered them. Would you rather I was silent?"

"I dinna' believe so. In fact, *nae*. I've been treated to it enough."

"You actually wish to converse with me now? Will you need your guard about, then, in the event I need to be silenced?"

"I already said I was na' arguing this. Come along."

"If I must have them about me, I guess I'll do my best to learn names and faces, then. Will you do the introductions on my shadows?"

"It will na' be necessary. You will na' need the Honor Guard. I've made another choice: I'll be your shadow."

"I . . . refuse." Her voice was as tight as the constricting band looping over her entire innards.

"Must everything be a fight with you? You can na' refuse. I'm your husband. You're my wife. You have to obey. Obey. Dinna' you remember that part of the ceremony, either?"

Elise tried another tack. She smiled seductively

before using a throaty tone. "Oh, please, this is all so unnecessary, Your Grace. I promise I won't leave my cell unless you or a member of your guard that I recognize comes for me. Won't that suffice?"

His face could have been made of granite for all the expression it had. Elise waited a moment longer before he answered her. "I've been lax. Tonight has educated me."

Her exasperation was showing in her next words. She couldn't prevent it before she was midway through. "To what, pray tell? I did exactly as I was bade, and now I'm threatened with your presence every waking moment. The punishment hardly fits, I would say."

He sighed and reached for her elbow to move her to his side. "I have enemies, Elise. I'm fairly certain I've already said that. I will na' repeat it again."

"Can't you just get me a dog, or something?" she asked.

"I will na' allow an abduction."

"Excuse me?" she asked.

"We can afford the ransom. They can na'. That's how we got in this predicament in the first place. I'll na' entertain this feud. It's gone on long enough, and I only sport if there's a fairness to it. If one side does na' play, the game is over. True?"

"Since I don't know what we're discussing, I can hardly answer that in an intelligent fashion. Ask me something I can reply to."

"Verra well. How do you know the term *Sassenach*?"

Elise's heart stopped for a moment, and then beat the blood fully into her cheeks. If she hadn't a headache already, she would have received one from that. She just hoped the flush wasn't as pronounced as it felt. "I have a maid with an uncertain temperament," she replied, hoping the warble of her voice wasn't as it sounded in her ear. "She's not fond of anything English and is not quiet with her sentiments."

"I'll replace her. Come along now. I've upset you over naught."

"Do I have a choice?"

"*Nae*, you dinna'. Now, obey like a good lass, before I have to come up with another punishment."

"*Obey?*" she repeated. She could learn to hate that word, too.

In a few minutes, she'd lost her composure more times then she could count, lost her new ally, Lydia, and gained the Laird of MacGowan at her side every moment. She was in luck that Torquil hadn't told her anything else about his plans.

"Must you do that?"

Colin looked over at her; he kept his gaze on her for several moments, before turning away and continuing his contortions as if she'd said nothing. Elise was forced to look back down at her book.

Dunvargas boasted a well-stocked library and an efficient staff. Elise hadn't any trouble picking out a few books that might not bore her too much. The large cotton nightgown and massive bed she was residing in were conducive to reading. She'd propped at least five pillows behind her, before setting the tome atop her knees. All of it was wasted. The book wasn't keeping her interest.

The banquet had gone well, earlier. If anyone reported to a newspaper, the article should be favorable. Elise had kept fairly quiet, allowing the wine to soothe her headache. She'd been placed between the duchess and a minor baron at her other side. She'd been aware of Colin the entire time, although he was more than forty place settings down at the other end, next to the Dunvargas, as was his place of honor.

She'd caught his eye on her more than once, too. He'd

probably been checking his property, she'd thought in disgust.

The sliver of his shadow caught her eye on the wall beside her, breaking her reverie. She glanced sidelong at him again. He was wearing his calf-length knickers and doing those strange exercises again. As slowly as he was moving, it shouldn't have brought a sheen of moisture to coat his chest, but it was there. Elise was angry at herself for noticing.

She looked back to the colorful drawings. She'd thought a picture book might keep her entertained. She should have known better. She shut it and put it on top of the others at her side. Then she folded her hands together on her knees and smirked at Colin.

"What are you doing, anyway?" she asked.

He stopped in a bent-knee position and looked down his arm at her. She caught her breath as he brought her into focus.

"It's called tai chi chuan."

Elise repeated it, then remarked, "That doesn't sound very Indian to me."

"It is na'. It's an ancient form of self-improvement from China."

"You've been in China, too?"

"My houseboy was. Amazing chap. Won me at hand to hand, easily. Became my instructor. Took seven years to get the basics."

He turned his head away, put his other arm out, and went back to ignoring her. She watched as he tipped his hand up and down gracefully.

"Seven years? Why would it take so long? The most intricate dance steps take less than a Season."

Colin sighed, then stood out of his crouch. He turned to her and lowered his head to pierce her with his gaze. Elise's eyes widened, and she couldn't look away from any part of his muscled, gleaming torso. She told herself it wasn't entirely her fault. He was breathing hard, and since he had nothing on his upper body, she had nowhere else to look.

"Why are you interrupting me?" he asked finally.

"I couldn't sleep."

"I thought you were reading. That was the reason behind persuading Dunvargas to show his library, was na' it? Or were you trying for another reaction from him?"

"Like what?"

"You're a beautiful woman with a black past and a hard heart. You're also a notorious flirt. Dunvargas is a lecherous old goat with an ugly wife. Do I need to go on?"

"You've a jaundiced viewpoint, Your Grace."

"That's hardly surprising, if you think on it. I'm wed to you, are na' I?" he answered.

"I'm sorry I interrupted you. You may return to your contortions. I went to the library because I wanted a good book, and for no other reason."

"Why are you bothering me, then?"

"I didn't pick interesting books, I guess, and I'm not tired."

"Are you as efficient at reading as you are at sewing? That could be the problem."

Elise lifted her chin. "I read fine. I simply haven't had to read with shadows continually falling across the pages. It makes it difficult to concentrate."

"Strange that you should bring up that word. It takes severe concentration in order to practice tai chi chuan. You broke into mine twice that I recall. I will na' be able to simply pick it back up."

"Do you want me to apologize?" she asked.

"*Nae*, I think I'd rather you entertain me."

Elise gasped, then spoke quickly to cover it up. "I beg your pardon?"

"Oh, you hear perfectly. Entertainment. Mine. I'm afraid I'm yours for what's left of the night, tomorrow during our visit to the sights of Glasgow, tomorrow night, and so on, and so forth."

"Is it too late to have a different MacGowan at my side? I wouldn't take your loss personally, I guarantee it."

"I'd na' let another man this near you. It would be stupid. I'm the Laird of the MacGowans. We're well-known. We're a political and financial stronghold in this country. One of my ancestors was a member of The Bruce's court. I've a reputation to uphold."

"If I haven't apologized yet for interrupting you at your outlandish self-improvement exercises, please allow me to do so now. I've changed my mind. I think I'm quite tired, too, after all." Elise rolled to the edge of the bed to turn down her lamp.

"And, despite this polite little conversation we're enjoying and your beautifully acted camaraderie with me earlier, I will na' let another man near you, because I'm still na' fond of claiming bastards."

She hooded her eyes and left the lamp be. She turned back to him and smiled falsely. "It's true what they say, isn't it?"

"Enlighten me," he replied.

"A Scotsman never forgets."

"You're a quick study, are na' you?"

"And you're a stubborn, self-righteous, judgmental fool."

"Glad to see I've risen in your esteem."

"I must have said it wrong. Let me rephrase it." Elise opened her mouth to do so, but he forestalled her with his next words and actions.

"Dinna' bother." Colin flopped onto the bottom of the bed. Several of her books fell off at the same time. Elise jumped. "I already know what, and how, you think me, and you know what I think of you. What I want to know is how do you feel about me?"

How did she feel about him? Elise's eyes widened.

She did her best to keep the reaction out of her voice. She feigned a yawn first. "I'm very tired all of a sudden, and this little talk is boring me. You'll not mind if I just close my eyes a bit and rest, will you?"

"I've gone over it hundreds of times in my mind, and I can na' figure it. What is it about you, Elise? There are a lot of women in the world. I've known lots of them. Some as breathtakingly beautiful as you, some of amazing intellect, and yet I find myself drawn to you. Why? Despite what a conniving bitch you've proved yourself to be, I close my eyes and I see you. I listen and I hear you. It's akin to a humming sound. I'm beginning to think that if I liked, I could concentrate and I'd be able to feel you. I studied mysticism because it fell into my life. It was Karma. I believe in the power of it. The problem is, you clearly dinna'. You dinna' believe in anything. So why is it you do this thing to me?"

Elise gulped. "I'm sorry. I quit listening after the conniving part. What was it you were saying?" She had to school herself to get through the entire sentences. Her breath had been stolen by his reference to the humming sound, and the gooseflesh running over her entire body was impossible to hide.

He sighed hugely and rolled over to look at the ceiling. Elise watched him.

"Sometimes in India, when the moon is just right, you can feel something. Call me fanciful, but there's a vitality and spirit to that place that can na' be ignored. It's in my veins now and forever will be. I can na' wash it out. It's like Scotland. There's a pulse beneath this soil that's impossible to ignore. It's like taking a huge breath and never letting it out. It's the smell of peat and damp, and it's the odor of wood fires and fresh bread and heather. It's the smell of all that is life—the joy and the pain. It's the throb of living. It's in the rain and the mist. It's even in the snow. It's the smell of renewal, the voice of heroism and bravery, the taste of adoration, and it's the feel of cold stone and warm blood! There's naught else on earth like it. You feel any of that?"

"Any of what?" she asked, between a heartbeat, and with such a carefully studied tone, she was absolutely amazed to hear it herself.

He tossed out his arms. One landed atop her ankle. Elise didn't dare move, in case he'd notice. Then he sighed again, heavier than before. She watched his chest rise and fall with it.

"Then there's the blackness. The indecision. The path that's chosen but not lighted along the way. I dinna' know why I'm talking to you. Oh yes, I do. It's late. And you're a goddess. That's right, I've got a goddess in my bed. She's sheathed in ice but formed with perfection, and she spews hate-filled words at me, instead of welcoming me with her lips, and her body, and her softness, and her warmth and moisture—"

He swore, sat up, and slid to the side of the bed. She couldn't make her eyes move from him as he stood with his back to her and adjusted the drawers about his waist. Then he went back to the spot in the center of the floor and began speaking in an emotionless tone.

"Tai chi chuan has been around for centuries. It can take decades to master it. I'm only a beginner. I dinna' have the luxury of studying full-time, although I would have liked to. I was supposed to be soldiering, remember?"

"Why learn it, then?" she asked.

"Because it was Karma. It fell into my life. Then again, my houseboy beat me, at everything. And he was a little snippet of a fellow na' much larger than yourself. He won me at every physical contest we tried. I dinna' have a choice. I wanted to know why. I wanted what he had. He made me start at the beginning. You've seen my meditation?"

"I'm not sure," she answered, when he stopped and waited.

"I practiced it in the carriage ride yesterday . . . or was it the day afore?"

"The day before," she answered.

"See? You do remember. I'm just a beginner at that, too. Mick found my teacher. He was a Holy Man. That's the highest caste you can be born into in India."

"Caste?"

"India has a caste system, rather like this English society with its peerages and lower classes. Only India's is more structured, more brutal. Who your parents are is who you are. If your father is one of the laborer caste, then so are you. Your friends will be laborers and your wife will be one. If you dare wed outside of your caste, then you *nae* longer exist to anyone. You become an Untouchable and are treated as if you're invisible."

"It sounds brutal."

"Worse than me, perhaps?"

Elise let his question stand for some moments. Then she picked up another of her books and practiced ignoring him. "This is all very fascinating, Your Grace. Perhaps you could start your tai chi chuan and allow me to resume reading."

He still wasn't facing her. Elise watched the muscles in his back and shoulders as he flexed his arms high above his head and started rotating them. Nothing in print could hold her interest from that. She didn't think he was going to answer her.

"You're a bit of an expert at changing the subject, I've noticed. It's an affectation I hope you outgrow."

The lamp's light tossed the man before her into relief on the far wall. The book lay forgotten in her lap as he angled himself sideways to the floor, and then supported his entire weight on one bent arm. Elise couldn't believe what she was seeing. She'd guessed at his strength, but actually witnessing it was stealing her breath and causing her acute emotional and physical distress.

There was no other word for the waves of reaction that flowed over her. Elise closed her eyes, and with each breath she tried to diffuse it. She could feel the beads of sweat gathering at her forehead and in the small of her back. Her breasts felt heavier, like they belonged to someone else, some wanton Elise who had nothing to do with the real one. *What is happening to me?* she cried silently.

There was no answer.

"Perhaps you should learn this, too." She opened her eyes slowly and wasn't surprised to see Colin standing upright, facing her again. He was beaded with moisture and glared at her with that greenish brown gaze of his. "Aside from being a system of self-defense, it's unequaled at relieving frustration."

"Frustration?" The word should have choked her.

"Aye, frustration. Surely you've experienced it at least once in your life."

"I'm not sure. Describe it," Elise said.

"Everything came too easy for you. That's the real issue, isna' it?"

"If you're describing the word, you're off the mark, Your Grace."

He lowered his head to look at her through his eyelashes. The same two furrows were in his brow at the movement. Elise had never seen anything to compare it with. Her pulse told her of it.

"Frustration is a human condition. Want. Need. Desire. Lack of fulfillment. Yearning and stifling of the same with no end in sight."

"Are you . . . frustrated, Your Grace?" Elise's voice caught midway through the question. She knew exactly what Colin had been talking about. She always had.

The humming was so loud, it blended with the heartbeats in her ears.

"Are you willing to accept me into your bed? Allow me your body, as your man, your mate, and your lover?" The words were flavored with his brogue. She could tell he knew the answer before she gave it.

If she'd not met Torquil? If Colin hadn't reacted like he had to Rory? If Elise didn't have one goal in mind, and one only?

"No." Elise's reply was more a groan, and she tore her gaze away.

"Then, yes, I'm damned frustrated."

Chapter 23

"What is this, please?"

Elise asked it as she stopped at the threshold of their tower room; her action was so abrupt, Colin ran into her from behind. She didn't wish to know what his arm felt like about her waist, but she found out as he wrapped it about her to stop their forward movement.

"What is what? It's our room. We left it but five hours ago." His voice wasn't amused.

"There's a hipbath." Elise pointed it out beside the fireplace.

"So it is. Come along. I can na' shut the door with you in it. It's against the principles of nature."

Elise frowned. He was making light of what wasn't. "I'm not bathing tonight," she said, in a tight, low tone.

"Of course, you are. You bathe everyday."

"How would you know?"

"Your water does na' appear and disappear by magic. I have to order it," he replied.

He had to move her out of the door's path. Her own feet weren't moving. Elise heard the resultant click of the latch. She gulped. "I can bathe in the morning."

"We leave for the station at first light. It's over two hours by carriage."

"I'm not bathing, and that's final."

"You are, and I'm na' arguing it. Turn around."

"You're not going to take the place of a lady's maid, either."

"Cease the woman-words. It will na' stay this." He was deftly undoing her hooks as he spoke.

"You're not to touch me. I won't allow it."

Colin made a sound like a snort and shoved the top of her dress down over her shoulders.

"You can unhand me. I'll not stand idly while you— you—"

"While I what?" he interrupted. "I already told you I'll na' take a woman by force. You fear for naught and waste good air on the argue. I'm giving assist be-cause I've seen when you lack it. You've a corset on? Bother that. You're small enough. This is extremely wasteful, and stupid besides. Some poor whale has lost his life so you could be pinched in two . . . and what? Be smaller than your dress? What seamstress designs fashion such as this?"

"I've lost weight," Elise replied.

"Then why wear the damned thing?"

"Because it's the proper thing to do."

He sighed in an exaggerated fashion. "Verra well, stay your woman-words while I unlace it."

Elise busied herself with pulling the cap sleeves over her hands and let the bodice drop onto the skirt over-lay. "Trust a Scot to call an argument woman-words. It isn't I standing in your chamber and assisting you with your disrobing against your wishes. Seems you'd have a better understanding of why if that were the case."

"Would you be a-caring to assist me? I'd na' say a word. I may even enjoy it."

Elise choked on her reply. Then everything stilled as his words sank in. "You're not bathing here."

"Yes, I am. The moment you've finished."

She couldn't answer. It didn't feel like her voice and

her breathing would be available to her at the same time.

"Does this mean my arrangement is finally satisfactory? Or have you run out of words?"

"This is impossible," Elise said from between her teeth.

"Only because you've made it so."

"What did I do?"

"What did you do? Associated with a MacKennah. Bedded with my brother. Birthed him a male bastard! Denied my husbandly rights! What have you na' done?"

"I know of no MacKennah," she finally stammered.

"Yes, you did. You just dinna' know it. Your maid? The dour one? She's the reason you slipped your guards yesterday. Dunvargas dinna' know of her leanings. He does now."

"You didn't see her dismissed, did you?" Elise asked.

"It's na' your concern."

"You can't do, and have, everything your way. I won't stand for it! Have her rehired immediately."

"What will I get in return?" he asked.

Elise caught her breath in surprise. She might as well have been outside, in the dead of winter, for the effect on her throat and chest. He wasn't finishing with the lacing on her corset while he waited, either. He was running a knuckle of his hand up her spine.

"You're abusing . . . my time, and—and . . . my good temper."

Elise didn't recognize her own voice stammering. It wasn't the effect she'd been trying for. She frowned at what he might infer. Then he sighed, feathering the feel of it over her bare shoulder, and went back to her laces.

"I dinna' have her dismissed, Elise. What do you take me for? I can only sack my own employees," he answered.

"Surely Dunvargas has maids that aren't associated with the MacKennah clan. Have one sent up."

"And have a hand starting up the feud again? I'll na' have it whispered of. The Honor Guard knows why that woman is na' attending you, but *nae* one else does. I gave out another excuse entirely."

"What glib one did you devise?" Elise asked; her voice sounded like her usual bored, uninterested self again. She eased the frown from her features. "This should be interesting."

"It is na'. I invented tales about love and having you all to myself. I added in that we're but newly wed and I'm unable to get my fill of your company. Bloody stupid of me, wasn't it?"

"I'd answer that, but you already did."

"Just think on it. I get to wait on you, when you could have been attended to by that dour maid, dressed modestly in your nightgown, and then sent off to sleep in a solitary bed, like a good little ice goddess. Instead of which, I get to receive the brunt of your arm's length personality. The papers were na' succinct enough."

"Perhaps you shouldn't have read them, then."

"In retrospect, I probably should na' have," he answered.

"You're not to watch me. I won't stand for it."

"I'm to do whatever I wish with you. Have na' you learned that much yet? You've *nae* reason to worry, though." He'd put up his finger as she spun to face him. That was stupid, considering the corset fell to the floor at her motion. Elise had to cross her arms about her chemise. The flimsy material was her own fault. She should have ordered them in the thickest cotton, instead of filmy lawn. He was frowning enough for both of them as he finished his words, "The inclination fits my own."

"This isn't a good idea."

"I've my fill of it, too. I've been denied so long, I've yet to decide which part of my anatomy aches the worst. Bloody hell! Forget I said that. Get into yon bath and allow me some dignity."

He spun from her and paced to the farthest wall. Elise didn't dare look to see what he was doing. She pulled the dress down and stepped out of it. She laid it carefully over a chair. It would be easier to pack that way.

She wasn't as careful with the petticoats. She pulled them off as quickly as possible and tossed them to the settee, where they shimmered like a storm cloud.

"Must you dawdle?" Colin snapped out.

Elise walked to the farthest side of the tub. The fire was blazing, yet she was shivering. "You . . . you'll need to turn aside."

"Like hell I will."

She lifted her chin. "Either turn, or I'll bathe in my underthings. You give me no choice."

He swore again, and she glanced over at him. His jaw was set, and he had his lips in such a thin line, they were nonexistent. "The count of ten. No more. Be modestly covered in that water by then."

Elise watched as he swiveled his entire body sideways to her and faced the windows. There were no drapes at either window, but it wasn't necessary. The walls were just shy of a yard thick. Elise knew it because she couldn't reach the glass, when she'd tried.

"Ten? I can't do it that quickly!"

"I'm already on two," he informed her.

Elise pulled down the pantaloons as rapidly as possible and shoved the chemise over her head.

"Why canna' I hear water splashing?"

"Give me a moment! I've never bathed under such conditions as these. You're making me quite upset."

"That exceeds expectations, since you've a very good idea of what you do to me, and keep doing. And then make up reasons to continue to do it. Time's up."

Elise ducked so quickly that water poured over the

side. She heard the sizzling it made as it emptied over the hearth and under the fire grate. The steam that rose dampened her hair and made it hard to breathe. It also effectively curtained her from Colin.

She didn't waste any more time.

Elise wasn't adept at washing her own hair because of the length. That meant it took longer than usual, but she couldn't be faulted for that. The steam had dissipated as she rinsed. Colin wasn't standing at the opposite wall anymore. He had turned one of the high-backed chairs about and straddled it to watch her. He wasn't but ten feet from her tub, too.

Elise should have done her bath the opposite method. She should have started with her torso and ended with her hair. It didn't help to chide herself, though. Colin's hooded, brown gaze wasn't moving.

"I still have to wash myself, Your Grace," she said as haughtily as possible.

"I'm na' stopping you."

"Oh yes, you are. And quite effectively, too. I'll not stand with you watching me."

"You've na' other choice that I can see."

"I'll just stay right here, then."

"You'd sit in that tub all night?" he asked, arching his brows.

"If need be."

"You're na' that good an actress, Elise, and I'm not partial to cold water. You'll finish, or I'll join you."

"What?" Her voice rose on the word, and he was right. She wasn't a good enough actress to hide it.

"Now's as good a time as any, I suppose."

Colin started unbuttoning his shirt, and Elise stifled the cry before she spoke again.

"Why . . . are you doing this?"

"I'm na' sure. Maybe I'm seeing how much I can stand, or I could be testing your denials. Either way, you're losing time."

He was shrugging his shoulders from his shirt, and it wasn't a gentle motion. He had a garment beneath his shirt, and when he was occupied with pulling it over his head, Elise stood. She couldn't face him. She watched the fire and soaped herself as rapidly as possible.

"Oh, Lord! Forget I said it. Forget—! Oh, hell."

Colin's words were garbled, and the chair slammed against the floor as he stood. Elise cursed herself for knowing that much. She hadn't had to look! She sank into the water and rinsed as rapidly as possible, upsetting more water onto the floor. It was his fault! He'd made her do it!

"Is . . . there a towel for me to use, Your Grace? Or are you going to make me dry myself in front of the fire while you watch that, too?"

"You scheming, little—! Yes! There's an almighty towel. It had better be large, too. Here." Colin had his side to her. One hand was over his eyes and the other held her towel out toward her.

Elise watched as the arm holding her towel trembled. Colin couldn't have disguised it. She pursed her lips in thought as she rose and stepped from the tub. She reached, then held the towel, but he didn't let it go. Elise stood beside him and watched the droplets dust the stone floor at their feet. Colin was watching them, too. She could tell by the shudder that shook him.

He hadn't gotten far in his own undressing. His chest was bare, but he still had full Highland wear below that. The hair on his chest glowed golden in the fire's light, and she couldn't tear her eyes away. She wasn't the least bit cold, either.

"What are you waiting for?" he asked in a savage tone.

"For you to unhand my towel. I can't dry without it."

His answer was Gaelic, but she had her towel. He'd released it with a raw gesture, and then left his hand outstretched, with the fingers spread apart. She would have thanked him, but instead held her tongue. She unfolded the covering, but her fingers fumbled more than they worked. She'd never been so close to anyone in her entire life, yet she knew so little of it. Colin's chest was turning red from the middle of it clear up his neck to his ears. Elise's eyes widened.

"Take the towel and go to the farthest wall from me. Do it now."

"But—"

"Do it!"

Elise backed away from him. It was colder the farther from him she moved, but the towel was helping; it was large, too.

"I will na' take a woman by force. As God is my witness, I'll na' do it. Not even if you are my wife in the eyes of all men's laws! Not even if you are a lying, unscrupulous, bed-hopping wench, with ice for a heart and thorns for a tongue. Not even if you are more woman than I can stand to watch. I'll na' take you by force. I swear it. Are you covered?"

"Yes." She had to say the word twice before it sounded.

Colin removed his hand from his eyes and raised both arms to the ceiling. Elise couldn't move her own eyes from the sight. The flush was receding from him the longer she watched. He had his breathing under control again, too. He lowered his head and found her.

"Dinna' watch me. I forbid it."

"What makes you think I was going to?"

"*Nae* flippant words this time. I forbid it. I'm finding out things about myself that I dinna' wish to entertain further. This torment is over, understand?"

"Bathe yourself, Your Grace. Trust me when I tell you, I'll put you completely from my mind the entire time."

"Turn around, then."

Elise did as he requested. Some past Duke of Dunvargas had smoothed plaster over this section of old stone, but it was uneven in places. She could tell where some of the old mortar had put the tower together. There were slight indentations in the plaster. She reached to trace one.

The splashing of water stiffened her back. Elise gasped, fought herself, lost, and then tipped her head to look.

He was standing with his back to her. He had a definite line separating where he was tanned from where he wasn't. He had strength evident in every line of him, and the hipbath wasn't deep enough to hide any of it. Then he turned sideways and raised one arm in order to soap himself.

Elise spun around and barely caught the cry. She pressed her forehead to the plaster and was thankful it was as cold to the touch as it was. Sweet heaven, but Colin was beautiful, and she had nothing to compare him with!

Sir Roald might have given her something to evaluate Colin against, had she asked it. It wouldn't have changed what she'd just seen. Colin MacGowan was careful with his body. He practiced forms of self-improvement, and only once had she known him to drink to excess.

"You can return to the fire. It's warmer."

Elise peeked before she turned about. Colin was sitting on the bed, attired in his red, green, and black plaid robe.

"Your hair will na' dry there. You have quite a lot of it, and it's all that silvery color, even when it's wet. Is that a family trait?"

"I have no family left with which to verify it." Elise spoke as she walked to the fire, keeping the towel about herself the entire time. It probably outlined her, but that couldn't be helped.

"You've a father, although I'm na' surprised you dinna' claim it."

"My father was dark, as was my mother. I didn't resemble either of them. My sister did, though."

"You've a sister?" he asked.

"I had one, once. She—she's dead. She died . . . last year." Now was the time to tell him, but she held back. If she did, there would be no escape for her, ever. There would be no abduction by the MacKennahs, no freedom, and from the exhibition she'd just watched, no possibility of an annulment, either.

Elise knew the shiver running through her was because of the last thought. Colin wasn't a man to be trifled with much longer. He'd been disturbing her since they'd met. The fistlike mass was back, wrapping around her heart and keeping it thudding with squeezing pressure. Elise knew what it was: her destiny. She suspected her loss of freedom would be worth it, just as Evangeline had once said. Elise opened her mouth to tell him, but he filled the space with words himself.

"I'm sorry, lass. Here, I had this made for you."

Colin was holding out a gray robe with rabbit fur about the edges.

"I'm not accepting anything from you," she whispered.

"What are you talking about? Acceptance has little to do with it. You're my property, and I'll not have you catch ill. My guess is, the towel's damp, and before long will be verra cold. Here, take it."

"But—"

"That towel does naught to cover you. Do you wish me to force you? I get tired of reminding you of your marriage vows."

Elise took the robe and turned from him. She'd find another time, and another way, to tell him. She still had tomorrow. "When do we reach Inverness?" she asked from over her shoulder.

"Why?"

She shrugged. "No reason."

"You wish small talk? After the teasing I just endured with yon bath? You've a wicked streak in you."

"I'm not interested in small talk with you." Elise tied the belt about her waist and let the towel drop. She heard Colin's intake of breath. The robe was made of a slick, silklike material and clung to each and every bit of her.

"What are you interested in, then?" he asked.

"Not what you are."

"And what would that be?"

"You've had women before. Figure it out."

"I'd rather hear it from your lips. Tell me you've na' interest in me. Tell me you find me unmanly and unattractive. Tell me why you won't welcome me as your lover, damn it!"

"You had me gagged and treated like a prisoner."

"I should have had you horsewhipped, except I'm na' that inhuman, and it would mar your lovely skin. You've such delicate-looking skin. Soft. Tender."

"Excuse me?" She was choking on the two words.

"You heard me."

"I'm not discussing this a moment longer. I'm more of a mind to find my bed for the night."

"Oh, your bed's right here, beneath me. I'll be here, too."

"This type of conversation is getting us nowhere."

"Only because you let it. You ken exactly what you do to a man. You practiced it. Perfected it. You're very good, too."

"I'll not sleep with you. Even with a bolster, I won't."

"We will na' be sleeping, Elise."

Her eyes went their widest, and she gripped the fur

lapel of her robe to her neck. "I—I won't allow it, Your Grace, and you never force a woman, remember?"

"Kiss me. We'll na' need force."

He stood from the bed. She would have backed away, except the chair he'd tipped over was in her way.

"Don't come a step closer,"

"Oh, please, stop that. Stay the teasing. I've no inclination for going where I'm na' wanted."

"You're not wanted. What are you doing?" The last of her question came out in a much higher pitch than she'd intended. She knew he'd heard it. It was in his voice when he spoke again.

"I'm stepping closer, and that robe was a splendid idea. It shows everything you're keeping from me."

"I've no idea what you're referring to," she said, and for once, it was true.

"Arousal. You're demonstrating the signs. I'm reading them."

She would have argued it, but he was too quick. Elise's cry made it into the caverns of his mouth, but no farther. It wouldn't have mattered. Colin's groan would have drowned it out, anyway.

Her palms were crushed against his gold-embroidered crest. From somewhere in her mind, she registered the absolute size of him, the difference, the hardness, and the heat. Her entire body was on fire with it. With one hand he'd pulled her against him. The embrace from the hand on her buttocks was colliding with the sensation of his groin pressed to hers and making her forget how to think.

"Oh, Elise . . . you're so much woman, and I'm *nae* saint. I'll na' wait another moment. Open for me."

Open? Open where? she wondered. He had the inside of her mouth enraptured, and she already had it wide open for air. "No . . . I can't. Colin—no. Please, no."

"Pretend I'm Evan."

Elise gasped as he nipped at the skin beneath her ear. Her mind wasn't functioning. "Evan?" she asked.

"Aye, Evan. Tall like me, but slender? You remember. He was na' one for exercise or work. You pretend and I'll fulfill it. Fair?"

His words were getting harsher, and she couldn't fathom why. He pushed the collar of her robe from her shoulder with his jaw. Then he was licking her skin. Then he blew on the skin he'd licked, making her use panting motions to pull in enough air.

"Beg me, Elise," he demanded.

"For . . . what?"

"For this." Now, he was sucking on her neck, pulling the skin into his mouth until she was certain she'd be bruised.

"And this." He gripped the sides of her hips and ran his hands up her body, pulling the material of her robe with him. He lifted his head.

"And let's na' forget this." He had both hands full of gray robe when he reached under her arms and lifted her above him.

Elise had her palms on his shoulders and her legs wrapped about the rest of him for balance. She could feel, smell, and sense everything. Taut strength rippled beneath every finger, clothed by skin resembling silk and satin, warmth and vibration, while each of his breaths was pushing the muscled knots of his abdomen against her inner thighs. Elise was scaring herself with the way she locked her ankles, mashing herself into him and sliding against him, to urge him onto more.

"Beg me for everything that Evan did to you." His eyes weren't brown or green. They were black with the size of the irises.

"Evan?" She whispered the name stupidly. "Why?"

"Dinna' he make you feel like this?"

"No, never."

"*Nae?* Never?"

His face settled into lines carved without a stone-mason's skill. Elise had to close her eyes to it. The chest beneath her was still heaving, and the hands holding her up were just as sure and strong, but something had changed. She didn't know enough about it to know what, either.

"What did I say?" she asked, looking back down at him.

He lowered his head. He didn't answer.

"What did I . . . do, then?"

Colin took the two steps to the bed and placed her on it, carefully averting his face the entire time. Elise pulled the robe down, nearly letting the cry make sound as it tangled about her hips.

"He meant so little to you, then?" he asked, in the coldest tone imaginable.

"No, it wasn't like that. Evan was—"

"If I gave you leave to say his name, I'm rescinding that, too! Lord! Why will I na' learn?" Colin pulled the sides of his robe together roughly. His motion to tie his belt had to hurt, as hard as he cinched it.

"Wait! It wasn't like that between us. I barely knew him. I didn't! He and—"

"Dinna' say one more God-damned, bloody word!"

Colin raised his hand, and Elise actually covered her face. She heard his intake of breath before he spoke again.

"You dinna' have to hide. Na' only would I never force a woman, I'll na' strike one, either."

"Will you have me gagged, instead?" she whispered through lips so numb she was surprised they functioned.

"If you shut up? *Nae*."

"I hate you, Colin, Your bloody Grace MacGowan."

"*Nae*, you dinna'. You dinna' have enough emotion in you for something so basic. Love's beyond you, too, no doubt. Go to sleep. I'll na' bother you again."

"You'll leave?" she asked.

"*Nae*, I've na' that much trust in you. I'm staying. I'll be right over here."

She watched him cross to the center of the floor and sit in that strange cross-legged position of his. The peace she'd sensed before wasn't anywhere in the room. Colin was too emotional; she could tell. He clasped his hands several times, over and over, sending ripples of movement across his chest until he was satisfied enough. He was ignoring her the entire time.

Chapter 24

"The carriage ride down went without incident, Your Grace. No sign of MacKennah. You traveled well?" Colin's servant Mick asked.

"I'm tired and sore. Her Grace is in a vile mood, too. Just see us into the car and me into my bed."

"I can answer for myself," Elise said coldly.

"There, you see." Colin gestured toward her.

Mick held the door open for them. Colin ignored all the social strictures and entered the car in front of her. Mick raised his eyebrows but said nothing about it. "Will you be wanting a light repast? If you were fed as little as we were at Dunvargas, you'll need it."

"I just need my sleep, and keep her from me."

Mick looked at where Colin was pointing. Elise lifted her shoulders.

"I thought he was my shadow, too," she supplied.

"When I need others to speak to my men, I'll advise you of it, Elise. I dinna' need food, Mick. I need sleep. I'm na' getting any with her near. Why the devil are we na' starting? I gave the order."

Mick couldn't hide his grin, and Elise looked to the floor. "We have to build steam, Your Grace. Perhaps you should spend your nights sleeping, instead of whatever you've been doing."

"Give my ears a rest, Mick."

"Yes, Your Grace. Oh, anything you say, Your Grace." Elise giggled.

"One word, Elise, and you'll spend the day in here with me. Understand?" Colin said.

"But I thought you wanted to sleep, Your Grace," Mick said.

Colin didn't answer. He simply glared at both of them.

"When will we be arriving at Inverness?" she asked in the silence that just seemed to grow.

"Why?" Colin snapped.

"I need to know how much time I have."

"For what?"

She shrugged but couldn't meet his eye. "Sleeping," she finally replied.

Colin and Mick exchanged glances. Elise watched them do it.

"Inverness won't be reached until just before dawn tomorrow. You've time for sleeping and eating and anything else you've in mind."

"Tomorrow morning? I'll not stay here with you that long."

"You'll stay as long as I say you'll stay." Colin was declaring it as he went into his room, and then he punctuated his words with a slam of the door behind him.

"His Grace is testy this morn. You've my condolences."

"I need a little sleep, too, Mick. I think I'll just find me a nice, comfortable spot. . . ." Elise let her sentence trail off as she spied an overstuffed sofa.

Colin's car was as far removed from the one she'd been in as could be imagined. Where she had plank walls, a plank floor, and but two windows, the Mac-Gowan car had black stuffed velvet lining the walls, rich furnishings, brass fittings everywhere you looked, and two sides devoted to large windows.

"Perhaps you could see the drapes pulled, Mick? It's too bright in here."

"You've na' mended things with him? What did you do with the information I gave you, then?"

"Nothing."

"That much is obvious. Why na'? He's an open wound, and I can na' heal it. He loves you, woman. Can na' you see that for yourself?"

"When I need a conscience, I'll alert you, Mick."

"Oh yes, Your Grace. Of course, Your Grace. Anything you say, Your Grace."

"Give my ears a rest, too."

He didn't answer. Elise pulled the tartan on the back of the sofa over herself and tried to stop her mind from thinking long enough to sleep. It shouldn't have been difficult. She'd not slept all night long. She'd spent the time watching Colin try his meditation, while she'd tried to stifle any emotion for him. She certainly didn't want to know now that Mick thought The Mac-Gowan loved her. She didn't want anything to do with the man. She'd spent the entire night convincing herself of it.

It hadn't worked then, and it still didn't.

She had to find a way to tell him the truth about Rory. She was going to post him a letter, but he'd dismissed her MacKennah maid, effectively trouncing that idea. Colin had to know about Evangeline and Evan, and Elise was running out of time to tell him. She had no idea what Torquil would be planning. She had no idea if she'd go when he came for her, either.

How was she supposed to know anything?

At first, all she'd needed to do was get near enough to Colin MacGowan to tell him of Rory. That plan had backfired. Then she'd needed to get to Castle Gowan. She was supposed to be making certain of Rory's reception with his clan. That much she'd promised Evangeline.

Now, she was so mixed up, she didn't know what she needed.

Colin had to know the whole truth, and not simply for Rory's sake. He had to know it so he'd know how wrong he was about his own wife. Maybe then she'd see that same look he'd given her at the altar at Crewe again. She just didn't know how to tell him, or when. Every time she was ready to shout it at him, he was shouting right back at her. And there wasn't going to be a time to tell him if Torquil abducted her. What had she been thinking? She'd been crazed to speak with Torquil. She'd been stupid with the toll of being a prisoner and treated like nothing more than a lying whore. That was the only excuse she could give for putting everything in such jeopardy.

Even if she wrote Colin a letter, what proof was that of anything? He deserved the truth, and every day she stalled was another she'd have to pay for. She'd been a fool. She'd been desperate. She'd been afraid. Sleep was a long time coming, and there wasn't one thing stopping her thoughts. Elise finally admitted it to herself.

She knew why she'd spoken to Torquil. She was a coward. She'd been afraid of what would happen the moment she told Colin, and she was terrified of what it would feel like . . . what it already felt like. She had every reason to be, she assured herself. She didn't think she could go through another night like last night. Although he'd been pretending to ignore her the entire time, she'd known it for the lie it was. The peace she'd sensed in the carriage ride hadn't been there, only anger . . . at her.

Elise didn't think she'd shut her eyes, and yet the train stopped so abruptly, she rolled from her sofa and landed on the thick carpet.

"I've *nae* idea what's happened, Your Grace. Are you hurt?" Mick helped Elise from the floor. She smiled her gratitude.

"Find the blasted conductor and have him lynched!" Colin must have had the same awakening she had. He pitched the door open as he spoke. He didn't look like he'd slept a bit. He looked more tired than before, if that was possible.

"I'm certain he wouldn't have stopped if he didn't have to," Elise said politely.

"Speak when spoken to, Elise."

"I'm tired of being treated this way. You can't expect me to continue this charade if you treat me like the lowest lackey."

"You'd be surprised at how I could treat you."

Colin was breathing heavily, and Elise returned his glare. If the scale of indecision in her mind had been weighing in to stay with him and refuse Torquil's abduction, he was rapidly changing her mind. She hoped it was conveyed in the look she gave him.

Mick looked from one to the other and rolled his eyes. "I'll go have a look-see at what happened, Your Graces. Try na' to harm each other afore I return."

He opened the door and stepped out. The door latching was loud in the stillness he left behind. Colin sighed and walked to his liquor cabinet.

"This is your fault, Elise. I'm na' usually of such mean temperament that my men flee me."

"Now, your mood is my fault? I'll not take responsibility for it. You've a strange train of thought to connect me. I did nothing."

"Yes, it's your bloody fault! You tease and tempt me sorely with each and every breath you take. Your wardrobe is fashioned to have such an effect, too. Just look at yourself."

"What? I'm wearing correct attire, and every button's done up."

"That may be true, but it's been slept in, and your hair's come undone, and you've the look of a wanton about you every moment of every day, and most of the evening ones, too."

"I can't believe I'm hearing this. Let me rephrase that. I can't believe you expect me to listen to it. I refuse!" Elise put her hands to her ears for effect.

"You put me into such a riot of frustration, I can na' think straight, and then you act as innocent as a maid," he said.

"If this is your idea of loving me, you're not very convincing at it."

"Who the hell said I loved you? I'll give the stupid bloke his walking papers!"

"No one told me so! Call it maidenly fancy, you overgrown buffoon!" Elise was yelling it back at him at the same volume.

"Maidenly fancies belong to maidens, not to courtesans."

"And blind judgments like that belong to ignorant boors!"

"You've lowered yourself to name-calling, now?"

"I'm giving as good as I get for a change. Perhaps when you preen in your chamber mirror next time, you should actually look at what you're seeing."

"Of all the—!"

The door opened, and Mick stuck his head in. "There's a blockage on the tracks, Your Graces. Oh, pardon me. Did I come at an importune moment?"

Colin's chest was heaving and his face was bright red. Elise didn't know what she looked like. She spun to the wall, so Mick wouldn't see.

"It will na' take long to clear it, Your Grace. Just you sit tight. I'll bring word the moment we have it."

"I'd rather help. The air's fresher out there."

The way it sounded, Colin's words were spoken through gritted teeth. Elise turned her head to him.

"Prisons have been known to feel that way," she said snidely.

"You're *nae* prisoner, Elise."

"Oh, please. When you to lie to me, at least make it convincing."

"I've na' lied to you . . . unlike your usual men."

"Can't you leave any quicker than this?" Elise's eyes were swimming with embarrassed tears.

"Can you na' see you're being protected?"

"Oh, I'm certain I needed protecting at Crewe, Your Grace. I'm just surprised you didn't notice that it was from you."

He lifted his head up and breathed in deeply, before his long sigh. Mick was looking amused at the door, and then she saw them. From behind Mick, there were yellow tartans coming from around every tree. Elise put her hand on her heart.

"Mick!"

Her cry alerted him, but it was too late. Elise watched in fascinated shock as Mick was hit from behind and slumped forward, his upper torso blocking the doorway.

"MacKennah." Colin's quiet, calm voice from beside her made her glance fly to him, and then to the door. "You're early."

"Your Grace."

Elise's eyes widened as Torquil stepped over Mick and entered the car to bow mockingly at first Colin, and then her. Several more clansmen climbed in after him. Colin hadn't moved. He was standing beside his liquor cabinet, swirling a brandy snifter.

"I dinna' expect you until Inverness," Colin continued.

"Plans change."

"You didn't expect him until . . . what?" Elise asked.

"Inverness. You're very easy to read, my dear; consequently, you make a lousy accomplice, among other things."

"But—I changed my mind. I'm not . . . going anywhere." Elise stammered the words in confusion.

"Oh yes, you are. Unless I miss my guess, The MacKennah is abducting you. He'll expect a hefty ransom, and I'll have to pay it. Then I'll call on my clan, and we'll see what we'll see. Dinna' harm her too much, MacKennah."

Torquil nodded. "Are you ready then, Elise?"

He reached a hand for her, and she looked from it to Colin. His mouth was set, but he looked more uninterested than anything else.

"I already told you two gentlemen, I've changed my mind," she said. Then she sat on a chair to prove her point.

"How much is too much harm, Your Grace?"

Elise's eyes widened as Torquil's words sunk into her mind. "I am not listening to this! This is 1876, not 1746. I am not listening to my husband and my neighbor chat about the niceties of kidnapping and ransoming. I'm not."

Colin's lips lifted into a half-smile, then he looked back to Torquil. "Tie the gag with a slipknot," he said quietly.

Elise opened her mouth to suck in air, and that just made it easier for them. The cotton material stuck to her tongue, and they didn't give her any time to spit it out. She reached to stop them from tying the band about her head, and his men simply tied her arms, too. Elise was screaming, but the only sound heard was whimpering.

"Have a care with my property, MacKennah. I'll repay every indignity threefold. I give you my word."

Colin's threat was the last thing she heard before a burlap bag was shoved over her, muffling every sound. Elise was too terrified to struggle. With her hands tied behind her back and a gag about her head, it would have been stupid, anyway. At least, her legs were free.

She knew she was being carried on a large shoulder. She knew when he tossed her across a horse, for the saddle horn bit into her side, and she knew when her captor mounted beside her. She knew it would be Torquil, too.

She was going to make him pay more than threefold.

The blood pounded into her head with each lope of the horse. Her legs swung into it in rhythm, too. The hand at the small of her back, holding her in place, was the most hated object she'd ever felt.

She couldn't believe she'd agreed to this! The moment Torquil released her, she was going to tell him his mistake. She'd been fully prepared to give him a very large portion of her entire fortune from Monte Carlo for helping her gain her freedom. Now, she wasn't handing over one bent shilling.

She'd make certain he regretted this. Abduction was one thing; commonsense treatment of a prisoner was another. If this was the Scot's version of capture, Elise would have to amend her viewpoint of Colin's. She tried to think, but with her head upside down, it was difficult.

Surely they wouldn't ride through the night. She wasn't sure she could withstand it. She couldn't tell what time it was anymore, or how long she'd been pinioned between Torquil's saddle and the horse's neck. Horses had trouble carrying double, didn't they? She wished she'd paid more attention to her lessons. No horse could run all night while carrying two, could it? The gag was getting soaked with spittle, and Elise concentrated on that. It gave her something to do while she planned her revenge.

Before he called a halt, she'd given up thinking of vengeance. She was only thinking to survive the pain of each thud in her temples until the next came. She no longer cared if the gag was wet. She couldn't stop the tears from dripping down into her hair and her nose from running, anyway. Now, she had some misery to compare with Colin's treatment. It wasn't a very pleasant thought.

The horse halted, and Elise was dragged from its back. She fully expected to feel the ground as she fell, but Torquil had as much strength as he looked to have. He swung her back over his shoulder and started walking. She knew he laughed about her, too, especially when he patted her buttocks familiarly.

If Elise hadn't prayed before, she started then. This was all her fault. Why hadn't she believed Colin when he'd said it was for her protection? If only she had it to do over again, how much different things would have been. She'd have told him everything the first chance she had, and she would have stayed at his side every moment since.

She was set down carefully. Elise recognized the restraint behind it. The hands about her were kind as the bag was pulled up and over her head, making certain none of her clothing was displaced as they did so. It was Torquil, and it was morning. The mists all about them were hued with a vague, green-tinted light. It was also raining.

"If you'll na' scream, I'll release you. Nod for aye."

She nodded.

The tie at her wrists was cut, and Elise cried out at the pain throughout her upper arms. She couldn't even feel her hands.

"Rub them together. Won't take long."

She started rubbing her hands together, although

it had taken two tries to connect them. The gag was undone, and she tipped her head forward to spit it out. Her hands were alive with spikes of pain. She gritted her teeth and almost wished for the gag back as the moans escaped her lips.

"I had *nae* other choice, Elise. I dinna' know what your husband had planned, or if you'd give us trouble. I hope you'll forgive me."

Torquil went on one knee in front of her as he spoke. Elise turned her head away. She couldn't reply. She was afraid the first words would be screams.

"Are you hungry?"

She shook her head.

"We've stopped for a bit of rest. We'll na' stay long. Your husband is a bright man, and we're na' safe here. We've two more days afore we reach MacKennah land. Stay here."

What a stupid statement from an equally stupid man! Where was she going to go? There were yellow-clad men all about her. She didn't know the country, her hands were barely starting to feel like they still belonged to her, her lower legs felt too weak to stand on, and she had only herself to blame. The last part was the worst. She bent her head and watched the drizzle falling from the ends of her hair to make a small puddle on her skirt.

She was in luck that she'd dressed in a heavy twill skirt and a broadcloth blouse. It was durable enough for her experience. It was quite plain and serviceable, too. She couldn't have chosen better if she'd known . . . and Colin had called it wanton!

Fresh tears filled her eyes, and she lifted her head to let the rain wash them away.

Chapter 25

They gave her a horse. There wasn't any way to sit sidesaddle. Elise realized that almost immediately. She hitched up her skirts, ignored the amount of leg she was showing, and picked up the reins. She was afraid of the alternative.

The rain continued throughout the day and she kept her head bowed to it. That way, the moisture drained onto the horse, and from there to the ground. She was directly behind Torquil, but he wasn't leading; some other yellow-tartan-dressed fool was ahead. She didn't want to know any of their names. When the time came for her release back into Colin's care, she didn't wish any more to come of it. Colin had been right about that, too. If one side didn't play, the game had to die.

They didn't stop when they passed Inverness. If Elise hadn't been such a ball of self-pity, she'd have looked about her and noticed when it happened, instead of having it pointed out to her.

She suspected they were simply making certain of their position, but it felt like an additional insult as far as she was concerned. Elise watched the spires of church buildings and the towers of what was probably

the university through the tops of trees below them. She
turned her head away. She'd only pine the lost opportunity if she let herself dwell on it.

She wasn't going to waste any more time crying. She
was going to need every bit of her strength. The
weight of her saturated skirt was giving her every indication of it. Hadn't Colin already warned her of the
dangers of Scotland's damp, and its chill?

There was a bite to the air that raised gooseflesh up
and down her back whenever they passed beneath the
shade of a tree. She wondered how much colder it
would get when night fell. She'd have to request a
tartan from Torquil if it was more than she could stand.

She should have eaten when he offered it, too. Part
of her chill was due to hunger. She only hoped it
wouldn't develop into an illness. She was going to
need her health. She was tired of being her own worst
enemy. She sighed and dropped her head.

They didn't halt until the sun set. Elise knew very
well how cold it was going to get now. The reins were
hard to hold, and her teeth chattered. When Torquil
came for her, she swallowed and told him of it.

"I'll need . . . a tartan, Torquil. It—it's cold."

"A MacGowan in MacKennah sett? A fine thing
that would be, to be sure. Here, I've MacGowan plaid
for you. 'Tis more fitting."

He tossed her a large blanket thing. Elise didn't
know how to wear it, and she ignored their amusement at her efforts to wrap it about herself. She
didn't care. The tartan was as sturdy and thick as it
looked. She was still wet, but it was warmer.

"Will you be eating sup?" he asked, when she'd
finished.

She nodded.

They'd killed a large deer, and then they roasted it,

despite the continual rain. She satisfied her curiosity at how, when Torquil went for her meal. They'd built a small, high-roofed affair of branches directly over the meat and fire. Elise watched them without saying anything. They were in great spirits. She supposed it was due to her capture. Torquil had been right: Abducting the MacGowan Duchess right from beneath the duke's nose was raising him in their esteem.

Of course, they didn't know she'd been in on the plot. Nor did they know that the duke had known. She hadn't planned on accompanying them to their stronghold, either. That hadn't been in the equation. Nor was anyone to be hurt, Mick included. Men shouldn't have control of everything. Look at how things turn out.

She wondered how much Colin would have to pay for her, and how much it would cost her to reimburse him. She was going to reimburse him, too. She was not going to have a debt of that sort over her! No man was going to be able to say he'd bought and paid for her! That would be the height of indignity. She leaned against a fallen log and latched her fingers together.

"Here, eat up."

Torquil held out more meat than she'd seen eaten at a dinner for four. Her slab of venison was hanging from a stick, and Elise's eyebrows lifted. None of her former society friends would have believed it. If she weren't watching the others eating, she would have had the same problem. She'd thought them barbaric before? There were no words for what she thought now.

She reached for her portion with both hands and started shoving it into her mouth. Elise couldn't believe she'd eaten the entire thing, when Torquil returned to her. She actually licked her fingers and debated asking for more as he stood there, watching her.

"You're raising my esteem of the dreaded Sassenach, woman. Do you ken that?"

"I don't wish you thinking of me at all," she replied.

"Fair enough. I've plans. Have you any?"

"On what?" she asked.

"What to do once the ransom's paid?"

"Don't you understand English? I don't wish you thinking of me."

"I'm na'. I'm thinking of the gold. I believe I'll refurbish the west wing. It's na' more than rubble at present. I already ken how much I'll ask. Do you want to know?"

"No."

"Too bad. You're na' uncomfortable?"

Only a heathen in yellow plaid from a godforsaken country would ask such an idiotic question. Elise bent her head to keep the disdain from showing in her eyes and hoped he'd leave.

"Get some sleep. The trail gets worse tomorrow. Pleasant dreams, Elise."

The devil's own nightmare to you, she answered him in her mind. Then she turned her back on him, pulled her knees to her chin to rest her head on, covered the whole with the woolen blanket over her head to sluice the rain, and tried to find a comfortable enough spot to support her against the log.

It was a muted thud waking her. Then vibrations of it were tingling all along the hollow log, into her side, and up her back, before finishing at the base of her neck. Elise raised her head from her knees, parting the fold of plaid over her face, and opened her eyes.

It was a MacKennah that had slammed against her log. Elise blinked as she looked at him. Actually, it was a MacKennah in an unnatural, folded contortion, completely bent at the waist. *That's strange,* she

thought. He couldn't possibly sleep like that. He'd be
a mass of sore muscles when he awakened.

There was another slight sound, like a breath of
wind through the leaves, and Elise's eyes widened as
she watched the MacKennah body that was the cause.
She gulped and turned her head.

There was still a steady drizzle of rain, which muted
everything. There were fingers of mist threading
throughout the trees about them and making a thinly
veiled whiteness coat the air. Then there was a shadow
slipping across the dying embers of their cookfire, slic-
ing the only available light with the movement. Elise
blinked. The shadow shifted again; the complete
blackness of it was the only indication of where it was.
Then it was gone, swallowed by the ground.

Another MacKennah made a soft sigh of sound, resembling a groan, and spun backward before falling
into his own contorted heap. The shadow was there
again, showing the reason for the MacKennah's propul-
sion. Elise sharpened her eyes, bringing what she
could see into perfect focus, and then she was wishing
she hadn't.

The shadow moved again, thickening for a moment
into a mass of depth, size, and volume. Then it solid-
ified into a demon. Then it was gone again. One of
Elise's hands went to her throat to hold the screams
in, whereas the other clutched at her plaid to mold
it about her skull and tighten the opening about her
nose. She didn't move as another MacKennah landed
at the other end of the log, transferring the same
tremor to her limbs as before.

It was a nightmare. It had to be. Elise watched the
force of nature that was contained in the one mass of
blackness and couldn't move. Silently, relentlessly,
and with a precision that defied the evidence of her
own eyes, Elise watched the black mass rotate, swoop,
and leap about, each move seeming to result in a

MacKennah collapse. Then there wasn't anyone left in the clearing, save her. The absolute silence was bad, and it was made worse by the way her heart constricted, filling her ears with its pounding and her own gut-choking fear.

The shadow had disappeared again. Elise's eyes flitted about the clearing, her breathing got hoarser and louder and faster, and her heart's thumping intensified, until she couldn't hear a thing over her own body's responses. Then the mist stirred; the demon at the midst of it rose from the ground to stand, etched by the dim light. Then it was moving toward her, floating through fingers of opacity, and when it got to her, it was opening the blackness enshrouding it and reaching down for her. The screams turned into a choking ball of burning pain right at the base of her throat, and the hand she still had there wasn't doing a thing to alleviate any of it.

"Oh, good. They gift wrapped you."

Elise heard the whisper, and even recognized it, as the ball of shape she'd been in was lifted and held against a very brawny, heaving chest that couldn't possibly be Colin MacGowan.

Colin MacGowan? she wondered.

In the nightmarish sequence of events, she'd never allowed that idea entry.

"Hush! We've almost a league to make afore they wake."

He was hushing her for no reason. Elise wasn't going to give any trouble, such as making any sort of noise. She had yet to force her own throat to swallow. She sucked in on her lower lip and relaxed her fingers from the grip they were still in on the plaid and on her own skin. He started running.

Elise was being held closely against mounds of hardness she recognized, which were thinly covered with a cotton shirt of some kind that was soaked with sweat and rain. The sound of heartbeats and a steady cadence of breathing got stronger and deeper the longer he ran with her. She put her nose squarely in the center of his chest, supported her forehead on the mounds of chest muscle he had, and stayed there. She had never experienced anything as wonderful.

The sensation strengthened, mutating into something different, something warmer and stronger, thicker and heavier. Elise could feel it, sense it, and taste it. She flicked out her tongue and touched it onto flesh that sparked the moment she did. Elise yanked her tongue back and enjoyed the tingling reaction that was still happening in her mouth.

"Colin?" She lifted her chin, rubbing her cheek along him.

A low growl answered her, and then a curse, and then a resultant slowing of his pace.

"I mean . . . Your Grace?" She tried again.

"Hush!"

"But, I have to tell you—"

"*Nae* time!"

He shifted her, removing her from the warmth and safety of a place against his heart, to drape her across his shoulders, securing her arms and legs with one arm. Then he started again, at a pace equal to, if not faster than, he'd already been running.

A branch hit her head, and then another, and another, in a never-ending sequence of annoyance. Elise lowered her head to hang it over his shoulder and promised herself to endure without a hint of protest. She even surprised herself by sleeping.

He was walking when she woke. Dawn was graying the skies and putting shape and substance to all the scattered boulders and thigh-high grass he was walking through. It took Elise a few moments to recollect where she was, and longer to recall why she was there. Colin's shoulders. She was across Colin's shoulders, and that meant he'd been hefting her all night. He was still breathing in a steady cadence of sound, but it was heavier, if the movement of his shoulders against her tender ribs was any indication.

"Col—I mean, Your Grace?" she whispered.

He cocked his head.

"Thank you."

"Gift me with such when we're safe."

"We're not safe?"

"*Nae.*"

He broke into a trot. Elise seized the intake of breath at the pain. She watched the sodden grass flatten and stay flattened as he went through it, making a trail that was easy to follow with the eye.

"Your Grace?"

"Hush!" he answered.

"But you're making a trail."

He chuckled. That hurt her ribs worse. She swallowed on the cry to still it but had to clench her teeth together to do so. Then she saw the reason for his amusement, as a herd of sheep entered the meadow, filling the grass with dots of white and easily erasing any sign of passage.

Elise felt like a fool. There was nothing about Scotland that was familiar, or easy to negotiate, or in her realm of experience. She was no ice goddess. Shivers heralded the tears, and she swallowed over and over again to stop them. When that didn't work, she had to accept the obvious. She wasn't just a fool, she was a self-pitying fool. The only thing left to her was to keep the knowledge from him.

She lowered her head back against the black material cloaking him and let it absorb the moisture.

At the other end of the meadow, he slowed and had to dodge hardier looking trees and denser foliage

before they were hidden again. It was darker, too. The
air was moist with the smell of damp and decay, and
the feel of life that he'd tried to describe to her what
felt like a year ago.

"We have a moment, Elise."

"A . . . moment?" she managed to ask, without alert-
ing him to the clogged nose and face full of tears.

"To relieve ourselves. Hasten to yon bushes."

He put her on her feet and released her arms. Elise
kept her face averted while she tried to find feeling
enough in her feet. Colin hadn't waited. He wasn't anywhere in sight.

Elise put her hands to her eyes, tried to stop the sobs,
and knew she wasn't successful as the last of it sounded.
It was better in the bushes. He wouldn't know of her
loss of control if she went and hid there. Branches
reached out and grabbed at her skirt, tugged at her
tartan, and scraped her cheeks. Elise ignored it all
and went in deeper.

She couldn't believe the path of her life. She who
had made it a standard to never go without a bath, followed by a rubdown with scented creams, was wearing the same wrinkled, sodden, and smelly attire
over a period of two days, and hadn't had a bath, a
decent meal, or even dining silver with which to eat
it. And she had no complaint to voice. Elise lifted her
skirts. Her petticoat was still damp, but it worked
well as a handkerchief. She mopped the ravages from
her face with it.

"Lass!"

He was too loud. Elise moved through the shrub-
bery, back to where he was standing, and pasted a
calm, composed look to her face before she got
there.

She didn't know what she expected, but the hooded
black robe shrouding him and his soot-covered face
wasn't it. She watched as he unfastened a tie at each

wrist, rolled each sleeve, and ended with fastening the ball of material by threading the tie through two loops at each shoulder and pulling on it to keep it there. Elise stepped from the bushes and dropped her glance. She couldn't meet his eyes. The carpet of mosses at his feet looked safer and less condemning.

"That really was you last night?" she asked.

"Aye."

"But how? Why?"

"Kung fu. I told you my houseboy won me. Every time. I had to learn it. I'm na' a master yet, as last night showed me."

"You were . . . nightmarish." Elise glanced toward him.

He was grinning, and from his blackened face, it was garish.

"I've never put it to the test with as much at stake, nor done as well. Come along. Enough talk. Climb up."

He went to a knee.

"Can't I walk?" she asked.

"I've mounts hidden. Near Dugan's Tower. We'll not make it by midday if we walk. Come here."

"I'll run, then." At his look, her chin lifted. "I can run, you know."

"We're na' far enough. The MacKennahs will be waking with sore heads and sorer limbs, but that won't stop them from tracking us."

"They don't know it was you."

"True, but a dram of whiskey or two, and they will na' care. You're too rich a prize. Now, climb up. Time's a-wasting."

"I'm too heavy," Elise countered. She didn't want to be anywhere near that chest and those shoulders. Not now. Not until she told him.

His lips twisted, to hide the amusement. "You're little more than six stone. Maybe seven."

"How much is a stone?" Elise asked.

"Fourteen English pounds."

She considered it. She should feel heavier than that. The secret was weighty, almost hampering her own intake of air.

"You said you were sorry earlier. Truth?"

She nodded.

"Then prove it. Come here. I'll carry you. We'll make better time."

"You'll trip."

She deserved the look he gave her.

"Dinna' make me come and force it. We'll be there in time for a nice hot sup, and a long soak, and whatever else you've in mind."

"I have to tell you something first."

"Tell me later."

"I promised myself that I'd say something. When I was ransomed, I'd tell you—"

"Say it when you're ransomed, then," he interrupted her.

"You always do that to me! I have something to tell you. It's not going to remain unsaid a moment longer. Surely we can take a moment or two for the telling. Right here. Right now."

"Very well."

He stood, crossed his arms, which tended to make the forearms bulge out from the unyielding mass of his stomach, and then waited. There wasn't a drop of moisture in her mouth.

"Well? Speak up. The sun will be up soon, making it easier to do a lot in, including track us."

Elise inhaled. The smell of the color green assimilated through her. Fresh. New.

"Is this some new ploy?"

"I'm not Rory's mother," she blurted out, stopping to suck in more air. "My sister, Evangeline, was. Evan was not my lover. He never was."

Everything about Colin MacGowan stiffened, clear
to the lines etched in the black of his face.

"You mean, you did this to me . . . on purpose?" he
asked, his voice sounding like it warbled for a moment,
and then cleared.

Elise couldn't continue meeting such damning
eyes. She looked back at the moss. "It wasn't like that.
I . . ."

He was waiting, and there wasn't anything she
could think of to fill the space.

"You vicious, vindictive, vengeful . . ."

He stopped his own words. Then he was making a
liar out of their need for subterfuge by yelling something unintelligible at her. Elise glanced up. He wasn't
yelling it at her. He had his head tipped back, his
throat tensed into cords of thickened flesh, and was
sending the cry to the treetops with a gruff, throat-tear-
ing sound. He finished. The throbs of sound died. He
lowered his head. Elise wasn't fast enough to dodge his
gaze and gasped before she could look back down.

"You walk. I'll na' touch you. Never again. You hear?"

Her eyes widened with the shock. She watched the
moss soften and warp, until it wasn't distinct anymore. It was a wash of greenish brown and sparkled
with touches of dawn. She nodded.

"You fall behind, you stay behind."

He wasn't waiting to see if she understood. He was
moving again, lumbering at a jog, through trees
branches that seemed to slash back at her and with
steps that slammed his feet into the ground. Elise was
at his heels.

Chapter 26

The pace was brutal. Elise welcomed it. The ground was uneven and treacherous, even when she could see it. That required attention. Elise welcomed that, too. It kept her mind off other things. Things like the rain finally halting, MacKennah pursuers, clan punishment . . . Colin's words when she'd told him. Never in her wildest imagination had she thought he'd react like that.

The moss beneath her feet wasn't truly moss. It was rocks, and holes, and fallen, rotting material that twisted her ankle more than once, and almost took her to her knees twice. On both occasions, Elise could have sworn a hand reached out and steadied her, but it couldn't have been Colin. Every time she looked, he was facing ahead and wasn't paying her the slightest bit of attention. Elise had shaken her head. It had to have been Colin. Anything else was too fanciful. It wasn't hard to see why. Everything was fanciful and mysterious in a Scots woods, with intermittent beams of sunlight piercing through, to dance on the last of the airborne mist and turn everything into a sparkling vista of wonder. It was entirely different from anything in England, even Barrigan's unkempt property.

Elise kept her mind on the beauty around her. It

was better than listening to her body's ill. The tartan was wrapped about her head and over her shoulders, and it itched and smelled as it dried. The skirt was still heavy with rainwater, and it chafed at her waist. The petticoat clung to each step she took. The blouse was drying to a consistency of thick paper, and the chemise she'd donned wasn't protecting any skin from the scratch of it. The boots she'd thought so serviceable before felt like they were full of holes. Her belly was echoing with emptiness. There was a twinge of ache in her left side that accompanied each breath. The front of her thighs were making certain she knew how much muscle was being overused and abused, and the middle of her chest felt like a bruised and battered cage of pain every time it beat.

She was vicious? Vindictive? Vengeful?

The trees started thinning, opening the woods more and more; then Colin was leading her down into another meadow. What was thigh-high grass to him, was waist-hugging on her. Elise had to use a sashay-style movement to get through it, which had nothing to do with the way she used to walk. There were purple clumps of flowers scattered through the grass and smaller white star-shaped ones.

She would have looked closer and appreciated how beautiful it all was, but Colin had increased his pace, and that meant she had to increase hers as well.

The morn wore on, growing to a full, blinding, light hue that hurt the eyes to look about. The sun was welcome, though. Halfway across the meadow, Elise flipped the stiffened wool tartan from her face and turned her face toward the sun, shutting her eyes and inhaling deeply of freshness, warmth, and the clean smell of everything.

"You'll burn your skin," Colin said, almost at her ear.

Elise started, then brought her head down to look over at him. He'd wiped the black from his face, so that only smudges of it existed near the creases, and he'd tossed his cowl off his head and onto his shoulders.

Elise kept his gaze for what felt like forever but was actually the span of three heartbeats, and then she dropped it.

"Dinna' make the mistake of thinking I care, for I dinna'."

"Very well," she answered, extremely proud of the cool, unaffected tone of her own voice. "I won't."

He made a grunt of sound, then he was handing her something. Elise eyed the flat, blackened squares, lifted her eyes to his, and dropped them again.

"Here, take it. Eat it."

"What is it?"

"Does it matter?" he asked.

"No." Elise took the two squares and devoured all but the last two bites. Those, she savored.

"They're griddle cakes. Overcooked. I always take them in the Highlands. Travel well. Filling. Hard to spoil."

"Oh," she replied.

"We've still a fair piece to walk."

The blisters in her heels, the muscles in her thighs, and, if she gave it enough time, every other inch of her would be protesting. Elise swallowed the last of her cake, licked her fingers, and waited.

"You sufficiently rested?"

"Does it matter?" she replied carefully.

She got a whiff of sound that could have been amusement but was probably disgust, and then got the back of him again.

They didn't reach the horses until almost sunset. It was probably her fault. It certainly couldn't have been his. He'd kept up his pace, and then he'd had to slow it for her, and then he'd made a liar out of himself again by coming back to her and hefting her back onto his shoulders. It was all so stupid. Her posturing. His vow. The lies. The secrets. The only thing that mattered was survival. Their ancestors had known it. Why didn't they?

Elise didn't have enough energy to lift her head from where it dangled at his shoulder, lolling back and forth with each of his steps. She didn't have a bit of fight left in her. He was stronger. He was more fit. He hadn't starved himself to fit into tight, little corsets, nor had he kept himself confined to indoors to protect his pale, unblemished complexion. He'd not made certain never to do a bit of exercise, for fear of making a physique that was other than ladylike and weak.

Colin stopped walking. Elise forced her neck to move and roll her head so she could see why.

There were horses. Lots of horses. And there were clansmen. Lots of clansmen. Red, green, and black plaid covered all of them; the patterns varied, but not the colors.

"You're late," one of the men said.

"Aye, a bit of trouble," Colin answered. Elise heard it with her ears and felt it with the rest of her. That was strange, she decided.

"The MacKennah?"

"*Nae*, the wife. She's not much for the clime."

There was a bit of laughter at that. Elise would have stiffened, but she was beyond that; besides, it was true.

"We just about sent a search party for you."

"*Nae* need. I told you such."

"Dugan expected us midday."

"Send a party ahead. Alert the man. We'll need food. A fire. A bath. Beds. Clean clothing. Go. Have Mick ready."

They didn't answer, but Elise heard hoofbeats. She focused her eyes on why. They were on hard ground, and there wasn't a hint of greenery or foliage any-where. She wondered when that had happened.

"Here, take the wife."

Elise's heart heard it before her ears did, as he tipped forward and slid her off his shoulders and into another man's arms.

"Please, put me down," she said.

He shrugged and put her on her feet, where Elise embarrassed herself by collapsing into a folded-leg pile. She bent her head over the whole of it and tried to dis-appear into the rock-strewn dirt of the hillside.

"Hand her up."

"You've your hands full with this one, Your Grace."

"Actually, lads, I've my arms full. Hand her over."

I'm sorry, Colin. I didn't mean to keep it secret. I didn't do it on purpose. I didn't mean to hurt you. Elise opened her mouth to say everything she was carrying in her heart.

"If you cling to me, I'll set you on another horse, with another man. I will na' care which man."

Elise hunched forward until her forehead touched the horse's neck and tried to find the heartless de-meanor she was famous for. Anything was better than knowing the man with his hand about her waist, secur-ing her seat, hated having it there. She told herself she was exhausted. That was it. She was too exhausted to even feel the soreness taking over her entire body. All she could feel was one thing: heartache. It was strange, but there wasn't anything worse than that.

Elise missed their arrival. She missed the fanfare of pipes, the torches that were lit, and the boar that was brought forth and eagerly sliced into and eaten. She missed her bath. She missed everything, save the luxury of linen-covered softness pillowed against her cheek and the feel of a mattress be-neath her body.

* * *

"Well! You certainly know how to give a body a shock."

Elise lifted her head, groaned at the poor use of her own neck, and plopped back down on the pillow.

"And if you think I'll come posthaste, on horseback, over mountains and around lakes filled with sea creatures, for anyone else, you're sadly mistaken."

"Daisy?" Elise's throat hurt to use it, too. That was strange. She couldn't remember working her voice.

"You were expecting someone else?"

"But . . . ? How? Why?"

"We were just getting settled in the nursery wing of that Castle Gowan place—Rory and I, and a whole army of housemaids and such. And my Lord, Elise, but when you see the state of this man's holdings, your own mouth is going to drop open, just like mine did. He's as rich as Midas. Has taste, too."

Elise moaned. It didn't stop Daisy.

"There's rooms of tapestries and furnishings . . . from France! There's marble and teakwood, and silver and gilt, and paintings. My, my, it's amazing. Would make Archibald's teeth fall out with the envy. And I didn't even see it all in the one look I got."

"Daisy," Elise said.

"What?"

"Why are you here? And, if we're so close to his home, why didn't he take me there?"

"Good questions. The first? His Grace sent his man Mick for me. You needed me, urgently. I can see the wisdom of that myself."

"I needed you? I don't understand. Where am I?"

"Dugan's Tower. Or so they call it. The man's an optimist. It's a square heap made of mismatched rocks. There's nothing towering about this sty."

"Sty?"

"The place needs a good cleaning . . . and a good sweeping. Actually, it's more in need of a good house fire. I could probably arrange one. We could blame it on you. It wouldn't be the first time."

Elise had been trying to lift her head but let it back down at the maid's words. They were true. "Where is Col—I mean, His Grace?"

"As far as I know, he's riding. Been doing that all day. Most of yesterday, too, from what I hear."

"Yesterday?"

"You've been asleep a day and a half. I can only surmise the horrors that man put you through that would lead to such a thing. Especially when I see the state of your clothing. Or what you're still wearing that I'll just assume is called clothing. What is this, please?"

The maid was lifting the end of the MacGowan sett that was still wrapped about her.

"It's a MacGowan tartan, Daisy."

"It's seen better days or had better use. What did you do with it? Scrub a barn floor?"

"I think it saved my life," Elise replied, speaking more to the down-filled pillow at her nose than to the woman moving about in the room behind her.

"I know something that will do one better. Coffee. I'll order it up. Some rolls, too. Some good cooked oats, heavy cream, and a bath. Do you need anything else?"

Colin, Elise answered in her thoughts. "No," she said aloud.

"Well, don't just lie there, wallowing in cloth that needs to be burnt to get the vermin out of it. Roll over. I'll assist."

"Roll over? Now?"

"Right now. You're laying on the ends of this tartan, blanket-thing. They're frayed. Is that a normal condition, or was it brought about by wear?"

Elise struggled to roll over, turning about so the maid could unwind her blanket. Her body was protesting, but it seemed to be doing a lot of that lately. Then she had to listen to what the maid thought of her wrinkled, unkempt blouse, with sweat stains beneath each arm.

"You actually slept this way? Sweet heaven! You?" The maid put her hands to her cheeks and her eyes were wide.

"There's a lot worse things than a bit of soil and sweat," Elise replied softly.

"What has that man been doing to you? I'll roast him! I'll flog him! I'll see every bit of flesh taken from every inch—no, that's too severe, and I don't have that much energy. He's got too many inches of it. It would hurt my arm."

Elise would have chuckled, but her ribs hurt the moment it started. She caught the gasp in a wheeze of sound.

"And he hurt you, too?"

"No, that was Torquil. More specifically, it was Torquil's horse."

"Who the devil is Torquil?"

"The MacKennah Laird."

"You've been with The MacKennah? Oh dear. That is not good."

"I wasn't with him because I wanted to be. He abducted me."

"He *what*?" Her voice rose an octave on the last word.

"Abducted. For ransom. They do it all the time. At least, that's what they tell me. I don't know if it's true."

"Oh, you poor love. Those barbarians tell me nothing! They expect to pull me out of a fine sleep and get myself ready for a brisk ride, without a word of explanation, other than you've gone and done it now with your secrets, and then I find out they let you get taken. By their sworn enemy? Where is he? I'll take a broom to his thick skull and my sewing scissors to

his heart! I hope it cost His Grace a fine pile of gold
to get you back, too."

"It didn't."

"Why not? Were you such a horrid prisoner they let
you go? Or better yet, did you escape on your own?
This is thrilling! I'm so proud of you!"

Elise giggled and stopped the instant she did. That
hurt her ribs, too. "Neither. Colin . . . I mean, His Grace,
rescued me."

"He did?" The maid's voice was rapturous. "I take
everything back about him. He's a handsome, manly
fellow, with a castle of treasures and a heart of gold.
If that man wants you, you're a very lucky woman, I'm
thinking."

"He doesn't want me. Not now."

"Oh, dear God. Please don't tell me that they took
you by force. I'll faint. I swear."

"They're Scotsmen, but they're still gentlemen,
Daisy. I'm bruised a bit, but unharmed. Honest."

"I'll just decide the truth of that, myself. Lie flat. I
can't unbutton you properly if you don't."

Elise rolled onto her stomach. It was getting easier
to move.

"You've lost three buttons, and four slipped their
holes. You're nearly naked."

Elise giggled again but caught it.

"And look at the state of your hair. I don't know if
I've enough oil to smooth this tangle. What am I going
to do about that?"

"Cut it," Elise replied.

"What? Cut it? Did you say . . . cut it?"

"Aye," Elise muttered, turning her head away from
the suffocating softness of her pillow. And then she
went perfectly still. She'd answered with a Scottish
sound on the word, and it hadn't been forced.

"The day I cut one inch from this hair is the day I
resign as your personal maid. I've a reputation at

stake. I've an ice goddess for a mistress, and there's none lovelier, nor with such a shade of glorious hair."

"I'm not an ice goddess," Elise replied. "Not anymore."

"Buck up, love. You've got an entire castle of folk thinking you are. They've read all about you. They can't wait to see you and meet you, and have their photograph taken with you, and a slew of other things."

Elise groaned again. She was finished posturing. She didn't think she had a bone left in her body that was willing to pretend to be anything other than what she was: a young woman in love who'd hurt the man she loved. She only hoped he gave her the time to explain.

There was a knock on the door. Daisy covered Elise, and then there was too much confusion and talking and movement as men in MacGowan sett brought in a tub, and then left for the buckets to fill it. There was another man bearing a tray with iced rolls, fresh from an oven; another one with a coffee pot; and yet another with a small silver pot that Elise knew contained her oatmeal. She turned her head aside and concentrated on the tight, fine weave of the linen at her cheek.

The MacGowan crest was on the end of her pillowcase, embroidered with gold thread, just as it always seemed to be. There were red, green, and black threads entwined at the center of the lion's feet, and flowing out from there to make ribbons of plaid. Colin MacGowan was rich. He was powerful. He was lost to her.

Elise caught the sob and forced herself to concentrate on tracing the golden lion, then one ribbon of plaid, then the other. The noise behind her settled, then died away.

"You can shed that blouse now, young lady, and I never again want to see you wearing a chemise that's the state of that one. Oh my! It's ripped. And you're bruised. Oh dear. Everywhere. This is not good. We'd best call a physician to look at you."

"I'm fine," Elise said, moving into a crouch; from there it was an easy maneuver to sit upright. She helped Daisy pull the blouse from her by putting her arms out straight. The maid was right about her chemise. The little ribbon adornment was hanging by a hair of a thread, there was a tear below her right breast, and the satin was stiff with use.

"Off with that, too."

"They'll be back any moment with water."

"Fine, then. Let them. You've a privy screen. Go there."

"I'd like a cup of coffee first."

"I'll serve it on your commode table. Come along. Stand up. Let me see to the damage. I've not got all day."

Elise stilled at the edge of the bed, where she sat preparatory to rising. "Why not?" she asked.

"Because His Grace wants you up and dressed and ready to converse with him at four. Prompt."

"Four?"

"Seems he's got a magistrate coming. I don't know what his plans are, but it's something to do with your wishes, and his granting of them. Whatever that may mean."

Elise's heart stopped, and then decided it really would continue to pump every ache-filled thud into her body. "It . . . means he's ridding himself of me." The sentence stumbled, but not any more than everything in her life was. She was in luck she hadn't stood yet; she'd have probably fallen.

"The nerve! I'll see him flayed with a cat-o'-nine tails—wait a moment. Isn't that what we want?"

"No!" Elise should have kept it to herself, as shivers flew through every limb before centering at her breast; then they did it again.

"We don't want to be free of him?"

"No," Elise whispered.

"And why not, might I ask?"

"Because I love him. I love him, and it's not a wonderful feeling, at all. It's horrible. I hate it."

"This is very good news. Very good, indeed. I think I'll just run along and speak with that Mick fellow after we've finished. He's a font of information that I didn't think pertinent to hear. Now, I think I'd best hear all of it."

"Mick?"

"His Grace's man. He came for me. Rode a day to get there, and then all night to get back, almost without stopping. I could hardly get my breath. They are definitely a hardy bunch, aren't they?"

"What did he say?"

"Something about how he knew you were hiding something else, and how he'd been afraid of what would happen, and then you went and exceeded his expectations all the way. Something along that line. It wasn't meant as a compliment. Quite the opposite. That was when I ceased listening."

"He was right," Elise replied, bowing her head and trying her best to keep the sickness that was curdling in her belly at bay.

"You want that man, Elise?"

Elise turned her head and regarded the maid, standing next to the privy screen that she should have been behind by now, shedding what was left of her attire. "Yes," she whispered.

"Then you'd best not waste a moment. I've got a goddess to create, and it's not going to happen with you sitting and wallowing in self-pity. Get in here. Give me that clothing. Get some victuals down your belly, and then get soaking in that tub. I'll do everything else."

"It's hopeless, Daisy. Absolutely hopeless." Elise

caught the sob on the last word before it became full-out sobbing.

"Pish! And stop that! No red eyes! No puffy cheeks! No signs of tears. You hear?"

"Why not?"

"Because we've got a scene to set, and you've got a part to play."

"I'm not playing any part, ever again."

"I think I like the new you, Elise. Not that I didn't like the old you. Bother this. Bad choice of words all the way around. I didn't mean to play a part. I meant seduction. You've got a seduction to plan. Full out. Floral scent . . . better yet, musky floral. Oiled hair, soft as silk skin. Trust me, love, it's not hopeless."

"I can't seduce His Grace. I don't know how."

"For some reason I don't think it's going to take much effort. Now, get on your feet. What are you waiting for?"

"I'm not playing anymore, Daisy. I promised myself. I'm not acting, and I'm not posturing, and I'm not anything other than what I appear to be."

"And what is that, pray tell?"

"A woman who just lost the man she loves."

"Make that another pish! Off with you. Into the water closet. Toss me that skirt! I'll see it sent to the compost heap, immediate-like. We've got work to do."

"I'm not going to do this."

"You're going to show him exactly what you are, and you were a bit off the mark, Elise, my dear." The skirt came over the privy screen. "Very good. Now the chemise. Do you have stockings? If so, hand them over. I'll burn them."

"What exactly am I?"

"A woman in love. That's what you are. We've just got to make it easier to spot."

"What are you talking of now?"

"Blindness. On both sides."

"What?" Elise peeked out the side to ask it.

"According to His Grace's man Mick, that man is so in love with you, he's been beside himself since you two first met. That doesn't sound hopeless. That sounds like a bad case of blindness."

"He said that? Truly?"

"Coffee?" Daisy asked.

"With heavy cream, and a roll, and the oatmeal. I'm starving."

"Now, you're talking."

"Oh, Daisy, I can't believe I almost gave up on him. I can't. We've got to hurry. What time is it?"

"Half-past."

"Half-past what?"

"Twelve."

Elise shrieked. "What? I've got less than four hours?"

"You've got less than three, love. We're calling His Grace for three. I'm not waiting for any magistrate man to put this asunder. I expect you to have that Highland man well under control by the time this magistrate arrives. You do understand what I'm saying, don't you?"

"What will I need?"

"We'll start with—"

The knock stopped her. Elise listened as water was poured into her tub, with a resultant cheerful greeting from Daisy. If Elise wasn't mistaken, it was Mick on the receiving end of it. She'd thank him later. She didn't have time right now. She had less than three hours.

Chapter 27

The room they'd given Elise was constructed of stone. It wasn't misfitted rocks, nor was it small, belying Daisy's words. It was either a very important guest room, or the maid was determining her definitions on Colin's Castle Gowan. There was a heavy oaken mantel, topping a large fireplace, which held three large logs, all burning. There was a solid-looking, carved, wood rocking chair to one side of the fireplace, with a braided rug at the hearthstone. There were two plump cushion chairs, facing each other, across a round wood table that had a tatted lace doily on top, with a vase of fresh-cut flowers right at the center of it. The firelight reflected off the vase, if she watched it long enough.

Elise noted it for the eighteenth time and moved to the next section of interest in her continual circuit of the room.

The privacy divider, screening off the water closet area, was made of more carved wood, although the woodworker hadn't been a master. It had a large amount of charm, however, and Elise recognized the tall purple wildflowers from the meadow, even if they were uneven and showed marks where the carver's knife had slipped. Elise looked it over, noticed the wooden dowels connecting the three sections of it, showing it was a movable piece, and then she moved on. The water closet didn't hold her interest.

The bed.

Elise gulped and turned away. It was twelve minutes past three now, and there wasn't a sign of Colin anywhere in the room. She checked her reflection again in the enormous mirror to the left of her privy closet. She was wearing a simple daygown of white, tied at the throat with a blue ribbon, matching the forget-me-knots embroidered all about the bodice, sleeves, and hem. Her face was bare of any cosmetics, and her hair was in a simple braid down to her hips. It was still damp but soft to the touch. The dampness couldn't be helped. They'd barely made the time as it was. Elise turned away. Now it was thirteen minutes past.

Dugan had a large hammered shield above his mantel, which was silhouetted against a dark green sett. She wondered if it was the Dugan family sett, and then answered it herself. Of course, it would be. No Highland laird displayed other than his own colors.

Colin knocked, and then entered. Elise spun about to face him, and then found out she couldn't. Her eyes dropped to the floor.

"You sent for me?" he asked.

She glanced up, memorizing the way he'd tightened his jaw; the way he'd pulled back his wavy hair; the wedge shape of his black doublet that looked like it had been sewn onto his frame, in order to draw every feminine glance; the white cascading lace jabot that set off the outdoor tone of his face, as the lace cuffs did for his hands; the red, green, and black plaid kilt, with a sporran worn low at the hip; the black tassels on his socks; black shoes; and the sword he had strapped to his left side, where his hand negligently lay.

It was imprinted on her eyelids even when she shut

them and looked back down to the floor. Colin Mac-Gowan was a stunning man. He was Scotland at her best. He was every woman's dream. He was her dream.

Elise welcomed the blush that overheated her throat and her cheeks, and even made droplets break out at her scalp line. She didn't know what was the matter with her!

"Well? Did you or did you na' send for me?"

"I . . . did." The words were stammered and unclear. Elise frowned as she heard them. She didn't know what she was doing.

"Why?" he asked.

Why? she wondered, stupidly tongue-tied yet again! Oh, Lord, to have a ready answer!

The door opened. The stone beneath her slippers swam with unshed tears as she heard it.

"Mick! Ready the horses! I'll na' be long."

The door shut again. Elise sniffed. A log shifted.

"Do you expect to leave me waiting all day?" he asked.

She gasped. He hadn't left. Elise quickly blinked the moisture away and looked back up. He hadn't moved.

"I need to tell you something," she said.

His face settled into the stone look she'd seen so many times.

"I dinna' wish to hear any more of your secrets. I've something for you. Something you'll need for your appointment."

"Appointment?" she asked.

"With the magistrate. I've taken my statement. There's been no consummation. You can have your annulment."

Elise took a deep breath and blurted it out. "What if I told you I didn't want one?" she asked.

That surprised him, for exactly the count of three; then his lip curled.

"Your maid described my castle to you, dinna' she? All right, how much do you want?"

"For what?" she asked.

"My freedom. From you. Right now. Name it."

"You think I . . . want . . . money?"

"Aye, and na' without cause."

That hurt. It hurt so much that there was no stopping the flood of tears that went straight from her heart to her eyes, and then slipped down her cheeks. Elise ignored them. "You think I want money?"

He frowned across at her. "I dinna' ken what you want, Elise. You have me so damned confused, I dinna' ken myself anymore. And you can cease crying. I know it for the act it is, remember?"

She turned her head aside and bit lightly on the piece of cheek she'd sucked in. What she wouldn't give for a glass of ice water and a handkerchief! She and Daisy had been lax. They hadn't seen to the most rudimentary of props in this stage setting.

"What are your plans for Rory?" she asked the floor.

"Rory?"

"He's my nephew, too."

"He's a MacGowan. He's my heir. I'm having papers drafted."

"Your . . . heir?" In all her imaginings, she'd never considered that for the babe.

"I'll na' wed again. I believe I've had enough of that state."

Elise caught the sob with her own willpower. She couldn't believe she had the strength for it.

"You sent for me, and you say naught. Verra well, I'll say it. I've known you a bit over a fortnight. I still dinna' ken why it was you. Why? Karma has failed me. I spoke of darkness? Na' knowing the path? Trust me. It's darker now than ever. It's filled with sweet lips spouting false words, while composure and beauty hide ugliness and deceit."

"Now, wait a moment," Elise began.

"*Nae,* you wait a moment. You asked to see me. Verra well, see me. See what you've created. A man who knows what lurks beneath beauty. Your beauty. I fell for you the moment I saw you, Elise Wyndham. I fought it. I dinna' want it, and I wish I'd had more sense."

"This is not all my fault!" Elise said.

"I beg your pardon?" he replied.

"You heard me perfectly. Every time I tried to tell you of him, you stopped me! You had me gagged; you nearly hit me. You stopped me."

"And yet every time you had a chance with none of that, you stayed silent."

"I dinna' trust you!" Elise replied, lapsing into his own brogue.

"You dinna' trust me?"

That had surprised him. She watched him pull back and glare at her. "Were you a man, there would be a challenge for such words."

"Well, I'm not a man! I'm a woman, and I'm your wife, and you're not going to be able to change any of that! You hear me, Colin MacGowan?"

Since she was yelling it at him, she shouldn't have needed to ask it. He wasn't glaring at her any longer. He was looking over her head at the high windows of her room. He was breathing heavily, and a nerve was bulging out the side of his jaw.

"There's something you need to learn afore you get much older, Elise. You've got to learn that you can't toy with some things. Things like hearts. You can't play with a man's emotions and expect to come out unscathed, and them unchanged. That's what happens. Things change. Feelings mute. Given enough time and pain, everything does."

"But I tried to tell you about Rory, and of Evan and Evangeline. So many times I tried to tell you."

"Why dinna' you, then?"

"I . . . was afraid."

The tears had stopped. She just wished her heart had stopped with them. The look of disgust was back on his face when he lowered it to look at her.

"I've seen you act, Elise. It's very convincing. Still. Verra."

"I'm not acting!"

"It was most convincing in Barrigan's chambers, when you claimed me for all to hear and see. I almost believed you. Pray dinna' test my patience more. I wish to be at Castle Gowan tomorrow eve."

"Don't walk out on me, Colin MacGowan."

"Say one thing to make me stop. One. Go ahead. Say it. Dinna' pretend. Say it."

It was the hardest thing Elise thought she'd ever done. She went pink with the blush; then she past that and went red. She didn't have to look at the mirror to verify it. The sweat beading her upper lip and then starting rivulets down her sides was enough verification. It was mortifying. It was dangerous. It was unavoidable. She opened her mouth and not one sound came out.

"Yes?" he asked, cocking a hand to his ear.

She opened it again. "I . . ." That word made sound, but it sounded like a little girl.

"I can na' hear you," he replied.

"All right!" She glared across at him. "I love you! All right! I said it. I love you! I wish I dinna', because I hate it, but I love you! You hear me, you big, brutish barbarian! I love you!"

His lips settled into a thin line, almost the match to his eye slits. Elise had never seen anything so frightening. Her heart was hammering from her confession, and then trying to leap from her breast with his reaction. She clasped her hands to it to stop it.

"You still seek to play the courtship game? With me? And for no other reason I can see than my gold. I dinna' think there's anything left to say."

"I'm not playing a game!"

"Good thing, for only a virgin would play it so poorly," he replied, with a snide tone.

"Well, maybe that's because I *am* one!" Elise clapped a hand to her mouth, but it was too late.

She watched as his eyes went from their narrowed state to a certain frown as he stared at her.

"Nae," he said finally.

Elise nodded. She didn't think her voice worked.

He tilted his head to one side and considered her closer. He shook his head. *"Nae,"* he said again.

She nodded again. Now, she had both hands on her mouth and was pressing back on the certain cry as he crossed the room to her with seven large strides. He stood above her, heaving with the strength of his breathing and sending shivers all over her with the feel of air on her nose and cheeks.

There was something indefinable there, too. Something he was asking, searching for, debating. Elise kept her eyes on his. She didn't dare blink.

He pulled back.

"Nae," he said again.

She nodded.

His lips twitched. He spun. Elise watched with eyes that wouldn't close no matter what order she gave to do that very thing, as he reached for the chamber door and opened it in seeming slow motion. She didn't think she was going to be able to survive past the slamming of that door, taking him out of her life. And she had no one else to blame. She hadn't had to tell him. He could have found out the same way every other man did—physically.

The humming sound grew in her ears. Elise moved her hands to them, instead, to keep it from getting out.

"Mick?" he yelled.

At least, Elise thought it was yelling, from the way the waves of sound penetrated across the floor and sought out where she was still standing. She was still standing? That didn't seem possible. Elise looked down at the beautiful, maidenly looking white day-gown, with the little blue forget-me-knots across the bodice, and she hated every bit of it.

"Aye, Your Grace?"

"Cancel the horses. I've changed my mind. And stay all from this chamber. The duchess and I are na' to be disturbed."

"As you wish, Your Grace. And Colin? Congratulations."

There was more said. Elise didn't hear it. The humming was covering it over.

And then it was gone. Everything went absolutely dead silent. The door clicking shut reverberated across to her, and then there was the sound of the bolt falling, which was louder than a shotgun blast from the foxhunt would have been. Elise jumped.

Colin had the door secured; then he turned, leaned against it, and crossed one foot over the other. Then he was unstrapping his sword, and she could swear she could hear and smell the leather as it moved. He leaned it against the wall, settling it into a groove in the rock. Then he crossed his arms, sucked in on both cheeks, which tended to put his lips into a pouting shape, and considered her. Elise's eyes widened. She dropped them to the floor and had to endure yet another blush.

"What do we do now?" she asked.

That got her a chuckle, then an outright roar of laughter. She didn't think it was that funny. Then she just asked it.

Her response was more laughter and the looming shape of Colin MacGowan as he neared. Elise surprised herself by putting up her hands, looking over her back, and then backing right into the privy screen. Not only was it a movable piece, it wasn't attached to the floor. She heard it crash and was with it the entire time as it came to rest, tilted atop the water stand.

Then Colin was right beside her, hauling her into his arms and rolling so she was atop his entire length, making the wooden screen creak with the added weight. He was still chuckling, too, and atop his chest, that was an interesting ride.

Then he sobered. Green-flecked brown eyes held her enthralled as he blew a kiss at her. Elise gasped. That got her a hearty grin.

"*Nae* man has ever been here?" he asked, his finger running up her spine, where there wasn't anything beneath the dress, save a chemise. Elise's eyes were huge. She shook her head. That got her a larger grin.

"And here? *Nae* man has ever been here?"

He was sliding his hand over her collar and resting his fingers beneath the back of her dress, while his thumb continued a rubdown of its own at the base of her jaw.

She shook her head again.

"Sweet Jesu'!"

His whispered words came with an accompanying groan from the wooden panel they were still perched atop, as he lunged slightly with his lower body against hers. She watched his eyes slit, his lips part, and then he was pursing them slightly to blow out, and then suck in, air. *Now, that's intriguing,* she thought.

"How about here?"

He was moving her higher along him; the wood was creaking in protest, but she ignored it. Colin was nuzzling his lips along her chin, and then down her neck; Elise arched her head up to allow him access.

"*Nae* man has ever been here, either? And here? And here?"

"Just you," she answered, and then she swallowed; the action moved the lump in her throat against his tongue.

"Your maid has put too much cloth in my way, Elise."

He murmured it against the base of her throat, where the little blue ribbon bow sat.

"Too much?"

"Aye, and she was verra smart to do so."

Elise brought her head down. He moved her again, sliding her the span he needed in order to place his chin against hers, his nose to hers, and his lips right against hers.

"She . . . was?" Elise panted the question.

"Oh, aye. A man denied for as long as I have been is a forthright man, an impatient man, an ardent, anxious, eager man. All of which would be a terrible mistake right now."

"It would?" Elise stammered the word.

"Oh, aye. But na' to worry, lass."

Worry? she wondered. He didn't allow her the time away from him for such a dense thought, as his lips pressed fully against hers, defined the shape and texture of them, and then tasted fully what she had to give.

Elise moaned. The screen creaked worse. Colin's breath mingled with her own, and his tongue touched hers. Elise jumped, and large hands brought her right back to stay perched right where she was, atop him. His mouth moved; he started talking to her lips, moving his against hers. The resultant twinge in her core pulsated right into an answering one in him. She felt it, and then experienced it as he felt it.

"Elise, darling, you're a goddess come to life. A vision. I thought it when I first clapped eyes on you. I think it now."

"You thought—?"

"Na' thought, I knew. You were the most beauteous woman on earth. Not were. Are. Dinna' move. Na' yet."

Elise lifted her head and brought him into focus. There was a dazed-looking expression on his features. His eyes were half-closed, and they were spark-ing green fire at her.

"Verra well. Disobey. Move. Dinna' say I dinna' warn you."

He didn't give her any time! Her gasp barely made sound as his hands moved from her back to grip her head and hold her in place. Then his tongue started marauding, pillaging and plundering, and making such a riot of sensation spark through every nerve in her body that Elise was writhing and moaning, slid-ing and clinging. Her knees slit, and then she was riding, roving and bucking, and listening to her own body's desires; she wasn't stopping until Colin moved his hands to grip her hips and bring everything to a standstill.

"Na' so fast, lass."

The words were mumbled indistinctly against her lips, and Elise would have hit him if she could have freed her hands enough to make the movement.

"But, Colin—"

"But naught. This here is to be our wedding night, and I'll see it treated as such. Did your maid include wine?"

Elise lifted her head, looked with out-of-focus eyes at where he was, and frowned. "Wine?" she asked.

"Aye, wine."

"What for?"

"To slow this down. 'Tis going to be an experience we'll remember all our lives, Elise. I'll na' take you quickly. I've waited too long. You dinna' understand, but you will."

"But I dinna' want to slow it down," Elise responded.

"What do you want?"

"I dinna' know!"

That got her another grin. The privy screen groaned ominously. Both of them looked sideways. He turned back first, and that placed his nose against her cheek.

"I ken what you want, lass. And I'm the man to give it to you. Trust me. You'll na' be unsatisfied, but it's na' something to rush."

"Colin—"

The sound of splitting wood stopped her. Colin was already moving and on his feet on the opposite side, with Elise clasped to his side. She watched as the dowels split, separating the wood where they'd just been, before falling open to let the water basin show through.

"You . . . move fast," she stammered.

His eyebrows went up and down several times. "You already saw that, lass. You watched me at the MacKennah camp. Now . . . where were we? I dinna' see any wine. I look about and I still dinna' see any."

Elise looked with him. The fire was still going, the vase of flowers was still sitting on the table. The bed . . .

She gasped and put her face against Colin's shoulder. He chuckled as he felt it, then he was running a hand up her back, and then he was lifting her into his arms.

"My thoughts exactly. Despite everything I try." He sighed heavily, and she went with it.

"Is it that bad?" Elise asked.

"Oh, *nae,* lass. It's that good. Your maid should have stocked wine to assist me with it."

"With what?"

He was at the bed. She hadn't even felt him move.

"Things."

"Things?" Elise asked.

"Aye, things. Desire. Lust. Passion. Those kinds of things."

He placed her on the bed, but he was right beside her. Then he was pulling her close, rolling to put her atop him again, filling her ears with his words, before capturing her lips to supply her senses with the feel, taste, and scent of him.

He didn't have her hands trapped this time, and

Elise needed no further encouragement than that. His doublet was just as tight as she'd suspected it would be, and despite trying, there didn't seem any pathway to burrow beneath it from the sides. She eased her hands around his waist, bringing them close together right at his belt line, and when she got near the front of him, he lunged, putting such strength and power against her palm that it frightened her.

"Oh, Jesu'! This is na' working!"

Then Colin was off the bed, standing with his back to her. Elise was the one giving chase.

"Colin?" she asked, wrapping her arms about what she could reach of him.

"I've a bit of a problem, lass. I've had it some time."

Her brow wrinkled. "Problem?" she asked.

"Aye, and it's dire, it is."

"What is it?" Elise held her breath.

"Love."

She frowned. "Love is a problem?"

"When it's as much as I feel for you, it is. Trust me." He grimaced.

Elise was glowing. She might as well be floating. Her ears heard every word, and her mind repeated them to her heart.

"You . . . love me?" she asked.

"Desperately. Even when I thought . . . what I thought of you."

"You did?"

"Aye, I'm afeared it's expansive, too. I'd not known that of it. Someone should have warned me."

"Of what?"

"How different it all is when one is in love, as I am with you. Only you. I'm beginning to understand why it was you. It makes everything a hundred times more poignant and a thousand times more intense. I only hope I have the strength to do right by you."

"I dinna' understand any of this," Elise replied.

Another grimace, and then she was off the ground and in a hug of unimaginable strength and care.

"I ken that you dinna'. That's what makes this so different. So special. So perfect. I'll na' ruin it with clumsiness, haste, and ineptitude. It's just so . . . it's tough, lass. Just holding you like this, right now, is making everything on my body betray me, and hate me, and curse at me. I'm trying everything I know to keep it tempered and held at bay until I can na' longer hold it."

"What?"

"Things. I just described them to you. Were na' you listening?"

She nodded.

"You ever try whiskey?"

She nodded again.

"Good, we'll try that. There's a dram or two in my sporran. Dinna' you dare!"

The last was abrupt and said because she was reaching for it. The part of him that he was keeping from her was alive and moving again. Elise was fascinated.

"Stop that, lass."

"But—"

"My sporran. Whiskey. We'll try that. It best work."

He was shuddering through his own words. Elise watched as he uncorked and drank until there couldn't be anything left. Then he was holding it out to her. She slipped her fingers along his, to reach the flask, and watched another shudder run his frame.

The answering gooseflesh went up her own arm.

Colin lowered his head and growled. And then there was no stopping him.

Chapter 28

"Divest yourself of your clothing, Elise."

Colin was pulling his jabot loose enough he could shove it to his temple, where it made a lacy, headband affair. He twisted it around.

"Now?" she asked.

"Right now. Without delay. Now."

She watched as his cuffs met the same end, although he got them over his hands, ripping material in the process. She couldn't take her eyes from the sight.

"Here, I'll assist."

He reached out, with a motion almost too quick to observe, and tugged loose one end of the ribbon bow at her neckline. He didn't let it go. He pulled her toward him with it. When she was within embrace distance of his arms, he bent his head and touched her cheek with his breath.

"Now. Finish."

There were buttons on his doublet, and his fingers were slipping them easily in front of her eyes. Elise's gasp, when he had it open and was yanking the material apart, showing the fine, cambric shirt he wore beneath, was loud and harsh and held a keen of sound to it.

"Elise?"

His breath brushed the stray hairs at her forehead. She looked up. Severe. His face wasn't granite-carved or stony. It was severe, though.

"Your virginity is near an end, and if you dinna' assist me with it, so is that gown. Now divest yourself of it. Now."

The shirt parted in front of her eyes next, and then her entire vision was filled with tanned flesh, rippled muscle, and a slight line of hair. She reached for him, spread her palms wide to him, and cupped her hands around every bit of his chest mounds she could reach.

The snort he gave made more breath rush over her head. Elise didn't care. His fingers pulled the laces from the front of her gown, and then separated it. She was defining how the strength beneath the skin moved, tensed, pulled, and flexed as he did so.

"Colin?" she whispered.

"Aye." Her answer was in a gruff tone, as if he wasn't paying attention. She knew it was because he had her dress undone and was moving up the opening to her shoulders to push open the material.

"You're beautiful. I mean—handsome. You're verra handsome. Manly. Immense. Beautiful."

He snorted again. Then he had his hands wrapped over her shoulders; using them as handholds, he had her in his embrace.

Satin-clothed skin touched warm, heated flesh. Elise slid her own nipples against him, enjoying the caressive pressure of the ropes of muscle at his abdomen, and from there she was moving up, smashing every bit of her against the strength of him.

She had her arms looped above his shoulders; then she was climbing, pulling herself up, and then latching her legs about that torso. Colin's groan filled the chambers of her mouth as she slammed it to his, using the motions he'd taught her.

It was delicious. Almost as much as the sparks that seemed to be flying from where her most feminine area was turning into all the consistency of a gelatin-like sensation where she was pressing against him.

"Elise. Elise."

She ignored him to launch herself up higher on him, wrapping her arms about his neck and imprinting her ownership on everywhere she could reach, taste, and touch.

"Yes, Colin! Oh yes!"

Elise's cry filled the room, reaching the ceiling as something expanded within her, and that was just the beginning of it. Colin pulled his mouth from hers, with a savagery she'd not known felt so wondrous, in order to lap at the satin cloth covering her breast. Then he was pulling the entire mass of it into his mouth and making her scream at how that felt.

Pipes started playing, haunting and loud, and filled with power and thunder, anger and strength.

Colin moved to her other breast, and he was yanking her dress from her body with four powerful pulls of his fists. Elise knew it because she felt them. Then he was moving and she was screaming again.

Moving. Screaming.

The bed had more bounce to it than she'd known, and he met her on the second upward one. It was the mass of his body forcing her down, onto her back, and then he was pulling her away from him by using her braid. The chemise was sliding up, baring one breast, then the other. She watched as Colin appeared to be devouring the sight with his eyes.

"I know, I've not . . . much meat to me," she teased.

"Shut up," he replied, hoarsely.

She heard further ripping, and from the corner of her eye, the red, green, and black plaid of his kilt went sailing to land in a puddle on the floor. Elise's wide eyes watched it. Then she moved them back to the entire male nakedness that was him.

"Colin?"

"Dinna' say . . . I dinna' warn you, Elise."

Hoarse breathing filled the chamber, joining the pipes and the hum in her ears and in her soul. And Colin was right there with her, filling her eyes and her mind with the glory of it. There was more, too. She knew there was, and she shook with the struggle for it, her body in an agony of want, desire, and lust that was worse than anything he'd described.

"Lass? Me. Look to me. *Nae*, not there!"

Elise only had a glimpse, and then she was shaking for another reason. Her arms halted the wild caresses of his back, and her limbs turned to absolute water where they were still wrapped about him.

"Colin?"

"Open for me, love. Now."

Elise had her legs locked about him, and there wasn't any part of her that wasn't open and ready and willing and absolutely terrified.

"No. No. Please? *Nae*."

It was her head wildly shaking, until he had to put his temple against hers to stop her. Heavy. His weight covered hers, and then he had his hands on her thighs and was parting her legs even farther, and then he was splitting her with pain, and blood, and absolute agony.

Time stopped. Nothing moved. Elise lay panting, her body filled with ache, and her eyes swimming in tears that slid out and were replaced by more. She hadn't even known she was crying. Colin lifted his head, and the movement made more of his weight press down on her.

"Elise? Love?"

"Love?" she whispered.

"Aye."

He gripped her hips tighter, and then she knew why as he pushed himself farther into her. Elise lifted her head and howled the agony at the ceiling.

"It'll ease, love. It will. I promise. 'Tis your maiden wall making it so. I promise."

He accompanied his words with yet another hold to her hips and another shove into her. Elise arched her back on it.

"You dinna' say there would be pain. Nobody said there would be pain."

"Elise. Love, look to me."

He lifted his head to say it, then moved both hands to both sides of her head, where he was smoothing stray hairs over her ears. His words turned into a croon of sound, full of strength, power, and pain.

He pushed himself again. Her eyes flew open.

"Why, Colin, why?"

"I'm na' fully sheathed yet, lass. 'Tis near insurmountable, this is. I dinna' know if we'll manage it fully tonight. I know I can na' keep it back much longer. Oh, hell."

He twinged something in the innermost, painful part of her. Elise narrowed her eyes and met his. They weren't green or brown or anything other than black. Elise clenched her jaw and bared her teeth.

"Then do it."

"I can na'—"

"Do it!" Elise moved her hands, and now it was her holding his head in place as she glared at him. His hair was wet, and the lace collar he still wore as a headband was wet with it. "Do it, Colin. Finish it. You say it won't pain further? Prove it. Do it. Now."

"Now?"

Breath touched her forehead as he lifted himself onto his arms, showing her every inch of sweat-damp flesh and sinew and muscle. Elise slid her hands from his head and molded them about the planes of his body, filling her senses with every bit of it, and then she tightened her legs about him and helped.

"Oh, dearest God."

Colin rolled onto his side, his hands pinioning her buttocks in place against him, and the release from his weight was countering the firelike feeling of their joining, until both sensations melded into one.

Elise sucked in air, let it out. Sucked it in. Let it out. Again. Over. Again. Her hands rubbed along his chest and belly, pushing against the solidity of him, until her palms tingled with it, and the blood in her veins sang with it.

Then he was moving her; his hands lifted her ever so slightly and let her fall back down. Embrace him. Lift from him, embrace him. The music of pipes floated into the room, coming from the opened window; the smell of new rain accompanied it, and Elise sucked in another breath full of it.

"Colin?" she whispered, opening her eyes.

"Aye."

He had his eyes closed to slits, and that span of chest was rippling with each movement he was making her do. And he was pursing his lips, as if for an imaginary kiss. Elise had never seen anything like it and wasn't willing to forget a moment of it.

"Colin?" she asked again.

"Aye?"

The word was said in the same modulated tone, and followed with the same kissing motion.

"I . . . dinna' understand."

One eye opened wider; then the other. The kissing motion was back, too, and she realized why. He was controlling his breathing with each motion he did with her body. He was pulling in a small bit of air, and with the next, he was letting it out.

"What . . . dinna' you . . . understand?"

He spaced the question between two of his motions.

Elise watched him do it and felt a powerful twinge deep within her at the sight. The moment it happened, Colin was in a sitting position, holding her immobile against him, and adding a bit of sound to his breathing.

"Colin?"

"Dinna' do that again, lass. I'm begging you."

"What? This?"

This time his breathing halted and was followed almost immediately by the lowest groan she'd ever heard. Elise bent forward and put her ear to his chest to hear it better, and that unleashed something so primitive and basic within him, that she had to clasp every limb in order to have any part of it. Colin filled her vision, his mouth holding hers, then her throat, then her breast. Breathing with her, glorying in the passion with her, and sending every secret so far into her past, she'd never find them.

Harsh breathing filled her ears, bagpipes joining it, and then there was the thumping rhythm of rain drumming on the sides of Dugan's Tower. And there wasn't any part of her that wasn't part of the storm outside, crashing, creating, living.

Elise held to Colin, fought with him, cleaved herself to him, danced with him, and when the rapture hit, it was her screams blending with his groans, her body sending the bliss of it back to his, and her soul matching everything of his.

A log fell.

Elise lifted her head from where it still lay, pillowed between the two mounds of Colin's chest, rhythmically rising and falling with each of his breaths. She thought he was asleep; the steady cadence of his breathing was a good indication of it. But when she tried to move, a hand snaked out and held her immobile.

"Dinna' move, my love. Na' yet."

"Why na'?" she asked, in a whisper.

"I've na' finished memorizing this."

"You, too?" she asked, laying back down.

He chuckled, and the sound echoed through to her ear. "Oh, aye. Me, too. Me. Forever. Dinna' you recognize it, yet?"

Elise frowned. "We can na' sleep like this, Colin."

"Why na'?"

"It will be cold."

"I'll warm you," he replied.

"You're beneath me," she replied.

"I'll crush you with my weight, otherwise. But I'm willing if you are."

"Wait."

Colin's chuckle answered her as she put her hands on both sides of him to stop any such movement.

"At least, let me shut the window. It will be cold."

"The window is na' open, lass."

Elise lifted her head again. "It has to be," she whispered. "I heard it."

"You heard an open window?"

"*Nae,* I heard pipes. And I heard the storm. Rain. I smelled it."

"I know you did, lass. As did I. Trust me, the window's shut and latched. Always has been."

"But—?"

He was chuckling again and pulling her back onto the security of him. Then he was smoothing a hand down the mass of hair that had once been a perfect braid and ending with the caress on her buttock.

"Colin," she warned.

"You've got perfect meat to you, lass. Perfect."

"That is na' what you said."

"You've picked up a delicious brogue, Elise. I rather like it. I do. But then again, I like everything about you. Especially this. Right here."

He had gripped her derriere and was using the

handhold to move her. His chest was flexing with it. Elise rose and fell with it.

"Come eve, I'll show you how much, too. You're so much lass. Almost too much, even for me." He stopped his motions and patted her.

"Colin—"

"All right, you win. You're perfect. For me. True?"

She nodded and settled back down. It was true. She was.